Strategic Engagement

CATHERINE MANN

Harlequin Mills & Boon

Intimate

First Published 2003
First Australian Paperback Edition 2003
ISBN 0 733 54849 0

Published by
Harlequin Mills & Boon
3 Gibbes Street
CHATSWOOD NSW 2067
AUSTRALIA

Printed and bound in Australia by
McPherson's Printing Group

CATHERINE MANN

writes contemporary military romances, a natural fit since she's married to her very own USAF research source. Prior to publication, Catherine graduated with a B.A. in fine arts: theatre from the College of Charleston and received her master's degree in theatre from UNC Greensboro. Now a RITA® Award winner, Catherine finds following her aviator husband around the world with four children, a beagle and a tabby in tow offers her endless inspiration for new plots. Learn more about her work, as well as her adventures in military life, by visiting her Web site: http://catherinemann.com. Or contact her at P.O. Box 41433, Dayton, OH 45441.

Dedication:
To military families everywhere.

Acknowledgments:

To Homer and Karen Tucker, treasured friends who are family in my heart if not by blood relation. Thank you for your never-faltering faith in my stories.

To Major Kevin "Bjorn" Brown and his wonderful wife, Leah. Thank you, Kevin, for your generous insights into the C-17 world. (Any mistakes are strictly my own!) Many thanks also to Leah, a talented author and dear friend, for cheering me on and keeping me up to date on Charleston AFB.

And as always, thank you to my very own hero, Rob, for making our happily-ever-after a beautiful adventure.

Chapter 1

Eleven years ago Mary Elise McRae had expected to fill a hope chest for Daniel Baker. But she'd never thought she would fill it quite so literally.

Her body currently folded inside a five-by-five-foot wooden crate, Mary Elise hugged the two small boys closer. The rough-hewn box jostled on the back of the flatbed truck, jarring bony little elbows and knees against her. Hard. Not that anyone dared do more than breathe in the cedar-scented darkness.

A lone horn honked along the stretch of desert road in their escape route from Rubistan. The truck jerked to a stop. A goat blocking the way? Or a cow? Either animal slow when Mary Elise needed fast. Headlights from the truck behind them shone through the tiny slits between the boards.

A Rubistanian guard from the embassy tracking them.

She'd heard his voice during thc loading onto the truck. Procedure didn't allow him on the U.S. government's vehicle, but those ominous beams sparked fear inside her as surely as if he'd been sitting alongside puffing away on one of those cigars he favored. Would he use this delay as an excuse to ambush them? Cause an "accident?"

The diesel engine's growl increased and the truck lurched to life. Mary Elise exhaled her relief in the stifling enclosure. Only another half hour, max, until she delivered Trey and Austin safely aboard a U.S. military cargo plane. Then she would say her tearful farewells to the two children being smuggled out of this Middle-Eastern hell in the back of Captain Daniel Baker's C-17.

Danny.

His name echoed in her mind amid the grind of changing gears. What would Daniel say when he saw her for the first time in eleven years? If only he had advance warning she would be with the boys, but she'd expected to stay at the embassy, not be in this sweltering crate.

With any luck, they'd be too rushed to talk. She would pass over her young charges. Thank Daniel for answering the emergency SOS she'd anonymously routed through the economic attaché. Then haul butt off the airstrip, back to her tiny apartment in Rubistan's capital, back to her teaching post at the American embassy school.

Back to her solitary life.

She wouldn't let memories of Daniel make her yearn for anything more. She'd worked damned hard for her pocket of peace away from Savannah. Peace bought with the help of Daniel's father. Trey and Austin's father, too. And today she would repay that debt.

"Mary 'Lise?" Austin whispered from under her chin. "Wanna get out. Gotta go."

"Shh," she urged as loudly as she dared. "Soon, sweetie. Soon." She hoped.

Sweat trickled down her neck, caking sand to her skin

as Mary Elise willed Austin silent. A crate of computers didn't whisper for a bathroom, after all. Sure, a diplomatic pouch was immune from inspection—a pouch being U.S. government property of any size from the embassy. Totally immune. Unless that "pouch" starting talking.

Her arms locked tighter around thin, preschooler shoulders on her left and the more substantial nine-year-old frame on her right. At least Trey was old enough to follow instructions, his shoulders pumping under her arm with each heavy breath. Little Austin was a wild card.

Bracing her feet against the other side to combat jolts, she suppressed the illogical bubble of laughter. Definitely a card. Wild. Precious. And looked so much like his adult half brother Daniel.

So much like the baby she and Daniel might have had if not for the miscarriage.

Of course she hadn't been able to turn away when Austin had pumped out tears at the sight of the crate. He'd begged for Mary 'Lise to crawl inside with him instead of his twenty-one-year-old nanny, a pale nanny who'd seemed all too willing to bow out.

The truck squealed to a stop. A tiny hand tucked into hers and clutched tight with chubby stickiness. She pressed a silent kiss to Austin's brow.

"Well, hello there, gentlemen," the masculine bass rumbled.

Danny.

Even with eleven years more testosterone infused into deepening his voice, she would recognize that hint of a drawl anywhere. No rushing. Even in the middle of an unstable country, on a darkened runway where threats lurked in countless shadows…Danny didn't hurry for anyone. Life followed him. He never followed life.

His ambling lope thudded closer. Could they hear her heart thump outside the box?

A second set of footsteps sounded. Faster. Cigar smoke wafted through the thin slits between boards. The distinctive scent of imported Cubans favored by the Rubistanian guard from the embassy snaked around her.

The slower bootsteps, Daniel's, stopped. "How downright neighborly of you to offer an escort, but my folks here can handle things now."

"We have procedure to follow in my country, Cap-i-tain," the guard clipped out in heavily accented English.

"Lighten up there, Sparky. I know all about your procedure. The paperwork's pristine...well, except for some ketchup on the edge there from my fries. Now back on up so my loadmaster can finish the transfer."

Daniel's affected flippancy reached into the box with calming comfort. And unwelcome arousal. His voice shouldn't still have the power to strum her numbed senses to life, especially not now. She wasn't a teenager anymore. She was a mature woman with control over her life. She'd moved on after the debacle with Danny. Married someone else.

Bad example.

Lighten up, 'Lise. Danny's mantra echoed in her head through the years. *Life's just not that complicated.*

She wished.

"Time to head on out, Sparky," Daniel called, casual and irreverent as ever. "The sooner Tag over there can load up and lock down, the sooner we'll get off your runway and out of this...garden spot."

A trail of tangy smoke slithered into the box. "What is your hurry, Cap-i-tain?"

"Hurry?" Daniel's bass rumbled closer, louder. The truck shifted with the weight of another body. "I need to head home for my annual pilgrimage to the Frito-Lay factory. Besides, my copilot's just a kid and it's past her bedtime.''

''Hey, now,'' a female voice called from below. ''Frito-Lay? I thought you were going to Hershey, Pennsylvania.''

''That was last month, Wren.''

''And you didn't bring me any chocolate? I'm crushed.''

''I thought about you. But what can I say? I got hungry on the way home.''

Their lighthearted voices filled the box, and Mary Elise resented the twinge of envy over his easy rapport with the copilot. She'd once shared that same relationship with Daniel until the summer their friendship had spiraled into something more. So much more.

Memories swirled in the murky box with oppressive weight. So Daniel still loved his junk food. They'd met twenty-two years ago over a chocolate Ho-Ho. She'd pulled the treat from her Holly Hobby lunch box to thank him for bloodying Buddy Davis's nose after the bully made fun of her Yankee accent.

Did Daniel still like video games, too? Hide his genius brain behind jokes?

Kiss with an intense thoroughness that turned a woman's insides to warmed syrup?

A hand patted the box once, again, and again, with slow reassurance. Daniel. ''And speaking of hungry,'' he said, his hand thumping a lulling lazy beat. ''There's a flight lunch and a bag of licorice with my name written all over it waiting in the cockpit. Let's step this up.''

Smoke spiraled inside, mingling with the ripe scent of fresh-cut boards. A low wheeze hissed from Trey. His head fell back against her arm as he sucked in air.

Tension stretched inside her. Mary Elise rubbed a soothing hand along his back, a poor substitute for his inhaler, but all she could risk. The smoke, cedar and fear were too much for anyone, much less a child with asthma. As if these kids hadn't already been through enough with their parents' ''accidental'' deaths and a Rubistanian uncle trying to claim them…and their inheritance.

All the more reason to get the children to their half brother on American soil. Screw official diplomatic channels where the boys could be in college before Rubistan coughed them up.

Mary Elise hugged the boys closer, her hair snagging along the wood. Pulling. Stinging her scalp. Hard. Her eyes watered.

Oh, God. Come on, Daniel. They needed to get rid of that guard so someone could crack open the box, let Trey breathe.

And let her out.

Another puff of cigar smoke tendriled inside. ''How interesting that your name tag reads Baker, Cap-i-tain. That is the last name of your ambassador who so recently died.''

The thudding stopped. Silence echoed for three wheezing breaths from Trey before the rhythmic tap resumed. ''Baker's a common last name over in America, Sparky.''

''Of course. If you were related you would be in mourning, not working.''

The vehicle dipped with added weight, then footsteps shuddered the truck bed. Not Daniel's lope. The clipped pace of the guard. ''Is that a loose board I see right—''

''Don't even think about it.'' Daniel's steely voice iced the humid air. The click of a cocked gun echoed. ''If you lay so much as one finger on that box, I'll blow your damned hand off. A diplomatic pouch is sovereign United

States government territory. Move back and get off this truck. Now.''

Bugs droned in response along with the low hum of the idling plane engines. Please, please, please, be careful, Danny. She hadn't wanted to see him and now she couldn't bear the thought of never laying eyes on him again. She'd brought him here, hadn't had a choice for the boys. But if things went to hell, she would never forgive herself.

An exhale sounded along with the retreat of boots and smoke. The gun snicked as it was uncocked.

The crate rolled forward.

Air rushed from her lungs. Not that she should be surprised at Daniel's victory. The teenager she'd known carried an untamed look in his eyes, the veneer of ten generations of Savannah wealth having worn thin for him. So often he'd flung himself into brawls like a scrappy street fighter in defiance of his pedigree. In defense of her. He'd always won, too. Except once.

I'm sorry. She winged her apology for then as well as now.

He'd taken a punch from his father when she'd been as much at fault for the unplanned pregnancy. Of course Daniel had never raised a hand to defend himself.

God, she wished she had the option of fighting back against her ex-husband, fists and brawn and bluster, instead of shadow dancing with insidious threats. He'd never actually struck her, just controlled her, betrayed her body in a way so soul rending she wondered if she could ever recover. And then when she'd dared leave him, he'd hired a hit man to take her out.

Not that the police would help her, thanks to her ex's far-reaching influence.

She wasn't a wilting flower, but she also wasn't stupid.

So she'd run. She'd even been willing to move to a hotbed of political unrest in the Middle-Eastern country of Rubistan to stay alive. At least in Rubistan no one thought it might be a nifty idea to kill her simply because she couldn't bear him children.

Visions of her Georgia home chilled the sweat sealing her silk shirt to her skin. Come on, come on, come on. Open the damned box.

The sides closed in with claustrophobic pressure. She shoved away the need to run. For the boys. The precious warm weights beside her who smelled of chocolate and sunshine and dreams she would never have.

The crate tipped. Mary Elise and the children slid, wedging into the corner with the minimal padding of a couple of blankets.

"Tag, go easy there," Daniel called. "Wouldn't want to crack a keyboard now, would we?"

"No worries, sir." A voice sounded beside them as the box jerked to a stop. "I'll treat it like one of my own."

A mechanical drone built. The dim streaks of light faded. The load-ramp shutting? The world faded around her to near black until the ramp clanked closed.

She forced her breathing to regulate. Maybe they needed privacy to open the crate. That made sense. Then they could slip her back off the plane under the cover of darkness. Not ideal. But doable.

Lazy footsteps picked up speed along the metal floor. A final thump sounded on the planked top. "Lock it down tight, Tag."

"Roger that, Captain."

The thud of boots faded. Chains jangled in the time fugue of waiting. Was it safe to talk? Engines roared and grew louder. Forget waiting.

Mary Elise opened her mouth and shouted. And couldn't hear herself over the engines.

Her heart hammered her chest. The boys wriggled closer. She screamed. A soundless shriek swallowed by the din.

The crate vibrated, joggled as the plane moved. Faster. Forward. Picking up speed. The roar built, swelled. Tension clenched her chest until each breath became a struggle like Trey with his asthma.

The box tilted back. Gravity slid her with the boys until she landed against the wooden wall as the plane…

Went…

Up.

Oh, God. They were airborne.

Airborne. And not a damned moment too soon.

Captain Daniel "Crusty" Baker maxed the throttle. Level at twenty-eight thousand feet. Time to plow through the night sky out of Rubistanian airspace so they could crack open the crate. He'd tried to keep the takeoff as smooth as possible for the boys and their nanny, but he couldn't risk letting them out.

Not while a pair of enemy MiG-21s flew an ominous escort in the star-studded sky.

Swiping aside the unopened bag of licorice, Crusty switched to closed interphone frequency. "Hold tough in back, we're almost over the border."

Where he hoped the MiGs would peel away.

"Roger, sir," answered Senior Master Sergeant J. T. "Tag" Price, loadmaster for the mission. "We're hanging in there."

Relief pilot, 1st Lt. Bo Rokowsky, loomed, strapped in behind Daniel, restless energy filling the cockpit.

Copilot, 1st Lt. Darcy "Wren" Renshaw, worked from

the right seat, punching numbers into the navigational system. "Five minutes and counting down."

No room for error with those MiGs hungry for an excuse to pop them with an infrared missile. Damn, but he owed this crew. Sure the mission had been CIA sanctioned—barely. Approved in a sped-through process that would likely leave heads rolling later when their new squadron commander returned from TDY—temporary duty.

Renshaw had signed on out of friendship. Tag out of honor. Rokowsky out of craziness. The wild-eyed lieutenant constantly gave new meaning to their squadron motto of Anything, Anywhere, Anytime.

Daniel adjusted airspeed, keeping his eyes trained on the holographic HUD—heads up display—perched at the bottom of his windscreen. He owed Renshaw double. Her boyfriend, who worked for the Air Force's Office of Special Investigations, had used his old CIA contacts to push through paperwork for this embassy run in less than forty-eight hours after the call from the economic attaché. The final mission orders had even included a couple of the Air Force's elite security forces, Ravens, to accompany them.

Who couldn't offer protection against the MiGs keeping pace alongside.

Daniel's gun weighed like lead in his pocket. The Rubistanians knew. Of course they knew. But their government couldn't search without concrete evidence the boys were in that crate.

His half brothers. A couple of kids he'd only seen a handful of times. Sure, he could blame that on being oceans apart, but he knew damned well it had nothing to do with distance in miles. It had everything to do with the distance between his father and him that had started eleven years ago. His father had been a senator in those days. Full of himself and his power, the old man had dumped his wife for a hot young translator from Rubistan and started a new family.

Later his father had assumed the position of ambassador to Rubistan so his wife could be near her family. Of course, then the old man had decided to dump her for a newer hottie model—until a blown-up embassy Mercedes had preempted the divorce.

Yeah, the old guy sure as hell had been a poster boy for the wisdom of bachelorhood. And damned if he didn't feel guilty as hell for the crappy, disloyal thought. If only they'd had a chance to come close to understanding each other.

Daniel's hand clenched around the throttle. Steady. They were almost to the border. The box was locked down tight, with the nanny inside to keep the kids calm and safe. The transfer had gone as smoothly as could be expected.

Except when he'd almost had a freaking heart attack over seeing a long wisp of red hair trailing from a crease in the crate. One glimpse of that strand glinting in the tarmac lights and he'd hauled ass onto the truck to put himself between the auburn thread and the guard. Hand behind his back, he'd given the telltale strand a quick yank—and prayed the nanny would stay quiet.

Daniel flicked at a lone red hair clinging to his sleeve. Again. He'd flung it away more than once, but the thing kept sticking to his flight suit. He shook his hand to dislodge it from his glove and tried not to think about another person with hair that shade of auburn. Why the hell was she right there in his mind today?

Mary Elise.

He damned well didn't believe in the mystical. He preferred the mathematical precision of his world of dark ops testing. But he'd never been able to explain the connection between himself and Mary Elise that had started over a shared Ho-Ho after he'd beaten the crap out of Buddy Davis for picking on the new kid about her accent.

Years later the connection had frayed because of a night of impulsive sex. Great sex. Impossible-to-forget sex with his best friend.

Then not friends. Not anymore. No friendship. No baby. No connection with Mary Elise. Until today.

The hair drifted across his control panel.

Renshaw keyed up the mike. "Ten seconds and counting down."

Daniel steadied his breath with each count. Focus. Fly. It must just be his father's death two weeks ago knocking him off balance. Since he'd been so deep in-country on an assignment by the time the message reached him about his father, Daniel had even missed the memorial service. A miscommunication snafu left out his stepmother's death, so he'd assumed the boys were fine.

Definitely a hellacious couple of weeks of surprises. At least he was in the homestretch.

"Three. Two," Wren chanted. "One. Over the Rubistanian border."

Daniel twisted to check-visual out the window. Like clockwork, the MiGs peeled away.

A collective sigh echoed through the headset.

In the clear. "Okay, Tag, go ahead and break open that crate now."

He would worry later about what to do with his brothers. Between their nanny and the brand-new pair of Game Boys in his flight bag, he might not even have to figure that one out until morning.

Daniel reached to punch in the radio frequency to notify Ankara center in Turkey that they'd crossed over into their airspace. The charge of having bested the enemy stirred an adrenaline buzz.

"Captain Baker?" Tag clipped through the headset.

"Yeah, Tag?" Daniel's hand fell away from the radio controls. "Problem?"

"As a matter of fact, there is. I think you're going to want to come down here and check this out for yourself."

Tension snapped through the crew compartment.

"Roger. I'm on my way." Daniel waggled the stick, the fighterlike stick in the C-17 a sleek upgrade from the steering yoke of older cargo planes. "Wren, you got the jet?"

The stick wiggled in his grip in tandem response as she signaled her control. Sweat dotted her brow, dampening her short brown hair to her head, but no hint of stress showed through her concentration. "Roger, Crusty, I have the jet."

Daniel unplugged his headset and charged down the narrow stairwell into the belly of the plane. Victory-sparked adrenaline ignited into a darker dread.

He may not know these brothers of his, but they were counting on him, damn it. They didn't have anyone else other than a megalomaniac uncle in Rubistan who wanted their inheritance to funnel into terrorist training camps.

No way in hell would that slime get his hands on Trey and Austin.

Daniel cleared the stairs and entered the cargo hold. His eyes adjusted to the dim glow of lights tracking the roof and illuminating the metal cave. The crate gaped open. Tag stood with boots braced, the bear of a man cradling a tousle-headed three-year-old like a seasoned parental veteran.

Austin.

Relief pounded through Daniel. His eyes jerked to the

grouping by the row of seats where Trey sat with his elbows on bony knees. Everyone alive.

Cricking his neck from side to side, Daniel strode toward the cluster hovering around Trey. The two Ravens stood guard in full battle dress camouflage, machine guns slung over their shoulders. Body armor padding their chests, both men scowled down at the willowy woman kneeling in front of Trey.

Red hair trailed down her back.

Daniel shut down thoughts of another woman. Everyone seemed okay and that's what mattered most. Some a helluva lot more than *okay*. The woman's brown silk shirt clung to her slim shoulders, to her elegant arms. And legs. Man, she had long legs, legs encased in tan pants smudged with dirt. Hugging a sweetly rounded bottom that begged admiration.

Daniel scrubbed a hand over his gritty—and damned wayward—eyes. Adrenaline played hell with a man's libido, especially after two days of no sleep. He did not need to be seducing the nanny, no matter how intriguing the idea of swiping aside all that silk and hair sounded.

He had other, more practical needs for her, rather than testing the waters to see if she might be interested in some uncomplicated sex. Uncomplicated sex was easy to find with any of the string of women who wanted to ''fix'' him—iron his wrinkled flight suits, make him eat right. Dealing with his brothers, however, would be complicated as hell.

Daniel shifted his attention to his nine-year-old brother. Trey hunched over, hands hooked behind his head on his buzz-cut brown hair as he sucked in gasps of air.

Crap. Daniel strode forward. ''What's going on here?''

Trey jerked upright. ''No-thing,'' he gasped out.

The nanny's shoulders rippled under silk. Still kneeling, she straightened her back but didn't turn.

His hand fell to her shoulder, wavy red hair snagging on his flight glove. A jolt shot up his arm.

Don't be a sap. There were at least a million women with hair that color. ''Ma'am? Is there something we can do for him?''

Slowly her head turned, her fiery hair tugging under his fingers. She looked up at him, and Daniel stared down into the greenest eyes he'd ever seen.

Holy hell.

There might be a million women with hair that color of auburn. But there was only one woman with eyes that particular shade of fresh-mown spring grass.

Mary Elise braced her shoulders with the same defensive bravado she'd worn when telling him the rabbit died.

''Hello, Danny.''

Chapter 2

Mary Elise decided the inside of that box might not be too bad after all. At least in there she could only hear Danny. Now she could hear and *see* him. All of him. Every damned fine inch of him.

Dim lights filled the gray cavern, glinting off Daniel's dark hair, casting shadows along the angles of his face. His lanky good looks had hardened into a lean body cut with whipcord strength that stretched just shy of six feet tall.

If only she could distance herself from his appeal, but the day-from-hell wreaked havoc on her normally rigid self-control. Instead, she could only stare at him and soak up the differences wrought by age.

One gloved hand flattened against the side of the plane, he lounged with that same loose-hipped carelessness he'd worn when she'd told him she was pregnant. As if her announcement hadn't meant the end of his Air Force

Academy dream since cadets can't marry until after graduation.

Except his dream hadn't ended. He'd won the Academy ring and wore the flight suit now, wrinkled though it might be at the moment.

Attraction be damned, she wanted to flatten him right onto his awesome butt. Care about *something*. Let it be important to see the woman you almost married. She'd never been head-over-heels *in* love with him, but she *had* loved him. Once. He'd been her friend, and the betrayal of how easily he'd let go after she lost the baby had hurt.

His indifference hurt now.

He shouldn't still have the power to wound her. Her ex had done so much worse to her and she'd held strong. She'd be damned if she'd let Daniel trample her heart with one distant look.

Mary Elise gripped the barred edge of the seat to steady her hands. She might not be able to regulate her pulse or her feelings, but she could control what she did about them. Bigger worries loomed, anyway, far more important than discovering if Daniel Baker still administered the most thorough, long and intense kisses she'd ever known.

"Danny, could you pass me the smaller bag inside the crate, please? The black canvas one. Trey needs his inhaler."

"Don't…want it," Trey insisted.

Daniel's forehead trenched. "The kid has asthma? Why didn't someone tell me?" He shifted away, mumbling, "And why didn't someone mention who the hell would be accompanying them?"

So it bothered him after all. Mary Elise stifled the urge to do an impromptu victory dance and rubbed soothing circles along Trey's back while Daniel reached into the crate.

His flight suit stretched across narrow hips that veed up his back into broad shoulders. Muscles rippled under taut green fabric with restrained strength. He pivoted around with athletic fluidity, pitching the bag toward her.

"Thank you," she said, avoiding eyes that told her too well she wouldn't be able to dodge talking soon.

Mary Elise yanked the zipper open and rifled inside the pouch until her fingers closed around the inhaler. She snapped off the cap and thrust her hand toward Trey.

He brought the medicine to his mouth and pumped once, twice, again.

She prayed they wouldn't be stranded in the air with Trey in a full-blown attack. "Come on, hon, take one more hit off the inhaler, okay?"

His shoulders heaved with a shuddering inhale.

Mary Elise waited for signs of relief. Years spent tending her chronically ill mother had left her with more knowledge about lung disease than some doctors. Her mother's illness had also left her unsupervised, free to tromp alongside the neighbor boy. Never once had Danny complained about a pesky tagalong two years his junior. He'd shrugged off any teasing—when had Danny cared what others thought anyway—and labeled her his mascot.

Daniel knelt beside her. The scent of bay rum mingled with the pervasive air of hydraulic fluid. "What else can you do for him?"

Mary Elise focused on the hydraulic fluid. Fat lot of good it did her with the warmth of Danny's arm inches away from her breast. "His nebulizer's in the other bag. We can set that up if the Albuterol inhaler doesn't do the trick."

Trey's heaving shoulders slowed.

She swept a hand over his pale brow. "Better, hon?"

The boy nodded.

Daniel held out his hand for the inhaler. "Hey, buddy, let me take that for you."

"You're not…my buddy. Don't even…know you."

Mary Elise stiffened.

Daniel stilled, then slowly retracted his hand. "That's right." His arms fell to rest on his knee. "We don't know each other. And we'll duke that one out later on terra firma back in the States. Right now you just take care of yourself."

Trey clamped his mouth shut and fixed his gaze somewhere over his brother's head.

Shoving to his feet by Tag, Daniel ruffled Austin's sweaty curls. "Hey there, sport."

Austin studied him with wary eyes, but at least not openly hostile. Daniel tugged off his flight gloves and reached into his thigh pocket. His hand whipped back out with a chocolate bar. "Snickers?"

Austin's brown eyes sparkled.

Mary Elise rose, Daniel topping her by only a few inches. A perfect fit. Double damn. "He's allergic to nuts."

"How about licorice?"

"He might choke."

Daniel's jaw flexed. "Three Musketeers bar?"

Mary Elise refrained from asking for an apple, a senseless request after the kid had already been offered candy. "That would be fine."

Daniel fished the treat out of his seemingly bottomless pocket for Austin, then turned back to his other brother.

Trey hunched back in the seat, arms tight across his chest. "I'm not hungry."

Uh-oh. The kid loved licorice. Mary Elise waited for Daniel's reaction. Prayed somewhere inside this harder new Daniel there still lived the Danny who'd sat with her during her bout with chicken pox, teaching her to play poker, tutoring her in math, making her laugh so she wouldn't scratch.

Shrugging, Daniel zipped his thigh pocket closed. ''Fair enough. I have to head back up to the crew compartment. If you decide you're hungry later on, Tag here can give you a hand.''

Mary Elise winged a silent thanks for the easy out Daniel offered Trey. Maybe they would be okay after all.

''Mary Elise?'' Daniel called. ''Got a second?''

Big-time uh-oh. She didn't want this talk right now, not when the old Danny still hovered in her memory.

Better pitch those sympathetic leanings back in the crate and maintain her distance. Keep it light. Do the *old friends* routine.

Old friends who happened to know every inch of each other's body.

Daniel cupped her elbow, his grip hot, firm—familiar. And it had been so long since a man had touched her. Her body absorbed the sensation. Stupid. Wrong.

But pulling away would lend too much importance to a simple gesture. She kept her eyes forward and suppressed a shiver. He was a good-looking guy, no question, in a rumpled way that defied her need for order.

Hormones, pure and simple.

The day's danger and stress left her vulnerable. That must be the reason she wanted to tuck against his broad chest, the only reason she yearned to savor the comfort of bay rum and chocolate.

Her eyes landed on the little round scar beside his brow. Two weeks after her recovery, Daniel's chicken pox had spread fast and furious. She'd brought a deck of cards to his house and reamed him out for not telling her he hadn't been exposed before. He'd just shrugged, scratching the corner of his eyebrow.

How could he be such a stranger and so familiar all at once?

His boots thudded along the metal tracks lining the belly of the plane as he put space between them and the boys. Tucked in a corner, he stopped, releasing her elbow. "Do I need to call ahead for an emergency landing?"

Mary Elise fingered the parachutes dangling from the wall for distraction. "I don't think so. Where would we land, anyway?"

"We can chance it in Turkey. Germany would be better."

"But?"

"It's safer if we press through straight for the States. Except of course Trey's health has to come first."

Intimacy wrapped around her, different from the sensual atmosphere of a few moments ago. Rather a more comfortable aura of two parents discussing their children. Each parent-style word sliced her insides with endless tiny paper cuts.

She forced herself to think of Trey. "I'll keep a close watch on him, especially for the next hour, but I think the worst has passed, now that he's away from the guard's smoke. Once we land, you could take him by the E.R. just to be certain."

"I'll have a flight surgeon waiting for us." Daniel lifted his headset from around his neck and readjusted the fit before plugging into the mounted outlet. "Wren, patch a call through to Charleston and have Doc Bennett meet us when we land. One of the boys has asthma and I want him checked out. Make sure Kathleen knows I'm the one asking."

Kathleen? An irrational jealousy stirred. Of course Daniel had women in his life, professionally and personally. Not that she cared.

Yeah, right.

Daniel flipped the mouthpiece away. ''All set. Anything else we can do?''

She was finished playing out this bizarre pseudoparenting game. She'd made her restitution to Daniel's father. No more guilt. The boys had their brother Danny now. He could feed them junk food until they spun out on sugar if he wished.

They weren't her children. Even considering assuming that role poured straight alcohol on every one of her internal paper cuts.

Mary Elise retreated deeper inside herself and away from Daniel's too familiar smile. ''We'll be okay, except he's usually physically drained after an attack. Please pull the blankets out of the crate for me to spread out here so he can sleep.''

Daniel watched her face tighten into the prim lines meant to distance him but instead made him want to gather up a fistful of her hair and kiss the look away. All the same, her autocratic coolness evicted their brief moment of connection.

For the best while he was trying like hell to find solid ground after being knocked on his ass over finding her in his plane. He wanted nothing more than to take an hour or ten to study this new Mary Elise in front of him. To understand her. But she wasn't a scientific equation.

A poised elegant woman stood in place of his freckled coltish friend. He'd be a fool not to notice her appeal. He'd be an even bigger fool to act on it.

Those two boys needed him. Austin would likely be a snap to figure out. The imp had a gleam in his eyes Daniel recognized well. Trey, however, looked so much like their imperious old man, he could already predict the head butting.

Time to get his mind the hell off unforgettable red hair and gentle curves.

Daniel dropped his hand from the side of the plane and allowed extra air to slide between them before he fell victim to the temptation to untangle a strand of her hair from her gold hoop earring. ''There are two crew-rest bunks. We can put the boys there.''

''Does that break some kind of regulation? What about the crew's sleep?'' She straightened both of the rings on her right hand—a ruby dinner ring on her middle finger and on her thumb, a large gold band worn only half way down.

Too large to have been her wedding ring.

What had she done with her band after her divorce? She'd mailed his engagement solitaire to him once he'd returned to the Academy, in spite of his insistence that she keep it.

The diamond ring burned a hole in his sleeve pocket even now, a constant reminder to learn from past mistakes. ''This whole mission breaks regs. I'm not overly concerned about a little technicality such as where they sleep. The crew can rack back here if they need to catch a nap.''

The plane jostled on an air pocket. His hand shot up instinctively to brace her waist. Her familiar scent of honeysuckle teased his nose.

His hand cupped her ribs, the underside of her breast heating his skin. Small, soft. Perfect.

Were her breasts as sensitive as they'd been in the early weeks of her pregnancy? They'd spent every one of those postpregnancy test days exploring each other's bodies without fear of consequence since the consequences had already occurred.

The heat of her now fired memories. Fired him. If he moved his thumb…

His headset crackled in his ears.

"Crusty?" Renshaw called. "Wanna finish that update, please?"

He jerked his hand away and flipped the mouthpiece in place. "The nanny opted not to join us and sent a substitute. We have a stowaway."

"Stowaway?" Bo Rokowsky piped up. "Man or woman?"

Daniel's hand clenched around the memory of warm silk and soft Mary Elise against his hand. "Woman."

"Is she hot?"

Yes. Hell, yes. "Not germane to the mission, Rokowsky."

"'Cause if she is, I'll take over down there and you can come up here."

"Can it, Bo."

"Touchy, touchy. Or maybe not enough touching lately in spite of all those women wanting to cook you dinner and iron your flight suits."

So what if he enjoyed a few casserole gifts now and again? Big freaking deal, and nothing compared to Rokowsky's history with women.

He wouldn't discuss Mary Elise over interphone with the squadron Casanova. A man who sure as hell wasn't getting anywhere near her during this flight. "Keep this up and I'll tell her what your call sign stands for, 'Bo.'" The guy's real name had long ago faded from memories as he'd gone by Bo since training days. "Meanwhile, how about working on flying the plane or something?"

Daniel flipped the mouthpiece aside again. "We need to talk."

"We are talking." Her spine pulled straighter—which exposed a tempting patch of graceful neck.

He nodded toward his brothers. "Away from them so they can't read your body language. I need to know more about what happened in Rubistan if I'm going to keep them safe."

Tension rippled through her.

He resisted the urge to stroke her arm, cup her shoulder and pull her to him. Worse than wanting to palm her breast, he wanted Mary Elise to fling her arms around his neck like so many times before.

Damn, he'd missed her. Missed their easy friendship. No surprise he'd screwed it up. A slew of failed relationships since with casserole-cooking and uniform-ironing women hammered home his shortcomings in the relationship department. The latest to walk had deemed him "emotionally unavailable."

Whatever the hell that meant.

Sure, he was sorry when each relationship self-destructed. But not one of them had left a hole in his life. Except Mary Elise.

His grip tightened as if he could somehow reinvent the past by holding tighter. She winced.

He raised his hands, backing away. "Sorry."

For so many damned things he wouldn't do any differently now. *Emotionally unavailable* worked well for him.

"Let me get the boys settled, Danny. We can talk once they're asleep."

At least she didn't argue or pretend they could ignore the fact that she stood in his plane in place of the boys' nanny from Florida.

He didn't know why she was here. Didn't know why

it mattered so damned much to him. But he did owe her. ‘‘Thanks for getting them out of there.’’

‘‘I’d do it for anyone.’’

Yes, she would. But she hadn’t done it for anyone. She’d done it for him. And just as when she’d passed him that Ho-Ho twenty-two years ago, he couldn’t walk away.

Mary Elise sagged into the seat across from the two crew bunks in the Spartan sleeping cubicle behind the cockpit. Trey tangled in the covers on the top, slack-jawed with exhaustion. On the bottom, Austin clutched his ragged sailboat quilt, sucking on a corner as if he could somehow taste home.

How much would the little guy remember of the ordeal, the crate, the escape?

Would he remember his parents?

Franklin Baker hadn’t been the best of fathers to Daniel, but he’d been trying to compensate with Trey and Austin. Their mother may have been a dim bulb, but she’d loved her boys. They’d loved her.

Trey and Austin had been shuffled so much in their short lives—born in the States, moving a couple of years ago, now back again. And the turmoil wasn’t over yet. A new home. A guardian they didn’t even know.

Their brother.

Danny.

The mammoth aircraft seemed to shrink, the gray beams and bolts closing in on her. Such a large plane shouldn’t feel so very small, nowhere to turn without bumping into him. They must be plowing through the most turbulent stretch of airspace in the sky. One more pitch against Daniel’s rock-solid chest and she would lose her mind.

Toying with her earring, she untangled threads of hair

from the hoop. He should *not* have the ability to unsettle her so much. She wanted to exchange a nostalgic smile and hug while they both acknowledged their lives had moved on for the best.

Except she hadn't. What about him?

A tingle started up her spine. She could feel *him,* standing behind her. Danny. Mary Elise glanced up and over her shoulder, already accepting she would find him.

Not Danny, but rather the stranger, Daniel, lounged in the doorway, rumpled flight suit making her long to swipe her hands over the wrinkles.

The muscles.

Silently he stared back at her. No doubt churning the whole mess around in his analytical brain, searching for a way to make sense of it all. Then opting to cover his confusion with a joke.

She didn't want that joke. She wanted a piece of the past to replace the awkwardness. "Remember the time you painted your face and decked out in cammo to see if you could break into the Savannah River Site plant?"

The C-17 droned for what seemed like an hour, probably closer to seconds, before a slow smile dimpled Danny's cheeks. He canted closer to be heard over the plane's roar, the privacy curtain swaying closed behind him. "Well, hell, Mary Elise, I was doing a public service. Anyplace constructing and testing the parts for nukes needed to have stronger security if a twelve-year-old could bust inside."

"No respect for danger, ever." Her eyes fell to rest on the children, checking the steady rise and fall of their chests, any snuffling breaths masked by the rumble of engines vibrating the plane. With each exhalation she thanked God for their sturdy little bodies, so resilient.

Five miscarriages had taught her well how fragile young life could be.

Although, Danny had seemed to possess a godlike invincibility in his youth. Or perhaps that had more to do with how he'd never groused over a tagalong tired of tiptoeing so as not to disrupt her bed-bound mother. "You wouldn't have been caught if I hadn't snuck along."

"You always did worry too much." His shoulders filled the portal and her eyes.

Mary Elise welcomed the escape into happier times with smaller childhood worries. "You could have left me behind when the alarm went off. I wouldn't have ratted you out."

"Which is why I couldn't leave you."

But he had. Eventually. After her miscarriage, she'd seen the caged look in his eyes, the need to run once he was free of obligations. She hadn't expected they would still get married—right away. She understood his need to finish school. But she *had* expected something more from him after all the times they'd made love following her pregnancy test. They'd moved past being friends, she'd thought. His need to escape her had hurt.

She'd hurt him right back. God, had she ever let her temper have its way with her as she'd sent him away.

Life had since taught her to contain more volatile emotions. "You always did have a soft spot for causes."

One hint of what waited for her back in Savannah and he would grease up in cammo to take on her ex in some commando raid. All the more reason to park her butt back in Rubistan. She'd quickly discovered how little help the police could be against Kent with his wealth and power. Even her parents hadn't believed her, instead buying into Kent's less messy explanation of postpartum depression.

The icy press of an assassin's gun to her temple had

not been a delusion. Only quick reflexes and an escape to Rubistan had saved her life.

Danny sank into the seat beside her. "I assume you were the one who nudged the economic attaché to call me."

His firm thigh molded to hers. She nodded, swallowed. "Uh-huh."

"Thank you."

"You're welcome." She pushed the words free from her cotton mouth.

He stretched his leg in front of him, rubbing a too long caress against her. "How the hell did you end up in that box in place of the nanny? Or are you their new nanny?"

She suppressed the urge to inch away. Not that she could go anywhere without slamming the wall. "I work at the embassy school, teaching English. I'm just close to the boys since they attend the school."

"How did you go from being editor of a newspaper in Savannah to teaching in Rubistan?"

"Excuse me?" she bristled. "I don't consider it a step down, thank you very much."

He elbowed her gently. "Cool your jets, 'Lise. I was talking basic geography."

She measured her words. "I wanted a change of scenery. Your father helped."

"My father." Muscles bunched visibly under the creased flight suit.

He'd never allowed himself to vent or rant, always taking on everyone else's battles and ignoring his own. Who would be there to help him through the grief over his father's death?

The Kathleen person he'd called for?

She couldn't begrudge him that. Especially when the boys would need a woman's influence more than ever.

They also needed their brother steady. Daniel's hero worship for his father had died in a rift they'd never bridged, which would only make the coming weeks tougher for him.

Mary Elise let herself touch him. Just his arm. Lightly. "I'm so sorry."

He didn't answer for an extended moment before he stood to leave, pulling away emotionally as well as physically. As she'd known he would. He had always been more at ease with simple. Uncomplicated.

Daniel paused in the doorway. "I'll take you up front to patch through a call."

She struggled to understand his words in the wake of the liquid heat pulsing through her veins. "Patch a call?"

"Home."

She frowned. "My apartment's empty right now."

"I meant Savannah. I don't have your parents' number or I'd do it for you. Unless there's someone else you'd prefer to contact." His eyes chilled. "Like your husband."

"My *ex*-husband."

"Right." His emotionless gaze pinned her. "Do you want me to call Kent McRae?"

Hearing her ex-husband's name sent a tremor through her. Followed by a completely different shiver over realizing Daniel had cared enough to track her transition from Mary Elise Fitzgerald to Mary Elise McRae. From a single college journalism student to the wife of a major newspaper publisher.

And who was she now?

Alive. Just how she damn well intended to stay. "I'm not planning to go home. I'll turn right around and return to Rubistan and my job."

''Think again.'' Familiar chocolate-brown eyes hardened into the different, darker Danny.

What in the world had he seen and experienced during their years apart? ''Excuse me?''

''We may have escaped Rubistan without being searched. But they knew. Once you and the boys come up missing at the same time, it won't take longer than a puff on that guard's cigar to link you to this. If you go back, you'll be jailed—or dead—an hour after you touch down.''

All those thousands of emotional paper cuts flamed to life in full-blown dread. The implications of the past hours swelled into certainty. She hated the helplessness. Most of all hated that she would have to turn to Danny for answers after a year of hoping never to need anyone again. ''What happens after we land in Charleston?''

''What kind of ID do you have?''

''I didn't have time to grab my purse before I got in the crate,'' she answered automatically, pushing the words through numb lips. ''But I always keep my passport on me.''

''Good, then you'll be processed through the base. In the meantime, you have to stay somewhere. With your parents or me?'' Daniel leaned closer, bay rum obliterating hydraulic fluid in a sensory tidal wave. ''It's your call to make, and quite frankly, I need you more right now.''

Chapter 3

"You need me?" Mary Elise enunciated slowly.

Daniel watched her brows pull together over confused green eyes. He wasn't feeling much steadier himself.

He braced a hand against the bulkhead and planted both boots for balance. Where the hell had his words come from?

There were probably a hundred different services he could call to help at a moment's notice. He knew at least a dozen women who would enjoy nothing more than mothering the boys as a way to entice him into being "emotionally available."

And none of them were Mary Elise.

He tried to tell himself his motives for keeping her close were rooted in protectiveness. That long-ago connection had kicked into overdrive in the past few minutes. Right about the time he'd mentioned calling Savannah.

He didn't consider himself an intuitive guy, a fact reinforced by his double-digit tally of breakups. But even he could sense something was wrong here. Her edginess should be easing with every mile they put between themselves and Rubistan.

Should be.

But wasn't.

Eleven years of distance between them didn't matter. He owed this woman, and until her frown smoothed, he wouldn't back off.

He was doing this for her. And for the boys. Not because he wanted to find out if the freckles dotting her smooth creamy skin had faded with age. ''I need your help with stuff like asthma meds and nut allergies. At this rate, the boys won't make it through the week with me.''

Mary Elise straightened in her seat. Daniel looked deeper into those lush green eyes that had once been so expressive and wondered when she'd learned to close herself off.

''I'll make a list.'' Her cool efficiency almost covered her underlying edginess. Almost. ''Starting with Austin's EpiPen.''

''Eppie what?''

''Epinephrine injection pen. Medicine in case he accidentally eats something with nuts or peanut oil or—''

''Stop.'' He made a giant *T* with his hands. ''Time out. You can compile lists all day long and it won't change the fact that I have no experience with kids. I need help settling the boys.''

She pleated her pants between fidgety fingers. ''You haven't made any accommodations for them?''

''Hell, Mary Elise, I was a little busy planning how to smuggle them out of Rubistan without getting our asses shot off.''

''Oh.''

''Apology accepted.''

Her hands flattened on her trim thighs, a smile playing with her lips. ''Uh, sorry?''

He winked. ''No problem.''

A smile and a wink linked them more than all his earlier speeches.

The deafening din of engines and the closed curtain offered a bubble of privacy and protection from being overheard. Not that he had thoughts of unrolling the past with her. He hadn't been much for emotional sharefests then, either.

Besides, he didn't want to trek back to the past. Too many memories waited there of a time he'd been less of a man. Too much his father's son—seducing an innocent, betraying a friendship. His father's wedding had marked a time of rotten decisions for everyone.

Halfway into a bottle of champagne, Daniel had found himself watching nineteen-year-old Mary Elise with new eyes. Another shared bottle and some consolation later, Daniel had found himself looking at all of Mary Elise with new eyes.

''What happens now?''

She'd asked him that then as well. *What do I do now, Danny?*

God help him, he'd shown her.

He'd been so pissed at his old man for going the whole trophy wife route. He didn't deal well with emotions on a good day, and a bad day had a way of playing hell with a man's self-control. Today marked another one of his worst days on record, but he wouldn't screw up this time. No matter how enticing the image of draping that red hair over his chest. Mary Elise over him.

Mary Elise sighing.

''Danny?'' She flung her hair over her shoulder in a

crimson waterfall. "If you haven't made arrangements for the boys, what do you propose we do once we land?"

"Hell if I know." Then or now. "And it doesn't look as if Trey knows what to do about me any more than I know what to do about him."

Her brows pulled tighter, deepening her perpetual frown. "You aren't going to give them up. Are you?"

"No. Absolutely not. I'll figure it out. Soon."

"Once you're through worrying about our asses."

He did *not* want to think about her ass. "Right." Daniel scrubbed a hand over his bristly chin. "I have leave time built up. I'll take it now until the boys and I can work out a plan. But I sure would appreciate your help for the next few days. Since you're an American Express card short of being able to check into a Motel 6, I'm thinking we can make a trade."

She shot him a disapproving look that had likely commanded boardrooms, then later classrooms. "Or you could do the gentlemanly thing and loan me a couple hundred bucks."

Already he could feel her slipping away. Damn it, the boys needed her. And while he might not be Captain Communication, he wasn't walking away without finding out what had her forehead trenched deeper than a fresh-plowed field. "Sure, I *could* loan you the money."

"But you don't want to." Mary Elise willed away the rogue twinge of excitement. She wanted to say her good-byes. Right? Danny had been a generous friend. An exciting lover.

And a lousy boyfriend.

Once that boyfriend/lover line had been crossed, recapturing the friendship became impossible. She knew keeping her distance now lent more credence to her feelings all those years ago. But her heart bore too many scars to risk opening it again.

All the same, guilt nudged her to say, "The boys *do* need me."

"Yes, ma'am, they do," he continued with a sincerity too reminiscent of past times conning his way out of trouble. "This is about more than asthma and EpiPens. Trey and Austin are alone and scared. They don't know me from Adam."

She didn't buy into the Danny-perfected con tones for even a minute, but his logic had merit. Turning away from Austin crying in the crate hadn't been an option. Why did she think now would be any different?

Scar tissue also made a person tough. She would hang on to that for the next few days with Danny and the boys. "Okay, okay! I actually agreed two arguments ago. You always were persistent."

"And you were always too nice."

Watching the dimples creep into Daniel's cheeks and past her defenses, Mary Elise decided "nice" didn't factor anywhere into her swirl of emotions. "Nice? Careful, Danny, or I'll change my mind."

"So you'll help me for a couple of weeks?"

"A couple of days." Hopefully enough time to formulate a new plan.

"Until I find another nanny."

Which would take at least a week. "For the boys."

"I never thought otherwise."

He ducked back into the crew compartment, leaving her alone with her thoughts and two sleeping children. The cubicle echoed without him, the repercussions of her decision crowding the confined space. Since Kent didn't know her location, a week should be safe before she risked alerting him by withdrawing money from her account. She could use the time to decide where to go and what to do with her life.

A week to stay with those two boys who'd first tugged her heart because of Daniel and then stolen her heart by being themselves. She wouldn't even let herself think about being a surrogate-mother figure to them. Her dreams of family were dead, thanks to Kent.

Mary Elise leaned forward and tucked the sailboat blanket around Austin, his puffy breaths whispering over her wrist. She started to pull away, but he grappled for her hand without waking.

Stroking a thumb over butter-soft skin, she studied the miracle of five tiny fingers and couldn't stem memories of all the babies she'd miscarried. She'd wanted to adopt, but Kent had insisted they keep trying for a biological child. She'd gone on the pill, anyway. For all the good it had done her. Then the surprise pregnancy had lasted longer than any of her other four first-trimester miscarriages.

She'd finally dared to hope.

Losing her son at twenty-four weeks had almost destroyed her. Discovering Kent had replaced her birth control pills with placebos months earlier finished the job.

Weariness swamped her along with the memories. She surrendered to the need for sleep and the tug of a chubby little hand. Mary Elise slid into the bottom bunk, curving herself protectively around Austin.

No, Kent had never raised a hand to her, which somehow made his menacing plans after she left all the more chilling. Hindsight told her she should have seen the warning signs. He'd been abusing her and controlling her in other ways for years, culminating in that final violation of her body and trust.

Now she had one week to find a new safe haven. And

pray seven days of playing house with Danny and two precious boys wouldn't slice past her scar tissue into what little soul she had left.

One booted foot resting on the bottom crew bunk across from him, Daniel sprawled in the unrelenting seat. Well, as much as a guy could sprawl in the tight space. Another half hour and he would take over flying while Wren sacked out.

He should be sleeping, but couldn't. Too wired. Seeing Mary Elise now when he was still reeling from his father's death rattled him. No question.

Daniel studied the three sleeping figures that had thrown his life into chaos. Sure he didn't give a damn about ironing his uniform or eating on a schedule, but he was in charge of his world and his emotions.

Or he had been until Mary Elise and the boys.

In the past hour he'd made strides in regaining control. She was staying. The boys would level out. And somehow that still didn't unkink the knot in his neck that had started right about the minute she'd turned those deep-green eyes his way for the first time in eleven years.

No risk of seeing her eyes now. She lay sleeping on the bottom bunk, her back to him, her body curved around Austin. Her hair tangled around the child and over the edge of the bed. The little guy snoozed on with his knees tucked to his chest, his blanket gripped in a white-knuckled fist.

Leaning, Daniel captured a lock of her hair and tested the silky texture between two fingers. He'd done the right thing asking her to stay. The boys had already lost their parents. They needed a familiar person to ease them through the transition.

On the top bunk, Trey rolled and shifted until he settled onto his back. All three, dead to the world.

Thank God they weren't dead period, only exhausted from the long hours and ordeal. A few more minutes of staring at them and he would have his balance back.

A shadow slid through the doorway. Daniel glanced up to find Tag waiting silently.

The Senior Master Sergeant nodded toward the bunks. "I'll watch over them if you need to catch some sleep."

"I'm set until we land. No worries."

Tag studied him silently, gaze falling to the lock of hair still twined around Daniel's fingers.

Well, hell.

Daniel dropped the strand. A lone determined hair clung to the wrist of his flight suit like before. He didn't waste energy refuting Tag's all-knowing expression. Why bother when he actually appreciated the older man's no-bull approach to life? The man appreciated facts and the uncomplicated.

Years of working top-secret test projects at Edwards AFB in California had honed Daniel's instincts. He didn't think of those instincts as anything of a woo-hoo nature. Rather, he made observations and processed them quickly. Efficiently. Two weeks into his transfer to Charleston AFB in South Carolina, Daniel had realized Tag was a troop to trust.

Even with something as important as Mary Elise.

"You know, Tag, I believe I'll take you up on that offer in another half hour." Daniel flicked aside the hair on his wrist. "I don't need sleep, but I have to head back up front soon and I'd rather not wake Mary Elise. So, yeah, I would appreciate it if you kept an eye on them in case one of the boys rouses before her."

Tag lumbered in through the door, curtain closing behind him, and lowered himself into the other seat. "Small world, her showing up on this flight."

And an even smaller world on base. No doubt, gossip would make the rounds three times over by the next nightfall. Not from Tag, but Bo would have a helluva time sharing the inside scoop at the club.

"Family connection. We knew each other a long time ago." Daniel shot him a half smile. "That 'Danny' of hers probably gave us away."

"Ah, so you're old friends."

Daniel hesitated a second too long.

Tag's quirked brow shot up toward the older man's salt-and-pepper hairline.

Finally, Daniel settled for, "We have…history."

Tag nodded again. Waited. Studied the sleeping trio. Finally shifted his attention back to Daniel. "Is the older kid yours?"

The notion blazed across Daniel's mind in a flash of horror. Had she faked a miscarriage? He'd never seen Trey's mother pregnant. He could imagine selfless Mary Elise cutting him free so he could complete his senior year at the Academy.

Simple math severed the irrational thought. Trey was over a year too young. "No. Trey's not mine." Daniel's head thunked back against the bulkhead. Damn it, why couldn't Tag have shown up fifteen minutes later once the world had stopped rocking under his boots? "Ours would have been ten now."

Hell, he hadn't told anyone about that time with Mary Elise. Something about the way Tag didn't push made it easier to talk during a day when the past crowded his brain.

Daniel hooked a hand on his knee, boot propped beside the trailing hair, and lost himself in the hypnotic sway of red. ‘‘She miscarried early, before we had a chance to get married. I would have married her though. No way would I have let her down.’’

But he had, in so many other ways, both of them too damned young. He’d been knocked on his ass by how much a few short weeks of making love to her had shaken him. So he’d run like hell the minute she’d given him the green light.

‘‘And here you two are again.’’

‘‘Not for long. She’ll settle back in Savannah and I’ll be in Charleston.’’

‘‘All of two and a half hours apart,’’ Tag’s dry tones mixed with the rumble of four engines. ‘‘Might as well be on different planets.’’

Daniel snorted. ‘‘I think I enjoyed you more when you stayed quiet.’’

‘‘My wife likely disagrees,’’ he answered, his dry wit more parched than normal. Not that the guy looked open to making the current sharingfest a two-way deal.

Tag canted forward, elbows on his knees. ‘‘While I’m on a roll, here’s some hard-earned wisdom you can take or leave. So you had a thing going once? But you were too young to hang on to it. Makes sense. That Mars and Venus stuff is hard as hell for an old guy like me to figure out. It can be damned near impossible when you’re younger.’’

Daniel shook his head, half believing, yet knowing he couldn’t let himself off the hook that easily. ‘‘Where were you eleven years ago when I wanted to hear something like this?’’

‘‘Making my own mistakes,’’ Tag answered with fatherly wisdom, even though his forty-one years made any true parental connection impossible.

‘‘She and I are history.’’

Tag stayed silent.

Crap. Did parents go to a school to develop that look?

Daniel followed Tag's gaze. Straight down to Daniel's hand that had somehow found its way back into Mary Elise's hair.

He untwisted his finger from the strands, not a speedy proposition. The hair unwrapped and unwrapped in a long unraveling stretch.

"History," Daniel repeated as if he could will it so.

"Sure. You can take that route. Let go, quick and easy like. Or you can use the second chance to get your head on straight about this woman. Your choice. Don't screw it up—" he grinned, standing "—*sir.* I'll be back in a half hour."

Tag swept aside the curtain and ducked out of the small quarters, his hard-earned wisdom lingering long after the curtain stopped rippling.

Daniel watched the pendulum swish of Mary Elise's hair and thought of that wary flash in her eyes at the mention of her ex. More cause to be careful around her, and it wasn't as if the woman wanted a commitment from him anymore.

He did "no commitment" damned well.

Tag's talk of second chances had merit. Now was Daniel's chance to right the past. He may have taken the easy route and let her send him packing eleven years ago. But he wasn't running away from her now.

With a cool determination that had carried him through countless secret test missions, Daniel fixed his mind on a dual goal. Nothing would happen to his brothers on his watch. And no one, most especially himself, would ever hurt Mary Elise again.

Kent McRae gripped his steering wheel until it hurt. From the comfort of his Mercedes, he watched the C-17 circle above the thick band of evergreens. Night sounds and darkness wrapped around him while he waited, tucked just outside the main gate of Charleston Air Force Base.

The drive up from Savannah after the call from the economic attaché in Rubistan had given him time to think, to strategize. He didn't like it when plans went off-kilter.

And Mary Elise had skewed his life once too often.

He forced his hold on the steering wheel to relax. No losing control. Stay steady and focused. If only she'd been inside that rigged car with Ambassador Baker as he'd been led to expect. That she'd survived, then turned to another man to help with the boys, stirred a cold wrath.

One explosion and his life could have been back on track, the past cleared away so he could start his future with a new wife. However, the week's events would only prove a minor setback for a persistent man.

Kent raised binoculars for a better view of the circling plane. Persistence paid off, after all. If only Mary Elise could have believed him about that. But her defective body housed a defective mind. She simply didn't comprehend, no matter how often he'd told her to keep trying and eventually they would have their perfect family.

He'd loved her, damn it. So much. And she'd left him. He'd thought he could win her back. Finally accepted otherwise. And if he couldn't have her, at least he would have a clean slate to begin a new life with a more malleable woman.

And Baker? Every crime needed a fall guy. The appearance of a murder/suicide between old lovers should satisfy authorities.

The oversize cargo plane straightened out of the turn, lining up with the runway, lower, closer, roaring overhead. Kent watched and waited. Patient.

Persistent.

Chapter 4

Her patience had worn thin.

Mary Elise wanted to call this day over. Now. The cargo plane had finally landed in Charleston, and they were seconds away from exiting the metal cavern that had grown more claustrophobic with each minute closer to the States.

Hitching the sleeping Austin higher on her hip, Mary Elise followed the loadmaster's lead through the belly of the plane toward the hatch. The remaining hours of the flight had dragged, drawn tight by anxiety over what awaited her once she exited the front gate. What would she do with her life and how would she deal with the possibility that Kent might find her?

Moreover, how would she handle a week alone with Daniel?

She tried to shake off the jangle of emotions. The fear of the unknown had to be worse than reality. Surely once she had a good night's sleep she could restore her boundaries and do away with the awful vulnerability pricking her insides.

The seal popped and swooshed as the hatch swung open. Her brief nap in the airplane barely made a dent in her weariness. Not that landing put her much closer to crawling into bed and sleeping away the exhaustion and frustration of the past hours. Trey still needed to check in with a doctor about his asthma.

The doctor. Kathleen. The woman who would drop everything just for Danny. Of course if he had someone else in his life, that would free her.

Yeah right, like she'd ever been free of this guy's ghost. Surely it had more to do with him being her first lover that earned him a special spot in her memories.

Daniel stepped into sight from the stairwell leading up to the cockpit. She eyed the stretch of his shoulders as she made her way toward the exit hatch. What about *her* spot in *his* memories? How much importance did she want there?

Daniel pivoted to her. "Let me take the little slugger."

Austin clung tighter in his sleep, his grip firm around her neck and growing dangerously tight around her heart. "I can carry him."

"The steps are steep. A tumble will land you both hard." He leaned to whisper against her ear, his warm breath scented with chocolate and the promise of passion. "Temporary truce. Everything doesn't have to be a battle between us."

Score one for Daniel. She passed over the sleeping child and forced herself not to smooth the boy's tousled curls.

Or the stray lock brushing Daniel's brow.

Steadying her hand on the metal rail, she descended the steps and inhaled the familiar Southern aromas in front of her mingling with Daniel's bay rum behind her. The early afternoon sun crested over the band of pine trees and live oaks bordering the stretch of cement. Nostalgia nicked her, the low country of South Carolina so like her Savannah home. A hungry longing filled her to inhale greedy gulps of both the place and the man.

Rubistan's isolation from temptation had merit.

Mary Elise steeled herself to move forward. The hum of engines from a distant bus, truck and ambulance mingled with the symphony of crickets and June bugs. Autumn in South Carolina resembled the summer heat in many Northern climes. Her silk shirt clung to her back by the time she cleared the last step.

A byproduct of the temperature, damn it, not the lure of home. She had to stop the past from dinging her control.

Guiding a groggy Trey to the side, she waited for Daniel and the others to clear the craft. She flipped a mental switch within herself, shifting from a too-vulnerable woman to analytical reporter mode. She would observe the world around her without getting involved.

One of the copilots, the young guy with a devilish twinkle in his eyes, strutted across the cement, guitar case slung over his back. ''Need any help there, sir? I've got extra seats in my car.''

He tossed a wink her way, his flirting complimentary without a threatening edge. She allowed herself a smile. Detached, but participating, interacting in normal human exchanges. Something she hadn't done in so long.

Daniel stepped closer. ''No, thanks, Bo. My truck has an extended cab. We'll be fine.''

''Okay, then. Take it easy, sir.'' Bo backed away, morning sun glinting off the copilot's jet-black hair and perfect features, increasing his fallen-angel air.

Actually more like an impish fallen cherub since the guy was probably all of twenty-five, making Daniel's hundred-percent adult male hard lines vibrate tension through the air.

Jaw set, Danny cupped her elbow as he guided her toward the waiting crew bus. "Did you want to ride with him?"

Jealousy laced his words. Surprising her. Thrilling her.

"Of course I didn't." The answer fell free before she could think to say something that would put more distance between them. Instead she just stared back as the thrill tripped through her, all the while blaming the yearning on a weakness born of exhaustion.

Running footsteps jarred her back to the present. The copilot, Darcy Renshaw, sprinted by toward the waiting military truck. The passenger door opened and a man stepped out, a civilian if his unconventional clothes and spiked hair were anything to go by. His seafoam-colored windbreaker clashed with flowered, knee-length swim trunks. Darcy dropped her flight bag and flung her arms around his neck seconds before he kissed her. *Really* kissed her, like a man who couldn't get enough of that one woman.

Screw distance. Analytical observations went up in flames as embers of long-dead dreams sparked. What would it be like to inspire that kind of passion? She and Daniel had been on fire for each other during those uninhibited weeks of lovemaking. But sometimes she wondered if years apart might have painted her memories a deeper shade of red as her discontent in her marriage grew.

Daniel cleared his throat.

Mary Elise glanced up. "They're married?"

"Nah, still in the newly engaged stage."

A rush of heat swelled through her. Yeah, she and Daniel had fallen well into that can't-get-enough engaged state. ''Oh. Uh, they seem well suited.''

He patted Austin's head to soothe the yawning child back to sleep and charged forward, the path past the necking couple the only route toward the waiting ambulance. ''They met last summer on a joint mission to Guam.''

''He's Air Force?'' She eyed the man's nonregulation hair with curiosity, hair currently getting a finger comb from an amorous lady copilot who wasn't overly concerned about public displays of affection.

''Was CIA. Now he's a civilian employee with the OSI—Office of Special Investigations. Kind of like the Air Force's own CIA.'' Daniel cleared his throat and urged her forward, not even breaking stride as they drew alongside the embracing couple. ''Thanks for your help, Spike. I owe ya one.''

Without slowing the kiss, the man pulled his hand off Darcy Renshaw's waist and held his palm up for a high-five.

As they strode past, realization crept over Mary Elise. Wren's spiky-haired boyfriend who looked more like a beach bum than an OSI Special Agent had played a role in the boys' escape as well.

Had known exactly how much danger his fiancée flew into.

Mary Elise couldn't resist glancing over her shoulder. The air crackled. Desire derived from a day filled with life and death stakes licked the air, scorching her even from a distance.

She turned her back on the image and thoughts of partnerships it inspired. ''Spike? A nickname because of his hair, I assume.''

''Yeah. Normally OSI guys don't get their own call

sign, but we made Spike an honorary member of the squadron once he and Renshaw hooked up.''

The air whirled with the dynamics of so many relationships, platonic as well as passionate. Her mind and body went into sensory overload after years of deprivation.

Kent had severed ties from people except in the working environment, later taking even that from her, insisting work-related stress caused the miscarriages. The past months in Rubistan she'd soaked up the teaching time with children like a healing balm after enforced distance from little ones. Even so, those relationships were superficial. She hadn't been a real part of any community for years.

And then it hit her what bothered her so much about this homecoming, why she wanted distance as a buffer from pain.

Daniel had moved on, made a life for himself with new friends, new direction, ever changing and growing. But she'd allowed herself to stagnate, frozen in time. How telling that when she'd needed help running from Kent's threat, she'd turned to someone from her past. Daniel's father. Sure, she'd escaped the immediate danger, but she still hadn't been able to lower the walls that sealed her from experiencing emotions. She'd focused on survival for so long, she wasn't sure she really knew how to live anymore.

Entering a world full of feelings, like love—anything—again was a scary-as-hell proposition. And not one she intended to attempt with Daniel anywhere near her.

The man of the hour beside her paused, a new tension radiating from him in waves. She didn't have to look to know. An instinctive understanding of him that had gone dormant over the years roared to life.

Mary Elise searched the windswept stretch of cement

for the source of Danny's tension. She didn't have to look far. From behind the driver's side of the truck, a man in a flight suit slid out with cougarlike stealthiness.

She didn't know much about military rank gracing the shoulders of flight suits, but even she recognized this man's air of authority. The adversarial vibes between them snapped along the air.

A shiver ripped through her. This sort of antagonistic relationship she had experienced and understood well. While she'd learned to haul butt in the other direction for self-preservation, she couldn't squelch a driving desire to fling herself between Daniel and the man stalking toward them.

Time for the crap to hit the fan.

Watching the new Squadron Commander stride forward, Daniel passed Austin to Mary Elise and braced his shoulders. Not that he intended to let things fly now in front of the kids.

He saluted the higher-ranking officer. ''Hello, sir.''

The last word bit on its way up and out, but he knew protocol. It was just tougher to swallow with some than others.

Damn he missed the boundary-pushing days of flying cutting-edge test missions at Edwards AFB. But he had to exist in a day-to-day flying job to fill time as well as maintain cover between the higher ordered, dark ops missions that periodically came his way. Like the one he'd just completed when the call came through to retrieve his brothers.

Yeah, he missed the freedom of his old job. But even the beginning of his transfer to Charleston AFB as Chief of Training Flight hadn't been too bad. Until the new boss took over. Lt. Col. Lucas Quade was nothing like their old commander, Zach Dawson.

The past summer had marked the end of Dawson's reign as Squadron Commander. While he'd opted to stay on at the base for another year for family reasons, Dawson had shifted to Assistant Deputy of Operations for the Wing. Quade had transferred in from the Pentagon to take his place.

Not a smooth transition in the least for the C-17 squadron. Quade lent a darker shading to the squadron motto, Anything, Anywhere, Anytime. This guy was everywhere, all the time, breathing down their necks. His ever-present scowl could melt the paint off an airplane.

Daniel stepped in front of Mary Elise and the boys, between them and the anger pulsing quietly from the commander. "I didn't expect to see you back from your TDY to England for two more days, sir."

At least he'd hoped not when he'd pushed this mission through in the commander's absence.

"No doubt," Quade answered, his low growl riding wind that didn't dare disturb his close-cropped dark hair. "Lucky I was able to cut it short and meet you on the flight line."

Daniel shot a pointed look toward the bedraggled children then back to his commander. "I'll be in your office first thing tomorrow morning after I settle them in."

"Yes, you will, Captain." Quade nodded to Mary Elise. "Welcome back to the States, ma'am." Spinning on his heel, he slid away as silently as he'd approached.

Mary Elise drew up shoulder to shoulder. Austin stirred, yawning, stuffing a fist against his eye.

"Crap," Daniel mumbled under his breath.

Mary Elise cocked her head to the side. "Problem?"

There'd been a time when he'd shared everything with

Mary Elise. Her insights had kept his wings level on more than one occasion. But opening that door to the past would invite a host of other issues better left alone when he needed objectivity to figure out what the hell was chugging through that brain of hers. ''Normal red tape. No big deal.''

He should be covered, thanks to Spike's CIA connections. Daniel shrugged off what couldn't be dealt with until the next day. He'd take the fall in a heartbeat if Quade started gunning for anyone else on the crew.

Daniel tapped Trey on the shoulder and pointed to the ambulance. ''You ready to get checked out so we can head home?''

Trey jammed his hands in his pockets and shrugged. ''Doesn't matter. Just wanna go to bed.''

More concerns. Where would he put everyone in his condo? A small condo with only one bed—a big bed that he could too well envision sharing with Mary Elise.

A headache started behind his right eye, like a tiny hammer rapping with irritating persistence. ''Not much longer and we'll hit the road. You'll be in b— Uh, you'll be tucked in before you can say Hershey's chocolate.''

Austin pulled his thumb out of his mouth. ''Crap.''

Daniel screeched to a halt. ''What?''

Trey smirked. ''I think he heard *you* say it.''

''Thanks. I figured that.''

Mary Elise tapped Austin's mouth. ''What's wrong, hon?''

''Got no jammies. Want my sailboat jammies. Crap.'' His thumb popped back in his mouth.

Daniel flinched over the curse, but couldn't bring himself to reprimand his brother. Poor kid had lost his parents and everything familiar in the span of a couple of weeks.

''You can both wear my T-shirts. I have one with an airplane on it, just for you, pal.''

''Mary 'Lise got no jammies, neither.''

An image he did *not* need, thank you very much. ''She can borrow a T-shirt, too.''

Another image no less tormenting than the last splayed across his mind in a tangle of long red hair and even longer legs. In his bed.

''And a toof brush and shampoo?''

Daniel blinked back to the present and Austin's latest question. ''We'll buy some.''

''For Mary 'Lise, too?''

Already he could see, smell her shampoo in his shower. The little hammer picked up speed and force in his head, pounding in time with each thud of his boots across cement. ''You bet.''

''And toof paste? Bubble-gum kind.''

''Yes,'' he promised, rushing to add before the three-year-old question machine could preempt him, ''for Mary Elise, too.''

Blessed silence echoed for four strides across the tarmac before Austin's thumb popped back out of his mouth again. ''Need my pull-ups.''

He turned to Mary Elise for interpretation. ''Pull-ups?''

Trey snorted. ''Diapers. For babies.''

''Am not a baby!''

''Are so.'' Trey sniffed. ''And no way am I sharing a bed with anybody who still wears a diaper to sleep. Yuck!''

The pounding behind Daniel's eye morphed into a jackhammer.

Mary Elise guided Trey alongside while explaining to Danny, ''They're like underwear.''

Daniel willed Austin silent. Please Lord, no mentions

of Mary Elise's underwear from the peanut gallery. "We'll make a quick stop by the base shoppette for necessities and buy the rest tomorrow. No worries, boys."

End of bedtime ritual discussions. Life back in control, Daniel forged ahead into the late-morning sun.

Yeah, order. Control. Gained from a logical act of the will.

He led them toward the military ambulance, his old Air Force Academy pal Doc Kathleen Bennett waiting as promised. His freshman year at the Academy, he and his classmate Tanner Bennett had both followed her around like lost puppies. Bennett had ultimately won. For the best, since those two were meant to be together, and he sure as hell hadn't harbored any feelings deeper than a teenage case of the hots.

The flight surgeon braced her boot on the bumper, tucking a stray strand of wind-whipped red hair behind her ear. Daniel paused in his tracks. How damned strange he hadn't realized something until just that moment. Every woman he'd ever dated or been attracted to had red hair.

Control spiraled into a nosedive.

Chapter 5

Mary Elise gathered her red hair in one hand and flung the rope over her shoulder. Amid a string of stilted houses, Daniel's condo complex loomed ahead through the windshield of his truck. Their visit with the doc had been followed by a quick-mart trip and a refueling stop at McDonald's, which stretched her never-ending day into late afternoon. Finally she could sleep.

In Daniel's home. Uh-oh.

She eyed the singles-type setup, a sleek soft-gray cement three-story complex complete with a pool, hot tub, tennis courts, set on marshy beachfront property that guaranteed they couldn't let Austin out of their sight for even a second.

At least Trey was healthy according to the flight surgeon, apparently an old classmate of Daniel's, a *married* classmate with a baby. Mary Elise stifled the rogue twinge of relief. No, she didn't need to confuse herself by combating strange twinges of jealousy over women like Kathleen Bennett or the copilot, Darcy Renshaw. Instead, she faced something far more unsettling. More proof of how Daniel had made a new life with new friends—friendship far more important than fleeting flings.

While she guided a bleary-eyed Trey toward the door, Daniel unbuckled the sleeping Austin and grabbed the shopping bag of pull-ups, silent. As he'd been for hours. Not that she intended to risk chitchat before a long sleep.

An hour later Mary Elise stood at the sliding balcony doors in Daniel's bedroom, Austin snoozing in the queen-size bed behind her. She pressed a palm to the screen separating her from the glistening breakers crashing against the shoreline. Egrets bobbed on spindly legs, long beaks pecking the sand while gulls dipped and soared to find a late-afternoon snack.

A prickle of awareness tingled up her spine as she felt *him,* Daniel, enter the room, and she didn't even have the energy to deny she felt him. He cruised to a stop just behind her, his heat warming her back in contrast with the gentle sea breeze caressing her front.

She glanced over her shoulder, the sleek silver and gray decor of his bedroom somehow matching the man's precise mathematical mentality. "Trey's asleep?"

Daniel definitely resembled the part of an overwhelmed father, hair askew, weariness stamping his handsome face. "Yeah, hopefully the dinner kept them up long enough to nudge them toward sacking out through the night. Trey didn't even balk at the prospect of a sleeping bag on the computer room floor once I mentioned the alternative was bunking with Austin in pull-ups."

Mary Elise offered him the obligatory chuckle he obviously expected and shifted her gaze to the artwork gracing his walls rather than the laugh lines crinkling the corners of Danny's eyes. The framed Escher-style print of a winding staircase seemingly leading nowhere pretty much summed up her life.

Daniel leaned a broad shoulder against the molding framing the sliding doors. ''You sure you don't mind sharing a bed with the little guy tonight?''

''Not at all. I'm too tired to notice he's there.''

Daniel eyed his bed, rumpled gray spread rising with each baby breath from Austin. ''That pull-up thing is leak proof, right?''

''Says so on the package.'' A smile tugged at her lips as she thought of Daniel's boggled expression when they'd bought the sleeper-diapers, a purchase so conspicuously different from that of the airman behind them intent on buying a bottle of wine, a plastic-wrapped rose—and a box of condoms.

Mary Elise banished that memory. Pronto.

Daniel speared a hand through his tousled hair until it stood even more on end, much like his buddy Spike's. ''I'll find bunk beds over at the base tomorrow. The BX furniture outlet has a decent enough selection.''

''Uh, the boys might want to go with you and choose for themselves.''

''Right. Of course.'' He shot her a wry smile. ''Not used to accounting to other people.''

He shoved away from the wall and crossed to the bed. Hands so comfortable flying an airplane fumbled a bit in fitting the bulky comforter around tiny shoulders, not that it stalled him in the task. He persevered until the shiny gray bedspread tucked as snuggly around Austin as any cotton sailboat blankie.

Her heart hitched.

Tension rippled up Daniel's back beneath the stretched green fabric. He reached toward Austin.

Swiped a tear off the cherub cheek.

Tears stung her own eyes. "He wants his mother."

A long swallow moved Daniel's throat before he dropped to the foot of the bed. Broad shoulders sagged for the first time in a day that would have leveled most men hours ago. "What the hell am I going to do with two kids, Mary Elise?"

His hoarse question filled the room. She crossed her arms over her chest to keep from gathering both Austin and Danny close. It would be difficult enough for her not to play mama to this motherless child. She damn well couldn't afford to play anything more than friends with Danny. "You'll make adjustments."

"How? My schedule's hellish. I'm gone for weeks at a time. This place is too small." He flicked a hand toward the glass doors revealing the stretch of sandy beach. "Even that's a hazard with Austin around."

His quiet anguish echoed, transporting her back to the time he'd asked her how his father could be so cliché as to opt for a trophy wife in his midlife crisis. Why couldn't the guy have just bought a freaking sports car?

Daniel rested his elbows on his knees while studying the mud-brown carpet as if it bore answers not likely held in the stack of books by his bed. "What kind of screwed-up world is this where those boys don't have anyone but me and a terrorist uncle ready to recruit them for his own special brand of 'summer camp'?"

Austin shuffled under the covers. With undue concentration, she closed the glass door and drew the steel blinds, trying to avoid other memories. Of knowing Daniel was trapped by circumstance now as he'd been years ago with her pregnancy. But even at twenty-one, he'd been a man of honor, putting others first. She'd known he would come through for their baby.

She just hadn't expected the surprise need for him to come through for her, too.

A tiny voice taunted from the far corners of her brain that she'd misjudged Kent. Horribly so.

She'd been looking for something different in those days. Her medical problems had increased, the endometriosis progressing to the point she'd realized bearing children would be doubtful. Her first miscarriage years ago hadn't been some fluke, and with the build-up of internal scar tissue over the years, even conception became difficult. She'd met Kent at a time when she'd expected to focus on her newspaper career since life had shifted her plans.

Kent changed the rules.

She refused to let her ex-husband take anything else from her, and that included what good memories she had of Daniel. Despite the traumatic last hours, she welcomed the distraction of thinking about someone else's problems, tackling concerns that didn't involve a stalker ex-husband.

Moving deeper into the room, she let her hands glide over Daniel's dresser, tap a change cup, an abacus. "The world isn't fair, Danny, and it's wasted energy expecting it to be. We make the best of what we have."

Mary Elise shuffled the abacus beads back and forth and back again. Whimsical memories slipped past her guard. "God knows, you always were one who could build a rocket out of a junior chemistry lab and a piece of your mother's Corning Ware."

A rusty chuckle slipped free. "I blew a hole in the yard big enough for a pig roast. Man, was my father pissed."

Too easily she could see Danny standing in the middle of his parents' landscaped lawn taking a reaming from his father. The son not recognizing his father's fear for his safety. The father not recognizing his son's need for freedom and acceptance.

"But you built a rocket, Danny, when most kids were still struggling to put together store-bought model planes or cars." Forget keeping her distance. She knelt at his feet so she could see his eyes. "You can do this. You'll move to a bigger place. A live-in nanny is probably their best choice, someone they can bond with. They have money, which gives you options."

"The old man's money." He grimaced.

She raised a hand to rest on his knee. He ducked away from her touch. From her offer of comfort.

Daniel strode toward the door. "There are extra towels under the sink. Sweats on the closet shelf, T-shirts in the top dresser drawer."

She trailed him, the two of them meeting in the suddenly too small portal, a pendulum in the hall ticking away the seconds. She should have expected him to duck past. The old Danny had dodged offers of comfort over his parents' split, seeking escape in her body rather than in her arms.

His eyes narrowed, his pupils widening. *Uh-oh.*

She stared into his brown eyes so deep and dark. He'd lost his father in a far more tragic way now than during the rift at his father's wedding. Would Daniel reach for her again? She wanted his kiss as much as—no, more than—before since she knew the promise of what they could experience together. Her body hungered for human touch.

His touch.

Except, she would have to stop as she should have done years ago. Because Danny with his restless feet didn't do forever well. Difficult enough to overcome even before she'd lost her ability to trust in forever.

In a move so quick she didn't see him shift, he pulled her to him. But not for a kiss.

Daniel gathered her against his chest, held her close and a little too tight. She wouldn't allow herself the indulgence of bringing her arms up. She simply absorbed the familiar feel and scent of him, absorbed the differences she'd observed earlier, the harder edges of a man instead of a boy.

Why was he doing this to her? To them?

Daniel pressed a brusque kiss to the top of her head, then softly spoke heated words into her hair. "Crawling into that box was the stupidest thing you could have done. You damn well could have died today."

He held her tighter for one final, eternal moment that ticked by with countless clicks from the pendulum. Then he thrust her away, the door snicking closed behind him.

She stood frozen, an odd contradiction since every nerve within her had flamed to life.

Stupidest thing? Not by a long shot. Crawling *out* of that box and agreeing to stay with Danny beat her other decision by a mile.

Pulling Mary Elise into his arms had to be the stupidest damned thing he'd done since his rocket blasted a hole in the yard and through the neighbor's stained-glass window twenty years ago.

Daniel thudded down the carpeted hall into his living room and dropped to the edge of the leather sofa. One foot at a time, he unlaced his boots and thunked them on the floor. Sleeping would be tough enough with Mary Elise a couple of doors down. Now it would be impossible with the feel of her body imprinted anew in his brain and a persistent auburn hair twined round his wrist.

So what if he preferred redheads? He had a "type."

Big freaking deal. Most guys had a type or a preferred female attribute that attracted them. Made perfect sense and had absolutely nothing to do with Mary Elise.

Slumping back on the sofa, he scooped up a Rubik's Cube from the end table and clicked through rotations while sorting through his life. He normally liked puzzles and the order they restored to his world. He might wear wrinkled flight suits and inside-out T-shirts, but he had reasons. He appreciated order and logic.

Yeah, he had a type—spunky redheads. Except Mary Elise's spunk had been tempered to a quieter, steely will. What had happened to the scrawny girl who followed him into a nuclear plant, jotting notes for a school newspaper exposé? The coltish teen who'd chewed him out for not staying away from her chicken pox?

And what had she been holding back from telling him during the flight?

His hands whipped across the cube, lining up a new row of blues before shuffling yellows. Her voice may have quieted over the years, but the passion in her expression when she'd looked at him hadn't diminished. He'd stood in his bedroom doorway staring into her eyes, green eyes alive with confusion and pain and yes, even a desire so strong an emotional half-wit like him could read it.

Then and now he could only think what it would have been like if the day's outcome had been different. Too easily things could have gone to hell. Tag's call on the headset to alert him of a problem could have been worse. Finding Mary Elise in that crate had shocked a year off his life.

Finding her dead in that crate would have damned near killed him.

He'd forced that image out of his mind all day. During those few quiet moments in the doorway, the scenario had blindsided him like a bogey flying in from a six-o'clock position. This incredible titian-haired crusader who snuck junk food to a kid with a health food fanatic mom and crawled into crates with frightened little boys at the risk of her own life could have died before he had the chance to hold her again.

So he'd pulled her close in honor of those good memories they'd shared. And his logical brain taunted him with an irrefutable fact.

He had to hold her again.

The next morning Daniel measured coffee grounds while listening to three weeks' worth of messages on his voice mail. He'd barely had time to fling his duffel bag on the bed after a covert TDY dropping CIA officers deep into Cantou before the call from the Rubistanian attaché had rung through.

Cordless phone tucked under his chin, Daniel returned the bag of coffee to the steel cabinet in his galley kitchen and tucked the paper filter into the coffeemaker. He figured he would have at least another hour to get his head together before Mary Elise and the boys rolled out of bed. He never needed much sleep at a pop himself, and the bunking conditions hadn't been the best. A fact that had more to do with a raging arousal harder than the sofa.

And a host of memories even more unrelenting. So persistent even his morning ritual of a five-mile run on the beach followed by a workout in the clubhouse gym hadn't helped. By the time he hit the cold shower and changed into a clean flight suit, he accepted the fact that Mary Elise had lodged herself in his brain again.

Daniel jammed the glass pot under the water purifier while listening through the seventy-five accumulated messages.

Two hang-ups.

The dry cleaners calling for him to pick up his service dress uniform. As much as he might wish otherwise, he couldn't get away with wearing everything wrinkled and unstarched.

Next message, an automated telemarketer.

Punching Delete, he shut the water off with his elbow, juggling the coffeepot before finally opting for speakerphone.

"Hey, Dan?" Sultry Southern tones crooned through the speaker, filling the sparse kitchen. "Hannah from upstairs in 18-B. If you get this message, give me a call and let me know when you'll be back. I can ask the superintendent to let me in so you'll have milk and stuff waiting when you get home."

Great. That "and stuff" would no doubt be unfit for kids' eyes, like the time he'd returned to find Hannah waiting with a shrimp casserole and a ribbed tank top that encased gravity-defying double-D's. And Hannah was *smart* as well as hot—a biochemist researcher at the medical university, for crying out loud—what more could a man want? Yet still he wasn't interested in the brainy blonde.

Blonde? Not redhead. Crap.

Two more hang-ups cycled through.

He flipped the coffeemaker on as the next message picked up. "Daniel? Elaine. Uh, just wanted to let you know I'll be in Charleston on business next week and, uh, thought maybe we could, well, have dinner or something. I'll cook. Well, call me."

An image of auburn-haired Elaine taunted him. Daniel glanced heavenward and barked, "Okay, okay, Big Guy. You've made your point."

He'd actually had a semiserious relationship with

Elaine, a chef at a five-star joint. He'd even donned a tie for her once, not that he hesitated in breaking things off six months ago when he'd transferred from California. He'd cited the long-distance-relationship reason, already realizing they wouldn't work out. She'd offered to pack up her ginzu knives and follow him.

Damn, but he felt bad.

Not bad enough to mislead her by letting her food processor back into his life. Like his life wasn't screwed up enough right now anyway. And then he still had to puzzle through whatever had Mary Elise so on edge. Daniel reached on top of the refrigerator for a box of Pop-Tarts.

"Is she a good cook?" Trey's voice drifted from behind him.

Pivoting, Daniel ripped open the pastry box. "Run that by me again?"

His brother stood in the archway, knobby knees showing just below the hem of a Thunderbirds air show T-shirt. Not a hint of bed-head in sight in his dark hair, the kid carried a puffed-chest air and haughty look that would have done their old man proud.

"Is that Elaine lady on the answering machine really a good cook?"

"Yeah, she's a great cook. If you're into stir-fried sprouts and snails." Daniel pulled out a pack of Pop-Tarts and tossed aside the box.

"Actually, I like escargot. Calamari too."

Figures. "Charleston has awesome seafood restaurants. Shrimp trawlers bring stuff in fresh every day."

Trey sniffed. "I've eaten in restaurants around the world. My mom taught us to like anything since we traveled so much. She also said that *healthy* stuff would help us grow."

The boy's condescending glance ran the length of Daniel as if that inch missing from making him six feet tall might have been added with more squid and fewer Moon Pies.

Daniel laughed. The kid was snotty, but gutsy. Gutsy, he could work with. Trey would need that grit to carry him through the transition.

"No worries, kid." He passed the pack of Pop-Tarts to his brother. "We'll find someone to cook for you between restaurant visits. Even I know a growing boy can't live on Twinkies and Mountain Dew."

Trey offered another of his snooty sniffs and shuffled to the refrigerator while days of messages clicked through in the background. Daniel didn't bother shutting off the speakerphone since nothing classified would come through his home phone. And aside from Hannah's message, he didn't expect anything R-rated on his voice mail this time.

Reaching over his brother's head, Daniel pulled a can of orange juice from way back on the top rack, an unconsumed leftover from one of his flight lunches. "Here, kid, vitamin C."

"*My* dad left us lots of money, you know, for shopping and stuff."

Daniel mentally counted to ten. "Thanks, but I can afford a few groceries."

His brothers could keep their damned trust fund. He didn't want a penny of his father's money, and he'd told his old man the same when he'd walked out the door to attend the Air Force Academy. Now he could support the boys fine on his own until they turned twenty-one.

If Trey didn't off him first.

Daniel unhooked a coffee mug from under the cabinet. "You feeling okay today?"

There. That sounded vaguely parental. He paused the

coffeemaker long enough to pour himself some much-needed java.

''I'm not a baby who can't tell you if I'm sick.'' Trey nibbled the edge of a Pop-Tart with a skeptical scowl.

''Okay. Okay.'' He'd let the doc handle that one. While Kathleen had given Trey the all's-fine yesterday, she still wanted both of the boys checked out by a pediatrician. After he shopped for bunk beds. And clothes. And food. Healthy food.

Damn.

When the hell was he supposed to go to work? Thank God Mary Elise was with them for a while.

''Mary Elise doesn't want to stay here with us.''

Had the kid taken up mind reading? Maybe Trey could figure the woman out. ''No sh— Uh, no kidding.''

Another thing to change about his life. His language. Just what he needed, Austin swaggering into preschool cursing like a crewdog.

Preschools? Double damn. What did he know about freaking kiddie day cares?

''Hello, Daniel.'' The deep bass rumbled from the speakerphone. His father's voice.

Shock sucker punched Daniel. His lungs constricted, tight. For a surreal moment he wondered if the past days had been a sick game. His father would come pick up Trey and Austin. Life would go back to normal.

Except for Mary Elise.

Trey's gasp slammed him back to the present. Daniel's gaze locked with his brother's saucer-wide eyes staring back from a pale face as they listened to the voice of the one man who joined them.

And it wasn't a dream or game. The message was more than two weeks old. Daniel listened to the words, the voice, couldn't make himself shut down this last link to a father he hadn't been connected to in years.

"Son, call back as soon as you receive this message. We need to talk about..." He cleared his throat.

Mary Elise? She had said his father arranged the job for her. How long had she been there? Maybe she'd only just arrived.

But why would his dad play Cupid when father-son chitchats were pretty much nothing more than a biannual affair? At best.

Daniel shook free the questions and, for his young brother's sake, reached to lower the volume. Trey sidled closer to the machine, his eyes glinting with a willfulness Daniel recognized well from the mirror.

Their father's voice continued to swell into the room. "I don't want to go into details over an answering machine. It would be better if you placed the call from the base on a secure line."

The message clicked to an end. Trey shifted from his guard post to let Daniel jam the off button.

Secure phones? The limited intelligence that had filtered in about his father and stepmother's deaths rolled through his mind. Their car had been caught in the crossfire between extremist dissidents and local militia. A tragic accident.

Right?

His heart pounded in his ears, each tight breath in sync with Trey's faster gulps of air.

Trey. Crap.

The nine-year-old stood rigid with his small can of orange juice in one white-knuckled fist and his Pop-Tart shaking in his other hand. Glassy brown eyes refused to shed tears. The T-shirt seemed to swallow him whole as his snotty air fell away, leaving behind a grieving little boy.

Daniel thumped his mug on the counter and knelt in front of Trey. ''Hey, bud, I hate that this happened to him, too.''

He cupped a comforting hand around the boy's shoulder.

Trey shrugged it off, chest filling his T-shirt again. ''Like you even care about him.'' He flung his breakfast pastry toward the sink. Missed. The Pop-Tart slapped the tile floor. ''I'll bet you just forgot to mail that 'World's Best Dad' card for Father's Day last year.''

Shot well taken, kiddo. ''Trey...''

''That's right. I'm Trey. Franklin Baker III. Third. Trey, after my dad. *I* was named for him, not you.''

Damn but the kid fought with the gloves off. ''I realize you're upset. Hell, I'm upset.'' Hell? Damn. Damn. Damn. Watch the mouth, Baker. ''You don't want to be here. I understand.''

''Like *you* want me here.''

What could he say to that? His brother needed reassurance, but would recognize a lie in a heartbeat.

Daniel stared at the blueberry Pop-Tart on the gray-flecked tile while the drip, drip, drip of the coffeemaker echoed. Finally he scrounged for words in a situation he'd never imagined facing.

''Trey, you're a smart kid, like the old man. You were well named.'' No bull in that statement. ''So I'm gonna be straight with you. No, this is not what I would have listed on my schedule for the year. Of course I wish you were with your dad and mom right now. That's the way things should be. But life didn't give us a choice, so let's help each other out here.''

Trey wavered forward. His bottom lip quivered twice. Daniel squeezed the boy's shoulder.

''No!'' Trey jerked back. ''I don't know you and I'm

not staying here.'' He spun on his heel and ran down the hall. The slamming door rattled dangling mugs.

''Damn.'' Daniel scooped the Pop-Tart off the floor and into the trash. ''Damn. Hell. *And* crap!''

The sight of Mary Elise in the archway halted the flow of bottled curses. Mary Elise in *his* clothes. His gray sweatpants and a T-shirt from a missile-testing project had never looked so good. Fire-red hair streamed over both her shoulders, pert breasts nudging the well-worn cotton to part the curtain of hair.

He needed air. He needed space. Both running low in his small condo.

Daniel turned away and hoped Mary Elise would get the not-so-subtle message that he wasn't in the mood for chitchat. Maybe she would go comfort Trey and leave him the hell alone. He realized his avoidance tactics were juvenile and didn't give a damn.

He jerked open the cabinet to look for…he had no idea what. He just knew he didn't want this attraction, and he definitely didn't want a soul-searching conversation about Trey and their father and the past with Mary Elise. He wanted to smile with her, joke about the incongruous notion of him packing Scooby-Doo lunch boxes and attending school plays. Anything to keep from facing so many truths.

First on the list, his relationship with his father sucked. With that as his only model, he didn't hold out much hope of his ability to parent two needy boys.

Next, and worse, came the gut-scraping knowledge that he hadn't done right by this woman, a person he'd cared about more than anyone then. Not that he had a clue how to tap into the emotional crap he knew she needed. Another blot against his parenting potential.

And damned if he didn't want to plunge right back into

the same mistakes, if it meant a chance to plunge into her one more time.

He let his hand settle on a jar of peanut butter and reached for the silverware drawer.

Apparently Mary Elise didn't take hints. Or plain ignored them as she appeared in the kitchen.

He recognized the tilt of her chin well. She might be a more subdued version of the animated spitfire who'd trailed his tracks and kept him from falling irretrievably into mischief with her dry wit and wisdom. Yet even subdued to half power, this woman had an unmistakable will. The furrow in her brow said it all.

She intended to talk.

Given his self-control lay in the trash right beside that Pop-Tart, he figured the bedroom door and wide expanse of bed waiting a few steps away didn't offer much hope for getting through their conversation with an inch of sanity left.

Chapter 6

Standing beside Daniel in the galley kitchen, Mary Elise forced her brow to smooth and edged aside her urge to offer advice. Danny should hone his own instincts in dealing with the boys. She could already gauge from the way he'd talked to Trey that his intuition was on target. Sure, she might approach things differently, but that didn't make his way wrong.

And therein lay the core truth. He needed to set patterns in place that *he* could maintain, not her way, since she would soon be gone.

She shouldn't tell him what to say to Trey, but she couldn't leave him alone with all that pain pulsing through the small kitchen. The echo of Franklin Baker's voice from the answering machine had shaken her, even if she couldn't hear the words. She could only imagine what Daniel must be feeling.

Given he'd dodged her comfort last night, she didn't expect him to start sobbing on her shoulder by any means.

Still she would be here for him. That much he would have to accept.

Danny folded his arms across his broad chest encased in a clean—albeit wrinkled—flight suit, obviously having finally accepted she wasn't going anywhere. ''What? No tips on how I should have handled that?''

She shook her head and padded across gray-speckled tile toward the coffeemaker. Colombian roast and freshly showered Danny scenting the air made an enticing morning blend. ''Why would you think that?''

''First day on the parenting job and I already flunked Kids 101.'' He braced a boot on the cabinet behind him and sagged back with a long exhale. ''Do you think I should go after him?''

She forced herself to ask instead of advise. ''What do you think?''

''Me? I want to get things settled. Now.'' He swiped an orange juice can off the counter and crumpled it in his fist before flinging it into a recycling bin with a resounding rattle.

A confrontation when they were both angry and on edge? Ick. She unhooked a dangling black mug to keep from grabbing his arm to stop him. To keep from grabbing him period. ''Do what you feel is best.''

''The kid's probably in there crying. Alone. I hate that for him.'' His boot jammed reflexively against the gleaming metal cabinet with a single thud. ''But he would resent me more for seeing it.''

Bingo, Danny. ''I would imagine so.''

''So I'll try again later.''

''And later again if that's what it takes.'' She leaned against the counter beside him and sipped the steaming coffee. ''He just needs time to assimilate everything.''

Daniel nodded.

Of its own will, her hand fell to rest on his upper arm. ‘‘I thought you did well in a situation that stinks no matter which way you look at it.’’

Muscles flexed beneath her touch. Her fingers itched to explore the broadened width of his shoulders. Silence echoed but for the hiss of the coffeemaker and more yearning zipping back and forth. The chill of tile floor seeped into her bare feet while the heat of his arm seared her fingers.

She jerked her hand away. Don’t get involved. They needed to make their own way.

And emotions hurt.

Daniel scooped an open Pop-Tart box off the counter. Five seconds later he was slathering peanut butter on top of the purple-and-white-swirled frosting. She quelled a wince.

He chewed through a bite before cutting a glance her way. ‘‘Aren’t you going to suggest eggs and wheat toast or shove me out of the way so you can whip up something healthy?’’

‘‘Daniel, you’re thirty-two years old. If you want to eat chocolate frosting on your bagel for breakfast, that’s your business.’’

‘‘So you’re not going to try to fix me or bake a casserole.’’

Confusion cut through the need to lick the peanut butter from the corner of his mouth. ‘‘Why would I want to do that?’’

‘‘Never mind.’’ He jammed the rest of his breakfast in his mouth and washed it down with a swig of coffee. ‘‘I should get moving. Thank you for staying. This morning is crazy enough without worrying about rounding up a baby-sitter.’’

Guilt swirled through her passion like the mix of that peanut butter through the frosting. She was using him every bit as much as he was using her. Except she wasn't being straight-up honest with him.

For the best, right? Then he wouldn't get hurt trying to sort her mess.

He opened a drawer, withdrawing a notepad and pen. "I appreciate that you let me reason through how to handle Trey."

She blinked away her surprise at his perception of her motives.

He thrust the pad and pen toward her. "But I could still use your input on their routine and those EpiPen things. Could you start a list of the factual stuff?"

She eyed the pen and paper. There'd once been a time she never went anywhere without a notebook handy for capturing the flood of words always ready to pour from her mind through her fingertips.

Written words trickled from her muse in short supply these days.

He waggled the small pad. "I won't impose on you forever. Just long enough to get through settling the boys."

A list. He wanted a simple list from her, not a creative writing essay or editorial or, God forbid, a story.

She gripped the edge of the pad without touching him.

"Thank you." He held firm, linking them through a silly little pad of paper with Gravity Sucks printed through an image of a crashing plane. "How weird is it that I have people I spoke to just last week, friends and old girlfriends who I should be calling to pitch in here. But yet here we are."

"I know the boys." She tried to explain away the connection with the logic Danny so valued. Fat lot of good it did her.

The silence swelled between them, filled with the

knowledge that their connection was more. Would it always be like this for them?

She studied the stitches, pockets, zippers along his flight suit as if the different clothing might help convince her this was a different man from the one she'd loved years ago. Her gaze traveled across his chest, to the strong column of his throat.

Her hand inched to the neck of his flight suit where the black T-shirt peeked free. With one finger she traced the raised seam of his inside-out shirt, a sight all too familiar. "I never thought to ask why you do this?"

Brown eyes deepened from milk chocolate to an intense, darker flavor no less enticing. "Do what?"

"Wear your T-shirts inside out. You've always done it and I never thought to ask you why before. It was just a part of the Danny picture that I accepted."

"Maybe I don't notice how I put my shirts on."

She shook her head. "I don't think so. If that were the case, you'd have your T-shirts on right side out some of the time. But you don't. You think through and have a reason for everything you do, Danny. You always have."

A smile crinkled the corners of his eyes. "Not everyone realizes that. You're scary, you know."

"Yeah, right. I'm intimidating as hell."

He chuckled. She joined in with ease, their laughs blending between them until she squeezed his hand.

His hand?

She looked down and found their fingers had entwined over the small pad. When? How?

They both yanked back.

He smacked the pad down on the counter. "The seams scratch."

"What?" She fisted her tingling hand by her side.

Daniel kept his back to her, scribbling notes along the

pad. ''The outside of a T-shirt is smoother than the inside with the seams. It's more comfortable to wear the shirt inside out. Damned silly to put the smoother side out just so the world thinks you look better while those seams are chaffing away.''

He spun to face her, lighthearted Danny firmly stamped across his features. ''Time for me to punch out of here, but I'll try to finish up soon. I have to swing by base legal and start paperwork for the boys before flight debrief, then a meeting with my commander. After that, we can head out to buy whatever you and the boys need.''

She watched him move, Danny so at ease in his own skin and with the world when his life had been flipped upside down. How much of it was pretense? ''You know, Trey's just like you.''

He snorted. ''You mean Austin, right?''

''No. You and Trey are both torn up over losing your father, and neither one of you can bear to accept a bit of comfort.''

The smile fell away, replaced by the newer Danny, the man who drew a gun in foreign countries with little or no backup. ''Like you're any different.''

A gasp caught in her throat.

Danny tapped her forehead. ''Exchanging troubles is a two-way street, Mary Elise. One neither of us seems comfortable traveling anymore.''

He waited, and for a weak minute she actually considered leaning against one broad shoulder and telling him everything. Except she understood Danny too well—rather than just offer help as his father had done, he would take over, guns blazing into the middle of her mess.

Or worse yet, he wouldn't believe her about Kent's threats any more than her parents had. Either way, for the sake of the boys, she needed to keep him as far away from Kent as possible.

She stepped back. Away from Danny and the temptation of broad shoulders.

He nudged the pad toward her, no risky hand-to-hand exchange this time. "Here are numbers where you can reach me. If there's a pressing emergency, call this one. The copilot, Renshaw, lives in this complex with her fiancé."

"Spike?" She followed Daniel across the living room to the door.

"Right. Up on the second floor. He's off today and can be down in seconds." Daniel paused under the porch overhang. "Promise me you'll call if you need anything. Not just for the boys. For you too, okay?"

"Okay." She lied. And suspected he knew it.

Daniel loped toward his shiny blue truck. Apparently he took more care with his vehicle than his flight suits.

She stood in the open door, mug cradled in her hands, and let the heated ceramic warm the chill that increased as Danny backed up and drove away. She stared at his empty spot long after the truck's rumble faded.

Shaking off whimsy, she spun toward the condo. Her feet tangled on the arrangement of flowerpots by the neighbor's door. Mary Elise knelt to right one lopsided pot and scoop stray soil. She patted it back into colored planters filled with ferns, pansies and impatiens. Her hand stilled on a final one tucked in the back in an incongruous bland terra-cotta pot.

False Unicorn. She fingered the small greenish-white flowers, their blooms having held on beyond summer blooming season. She'd been so touched when Kent brought her a small pot similar to this once, the simple romantic gesture more special than the dozen roses he'd given her after the second miscarriage. Or so she'd thought. Then he'd explained how False Unicorn root supposedly increased fertility and prevented miscarriages.

By the end of the year, he'd bought her a window garden full of other such plants like red clover blossoms and blue cohosh. Not that he actually expected her to use them. He'd hired specialists, after all. Eventually, hope had withered along with words and creativity while her window garden blossomed in mocking contrast.

A chill iced up her spine. Rising, she searched the parking lot. Found nothing unusual. Her fingers slid from the tiny flowers and sought the warmth of her coffee mug.

Quit imagining things. The plant had nothing to do with Kent. She hadn't heard even a whisper from him in the year since moving overseas. He'd either lost her trail or the edge to his insane fury had dulled.

But those fears were difficult to shed. Trust was hard to recapture.

Mary Elise bolted inside, locked the door and tried to blot the image of the tiny plant outside. Tried. Failed. Hand gripping the knob, she sagged back.

Her gaze trekked across the living room to the bar separating it from the kitchen. Pop-Tart wrappers lay scattered across the counter with an open jar of peanut butter beside them.

Daniel's life might seem wrinkled and disorganized from the outside, but his disorder was a choice for comfort in a man totally together on the inside. While she knew her dry cleaned and wrinkle-free silks shrouded a woman with a mess of a life.

"Crap." Daniel bit out the crewdog-worthy curse with precision since there wasn't anyone *but* crewdogs to hear him in the squadron corridors.

In seconds he would receive an ass-chewing from the Squadron Commander for skirting rules. Technically Daniel hadn't busted a single regulation. But goodwill protocol on the other hand…

Damn, but he hated playing politics. He left those niceties and games to his old man.

Or rather once had. Daniel ignored the pounding ache in his head and in a place some might call a heart while focusing on the more literal pounding yet to come.

He lengthened his strides along the industrial carpet, past photos of previous commanders, by a planning room filled with crew members at work—the kind of toe-the-line officers who made life easier for men like his father and Lt. Col. Quade. Voices drifted into the hall—Marcus "Joker" Cardenas and Jack "Cobra" Korba. Solid flyers, intense and by the rules.

Unlike himself.

The Squadron Commander's closed door loomed ahead. Man, the old open-door-policy days of Zach Dawson's command were long gone. Just grit through it. Not the first reaming and sure wouldn't be his last. Daniel rapped his knuckles twice.

"Yes."

Okay, guess that meant enter. Daniel stepped inside the spacious office, stopping short of an oversize wooden desk looming with flags behind it. "You wanted to see me, sir?"

Lt. Col. Lucas Quade didn't glance up from the file in front of him, the subtle put-down not lost on Daniel. He waited. Studied the rows of airplane photos, a C-17 framed alongside a print of the C-141 Quade flew earlier. Cornell diploma. With honors. Figures.

His old man had wanted him to go there. Actually, his father had wanted him to attend Harvard or Yale, but they didn't have ROTC programs, so the prestigious schools didn't even make Daniel's list of possibilities.

Quade closed the file with precision before raising his gaze to Daniel without standing. "Is that how you report in a military manner, Baker?"

Ah, so that's how the guy wanted to play it. Quade's turf, they had to play Quade's way. Just like days of old with Franklin Baker.

Daniel drew to attention and snapped a sharp salute. "Captain Baker reporting as ordered, sir."

Quade returned the salute, no invitation to sit on the sofa followed like with the past commander. This guy wouldn't be pulling a secret stash of Little Debbie cakes out of his desk drawer to share either. Yeah, he'd received a few "chats" from Dawson about how to better balance the secrets ops Daniel pulled with the commander's need-to-know basis. Chats, not this standing-at-attention bull.

"Baker, I'm sure you realize why you're in here."

"Yes, sir." He kept his eyes on the flag just behind Quade and consoled himself with the fact that a squadron commander usually only held the position for eighteen months to two years.

About how long it felt like this "chat" would last.

The commander jabbed a finger on the closed file with a red cover sheet declaring "Secret." "You're lucky you covered your ass planning this one."

Daniel didn't bother making excuses. Air Force Academy days had picked up where Mary Elise left off in drilling some caution into him.

Quade continued, "I don't question the mission's importance. And I know damned well there are times you can't be straight-up about where you're going. But, *Captain,* that was my plane and those were my flyers. No matter how much paperwork you filed or how many strings you pulled, their safety is still on my shoulders. You should have placed a courtesy call to me.''

The past blended with the present, too many such confrontations with his father hammering his memory at a time when the last thing he wanted was to think of his old man currently dead in the ground.

Quade blinked slowly. ''Answer me one question. Would you have given Dawson a courtesy call?''

Nailed. The question and its obvious affirmative yanked Daniel right back to the present, a not so comfortable place to be. He kept his eyes forward and mind centered on the shopping trip he and Mary Elise would make with the boys.

The Squadron Commander released him from answering by planting his hands on the edge of his desk and standing. ''You didn't call me because you didn't want to risk my having a different take on your plan.''

Silence seemed the wisest course of action. Bunk beds. They would shop for those first and then pick out sheets. Austin said he wanted sailboats. Fine. Mary Elise would help Trey open up enough for the kid to choose what he wanted, too.

Quade pushed a paper across the desk. Daniel glanced down. The guy couldn't actually intend to write him up without grounds? Daniel looked closer and found...leave papers. The commander was giving him two weeks vacation.

''Get your household in order.''

Confusion shifted the ground under his feet. He'd expected to have to beg for leave. ''Thank you, sir.''

''Don't thank me. This isn't some kind of personal favor. You're no good to my squadron if you're distracted.'' He clipped through the words, snagging a fresh file to open. ''Dismissed, Baker.''

O-kay. Daniel spun on his heel to leave, the prospect of bunk-bed shopping suddenly not so daunting after all.

"Baker?"

Slowly Daniel turned.

Quade stood with his back to the door, shuffling pages in the file as if Daniel only warranted half of his attention. "Boundary pushing is necessary to expand the airframe's capabilities. Confidence in the air is admirable." He tucked another page to the back. "Intellectual arrogance, however, will put you face-to-face with an enemy missile someday."

The words chaffed more than any right-side-out T-shirt.

Quade reached for the file cabinet. "Close the door behind you."

Daniel stepped into the hall, shoulders tensed just as after countless confrontations with his father. Hell, yeah, he had trouble with authority figures. Didn't take a freaking Sigmund Freud to figure that one out. Still, he managed. Pushed his boundaries, stayed alive and kept his career on track, accepting the occasional chewing out as the price to pay for freedom.

What baffled him, however, was how easily he'd fallen into the old habit of keeping his temper in check with the promise of seeing Mary Elise.

Much more "seeing Daniel" and she would lose her mind.

Mary Elise plastered herself against the truck door, the back now full of bunk beds, linens, enough food to feed an army, four bags of kids' clothes and two bags for her.

Never had he grown impatient, even when Austin had screamed himself purple with a temper tantrum in the Base Exchange. Not once had Daniel snapped or glanced at his watch, darker emotions apparently shunted away.

Playful Danny had reemerged with a charm and ease that simultaneously dazzled and tormented her. He slid into the family routine without a misstep, as if he lived to purchase new video games and supersize an order at the golden arches.

Which of course he did.

Palmetto trees whizzed by the window along the barrier-island road. Sailboats, a barge, a shrimp trawler bobbed in the distance until she lost herself in the hypnotic regularity. What if she and Danny had stumbled on each other again through a simple passing on the street, no dangerous ex-husband lurking in her past? Could they meet for coffee and discuss their engagement and lost baby with adult perspective, then slide back into their old friendship? Maybe something more.

But she had met Kent. Married him. And knowing him had marked her—transforming her into a different woman, one as incapable of committing words to paper as she was of committing herself to another person.

Threat or no threat, she'd changed. Not for the better. Even if she scraped deep inside herself for the pieces to try, the risk wouldn't be hers and Danny's alone. Echoes of Austin's screaming fit still reverberated in her head, his anguish because he'd lost sight of her for seven seconds when she stepped around an aisle. She wouldn't mislead those two grieving boys into expecting her to stay. They'd lost enough.

Two grieving boys in the process of beating each other to death with blow-up baseball bats that had been on special with the kids' meals at the Base Exchange food court.

Austin thunked Danny on the back of the head.

Daniel ducked. "Hey, short stuff, you're gonna land us in a ditch. Hold off another minute while I park the truck and we can cross swords on the beach."

He wove the truck past an unusual abundance of cars lining the street leading into the complex. He crept past every full visitor spot and finally nosed his Ford into a tight space on the end.

"Someone must be throwing a party," he noted offhandedly as he reached back to unbuckle Austin.

Mary Elise couldn't help but think how a week ago he would have likely been joining the party. Still, he didn't say a word or show even a hint of the frustration he must be feeling.

Don't be so wonderful, Danny. Please.

She stepped out of the truck just as one of the second-floor condo doors flung open to emit music and laughter.

Spike strode onto the balcony, his arm hooked over his fiancée's shoulders. "Come on up, Crusty. Most of the squadron's already here and ready to party."

Daniel pulled Austin out before shouting, "Thanks, man, but I need to unload the truck and start putting together furniture so we're not bunking on the floor again. Besides, uh, I've got the kids."

"No problem," Spike insisted, tucking a bathing-suit-clad Darcy Renshaw closer. "There are plenty more rug rats here."

A carrot-topped little girl crawled between Spike's legs seconds before a linebacker-size man plowed past to scoop her up. Mary Elise forced herself not to wince at the sight of a baby that too easily could have been hers and Daniel's.

Darcy stepped forward to lean over the balcony. "Didn't you hear us, Crusty? Most of the squadron's here. Surprise! We're throwing you a baby shower."

Chapter 7

Three hours later, Mary Elise dangled her feet in the pool and tried to soak away the tension of attending a "baby shower" eleven years after the fact with Daniel. Actually, a truly thoughtful gesture on the part of his squadron friends, and she refused to allow past baggage to taint it.

And man, did these people know how to party.

Chlorine drifted along the salty air while Mary Elise kept guard over Austin splashing nearby in the shallow end with his newly christened pair of inflatable water wings. Tables and loungers filled with adults and kids, the pool packed with squadron guests bearing gifts of toys, clothes, even a surprise extravagant present of two bikes.

Three couples strayed beyond the fence to the marshy coastline, gushing tidewaters surging against the beach with circling gulls and herons overhead. Darcy and Spike's condo had overheated quickly with the press of people inside until they'd moved the party, complete with

Bo's guitar entertainment, to the pool in hopes of cooling off.

Feet swishing through the lukewarm water, Mary Elise watched Danny step under the pool shower. Cutoff jean shorts rode low on his slim hips until she could count every ridge of his six-pack abs. Spray streamed down his face, between his defined pecs in a trail southward that left her swallowing hard.

She jerked her gaze away before it followed that water straight down. Geez, how totally embarrassing, not to mention insulting. She liked to think of herself as a normal woman with healthy urges, but also a thinking woman and not an out-of-control bundle of hormones.

As she'd once been around this man.

Gentle guitar pluckings floated along the ocean breeze in a sensual serenade. Great. Apparently, bad-boy Bo had decided to turn his talented fingers to a sappy love song as he sprawled in a chair at an umbrella table. No doubt playing in hopes of luring the splashing hot tub mermaid back to his place.

Couples. Couples. Couples everywhere. Ugh.

At least she and Daniel wouldn't be swimming together half-naked as they'd done so often in his parents' pool. Darcy had offered to share an extra bathing suit with her, but Mary Elise found lazing by the pool the perfect way to end a draining day.

She accepted that some of her lassitude could be attributed to her lack of medicines since her supply now sat useless in her cabinet back in Rubistan. She would have to check in with a doctor soon about new prescriptions. At least the over-the-counter, iron-fortified vitamins she'd bought would help with the anemia that accompanied endometriosis in full tilt.

Her body chemistry might be out of whack, the building

pain only mildly numbed by extra-strength Motrin. But she'd lived with the fallout of her illness for so long, she refused to let it rule her anymore. She would enjoy the moment before her life shifted into another unknown direction.

Besides, since Austin had a conniption fit any time she stepped too far out of his sight line, napping back at Danny's condo wasn't an option.

Across the stretch of cement, Danny yanked the shower chain, ending the spray in a trickle. Shaking the droplets from his hair, he strode toward Mary Elise, the loose-hipped grace of his walk leaving her longing to trace the band of those low-riding cutoffs.

''Are you okay here while I swim? You know Darcy.'' He jerked a thumb toward their tomboy bombshell hostess sprawled in a lounge chair with a beer at her ringside seat for Bo's concert. ''And you've met Julia Dawson, right?''

''Come on over,'' Darcy called from beside the woman Crusty had called Julia—wife of the prior Squadron Commander. The earthy blonde—Julia—wriggled her red toenails while her toddler son gripped them and giggled.

More families. More couples.

Mary Elise shook off the senseless frustration. Time to cut the self-pity crap.

Crap?

Geez, already Daniel was sneaking into her life and mind in so many ways. And now he had to soften her heart with sensitivity in making sure she didn't feel abandoned or awkward in the group. Yet, he achieved it without plastering himself to her side possessively as Kent had done.

No thoughts of Kent. Not tonight. Just enjoy the moment. ''I'm fine, thanks.''

Daniel knelt beside her. ‘‘I’ve got Austin now. Go visit or whatever.’’

Music and swirling water whispered a wake-up to her dormant creative muse. ‘‘In a minute.’’

He canted closer. ‘‘Are you okay? Everyone’s being nice, right?’’

Mary Elise struggled to keep her eyes on his face. She surely didn’t want the sensual domino effect that would come from roving eyes, anyway. She’d seen his chest quite well a few seconds ago.

Now to try and forget those muscles. Just a body right? And she knew well what he looked like *without* the jean cutoffs. How really good he looked without them. Her heart rate kicked up a notch.

She willed her eyes to stay locked with his. ‘‘Everyone’s been great.’’

And they had, welcoming her, yet not asking the umpteen questions that scrolled across their eyes every time she slipped and called him Danny instead of Daniel.

‘‘Yeah, they have been awesome.’’ He glanced back at his guitar-plucking buddy. ‘‘I’m still wondering how Bo financed both those bikes on his salary. I’m thinking lieutenants must be making more these days.’’

She couldn’t help but marvel at the surprise thoughtfulness of the young bachelor, the pair of shiny mountain bikes a fun gift these world-weary kids would probably never forget.

Bo’s speeding fingers slowed on the strings. ‘‘Every kid should have his own bike. Better for the little fellas to cruise the local sandbox for hot chicks,’’ he said, dismissing his own generosity while he packed away his guitar.

Darcy wadded up a napkin and pelted him. ‘‘You’re

just trying to score points with unsuspecting women like Hot Tub Hannah over there.''

A wicked twinkle lit Bo's baby blues. ''Do you think it's working?'' He directed the power of that lady-killer gaze toward the blonde in the steaming oasis at the end of the pool and received an encouraging grin in return. Bo stood. ''My cue to soak away my troubles. Thanks again, Crusty, for introducing me to Hannah. I owe ya one. Don't hesitate to call me if you need a sitter.''

Daniel pushed to his feet. ''So you can hit on my neighbor, then take my brothers cruising sandboxes?''

''The park's a great place to meet women. Joggers and dog walkers and babes lounging on picnic blankets.'' His twinkling eyes took on a rapturous gleam before he landed back in the present. ''Not that you need any of that now. Have fun you two.''

Winking, Bo pivoted away to jog toward the hot tub, lowering himself into the frothing bubbles beside Hannah.

With everyone assuming she and Danny were a couple in the making, it would be simple to let herself slip into that notion, as well. But while she might be willing to take pleasure from living where she could, not at so high a price. If she allowed herself to soften around Danny any more, she would crack and spill all.

The temptation was rapidly growing as strong as the desire to press her lips to his warm skin with beads of water begging to be sipped. ''Go. Swim. Play. Whatever.''

Please. Now.

He searched her eyes for an extended second before backing a step. ''All right.'' He turned to Trey, the boy scowling in a pool chair with his knees hugged to his chest. ''Hey, kid? Can you swim?''

Trey sniffed. ''Of course I can.''

"Good. Hold your breath." He scooped his brother up and launched him airborne toward the center of the pool.

Trey shrieked, closing his mouth with a gasp seconds before he landed in the water. Daniel cannon-balled a foot away from him. Spray sluiced a giant wave over the side.

Years slid away to the countless times they'd played in his parents' pool. God, she'd hated it when he'd dunked her. Until she'd learned to dunk him right back.

Daniel exploded to the surface beside Austin and shook the water out of his face.

Austin paddled, his water wings bobbing, and shouted between huffing breaths, "Mary Elise, come in. We're gonna play baseball."

Trey splashed him. "Volleyball, you dweeb."

"Yeah. That."

Mary Elise pulled her feet out of the water. "I'm not swimming today, sweetie. You just have fun with your brothers."

She backed away, mentally recording the image of Danny swimming with Austin's spindly arms locked around the strong column of big brother's neck. Daniel, a man so different from the steely warrior who'd drawn down an enemy guard in a foreign country to save his brothers less than forty-eight hours before. The dual image left her dry-mouthed. Rattled.

Intrigued.

She could watch. And she would enjoy. But she needed to keep enough distance so she could still leave.

Daniel spiked the ball back toward Tag. For all the good it did him. The loadmaster tapped it in the air with ease, setting up the next shot as he passed the volleyball to his teenage son.

Who missed it—hallelujah—since the boy was too busy

ogling the high schooler springing off the diving board, Zach Dawson's daughter, Shelby.

Teenage hormones packed a ferocious punch.

Daniel's gaze drifted back to Mary Elise. He looked beyond the new lines of worry and fatigue around her eyes to the clear green gaze he'd fallen hard for in his youth. Remembered how they'd known everything about each other. Shared every thought, no matter how personal.

Maybe it was the swimming scenario hammering him since they'd enjoyed countless hours in his parents' landscaped backyard and kidney-shaped pool growing up. He'd shut down those memories after they split, but now he'd have to learn to live with them bombarding him from more directions than antiaircraft fire.

"Crusty?" Tag shouted. "You with us, man?"

Daniel nodded, rejoining the game, his mind lofting back to the past as surely as the ball sailing through the air.

"I'm not swimming today, Danny."

Daniel stroked his way through the numbingly cold pool. His teenage body hungered for exercise outside the stifling formality of his parents' house. Early spring weather in Savannah made for chilly water, not that he cared. And usually Mary Elise didn't care, either.

"Why not?" He stopped inches from the cement edge where Mary Elise perched gripping her knees. "Scared of a little freezing water?" He flicked drops in her face.

"Yeah, right."

He hauled himself out to sit beside her. "What's the matter? Really? Come on, spill, because I'm not buying the scared-of-cold-water crap for even a second."

She scooped her hand through the pool and flicked his face right back. "Your dad hears you say crap again and you'll be needing that cold water to rinse out the soap."

"Yeah, yeah, whatever. He hasn't tried that since I was in junior high. Now come on. Swim with me. There's an extra suit in the pool house."

He reached to tug the rope of red hair trailing over her shoulder, then paused. When the hell had Mary Elise gotten breasts? Not much to them, but they sure as hell were there. He jerked his hand away.

"I can't, Danny. Can't. Okay? I'm a girl and there are days it's just easier for a girl if she doesn't swim."

He felt the color drain from his face and knew it didn't have anything to do with the freezing water. Some stuff a guy just didn't want to know. "Oh."

"Yeah, oh. Now go swim and enjoy the fact that you're a boy and can swim all thirty-one days of this month. I'll soak my feet here while we talk about something else."

And he wanted to do just that. Well, until he saw the downward tilt to her mouth, the minifurrow on her serious brow.

Who needed to swim laps, anyway?

Standing, he extended his hand without a word while he waited. He could handle this. Sure, he wanted to dive to the bottom of the pool where he wouldn't have to even think about this discussion. But he was a practical guy and, hell, this was Mary Elise after all. They could talk about anything.

Even if she had developed breasts overnight.

He shoved his hand closer.

She eyed his outstretched arm. "What?"

"Chocolate."

"Huh?"

"Let's go get some chocolate. I hear chicks like to eat a boatload of the stuff when they're, uh—" he stifled his wince for Mary Elise's sake "—not swimming."

A smile so perfect crept across her face and right up

to her eyes that a charge of victory shot through him until Daniel forgot about the pool behind him and the swim he'd waited all winter to take.

Mary Elise fitted her hand in his and stood. ''Yeah, right, now I get it. You've just got your eye on that box of Hostess Ho-Hos in my mom's pantry.''

''Busted.''

Her laugh swelled then faded as they pushed their way through the ivy-covered gate separating their yards. ''You're not totally grossed out?''

''Maybe a little.''

She punched his arm.

''Hey, joking!'' He rubbed his arm, relaxed. He could always do that with Mary Elise, relax, be himself with nothing to prove. Daniel slung an arm around his best friend's shoulders. ''This just means you're gonna be able to have kids someday. Right? Nothing gross about that.''

She tipped her face up to his. ''Thank you, Danny.''

Mary Elise arched onto her toes, a soft breast pressed to his side as she grazed a kiss against his cheek right at the corner of his mouth. If he moved his head even…

''Hey! Heads up, Baker.''

Daniel blinked. The volleyball whizzed through the air, straight toward his face.

''Crap.'' He launched to the side and swung his cupped hands up into the ball with a microsecond to spare.

And damned if his gaze didn't land right back on Mary Elise to see if she'd been watching. He wasn't any better than Tag's son, Chris, drooling over a girl until he lost focus on the rest of the freaking world.

Chris punched the air with a victory shout. ''Point, game and match for the visiting team.''

Tag eased out of formation over to the side of the pool. ''Perfect timing. We need to hit the road. My daughter's driving home from college for the weekend, and I promised Rena I'd move boxes out of Nikki's room before she gets here.''

Daniel waded closer to Tag as Darcy launched out of her chair to join in the game. No doubt those boxes had been pulled down on his account as the loadmaster and his wife sorted through their son's old clothes to help fill Austin and Trey's empty closet. He stifled another wince at everything he owed his friends. He was a hell of a lot more comfortable being on the giving end. Did Mary Elise feel the same way?

And when the hell had he started analyzing *feelings?*

He shook off the thought faster than beading water in his hair. ''Hey, make sure you pass along my thanks to Rena for the kids' clothes.'' Since the other marrieds had attended together, he couldn't help but notice Rena's absence in light of the conversation with Tag on the flight. ''Let Rena know I'll send 'em back your way once these guys get through with them.''

Tag shook his head with a look of horror. ''Don't come near my house with those things, man. We've almost got our nest empty. Our baby-making days are over.'' He hauled himself out of the water. ''You ready Chris? Chris?''

Christos Price jerked his gaze off Shelby Dawson's belly button ring and back to his father. A dazed look in his eyes glinted like the water streaming down the olive complexion inherited from his mother's Greek roots. ''Yeah, Pop. I guess so.''

The teen hefted himself from the pool. Right by Mary Elise. Which offered Daniel a convenient excuse to check on her. Just making sure she was comfortable with everyone, of course.

Yeah, right.

She'd settled in with his friends as he'd known she would, already absorbed in conversation with Julia Dawson while they both held sleeping children. Austin snoozed away on Mary Elise's lap, his soggy body soaking her silk shorts set. Not that she seemed to care or look in the least ruffled. Just natural. She should have kids of her own with some lucky bastard who would get to touch her incredible red hair.

Crap.

Daniel backed into the resuming game as they swapped sides, which gave him a perfect view of Mary Elise's night-lit lounge chair. When she'd told him about being pregnant with his child, he hadn't given much thought to the baby itself, or life after the wedding. He'd focused on shutting down thoughts of the future because they contrasted too much with what he'd dreamed for so long.

Yet once she'd lost the baby, once he'd lost Mary Elise in his life, he'd spent the next year thinking about what their baby would have looked like. What she would have looked like holding it.

And that image mirrored the one he was seeing too damned closely for his peace of mind.

He considered waking Austin up for another round of chicken just so he wouldn't have to keep staring at Mary Elise holding the little guy. But the boy's needs came first and God the kid pitched holy hell when taken away from Mary Elise. The boy was breaking his freaking heart with the tight-fisted clinginess to the only mother figure in his world right now. Maybe he could convince Mary Elise to stay in the area.

And then she'd be too busy to meet that lucky bastard who would father her children.

The rogue notion chugged through him as he pumped another serve into the air. She had to settle somewhere, and apparently their Savannah hometown no longer held any allure for her. The idea took flight, leveled out like the ball lofting over the net.

He staunchly ignored the insistent voice telling him he was doing this for himself. So what? Yeah, he wanted her around, but because he needed her to stay put. Made logical sense that she should stay in Charleston. Two plus two equaled four.

His gaze zoned back in on Mary Elise smoothing a hand along the sleeping child's back while her laugh carried on the ocean wind.

The next ball whizzed right by Daniel's head.

Kent McRae closed the Mercedes door—forced to park out on the street where some damned fool might scratch the paint. A nuisance, but an overabundance of vehicles packed the condo lot.

He wove his way through the maze of trucks and SUVs with military ID stickers on the windshield. Adrenaline snapped through him until he wondered why he'd ever bothered to pay someone to take on these tasks before. And to think he never would have known this quiet thrill if necessity hadn't forced him. Help wouldn't be arriving for another four to five days, and he'd sworn not to act decisively until then.

Striding along the lengthy row of Palmetto trees, he checked again to ensure Mary Elise was still engrossed with the pool party and her old lover. Her lover now?

Kent kept his strides even, loose, his hands unclenched. He wouldn't allow her the power over his emotions. He was in control.

He neared the line of mailboxes. As much as he might enjoy ending it now, he couldn't. The boys were off-limits, as per his accomplice's demands. He owed his accomplice too much in tracking Mary Elise's every move to step off their designated course now. And he always paid his debts.

As if he would hurt innocent children like some monster, anyway. He focused his revenge on the deserving.

Meanwhile, he needed Mary Elise off-kilter so she wouldn't become overconfident and opt to disclose her tale of woe to an old boyfriend. Having been married to the woman for three years, he knew which buttons to push. Watching her hand tremble as she'd touched that False Unicorn plant had been…satisfying.

Locating the correct box number, Kent straightened the knot on his favorite tie, silk with pelicans patterned in diagonal lines. A gift from Mary Elise two years ago and now a reminder of unfinished business. A final swipe to smooth his tie crinkled papers inside his suit coat pocket. He tugged out the folded pamphlets guaranteed to make more than her hand tremble. Innocuous fertility clinic literature to most. Pointed for her since she'd visited the same chain of clinics more than once.

A quick glance over his shoulder assured him no one watched. Kent slid out his lock pick and set to work on Baker's mailbox. Given how involved they were in their pool play, he should be well in and out before anyone noticed him. He wouldn't want to upset the boys. No, he wasn't a monster.

Just a man in control of his destiny with a debt to repay.

Chapter 8

Danny blasted out of the water like a sea monster, swiping his arm across the pool to spray Trey before he ducked behind Darcy. Mary Elise watched, smiled, couldn't help herself. Even allowed herself the pleasure of following his leap from the pool, his loose-hipped stride to the ice chest illuminated by a halogen lamp and crescent moon.

Oh, God. Danny was so cute, the boyishness somehow all the more charming coming from a muscle-bound man. Evenings like this made it easy to forget the ways she and Danny had annoyed the hell out of each other.

Distance, she reminded herself. Make lists and keep her distance from the enticing, playful Danny. For starters, her list making used to bug him. Go with the flow, he would tell her. Explore. Find adventure.

She'd found more than enough adventure with Daniel Baker and a bottle of champagne, thank you very much.

The party had wound down to half speed, quiet laughter no longer overriding the shush of gentle ocean waves. As much as she'd enjoyed conversation, she didn't mind the moment of peace.

Rubbing Austin's back, she tried to ease his fitful sleep, letting him snooze on until she could tuck him in his own bed. She could only risk four more days to smooth the transition and then she would have to leave.

Survival instincts screamed at her to run. Now. Long-denied maternal instincts, however, insisted she protect this precious little boy's wounded heart by staying as long as she could risk.

Enough cash waited in her account to carry her for a month, even finance a visit to a clinic to update her meds. Franklin Baker had managed to reroute her transactions while she was overseas so Kent couldn't trace them. She had no way of knowing if Franklin's accounting cover stayed in place. Once she presented ID to withdraw money, she would have to go.

Damn, she was tired of living like this, but what else could she do if even her own parents didn't believe her? Postpartum delusions, Kent had told them when she'd had no choice but to break her long silence over the growing problems in their marriage. Depression from the final late-pregnancy miscarriage.

Yeah, she sure as hell was depressed over losing her child and her marriage. But no way had she imagined the cold steel of a gun barrel pressed to her head as an assassin tried to coerce her into the car so he could launch her vehicle off a bridge in a fake suicide.

All on Kent's payroll.

She'd fought. Escaped. And no one had believed her. The more she'd insisted, the stronger the accusations of paranoia became. One mention of putting her in an institution from Kent with his monied influence and she'd hauled ass out of the country.

Unease tickled along her spine, like a caterpillar making its way ever so slowly up her back. The sense of being watched. Mary Elise held herself still, refusing to cave and look. Much more of this and she would be acting as crazy as Kent convinced her parents she was.

"Mary Elise?"

She jolted. Looked up and found Darcy Renshaw climbing up the pool ladder.

Relief shuddered through her, shaking the caterpillar sensation free. She *was* being watched, by one of Daniel's fellow flyers.

Dripping wet, Darcy sank to the middle of the lounger and sat cross-legged with a long-legged grace that had her fiancé eyeing her with smoky appreciation from across the pool. "Can I get you something to drink?" She stretched to offer up a bag of sunflower seeds from the smorgasbord on the table. "Or anything to eat?"

"You've already done so much. All of you have. I'm a little overwhelmed by it all, so many gifts and so many people. Please say you wrote everything down, like the clothes Tag brought, or was his name Jim or J.T.?" The loadmaster with shoulders as broad as Danny's. God, she hoped his wife knew what a lucky woman she was. "See, already I can't remember half the names, and men can be dense about things like thank-you notes."

"Don't worry about it. No one expects thanks. This is what we do for each other."

"Still..."

Darcy's finger sawed along her dog tag chain pensively. "I'll bet you're tough to help."

She shrugged. Help meant dependency and debts, and she was through with that.

Darcy's laser gaze eased. "There are a lot of us to meet at once, with call signs and real names doubling up what you're trying to learn. You're probably best off just remembering the call signs.'' She gestured with her fistful of sunflower seeds. ''Over there, the big blond guy with the baby who brought the football, that's Bronco. He's married to the flight surgeon Kathleen—or Athena, if we're using nicknames—who took care of Trey when you landed.''

''Bronco?'' She glanced over at the man with his wife, packing up their baby daughter to leave. ''Because he looks like a bull?''

''No,'' she said with a wicked glint lighting her eyes. ''Although I'll have to use that on him next time he rolls out a crewdog prank. Actually, he turned down a pro ball contract with the Broncos to stay in the military.''

''Wow. Mind-boggling that he would give up that much.'' Of course Daniel had also given up his family money to pursue his own dream. A calling more than a job, he'd once explained to her as he filled out his application to attend the Air Force Academy. ''So there are stories behind some of the names. I guess I just thought they usually linked to someone's personality or the last names, like yours, Wren Renshaw. Or like Danny's, Crusty Baker.''

''Sure it goes with his last name, but also with the fact that he's a bit of a mess.'' Darcy grimaced. ''Uh, I don't mean that as an insult. His scruffiness is kind of cute.''

And yet there was so much more to this man who flew military planes and commanded respect from a crew with as much ease as he unraveled equations—or dunked Trey.

God, if only she could view Daniel as simply scruffy or cute it would certainly save her a lot of yearning she had no choice but to ignore. ''No offense taken. I've known Daniel a long time.''

Curiosity flared in Darcy's eyes again. ''Then, like

Bronco, other names are tied into a watershed event.'' Darcy pointed to the Nordic-looking guy moving in on Hannah while Bo's back was turned. ''Scorch set his mustache on fire once in the Officer's Club bar with a drink called a Flaming Dr Pepper.'' Her finger shifted toward a laughing hulk of a man digging into the ice chest to fish out two beers, passing one to Crusty. ''There's a great story about Cobra over there, but it's best not to share the details with kids around.''

Slowly the men and women became more than a few names and loud revelers for Mary Elise. They took on personalities in a tight community she'd invaded.

Absorbing the pieces of Daniel's world, she realized distance didn't seem to be helping anymore. He'd exploded back into her life and mind. She wouldn't be able to stop envisioning him in his new environment, wondering about him, how he was handling the changes. Even with a live-in nanny, he would be thrown feetfirst into parenting those boys. At least, she hoped he would.

Her hand gravitated to cup the back of Austin's head, protectiveness twining through her as surely as the boy's silky soft curls wrapping around her fingers.

Would Daniel find some hot-tub Hannah woman to share his life with and ease his load? Would the woman love these two precious little boys?

And one very grown man.

''Okay, fair's fair.'' Darcy's voice sliced through the green haze of jealousy. ''I've ponied up some gossip, now how about trade some in return. Starting with how you met Danny.''

Mary Elise yanked her gaze off broad bare shoulders and over to the hostess snacking on sunflower seeds with undisguised curiosity. What would it hurt to share a few harmless stories? She could leave something of herself behind in his world from her younger days, the part of her that had been fearless, strong. Willing to risk the occasional broken bone or heart.

"We grew up together." Mary Elise searched for words to explain a relationship she wasn't certain she understood anymore. She stared out over the beachy expanse, the winding island coastline glittering with lights.

When Darcy's fiancé eased into view, Mary Elise couldn't help but welcome the distraction. She scrambled to gather thoughts scattered further than the expanse of ocean with tiny dolphin fins slicing lazy paths in the moonlit distance.

Silently Spike dropped a quick kiss on Darcy's mouth, the wren tattooed over his heart proclaiming his devotion as loud as any bullhorn. "You got the party for a while?"

"Yeah, hon, everything's winding up."

"Thanks. And no grilling the guests, okay?"

She slugged his tattooed arm, dead center on the diver-down symbol. "Love ya."

"You, too." He dropped another kiss on her lips before sprinting away.

So much devotion glowed in the woman's eyes, as she watched her spike-haired fiancé hop the fence to make his way toward the ocean, that Mary Elise felt like an intruder. "Why don't you go join him? I'm fine on my own."

Darcy shifted her attention back. "No way. We're having girl talk, and God knows I don't get much of that around these bozos." She shook her head. "Honestly, Max was pretty much an antisocial hermit when I met him. And while he's come out somewhat, he still needs his cave time on occasion. He has a cabin on one of the more remote spots of a barrier island for when the surfer dude within him needs to have a Poseidon moment," she explained with an understanding that boded well for the long term.

"I'm sure he appreciates your accepting him as he is."

"He does. And honest to God, it's a two-way street. He's given up so much for me, changing jobs, relocating from the West Coast to Charleston. He even wears a coat and tie to work when he's not out on assignment."

Darcy reached across to Austin to smooth baby-soft curls, a wistful look in her eyes. Her hand fell back to her lap. "Okay, I confess, I'm so ga-ga happy with Max I can't help but see romance everywhere. But folks really are dying to learn more about you two."

"Guess my calling him Danny gave things away." In spite of her decision to share, Mary Elise found the words tougher to spill than she'd thought. She seldom granted herself permission to look back on those times. Hadn't dared look, knowing the strong person Danny had challenged her to be then might not approve of the more cautious creature she'd become.

"We call him lots of things. But never Danny."

"Old habits are hard to break." In more ways than one. She forced herself not to let her eyes linger on the crinkle in the corner of Daniel's eyes as he smiled. "My family moved down south when I was eight. My mother's lung specialist was located in Savannah, so my father made the transfer there."

"Crusty's from Savannah? I thought he might be from the South with that hint of an accent, but I wasn't sure."

A twinge of surprise nipped her. Danny seemed close to these people, and yet they didn't even know the most basic facts about his background. "We were neighbors. Best friends since elementary school."

Laughter rode the wind, Bo flirting with Hannah as she cooed over his generosity with the bicycles.

Mary Elise smiled, pool memories merging with bike-riding jaunts. ''Daniel even taught me to ride a bicycle. I was catching a lot of ribbing from the neighbors over being eight and still using training wheels. I'd fallen once before.'' She pointed to the scar on her knee. ''One day he got a wrench and took off the training wheels, presenting me with my shiny, dangerous two-wheeler. No way did I want to climb back on that bike again. But somehow when Danny told me I could do it, that this time would be different, I believed him.''

Again Daniel scooped a passing Trey into the air for a canonball splash, but without any repeat protests from Trey. Daniel inspired trust with his oozing confidence and invincibility. Only, the stakes were so much higher now than a dunking or scraped knee.

Darcy angled back on her elbows. ''I can just see you sailing down that sidewalk, red pigtails streaming behind you while Danny whooped it up cheering you on.''

Mary Elise smiled at the memory close to the one Darcy described. Those soaring two minutes of freedom were incredible. Until… ''I broke my wrist.''

Handful of sunflower seeds pausing midway to her mouth, Darcy flinched. ''Ouch.''

Mary Elise nodded. He'd gotten her right back on that bike again the minute her cast had been sawed off, albeit running alongside her to steady the handlebars. But unbending in his assertion that she could do it. She wasn't going to enter the fourth grade with training wheels.

''I was a real klutz in those days, arms and legs tangling. I did fine pedaling downhill on the straight and narrow, but once it came time to turn. Bam. Right into a hundred-year-old tree. Man, did his father ever chew him out.''

''Kinda like Darth did today at the squadron.''

"Darth?"

Darcy rolled her eyes. "Our private name for the new Squadron Commander. Daniel decided Evil Emperor was too long and opted for Darth, as in Darth Vader."

Mary Elise shivered, remembering well the stealthy man on the runway, dark, a little menacing—and conspicuously absent from a gathering where even the prior Squadron Commander had attended.

How bad had the reaming been? Yet Danny hadn't shown the slightest sign of tension all afternoon while shopping. Had he needed support or a confidant earlier, and she'd been too wrapped up in her own problems to notice? She would have never let that happen in the old days.

Of course they'd been more in tune with each other then. Still, she was surprised how much it ruffled her feathers to think of someone giving him a hard time. "Is he in trouble at work over the flight?"

"Sort of, but not really." Darcy waggled her hand. "Crusty has...connections. And he knows how to skirt the rules, push some boundaries, but he's careful not to risk his job by stepping over the line."

Apparently, Daniel hadn't changed much after all, merely upped the stakes of his boundary pushing.

Darcy laced her fingers over her stomach. "Sometimes Crusty reminds me of my Max, willing to bypass recognition for the higher good of the mission. Men like those two don't care about pinning on general. And from the shadows they make the world a better place."

A faraway smile played with her face before she turned to Mary Elise. "So? Will you be sticking around here? There's always a market for good teachers, and with your overseas experience—"

"I'm not staying." Enough confiding. She needed to

erect some barriers before she slipped into Daniel's world along with those stories. Mary Elise cuddled the warm weight of sleeping Austin closer, her arms already aching at the impending emptiness.

"Does Crusty know that?"

"He will."

Across the chlorine waters, Daniel's eyes met hers. Held. Mesmerizing. Unrelenting.

For all his easygoing ways, Mary Elise knew Danny possessed a steely will. Well, so did she now—at least when it came to keeping herself and those around her safe. She just hoped the battle took place with them both wearing a few more clothes.

Friendship could sure be a mixed blessing.

Walking beside Mary Elise in the late-night surf, Daniel wasn't certain whether to thank or curse his squadron buds. As if Darcy and Spike hadn't already done enough for him, now they insisted on watching Trey and Austin while the boys slept so Daniel and Mary Elise could take a breather. Stroll down the beach. In the moonlight. Alone but for the occasional passerby and dim lights of distant houses.

Thanks, pals. He jammed his fists into the pockets of his damp cutoffs. Clammy jean shorts didn't help cool the steam of frustration. The need to act.

Moored sailboats bobbed, wind snapping and pinging slack lines against the masts in an erratic tune. More than a walk, he wanted a solid twenty minutes with Max for feedback on the answering machine message from his father. Could be nothing. Could be something. He should be talking to Max. Or loading new games on his computer for the boys. Or plotting out flight plans to Timbuktu, just in case he got any ridiculous ideas about his new houseguest.

Anything except taking a cornball, romantic, seaside walk with Mary Elise, their shoulders brushing every other step.

He kept his eyes locked on a wooden dock fingering into the ocean. Yeah, he needed to make something happen, take action. Now would be the perfect time to lock in persuading Mary Elise to stay in the area. For the boys. Not for more moonlit walks and shared peanut butter Pop-Tarts, damn it.

Practical, right? He would still manage the boys on his own, but could check in with Mary Elise. Maybe they could find that friendship again. As adults. Wiser adults. Without the messy emotions. He opened his mouth—

"You are loved, Danny."

His jaw slammed shut. He risked a look at moonlit Mary Elise. "Uh, wanna run that by me again?"

She slung her hair over her shoulder, the gentle curves of her breasts straining against silk as creamy as her skin. "All these people jumping right in to help you. It's amazing to see how quickly they turned out with the perfect presents. More than just liking you, they know you and perceived your needs. That's a rare gift and you have it in abundance."

He might not be the most sensitive guy on the planet, but even he could see the woman had her brain wrapped around something heavy. Upsetting.

Please, Lord, no tears. Those made him long for the bottom of a pool more than discussions of "not swimming."

And then the memory hit him. An image of Darcy leaning over the porch rail to shout her announcement of a baby shower, tension promptly rippling up Mary Elise's spine. ''Are you okay?''

''What do you mean?''

Hell, even he'd been knocked back a step by the notion of attending a baby shower with Mary Elise eleven years too late. ''I gotta admit the whole baby-shower thing blindsided me.''

She strolled without speaking, her arms swinging as she splashed through the low sipping surf. Suddenly he found something he feared more than her tears—knowing she might have tears locked inside. The girl who'd been a willing crusader for others had always been reluctant to share her own fears.

Words he hadn't known were within him churned. Wanted out. More of that old connection urged him to fill the silence rife with her hurt. Even if he was eleven years too late in addressing a subject that no amount of back-pedaling could fix.

For a man who thrived on logical solutions, that bit.

Once upon a time prior to their sexual marathon days, they'd been able to talk about anything. Surely he could recapture that ease for a short walk.

For Mary Elise, he pushed the churning words free. ''I think about him or her sometimes. Wonder what our kid would have looked like. What we'd be doing now, if...'' And the question he wondered about most, even if he suspected the answer. ''Whether you and I would have made it.''

She tipped her face up to his, red hair streaming across skin turned translucent in the moonlight. ''Likely not.''

Regret dulled her eyes, stirring protector instincts stronger than any he'd felt in a job that had taken him to some of the most twisted hellholes of the world. He wanted to fight a tangible battle to swipe away the stain in her eyes from memories past. Which of course meant taking on himself.

Way to go, bud.

He forged ahead. "You're probably right. My relationship history hasn't been any better than my father's."

"At least you were smart enough not to marry your mistakes."

He grabbed her arm and pulled her to a stop. "You can shut that talk down right now. We may have made mistakes, you and I, but knowing you was the best damned thing that ever happened to me."

A tender smile crept over her face. "You are so sweet, Danny."

"Sweet?" Crap. She obviously had him mixed up with someone else.

Her hand eased away as she trailed ahead. "But I wasn't talking about us. I meant my marrying Kent."

Her words carried so quietly on the night air, he let them kick around in his head for a few seconds to make sure he'd heard her right.

"So Kent McRae was a mistake?" He couldn't stop the question. He was human after all.

"Obviously, or I wouldn't have divorced him." She pulled ahead with long-legged strides that drew his eyes and his libido.

And then her words soaked into his brain. He stopped. "*You* left *him*." A fact that meant a lot more to him than it should. "I never knew for sure."

She continued ahead for five tide-swishing steps. He stood unmoving, seaweed twining around his ankles as tenaciously as thoughts of this woman. Thoughts and curiosity about the man she'd chosen to marry without the coercion of a shotgun wedding.

Finally she spun to face him, all traces of regret and

could-have-beens erased from her face. She was getting better at hiding her emotions. Much more practice and she'd be gone from him altogether, even if she never crossed the county line.

A bizarre thought for him, a man who kept life simple. Fact based. But he knew. She was easing her way out of his world. She'd thrown him out last time. This time she would stride away with a long-legged grace.

She smiled, signaled her end to deeper discussions, another freaking odd thought since that was usually his role.

"Anyhow, it's wonderful how everyone turned out for you with more than just gifts. They're here with support, for you and the boys. You're going to be fine." She held his gaze for one of those long, Mary Elise moments that carried peace and intensity all at once. "I'm so happy for you, Danny. You deserve to be loved."

"So do you." Where had that come from?

Well, hell. Of course he'd never been the right man for her, but that didn't mean he didn't want her to be happy. He'd always wanted that for her.

Her mask slipped, not much. But enough.

He pressed his advantage. "You don't have to go." Daniel closed the steps between them. "I know you'll need your own place and a job, so why not settle in Charleston? I'm not looking for you to take on my responsibilities, but it would be good for the boys to have you near. And I could help you relocate."

She backed up a step, tidewaters swirling between them. "I'm not staying here."

He'd expected that, realized he'd have to push her on this. He hadn't, however, expected the jab of disappointment. Eleven years had passed just fine without her.

Well, maybe more like the last nine of them.

Why the hell should a handful of days together change

that? "Where are you going? Back to Savannah after all?"

She shook her head. "I want to start over somewhere new, fresh."

"Where?"

Since when was she the kind of woman who wanted to see the world? She'd been the girl who planned to settle in Savannah and fight battles with award-winning editorials that would shape the future of her hometown.

"Midwest or up north," she answered evasively.

Enough of this bull. He gripped her shoulders and drew her close, closer until the current made circles around their ankles. "What's going on here, Mary 'Lise?"

He tightened his hold before she could slip away from him again like the sand under his feet; and tried like hell to ignore the sense that if she left, that would be the end. No more second or third chances to get her out of his head. He would be stuck with her haunting his mind with regrets, clinging to his thoughts like one of those whispery strands of red hair blowing over him for the rest of his freaking life.

They might not be able to recapture their friendship. The soft give of womanly flesh heating through his hands and sending blood straight south fast confirmed that. But damn it, he would not let this woman go until he knew she was settled, editorial pen in hand, crusades in place.

Smiling again.

He stepped closer and let the heat of his body filter through the air and his words. "Why haven't you called your parents? Or anyone other than me? Don't get me wrong, I want to be here for you, whatever you need, you know you can count on me. Doesn't matter what the hell happened eleven years ago. One call, and I'm there."

"The call was for the boys, Danny."

Anger chafed like the broken shells under his feet. "I know there's not a chance you would have contacted me otherwise."

"Because I don't need anything." She softened her steely declaration with a gentle smile and hand on his forearm.

A hand that shook.

"You're a good liar. You say it with a straight face, no wince, looking me right in the eye. But the thing is, I know you learned that from me after the trouble I pulled us through as kids."

"Then how do you know I'm not telling the truth?"

"I'm a better liar now than I was before." Military training and covert ops had taught him well. He raised his hand, pressed two fingers to the side of her neck, her pulse throbbing against his skin. "I can feel your lie right here."

Her heart rate kicked up a notch under his touch, a wariness tinting her eyes that almost stirred guilt. Almost. He wouldn't be deterred from prying answers out of her this time.

Eleven years ago that cornered look in her eyes might have swayed him. But not now. He'd seen the worst the world had to offer. Fought it. Conquered it more than once, and damned if he would let this woman bring him down with a simple wince.

He was doing this for her.

Then the flash in her eyes shifted, she shifted, changing into a different woman, a steely, determined woman who may have visited some of those hells he'd seen. He saw a different Mary Elise, but one who still sent jolts of awareness rocking through him until his gut clenched with need, his pulse now echoing hers. Hard and fast.

Definitely hard.

Mary Elise gripped his wrist and pulled his hand down, trailing his fingers over her collarbone until his palm flattened over her heart. "There are plenty of reasons a woman's heart rate speeds up, Danny."

Chapter 9

Desperation chewed through her. Mary Elise wrapped her hand tighter around the warm strength of Danny's wrist, his fingers riding the beginning curve of her breast. Heat seared silk.

It had to be desperation and fear of her past being uncovered, of others taking on the risk and danger of her foolish mistakes. She wouldn't allow the emotions burning through her to be anything else.

Still, why hadn't she opted for a different distraction from Danny's persistence? Like a leg cramp? She'd walked off the real cramps and backache, but why hadn't she faked they were back again? Even a mad dash in the opposite direction would have made more sense than this.

Touching. Wanting. Needing. And there weren't nearly enough people on this patch of beach to offer chaperoning, a lone dog walker already disappearing around a dune.

At least she had the satisfaction of knowing she'd

shocked Daniel as much as herself because the man stared down at her with dark eyes, stunned silent—but not moving away. Desire curled smoky paths through her veins.

She wanted to believe the pulsing heat came from abstinence. Except she knew better. Never had she wanted a man's touch as much as she wanted Danny's. Now. Right now, with a surety that if it didn't happen soon, she would spontaneously combust.

Danny's brows lowered and his hand twitched back, away, callused fingers snagging on silk. Involuntary muscles held his hand firm with a strength she hadn't known she possessed.

And suddenly, more than ever, she wanted something to take with her when she left in four days. A memory. A kiss. The question answered about whether her imagination had exaggerated the impact of his mouth against hers.

She couldn't stay, so what the hell did it matter now if she blew any chance of friendship? Her peace of mind was already shot. Yes, even fleetingly, she definitely deserved something. This. Him.

"You should know what you do to my heart rate, Danny. And I think maybe I do the same to yours." Mary Elise arched up, into him, against him, not a far stretch as he topped her by no more than four inches.

Surprise nipped. This new man seemed so much larger than the young lover from her memories. But in her arms, he was her Danny. She took comfort in that as she leaned in to take his mouth.

And then he wasn't her Danny at all.

A hungry growl of possession rumbled low in his throat. His mouth took hers right back in the kiss of a man. Not a hungry youth who, yes, had style and exuberance. But a man of intensity, strength.

Experience.

All man. And he made her feel all woman. A sensation she hadn't experienced in so long she'd forgotten the heady rush of being wanted. Desired. Even while sex with Kent had been physically satisfying at the beginning, all too soon any mating had become just that. Mating. She'd been nothing more than a vessel to bear his child, and somewhere along the way had lost the wonder of being a woman.

Danny reminded, reassured her with the bold possession of his mouth, tongue, hands traveling down her back to urge her closer to the undeniable proof that he desired her. A precious gift she hadn't realized she needed, and now she couldn't face losing it.

Losing him?

She shunted that thought away, too much, too dangerous, and focused on his kiss, the warm play of muscles under her hands. The roar in her ears swelled like ocean echoes in a conch shell. Somehow she knew that in years to come she would listen to a shell whisper reminders of passion.

Mary Elise hooked her leg around Daniel's bare calf and gloried in the gentle rasp of his bristly hairs and sand against her sensitive skin. Reveled in the masculine growl the rub of her heel elicited low in his throat.

Drinking in the taste of him tinged with beer and memories, Mary Elise clung to his broad shoulders and the moment. A moment so much hotter than her memories, and her memories of wrapping herself around Daniel Baker had been mighty damned hot. Keeping her awake and hungry and longing on more than one night.

And now after just one kiss from the adult Daniel, she feared she might never sleep again.

* * *

Daniel gathered a fistful of Mary Elise's hair, anchoring her sweet mouth to his, and wondered how he was going to sleep through another night on that damned sofa. Then thought about how much he didn't want to sleep tonight, wanted to spend the night peeling those silk shorts down Mary Elise's long legs.

What the hell was wrong with him? He couldn't freaking control his shaking hands or the consuming drive to possess this woman. Now. Here. Who needed a wide inviting stretch of bed where a couple of nosy kids might spring in on them anyway?

Kids.

The boys. Responsibilities and life and a woman with problems she wasn't sharing and plenty of his own she didn't need to shoulder.

He tore his mouth from hers, a tougher proposition than slipping past enemy radar in a combat zone. Her foot glided down his leg back into the water, moonlight sparking fiery glints in her hair. His forehead fell to rest on hers and he inhaled the scent of her honeysuckle shampoo. Of her.

His arms draped over her shoulders, their hips still grazing a tantalizing dance against each other as his libido defied his reason. ''Good God, Mary Elise. What was that about?''

''You didn't want to kiss me?''

Oh, he wanted to and a lot more, but that didn't make it any wiser. Not that he could lie to her. This was his doing as much as hers.

He pressed her fingers to his neck where his pulse double-timed. ''What do you think?''

Femininity and more desire flared in her bottle-green eyes searing through half the slipping threads of his self-control. He cupped her shoulders to keep from sliding his arms around her back again. ''But I don't understand why you initiated this when you say you're leaving.''

She traced the line of his jaw, square, stubborn and the one thing he'd inherited from his father. He suspected he might need every ounce of that stubborn will to make it through this conversation.

''Chalk it up to a weak moment brought on by moonlight and old memories.'' She cupped his cheek, her finger tracking up to trace the chicken pox scar on his temple. ''We did make some wonderful memories together, and right now I *so* don't want to think about the bad ones, if you don't mind. We can get to those another time.''

He waited, searching for the tiniest chink in her defenses, but this woman was tougher to read than the open Mary Elise from before.

Finally her fingers fell to rest on his chest, branding his skin, except she was pushing him away.

''Danny, as wonderful as that was, I really can't stay.''

He looked, studied. She wasn't lying.

''Damn it, why not? I don't expect you to move in with me or take on responsibility for the boys. They're mine now. But it would be nice for them to know you're close. There are schools and newspapers here where you could work, and it's not like you want to go back to Savannah. Heard and understood on that point. But you haven't come up with a place you do want to be since Rubistan is out.''

''What happens when you're transferred? Am I supposed to follow you forever because the boys need my help? You're not making sense, Danny, and that's not like you.''

Hell no, he wasn't making sense. Nothing tumbling around inside him made sense right now and that pissed him off. His whole freaking world was flipping, first his father dying, then the boys moving in. Now Mary Elise was back in his life. Once he'd depended on her to be his voice of reason and now he didn't want to grant her any more importance in his life, power over his thoughts.

But he couldn't let her walk away again with things so unresolved. He couldn't live the rest of his life chasing redheaded women who weren't her. "You're going to make me say it, aren't you? The real reason I don't want you to go."

Panic flared in her eyes. She backed away. "No. Forget it. I'm not trying to do anything except convince you to—"

He clapped a hand over her mouth. "*I* want you to stay."

Her eyes closed as if that would distance her from him.

Screw this evasive crap. He might not be Captain Happily Ever After, but he wasn't a coward. He would find some closure for both of them. Even if it meant—he shuddered—talking about feelings.

"The first year without you was the strangest damned year of my life. I kept looking for you. Picking up the phone to tell you something. Hell, sometimes I even started talking before I realized you weren't there. But the next year was a bit better. Then I hit a groove, moved on. Yeah, I thought about you sometimes, but I was living my life." A life full of redheaded women. "Now it's like those eleven years are gone, and the thought of telling you goodbye is tearing me up."

Her eyes drifted open, so full of pain it hit him like a load of shrapnel to the gut.

"But, Danny, those eleven years did happen. We're different people now."

Damn, he was in over his head here. But he had her talking, and he intended to press whatever advantage he could. "I'll be straight up with you, Mary Elise. You can check my pulse if you want to prove it.'' He gripped her wrist and flattened her palm to his chest again, over his heart. ''I still suck at romance. Don't want it and usually manage to screw it up if it comes my way. But I make a damned good friend. Just ask that pool full of people.''

Her fingers flexed in an involuntary caress. ''I don't have to ask them. I remember.''

''Let me help you.'' He gripped her shoulders to keep her from running.

What the hell had gotten into him that she'd become so important to him all over again? Maybe that call from his dad had messed with his head—his control—more than he'd realized. He wasn't the kind of guy who needed more than superficial friendships, fun pals, often. But damn it all, between inheriting two kids to take care of and the cryptic message from his father that he couldn't follow up on because of those two new responsibilities, this was one of those times he could use a little backup.

Preferably from someone he knew without question he could trust. ''Tell me what's wrong so you can stay and be my friend again.''

The tide tugged sand from beneath their touching toes for four ripping waves and he thought maybe, just maybe he'd gotten through to her.

A sigh shuddered through her and into him. Her fingers dug deeper in his skin, held. Each breath moved harder, faster through her until… What the hell was tearing her up so much?

Forget distance. He hauled her to his chest before she could blow him off with an evasive remark. Folded his arms around her and absorbed the tremors racking through her. ''God, Mary Elise. What's going on here? Talk to me.''

Her fingernails bit deeper into his skin, as if she

couldn't get close enough. "I'm so damned scared, Danny."

Mary Elise's thready words barely whispered against his neck until he might have questioned his hearing. But he felt each word and all her fear soak into him along with the heat of her rapid breaths.

His hands roved her back, no bold lover's caress this time, instead resurrecting that friend within him. "Tell me," he coaxed. "Tell me what to do for you."

She inched back, her hand sliding up his face again. "Oh, Danny, can't you see that you and all this," she slipped her hand around his neck in a sensual glide, "this tension between us that we can't ignore is a big part of the problem? You need to believe me when I say I just can't risk staying here with you."

He sifted through her words, thought back to her sparse confidences about her divorce—marrying her "mistake." No question she closed off any time the man's name was mentioned. How badly had the ass hurt her?

Hell, who was he to talk when he'd hurt her himself years ago? And apparently she wanted to avoid an encore.

His arms around her twitched, muscles convulsively tensing to hold her closer, safer. As much as he wanted to reassure her, he couldn't. He knew himself too well. So he held her and stroked her back.

How long they stood there he didn't know. Yeah, the sex and friendship might be tangled in his head, but it felt damned good to have her back in his arms.

Finally, her breathing slowed to normal. She pulled away to let the wind slide an invisible wall between them.

Her mouth tipped in a half smile, a friend smile as if trying to jam more bricks on that wall between them. "Since I can't stay, do you want to have a quickie affair before I go?"

In spite of her kiss, she didn't mean it and they both knew it. And, hell yeah, while he wanted to sleep with her, stay awake with her, no way could he answer that one truthfully since it would send her running.

He might be confused about a boatload of things at the moment, but he knew one thing for certain. She could spit out excuses until sunrise, jam layer after layer of bricks between them, and it wouldn't change his course. More than ever they both needed closure so he didn't spend his life chasing redheads.

He would convince her to stay. He considered himself a master at tactics, his logical mind paying off big time in that arena. And a strategic retreat to regroup seemed the wisest battle plan.

Picking up her attempt at a lighthearted escape out of a land mine discussion, Daniel resurrected his best-bud smile and slung his arm around her shoulders. "Well, friend, if we do opt for that quickie, let's make sure at least one of us thinks to bring condoms this time."

Four days later, Daniel poured his third cup of coffee and scooped up a second peanut-butter-topped Pop-Tart. Only a week into his leave time and he'd made decent strides at settling the boys, thanks to Mary Elise, the master list maker.

Her lists picked up speed and length by the minute as if she had to get everything documented for him before she left. If they brushed chests passing in the kitchen, she logged the boys' favorite foods. An accidental walk in on her in her underwear—lime-green satin, heaven help him—and she'd spent an entire afternoon penning every childhood story she could remember the boys' parents ever sharing.

And he was running out of excuses for her to stay.

The boys were enrolled and ready to start school in another week, after Thanksgiving break. House hunting would come after Christmas. He'd interviewed a battalion of nannies and lucked into a woman he could swear was a clone of Alice from the Brady Bunch, no less. Hell, if things went much better, Mary Elise would hit the road by sundown.

Which should be cause for rejoicing since he was losing his freaking mind locked in the condo with her. The bunk beds might be offering the boys a better night's sleep, but visions of Mary Elise alone in his queen-size bed had him twisted into trigonometric knots.

Their attraction multiplied exponentially by the minute, thanks to one kiss on the beach. Ending up horizontal together was a given before much longer.

But she would be gone soon. He could see it in her eyes even as she smiled and went through the motions of helping the boys start a new life. He knew her too well, and what parts he didn't remember from before or had changed over the years, he'd relearned with alarming speed.

That same crusader spirit of hers also made for a damned stubborn woman. It could well be his smart, crusader buddy knew what a rotten risk he was and thus had opted to stay staunchly vertical.

Of course he could see definite possibilities in vertical as well.

Sagging onto his sofa, Daniel sifted through the junk mail he'd ignored earlier in the week, tearing and pitching now that he finally had a free moment.

Free minutes sucked. Busy was better. He'd already run, worked out, showered and changed into his flight suit for a quick stop by the squadron.

But still the rest of the house snoozed on, so he would

keep quiet. He felt guilty enough over how much he was demanding of Mary Elise. Her pale exhaustion tugged at him. Sure he wanted her to stay, but not because he and the boys had made her sick, for God's sake.

Shuffling the pile, he saved pizza coupons. Tore a vacation giveaway sweepstakes. Flipped over a flyer on a local women's clinic, complete with stats on infertility and other birth control factoids. He ripped that sucker in half. "Where was this when I could have used it eleven years ago?"

Daniel pitched the rest of the stack back onto the coffee table, brochures and flyers skidding into a fan across the glass top. A quick glance at the clock told him Spike wouldn't be up yet. Of course, the guy would have come by the night before if there had been any more on the answering machine message, since he'd turned the tape over to the CIA for analysis.

He had to hope his father had simply called about Mary Elise and not anything related to his death the next day. Otherwise, the international implications in an already rocky region boggled his mind. As if the military wasn't already maxed from the recent conflicts. Just what they freaking needed, another Afghanistan on their hands.

Feet shuffled down the hall, easing Daniel back to the present, home life overriding big world. He glanced up and found…a buck-naked Austin.

He sighed. Crap. Another load of laundry. Who'd have thought two kids could quadruple the wash load? The math defied logic.

Austin danced from bare foot to foot. "I gotta go."

Uh-oh. The potty dance. No arguing with that.

Sprinting across the carpet, Daniel scooped his brother up under his armpits. No direct pressure to the bladder. And face the kid forward. He'd learned that one the hard way. Nope, he didn't plan to add his own clothes to the packed hamper before he'd even finished breakfast. "Why'd you take off your pull-ups, pal?"

"Gotta go."

Ah, hell. He didn't even want to check out that bed. His revamped budget would have to stretch to cleaning help as well as a nanny.

Daniel sidestepped discarded pj's and performed a military pivot round the corner into the bathroom. He plopped Austin on the tile floor.

In front of the neon-green plastic attachment to the john.

God. His bachelor digs now sported a freaking training seat. He liked the kid and all. Even Trey wasn't a major pain in the ass anymore, his snotty attitude having downgraded to *minor* pain in the ass, with the occasional quip that actually had Daniel laughing the minute the kid left the room.

He was managing. Doing okay. But that training seat pushed it.

Austin climbed up the step and took aim. Daniel leaned against the doorjamb and waited. And waited. Man, the kid was going like a racehorse. Daniel snagged the footed pj's off the hall carpet along with the pull-up.

Huh?

Well, hell. The thing was dry.

He spun back to Austin. "Way to go, bud."

"Oo-rah." With a big-toothed grin, Austin reached over the sink and pumped purple soap from a dinosaur dispenser.

The spare room door cracked open, Trey stepping out, his yawn closing into a frown. Big surprise. Not. "Wanna hold the party down? Some of us are trying to sleep."

Austin's smile faltered, and Daniel vowed he'd slip

peanut butter and marshmallow sandwiches in the kid's lunch for a week if Trey didn't ditch the attitude at light speed.

''We're celebrating Austin staying dry through the night. And so should you, pal, since Austin sleeps on the top bunk.''

A grin tugged Trey's somber face. He held up a high-five palm.

Austin launched off the footstool and smacked his brother's hand, shouting, ''Oo-rah!''

''Hoo-ya,'' Trey parried with the Navy grunt, anything other than a nod to the Air Force.

Yesterday Trey had chanted an Army cadence as he circled the pool. The day before that he'd taped a computer printout of the ''Marine Hymn'' to Daniel's bag of licorice—a bag that was suspiciously light.

Trey let loose another hoo-ya. Daniel snorted on a chuckle. Trey turned, a wicked glint sparking his brown eyes. The way would never be easy with this kid, but at least Trey had found his sense of humor.

Daniel burrowed a hand into a laundry basket—of clean stuff, he hoped—and yanked free a pair of Austin's shorts and a T-shirt. Once they passed a quick sniff test, he tossed them to the little guy. ''What do ya say we head out to IHOP for breakfast before I swing by base so Mary Elise can sleep in?''

Guilt bit over how he'd kept her up late more than once grilling her about where she'd go. What she'd do. Of course, now he wondered if maybe she did have a plan and just didn't care to share it with him.

''Pancakes?'' Austin cheered, pushing his head through his wrong-side-out T-shirt.

''IHOP?'' Trey echoed with a shrug and an almost disguised grin. ''Yeah, I guess that's okay, even if it is a regular hangout for you Chair Force dudes.''

''Don't push your luck, kid.'' He thumped Trey in the stomach with his shoes.

Eyes well off the master bedroom door, Daniel charged down the hall. Leave a note and let her sleep. He wasn't up for resisting a sleep-mussed Mary Elise, anyway.

She might be stubborn, but so was he, and he had reinforcements. Each day that passed, it was obvious she loved Trey and Austin. The boys were his trump card for convincing her to stay.

He locked the front door while his brothers sprinted toward Darcy Renshaw's Firebird easing into her parking spot after her night flight. The boys launched at her as she stepped out. She had to be dead on her feet but didn't wince. He owed Wren and Max more than he could repay.

Daniel finished bolting the door and turned to thumb the remote on the truck lock. ''Come on, fellas,'' he called, striding down the walkway past the mailboxes. ''Leave Wren alone so she can go to sleep. Let's get a move on, or I'm ordering Trey chocolate chip pancakes.''

''Eww!'' Trey's exaggerated gag drifted across the lot.

''You're talking to a man who ate rabbit eyeballs in survival training. I'm not impressed with your bellyaching about the menu, kid.''

When Trey didn't snap a ready comeback, Daniel glanced over his shoulder. Wren was long gone, Trey and Austin now standing with some businessman, tie flapping in the breeze over his shoulder.

Alarms jangled in his head. Not the work instincts he'd come to expect and trust, but a strange new protectiveness. Didn't schools teach kids not to talk to strangers?

Daniel charged forward. ''Come on, boys. Now.''

Trey jogged toward him, dragging Austin by one hand.

"That man was just asking about the condos, said he's thinking about moving here."

"Yeah, well, the guy's outta luck, then." He knew damned well there weren't any condos available since he'd already called to check that out for himself in the midst of a stupid whim thinking maybe he could coerce Mary Elise into staying a few doors down.

Just to be close to the boys, of course. And because he wanted to help her as much as she'd helped him. Not because he damn well couldn't stomach the thought of her long-legged stride walking out of his life.

Daniel scooped Austin up under one arm and "flew" him to the truck. "We'll talk about staying away from strangers some more over your milk, kid."

Austin stretched his arms out, airplane-style. "Man's got funny birds on his tie."

"Yeah, yeah." Daniel swung Austin upright and snapped him into the car seat with a newfound skill.

Tucking behind the wheel, Daniel watched the man cross the parking lot to the main office. Okay, that seemed to support his claim of condo hunting. Instincts were there for a reason, however.

He popped open the glove compartment and snagged a pad and pencil, jotting the license plate number on the guy's Mercedes. He'd get Spike to run the number when he checked in about the answering machine tape.

Daniel shifted the truck into reverse and glanced over his shoulder. Two pairs of brown eyes stared back at him.

Those eyes filled with trust, albeit begrudging on Trey's part, until something twisted inside Daniel. He'd been so damned busy thinking about how he would do his duty and take care of them, he'd never even seen it coming.

These weren't trump cards.

They were his brothers, his blood, not just some burdensome responsibility. They needed more from him than a set of bunk beds and a ride to school. God, if he felt this much for the two runts after only a week…

As much as he wanted to break through whatever walls Mary Elise had erected between them, if he screwed up again—a likely scenario—two sets of trusting brown eyes would pay as well. A prospect a helluva lot more daunting than the addition of a neon-green training seat to his bachelor condo.

Chapter 10

Mary Elise tugged the T-shirt over her knees, chin resting on her folded arms, and listened to the door slam as Daniel and the boys headed out for breakfast. The scent of bay rum—of Danny—drifted up from the rumpled sheets where she'd lain awake, too aware of him with every breath.

As if sleeping in the soft warmth of his shirt wasn't tempting enough. Almost as tempting as the fading echo of his laughter mingled with Austin's giggles and a repeat hoo-ya from Trey.

She was so damned proud of Danny.

He'd pulled it together with his brothers. Sure, they'd only been together about a week, and no doubt more bumps would jostle them in the future. Trey was still prickly, but Daniel had his number. Austin would adjust faster because of his youth. The rest would sort out, now that they'd begun to forge a family unit.

They didn't need her anymore. Her suitcase waited in a corner, calling to be packed.

She'd known he could manage—smart, determined, with a heart bigger and softer than he realized. She worried more about him submerging his own needs. The boys would be fine. But what about Daniel? The friend inside her wanted to be the one to take care of him in what would still be an ungodly stressful time.

The woman within her just flat-out wanted to take him.

Her gaze gravitated toward the half-open closet to Daniel's uniforms dangling across two-thirds of the space. How such neatly hung clothes could end up wrinkled within seconds of hitting his body defied logic.

But then, Daniel was as complex a puzzle as the artwork and toys he favored.

From the closet rod, the deep blue of a formal uniform gave way to the lighter blue shirts, shifted to splotchy green military camouflage, desert-tan cammo, then flight suits in both green and beige. All shapes of hats. Vests with canteens dangling and a scary-looking knife attached but sheathed in black leather. The Daniel who'd streaked grease paint on his face to jump a fence had turned his hobby into a profession.

Or perhaps it hadn't been a hobby, just a sense of direction from the cradle.

Pride hummed through her anew over the man he'd become. And, oh, my, was he ever a man. The heat of his kiss from the beach still tingled along her nerves. Tough not to think about it while she sat in his bed. Wanting him.

Mary Elise thunked her forehead against her hands folded over her knees. She could laze around feeling sorry for herself. Ick! Or she could shake off the blahs and get her butt in gear. Be satisfied that she had helped Danny build a strong foundation for a future with the boys in a few short days.

Get up, get a move on. And pretend her heart wasn't breaking in two.

Snick. The click of the front door opening echoed through the condo. Daniel must have forgotten something. Facing him now when sleep still mussed her defenses seemed a reckless move. Time to hit the shower.

She swung her feet over the edge of the bed and arched up to stretch out sore muscles, vowing to visit a clinic first thing in the morning. But after her mother's endless doctor appointments, live-in nurses, medicine bottles lining the kitchen windowsill, Mary Elise hated admitting to a physical weakness.

Prideful. Silly. Reckless. She could almost hear Danny ticking through her illogical reasoning.

Whipping the well-worn T-shirt over her head, she padded to his master bathroom. For the last time. Once Daniel and the boys returned, she would have to say her goodbyes.

The shower spray hit her with stinging needles of heat.

Stay.

Danny's words from the beach rolled over her in a tidal wave. Give their friendship another chance.

Friendship? Thoughts of him walking around the condo looking for Austin's favorite blanket while she stood naked in the shower led her mind to thoughts far from friendlike.

Honestly, she wanted to stay. And, yes, she even wanted to try again. The friendship. Maybe even more. The past days with Danny and the boys had been… everything.

Mary Elise snagged her bottle of shampoo from beside Daniel's. How could she escape the fact that she had to leave? To stay another day would be selfish and not worth the risk. Life seemed to be telling her in a hundred different ways that Kent was still out there.

Returning to the States had brought old memories forward. Stronger. Which likely heightened her emotions to supersensitivity. Or perhaps her subconscious was tormenting her so she wouldn't be tempted to stay.

And that pissed her off.

Her hands slowed in working the shampoo through her hair. Where was the fear? The ache over Kent's betrayal? All she could feel was a stinging anger like soap in her eyes over all Kent had taken from her.

Well damn. She'd gained something from the past days too.

Seeing herself through Danny's eyes reminded her how far she'd strayed from her essential self. First, losing pieces of her will through Kent's subtle control, then later by hiding while she licked her wounds.

Strength seeped into her with each waft of steam carrying the lingering scent of Daniel's aftershave. Yes, she had to leave. She accepted that. But she didn't have to cower.

She would fight back, scavenge for a plan to reclaim her life. Plans were in short supply at the moment, beyond saving to finance a private detective, but already the renewed strength fueled determination. How odd that until a few days ago she hadn't realized just how much had been stolen from her.

And once she had her life back?

Simply because she'd reclaimed her inner self didn't make her any more right for Danny than she'd been eleven years before. Not that he was even the same person. Parts of Danny remained, mingled with the newer, darker Daniel. Even if he stayed single after however long it took her to reclaim her life…

She didn't know. But for the first time in years, she knew she wanted to dare. To dream.

And the steamy whispers of possibility made packing somehow easier and tougher at the same time.

"Hey, Mary Elise, where ya going?" Austin piped from four steps ahead as he sprinted into the condo, his blankie dragging.

Going? Daniel's brain went numb.

He stood in the open doorway staring at Mary Elise's suitcase, and freaking couldn't process what he was seeing.

Didn't want to.

Hell, his mind never stopped working. Never. His thoughts always operated three paces ahead of his feet, and his feet were mighty damned fast even on a bad day.

And thanks to Austin's question, this promised to be a sucky day. Once again Mary Elise flipped his world.

Daniel double-timed into the condo, his boots traveling ahead of his reason. He charged past the boys, stopping toe-to-toe with Mary Elise and her small suitcase.

Austin shuffled to a stop in front of her, his bottom lip trembling.

Mary Elise knelt eye level with Austin's blueberry-syrup-stained face. She licked her thumb and swiped it over his cheek until the smudge disappeared. "Well, sweetie, it's time for me to get a place of my own."

"Why ya gotta go? I want you to stay."

"I'd like to stay, too. But this isn't my home."

He hitched his blanket under his nose and sniffed. "Are you gonna be close? Are we gonna see you again?"

She smoothed back sweaty brown curls off his forehead. "You bet you will." She answered the latter question while avoiding the first. "It may take a while for me to get everything...settled, but I'll be back here to see you sometime. And when I come back, I want you to show me all your new dives into the pool, and I'll bet you won't even need water wings anymore."

Damn it, he could see the tears in her eyes. Why was she doing this to herself? To the boys.

To him. "Mary Elise, let's talk without the boys here."

"Daniel, I'll be sending you the money I owe you for all the clothes and such. And I made a list of things Austin and Trey have mentioned wanting for Christmas." She avoided his eyes by rifling through her suitcase with jerky agitation. "Where did I put them?"

Trey leaned forward to tug the side zipper pouch. "Are they in here?"

"No. I don't think so. I haven't used that pocket yet."

"But it's half-zipped."

Hell, did the kid have to flipping help her out the door with a hoo-ya just to piss him off?

"Hmm." She yanked open the zipper and jammed her hand inside. "Maybe I put it in here without think—"

She shrieked. Her hand whipped back out of the bag. Blood dripped from her fingertip. "Ouch."

Daniel knelt beside her, pressing his thumb to the pinprick. "Trey, run back to the bathroom and get one of those Winnie the Pooh Band-Aids."

Maybe he could stretch this into a trip to the hospital for a tetanus shot to buy him time to talk her around. Or he could stand here and hold her hand for another hour and stare into the damned prettiest eyes he'd ever seen.

Mary Elise tugged her hand free and stuck her finger in her mouth. She looked away, taking all that endless green with her.

Prying open the side pouch, she peered inside. Color drained from her already-pale face. Swaying, she withdrew a small medicine bottle for a shot.

Daniel supported her shoulders with one arm and grabbed the bag from her. A syringe lay in the side pouch, and from the stunned glaze in Mary Elise's eyes, it didn't belong there.

Instincts went on full alert. Something wasn't right.

Trey charged back down the hall, Band-Aids waving from his hand like banners. "Got it. Two of them. One Tigger and one Ee-yore."

"Thanks, pal." Daniel snagged the bandages and wrapped an orange Tigger Band-Aid around the tip of Mary Elise's finger. "How about you fellas take your Game Boys to your room for a minute."

Austin's bottom lip trembled. "But I wanna say goodbye to Mary Elise."

"I promise you'll get to." He scruffed a hand through the tousled curls. "Meanwhile, let me see if I can talk her into staying a little longer."

Mary Elise exhaled, shaking free whatever had gripped her. "Please, Trey? Could you keep Austin busy for a bit? I promise not to go anywhere without talking to you first."

Trey shuffled from foot to foot, then shrugged. "Yeah, okay, but I want eggplant parmesan for supper."

Daniel faked a smile. "Sure kid, whatever."

Trey yanked his little brother by the arm, promises of Pokémon Nintendo fading with the close of their bedroom door.

Anger on a tight rein, Daniel jabbed a finger toward her. "Cut the crap. I'm not letting you walk out until you tell me exactly what's going on."

Mary Elise sunk back on her bottom. "Oh, God, Danny. I've screwed up so bad."

Mary Elise forced her hand to stay steady around the empty bottle, willed her teeth not to chatter. Still, the shaking swelled inside her.

She'd tried so damned hard to weigh the options and make the right choices to keep the boys from being traumatized. Yet, once the cargo plane had become airborne, her life had spiraled out of control until every option absolutely stunk.

Even if little Austin hadn't been frightened to the point of being immobilized and she could have run right away, Daniel would have been curious. Which would have led him—and therefore the boys—directly to Kent.

Except Kent had found her anyway.

She'd expected fear, and hell yes, fear stirred a storm within her. But she hadn't anticipated the blind explosion of fury.

How dare he do this to her? To the family she'd grown to care about so much? Rhetorical questions that served no purpose. Kent dared anything. And now she had to tell Daniel. Surely he would understand he needed to stay near the boys, protect them. Once he heard the truth, he would realize the farther all three were from her now, the better.

A horrific notion took root. She knew Kent had planted the bottle, but when? Her mind echoed with the rustlings when she'd showered. "Danny, once you and the boys left for IHOP, did you come back to pick up anything?"

"No." Impatience stamped his face. "The boys stopped to talk with Wren for a minute and then we left. What the hell's going on here?"

She flattened a hand to the carpet, slumping back against the couch. Nausea roiled. Bile burned. She dropped the bottle like a snake onto the glass-topped coffee table. "This isn't mine. Someone broke into the condo and put it here."

Kent, the man who dared anything and respected no boundaries, had placed it there. While she was naked in the shower.

Incredulity furrowed Daniel's brow, feeding her worries that he wouldn't believe her, either.

"What the hell for? Ah hell, whatever the reason," he reached for the phone on the chrome end table, "we need to call the cops, now."

"Wait!" She lurched to the side, flinging her hands over the telephone, the pinprick forgotten in a new panic.

He paused midreach. "The longer we wait, the farther away whoever it was will get."

"I know who it was, and no way is he anywhere near here now. He's left his message and will undoubtedly leave another, but not today."

His hand fell back to his knee as he sank down beside her. "Run that by me again?"

"I know who planted it there. Or at least I know who was responsible." And damn it, she prayed she hadn't made a huge mistake in lingering at Danny's this long.

"Want to share that nugget? Because I'm getting pretty torqued off thinking about someone slipping in here when the boys may have been around."

"The boys are fine." She would have never stayed at Danny's for so much as one night if she'd thought for a second Kent would come near the boys. He'd always been precise in his sanctimonious anger. "It's me he wants to rattle."

"He?"

"My ex-husband."

"Your ex did this? How can you be sure? You haven't

even let him know you're here.'' His eyes narrowed with a glint of…jealousy? ''Have you?''

''No! Of course not. But somehow he must have found out.'' She nudged the bottle beside a stack of junk mail on the table. ''Only he would think to leave behind a medicine bottle with my name on it, used back when we were married.''

Medicines to increase fertility.

A bottle from one of her daily shots.

As much as she hated giving Daniel details, she had to convince him, for his own safety and the boys'. ''Kent didn't take our breakup well. He pulled stunts like this all the time right after I left him.''

''You still haven't explained why you know this is from him.''

''I had difficulty conceiving. We tried…everything. I wanted to adopt. Kent wanted to keep trying for a biological child.'' She couldn't make herself tell him about the miscarriages. Her precious son born too early. But Daniel needed to know her suspicions, no matter how paranoid they sounded. ''I think maybe this wasn't the first time he's attempted to rattle me since I returned to the States. There was a plant mixed in with your neighbor's potted garden, a plant that's supposed to promote fertility. I thought it was a coincidence, and now I'm not so sure. I'm so very sorry for not telling you then.''

Daniel's hand fell to rest beside the bottle, inching over to straighten the stack of junk mail beside it with an odd precision. ''Why not just contact you?''

Long-buried resentment clawed its way to the surface, having been denied light too long, due to her more basic survival needs of the past year.

''Because he's a sick bastard who enjoys tormenting me. God, I could go on forever. Regardless, he's a nut case, Danny. And I'm so, so sorry for bringing him anywhere near the boys. I didn't think there was any way he could know where I was. Even if he'd tracked me to Rubistan, it's not like my leaving the country was exactly out in the open."

"You went to Rubistan to get away from him?"

"I'd have gone to the moon to get away from Kent McRae." She pushed out the words she'd told her parents, only to be patted on the hand and ignored by them. "Danny, my ex-husband was more than just a mistake. He's dangerous."

"The bastard hit you?" Daniel's eyes flamed.

He canted forward, already on the offensive just as she'd predicted. As much as her heart cheered his ready acceptance, she also feared his reaction.

With her own anger building by the microsecond, how would she stay calm enough through the rest of her explanation to keep him from going ballistic? She forced herself to sit still when her feet wanted nothing more than to pace out the edgy bite of emotions.

She shook her head. "No. He never raised a hand to me. He's much more subtle than that, like with leaving this old medication bottle. You can call the police, but what are they going to do? Unless we can prove he broke in here, they'll just issue another restraining order, all the while looking at me like I'm a hysterical woman because I don't have bruises to show for proof."

Sometimes she wondered if things might not have spiraled down so if only she'd left sooner, once Kent started changing from the charming man she'd married into a manipulative control freak. Easy to second-guess now with hindsight, but at the time she'd let guilt blind her to the signs. Deep in her heart she'd been certain the fault was hers because, God help her, she didn't love Kent as much as she'd once loved Daniel.

The guilt had torn her. She'd chosen to marry Kent, after all. She owed him better than she'd given him, half of herself. Now from the clearer perspective of distance, she wondered if he'd somehow sensed her feelings and manipulated them all the more to persuade her to give him whatever he wanted.

Daniel shoved to his feet, pacing enough to wear tread marks in the carpet with his boots. "We'll get another restraining order. I'm here to help keep space between you and the jerk before things turn violent. Mary Elise, you can't just keep running."

"It's too late for that. I know this may be difficult to take in. There are certainly plenty of people out there who think I'm only out to tarnish his reputation. But Kent went off the deep end when I left him." She closed her eyes and sucked in air to keep her voice steady. What would she do if Danny didn't accept her story?

Mary Elise rose to her feet. She didn't have a choice but to make him believe her. He stood with his back to her, which seemed the perfect time to tell him. She wouldn't have to see his skepticism. Not right away.

"Danny, I moved to Rubistan because Kent hired a hit man to kill me." Even the words chilled her. She tamped down the images and concentrated on reading Daniel.

Tension rippled the muscles along his shoulders in visible waves under his flight suit, but still he didn't turn. Thank God, because she wasn't sure she could keep talking if she found disbelief on his face. But she would talk, had to. Damn Kent straight to hell, she wasn't the wounded woman who ran to Rubistan anymore.

"Shortly after I left him, I suspected I was being followed, but I thought it was just Kent and more of his hurtful *messages,* like the bottle or the plant. Then a man with a gun caught me getting out of my car in front of my apartment. He planned to fake my suicide.'' The remembered cold press of the gun to her temple pushed through her concentration. ''He told me Kent had sent him. Even gave me a message from Kent no one else could have known.''

Her secret name for their last child, a name she hadn't dared share with anyone except Kent because she couldn't take the hesitant looks from people if she dared be hopeful.

''I realize it sounds crazy. God knows the cops and even my parents were skeptics.'' She winced. Great. Way to go giving him the idea if he hadn't already thought of it himself. ''I never dreamed something like that could happen to me. It seems the sort of story you only hear about from celebrities or in tabloids. But it happens. It happened to me.''

She waited.

And waited, reassuring herself that no matter what his reaction, she would hang tough. She would be strong and walk out the door today despite Danny's offer to help. The time had come for her to deal with the shambles Kent had made of her life, but she couldn't do it here. She'd leave to protect the boys. To protect Danny.

Slowly he pivoted on his boot heel with military precision. Fury vibrated through him, so tightly reined the low hum of rage reached to her from across the room. Not at her, but for her.

He believed her.

She reached back for the arm of the sofa and let herself sit. Relief rattled her teeth for three blessed seconds. Until she realized that yes he believed her, and planned to right the wrong done to her.

Any veneer of civilized niceties peeled away from him in strips, leaving behind raw man. Man at his most elemental protector self, a primal essence that centuries ago enabled him to charge into battle with only a sword in his hand or a knife between his teeth.

To protect.

What should have brought her breath-stealing relief instead chilled her. Daniel—she couldn't think of him as Danny right now—yes, Daniel would throw away his life to keep her safe. Looking deep into his eyes, she knew without question.

Kent was a dead man.

Chapter 11

Daniel deadened his emotions.

His brain assumed control, assimilated information. Video chirps and blasts reverberated from behind the boys' closed bedroom door. Two little boys he was almost certain had come inches away from Kent McRae in the parking lot earlier. A sick son of a bitch who'd dared to walk into Daniel's apartment. Who'd dared breathe the same air as Mary Elise.

A tic twitched the corner of Daniel's eye. Yeah, deadened inside was better. Otherwise the molten rage bubbling deep within him would melt his logic with a burning need to take out the bastard.

Damn straight Kent McRae had tried his scare tactics before with that junk-mail brochure. Coincidental that it landed in the mail this week? Not a chance. And he would pay.

But first, get the facts straight. Make a plan. And don't

fall victim to the distraction of vulnerable green eyes. "How long?"

"How long what?" She lifted the telephone from the end table and placed it on her knees, as if that could keep him from dialing the cops if he chose.

He let her have her phone victory for the moment. He needed every ounce of information he could wring out of her before he spoke to them, anyway. "When did you leave for Rubistan?"

"I started the teaching job at the embassy school a year ago."

A job his father had arranged for her.

More anger piled on top of a towering load. She hadn't even considered coming to him with this.

Later he would deal with the fact that he would have to reassess his father's call from Rubistan shortly before his death. His dad hadn't been informing him about Mary Elise's arrival. In fact, had known about her slimeball ex and hadn't bothered to share with Daniel, another betrayal from a man he already resented like hell. A man he would never have the chance to chew out.

But Franklin Baker had kept her safe.

As much as Daniel wished he could have been the one she'd run to, he owed his father a debt for keeping her alive so she could sit there on his sofa and frustrate him with every defensive twitch of her head. Sunlight through the window glinted along the wet sheen of her hair.

She'd been in the shower.

Mary Elise had been vulnerable in the shower while McRae had rifled her bags. Walked through Daniel's place. Touched everything that was his.

Whoa. Full speed emergency stop on a short runway. Mary Elise was *not* his.

Wrong.

She was under his roof. Under his protection. And hell yes, she'd once been his. If he hadn't allowed the ties to be severed between them, she would have come to him. This might well have never happened at all.

Anger and guilt tangoed big-time. ''You should have told me everything when we landed. Hell, before that.''

''This isn't your problem. It's mine. I didn't mean to bring you in at all. You were right that crawling into the crate was a mistake.'' She speared her fingers through her tangled mass of wet hair. ''But I still don't know how I could have sent those boys off with Austin crying. The guard would have been on them in a minute. And once I was in that crate, everything rolled out of control so fast.''

He backed up a step to keep from yanking her close again. Thoughts of her risking her life a few days ago hammered too hard and fast on the out-of-control mess at their feet right now. ''That's a crock, Mary Elise. You know I would have been there for you. Why didn't you tell me?''

''Maybe there's a better answer somewhere, but I did the best I could.'' She freed a lock of damp hair twisted around a gold hoop earring, no doubt to avoid looking at him. ''God knows Kent told me what a screw-up I was often enough. I know better, damn it. I do. But sometimes it's just hard as hell to trust your instincts. Not everyone can be so all-fired certain their choices are perfect, like you are, Danny.''

Daniel's slowing steps drew him to her with the seeping realization from her words. He may not agree with her choice to stay silent, yet there was no question but that this woman selflessly had his brothers' best interest at heart. Always.

She was scared and he was grilling her. Way to go, bud.

He brushed her hand aside and finished untwisting the hair from her earring. ''Damn it, Mary Elise, don't clam up now. This is too important for you to deal me half parcels of truth.''

''Yes, Danny, I do know you, and I knew you'd be just like this. That you'd throw yourself in the middle of my mess, which is the last thing I want for you. Or for those boys.''

His fingers gripped tighter around the silky lock. ''You would have left today, without telling me.''

''Of course,'' she answered without even a blink.

More of that anger and something else he damned well didn't want to define scratched through the numbed state. Letting her go eleven years ago had been the toughest thing he'd ever done. And yet she could just write him off. She'd put the boys first and once they didn't need her anymore, she was gone. Over and done without a wince about losing him.

That bit. Too much.

''Yes, I would have left. Would that have been the right decision? Have any of my choices been the best option? God, I don't know.'' Her steady gaze pinned him. ''Where is it written that every choice is clear cut? Even in your logical brain, there's got to be room for shades of gray. And who says that we're perfect and had better damn well make the perfect, right decision or we're too stupid to live?''

She fisted her hands by her sides. ''Kent told me for years I was defective. Incompetent. Incomplete, if I didn't live my life his way. I almost bought into it. Almost. But I got away. And I'll be damned if I'll let you take away something harder to rebuild than you'll ever understand.''

Her voice didn't so much as quaver. But pain laced her words.

Psychological warfare on the home front.

He'd studied and experienced the power of mental mind games in the POW phase of military survival training. And for her, the propaganda crap had come from someone she had every right to trust, someone who'd vowed to love and cherish her.

When had anyone cherished this woman?

Damn straight he didn't agree with her decisions, but he understood how she'd arrived there. She'd been betrayed by her husband and her parents. Why should she trust him, someone who'd already let her down before?

Yet even as he saw the wounded pieces of her, he couldn't mistake the grit. Hell, yeah, she may not have made his kind of choices, but she'd kept right on moving.

He'd seen bravery and cowardice in a hundred different forms. And, God, was he ever in awe of this woman right now.

She inched her hair from between his fingers. "Are we clear? I'm leaving, and I'll be careful. I'm going to find a private investigator and try to put an end to this. But I can't let it touch you and the boys anymore. I only told you this much so you're aware and can be careful for their sakes. I did *not* tell you so you could launch into a commando protector and solve my problems for me. I *am* leaving."

Like hell.

She wasn't taking one step out that door without him five steps in front of her, between her and whatever waited. Daniel shook off the sentimental fog, emotional crap that would distract him, get her hurt. She could make this easy. Or she could make it tough.

Mary Elise picked up her suitcase.

Okay, so it would be tough.

Ducking a shoulder into her stomach, Danny hefted her up. She gasped, deep. Damn. She was gonna get vocal.

Planting a hand on her bottom—ah, hell—he forestalled her with, "Shout and you'll upset the boys."

"Danny," she threatened through gritted teeth. "Put me down." Her suitcase thumped his leg.

Deliberate? Or accidental.

Ow, damn it. Deliberate.

Daniel flung her on the sofa. On her back. Already she arched up.

Something snapped in her eyes. All that Mary Elise calm and restraint unraveled into a tangle as convoluted as her hair twisting through her hoop earrings. Any minute she would lose it, and he couldn't let that happen, for her or his brothers.

Daniel dropped, flattened her fast. His body pinned hers in a full-length press to the sofa. "You're not going anywhere."

She bucked under him. "I'm damned tired of people controlling my life."

No way could he let her fly out of the apartment like this. He struggled to make sense of her words, a hard-as-hell proposition with her writhing under him. The glide of her body against his numbed his brain while heating other parts of him.

She clipped him on the chin.

All right, then. Passion tempered. He grabbed her flailing fists, manacled them with his hands over her head. "You need to rein it in, Mary Elise."

"Get off me, you son of a bitch, and I'll be just fine."

She glared up at him, her green eyes sparking with a mix of fury and a desperation that knocked him harder than her punch. She wasn't fighting him but some demon he couldn't combat until she let him in.

God, he never, never wanted to frighten her. As much as he knew of the old Mary Elise, he was beginning to realize he would need new instincts in dealing with this wary woman.

He gentled his grip. "Southern boys get particularly pissed when you talk bad about their mamas. Now hush up and listen for a minute." He trailed a finger down to loosen a strand of hair clinging to her full bottom lip. "You know I would never hurt you."

She stilled under his touch, breasts pressed to his chest, legs twined. Back and forth, he traced the pad of his thumb over the giving softness of her mouth, felt the steamy rushes of breath gust over his skin.

Into him.

Her eyes darkened to that deep green of late summer grass. Oh, yeah, he remembered the shade well, felt the hitch in her breath that had nothing to do with fear and everything to do with wanting.

Adrenaline-fueled desire. Logical explanation. Not that logic would stop him from—

Her face rose to meet him as he angled down. Mouth to mouth, open, ready, hungry. More adrenaline and heat and too long not touching sent his hands into the pooling mass of her hair.

He needed to hold her again and kiss her senseless and find out if being inside her was as un-freaking-believable as he remembered before she hauled ass out of his life. Not that she seemed pointed toward that door at the moment.

She was damned near tearing his flight suit off. Her fingers yanked at his zipper, crawled inside to stroke his shoulders. Sweeping the warm recesses of her mouth with his tongue, he tasted Mary Elise, wondered if the honeysuckle sensation was taste or scent but couldn't tell with her jumbling all his senses.

Daniel struggled for reason. He couldn't let this spin out of control, as much as he might want to roll her to the floor and lose himself inside her with a deep rightness he hadn't felt since…her. He needed to get his head on straight. Two boys waited down the hall, and regardless of what she said, the cops would have to be called. They would have to face her past.

Together, damn it.

He let her soft touch seep into his anger, even feed the protective urges. Whatever it took to keep her safe, he embraced it.

Daniel pulled away, let his gaze land on her, immobilizing her with only his will. "You're not going anywhere without me."

The cloudy passion in her eyes dissipated. "Danny—"

"How closely did you look at that bottle?"

Her head angled to the side, toward the coffee table where the bottle rested. Her hand inched closer to graze the numbers handwritten across the label.

He forced himself to say the words, even knowing they would scare the hell out of her.

Whatever it took to keep her safe.

"You can talk about walking away to protect me all day long, but McRae has already made the choice for you." Daniel pointed to the penciled scrawl across the label on the medicine bottle. "My social security number. He's not just after you anymore."

Time passed in a haze.

Standing by the queen-size bed, Mary Elise sorted through the laundry basket, folding the boys' clothes into a suitcase, her body on autopilot. Beside her, Daniel jammed gear into a big green bag—a webbed vest, canteens, knife.

A gun.

His stark announcement about his social security number on the bottle still thundered through her head. She'd brought Kent's wrath to Daniel.

She would never be able to forgive herself.

Danny had insisted on calling the cops and filing the official complaint. Prints had been lifted. A restraining order requested. She'd been this route before.

At least the boys would be protected, safely hidden away with Darcy and Max until the threat passed. The engaged couple had already planned to spend Thanksgiving with Darcy's sister stationed at Seymour Johnson Air Force Base in Goldsboro, North Carolina. The boys would be ensconced in a family full of service members and an OSI special agent. She would stay alone with Daniel in a secluded fishing cabin Max kept for his "cave time" as Darcy called it.

Totally alone. Gulp.

Daniel had calmly explained this would give him and Max time to track information through CIA and OSI internet files. The remote locale would also keep the threat away from others if Kent found them.

Mary Elise willed her hands to keep folding little boy boxers and pairing up socks. Darcy and Max would finish their own accelerated packing soon. It still boggled her mind that Daniel could ask this of them and that they wouldn't even hesitate to help. The level of friendship went beyond anything she could fathom.

Made her question the depth of her friendship with Danny.

She tunneled a hand into the basket and came up with…one of Daniel's shirts. Hard Rock Café: Bangkok.

Once they'd shared so much, and now there were countless unshared memories and experiences between them. She smoothed a hand over the logo, then tugged the shirt inside out for Danny before folding it.

They *had* been close, damn it. She'd only turned to his father because she'd known Franklin wouldn't ask too many questions.

Or had she secretly been hoping Franklin would notify Danny? A disturbing notion that left her swaying on her feet.

"Would you quit before you fall over?" Daniel palmed her waist, stirring embers barely banked after their kiss earlier.

The two of them would be alone together soon. No more secrets. Well, not many. Already she could feel the inevitable draw they hadn't been able to resist eleven years ago.

She didn't want this. Especially not now.

Mary Elise ducked from under the temptation of his broad palm. "It's only a little laundry. Do you really want to subject Darcy and Max to the sonic shriek that will come if you forget Austin's blanket?"

Daniel jammed a pen and paper in her hands. "Make a list. You're great at details. There's plenty of crap Darcy and Max don't know about the kids that you didn't need to include on my lists."

What? He didn't think she could even handle climbing Mount Washmore? Being relegated to nonactive roles stung on a day where she'd taken a few too many hits. "I've already written everything out."

His hands landed on her shoulders, urging her to sit on the bed. "Do you have any freaking idea how pale you are?"

Yes, she did. The mirror didn't lie as well as she could.

"It's been a helluva day. Maybe I'm a little shaky, but then, who wouldn't be?"

Slowly he shook his head. "What the hell else aren't you telling me? Why would your ex leave a medicine bottle in your bag? And you'd better come clean now because I don't want any more surprises knocking me on my ass for at least another twenty-four hours, if you don't mind."

Two fingers slid from her shoulders up to the bare skin of her neck. "No lies."

Mary Elise swallowed her anger. The last thing they needed was more sparks. She stared into his smoky-brown eyes and found plenty of anger…and concern. The guy genuinely thought there might be something wrong with her.

She'd pushed him far enough.

"I mean it when I say I'm fine, Daniel. I told you already that the bottle was linked to fertility drugs. I just have a…condition…called endometriosis. A chick thing, and you really don't need to hear all the details. I hadn't planned on this trip back to the States, and my meds are still in Rubistan. But it's not like I'm terminal. Women lived with this for centuries without any more medical help than herbs and a warmed brick."

"Well you look like hell."

Just what a girl wanted to hear from an old lover who was even hotter eleven years later. "I get a little achy." Understatement of the year, but hopefully she'd kept her pulse steady enough. "I'm a tad anemic, too, which is why I seem run-down to you. And thank you very much for letting me know I'm a hag. That makes me feel much better."

"Nice try with the diversion. Not working. Although later I'm going to want to hear what the hell the brick was for.'' He tapped her nose. ''You know you're beautiful, so don't fish for compliments. Do you need a specialist or can any doctor take care of this?''

Beautiful?

''Mary Elise? I want an answer.''

Oh. Yeah. She shook off silly vanity.

She had a specialist, but… ''This can wait until we have everything settled.''

His stubborn chin jutted. ''A specialist or a regular doctor.''

''A regular doctor can handle this, but Danny—''

''Fine.'' He wrenched the zipper on the green military-issue bag closed, then slid a laptop computer off the dresser to rest beside the suitcases. ''We have to swing through base, anyway, to mask our tracks and make sure no one sees us trading the boys off to Wren and Spike. We'll check in with Kathleen while we're there. Now that I think about it, Bronco's TDY—temporary duty—to McChord for two weeks. We can swap out my truck for his SUV when we leave base. I can clear a tail even if McRae's got help, but changing cars wouldn't hurt.''

Damn it, she understood he had more expertise in these things, but she wouldn't be relegated to a sick bed with her pen and paper. She could pitch in with something besides lists.

She respected that Danny was loading his gun and packing for the worst, but he didn't realize Kent would never fight the kind of head-to-head battle that Danny must excel at. ''Do I get *any* say here?''

''No.''

Frustration swelled. Built. She owed him, but why did he have to be so damned stubborn with the whole his-way-no-matter-what attitude?

The doorbell pealed once, twice.

Daniel backed one step at a time. "You won't be any help to me if you pass out."

He spun away on his boot heel.

Great. He got to be bossy *and* right. As if the hag comment wasn't bad enough, damn his cute departing ass in a wrinkled flight suit, he had to go Cro-Magnon on her.

She should be thanking him for fixing her mess of a life, not cursing him. Except rogue thoughts of the future kept teasing her with how much these boys would need a mother's softening influence long-term so their knuckles wouldn't drag the ground on occasion, as well.

Compressing the stack of clothes, Mary Elise tucked Trey's nebulizer, an extra inhaler and the rest of his asthma meds on top, and zipped the suitcase closed.

"Boys?" She crossed the hall and opened the door to find both children perched on the bottom bunk with Game Boys in hand. They'd been told about the change in plans, but with so much to assimilate in the past week, she wasn't sure they fully understood.

Hell, she still didn't understand everything.

She held out her arms. Flinging aside the video game, Austin launched toward her and hopped up. He clung to her, spindly arms and chubby cheek pressed against her neck while Trey's thumbs flew over the handheld video.

Voices drifted from the living room, Darcy and Max with Daniel. Austin's hold tightened. Tears burned her eyes. Oh, God, she couldn't lose it in front of the kids.

"Don't wanna go wif' Wren and Spike." Austin's muffled voice rang with the steely resolve of a temper tantrum on the rise.

Guilt jabbed her like the unrelenting stab of endless needles.

She pushed back her tears and straightened his Winnie the Pooh shirt. "I'm sorry, sweetie, but it's just for a little while. You'll have fun playing with all of Darcy's family.''

He shook his head against her neck. ''Don't know them.''

''But you do know Darcy and Spike.'' She sank to the edge of the bottom bunk amid rumpled sailboat sheets, ducking her head to accommodate the upper bed. And you'll get to play with Darcy's big sister and brother and her dad. I'll bet they even take you to McDonald's, and Danny's going to give them money to buy two new cartridges for your Game Boy Advance.''

Chiming bells from the video signified a leap to the next level. Trey's fingers flew. ''You might as well give it up,'' he confided without pausing. ''He doesn't want to leave you and go with them.''

''Trey,'' Mary Elise warned low.

''He's just a big baby.''

Mary Elise gasped, reached to clap her hand over Trey's mouth. Just what they needed. An all out battle on their hands.

Austin's head popped up from Mary Elise's neck. ''Am not a baby.''

''Are so.''

''Am not.''

''Then why are you hanging on her like one?''

Realization clicked. The kid was maneuvering his brother with tactics reminiscent of his big brother scamming an extra helping of ice cream out of a neighbor. She stifled the urge to give Trey a tight hug and blow the whole gig.

Trey flipped the off switch on his game. ''Danny and Mary Elise need some time by themselves, you big bozo. Like Mom and Dad did.''

''So they don't get a di-borce.''

Divorce? Franklin Baker had been heading to divorce

court again? She'd known they were having trouble, but apparently not how much.

Trey nodded. "Yeah, dweeb. Come on, I want that new Zelda: Ruler of the Universe game really bad." He rolled his eyes. "But it would probably scare you, anyway."

Mary Elise held her breath. Had Trey overplayed his hand with that one?

Austin squirmed, working his way down and out of Mary Elise's arms. Apparently sibling rivalry was a mighty strong motivator. She mouthed over Austin's head to Trey, "Thank you."

A grin creased his face.

Well, hell. He did look a little like his big brother after all.

Austin tugged her shirttail until she leaned forward.

"Love you. Have fun with Danny." He planted a wet kiss on her cheek along with a final hug.

Footsteps sounded down the hall just before Darcy poked her head into the room, looking rested from her power nap after her night flight. "Hey, kids, let's go raid your brother's junk-food cabinet and find some snacks for the road."

"Treats? Oo-rah!" Austin launched into Darcy's arms.

Mary Elise forced her feet to stay still while Darcy led the boys away. Austin was settled and she would only make it worse by following Darcy and pointing out what Austin and Trey preferred.

Relief and jealousy duked it out inside her. Thank God Austin would be okay for now. But damn it, she wanted to stop making lists and start living life. She wanted to be the one packing snacks for those two boys who'd first tugged her heart because of Daniel and then stolen her heart by being themselves.

No way would she let Trey and Austin lose their big brother. Captain Commando would have to learn to accept her help whether he wanted it or not.

Chapter 12

In the home stretch.

Tucked in a corner of the living room, Daniel memorized security codes from Max, for the fishing cabin, for joint computer access. Only a few more minutes and he could hit the road, hide Mary Elise safely away, then forge ahead with his plans to neutralize Kent McRae. Ensuring that ex of hers stayed locked up for life offered the only guarantee of safety.

With a little luck, he and Spike could dig deep enough into intelligence files for some kind of connection between Kent and a too-damned-cold trail for a hired gun. And pray the police landed a lead, as well. If the dusting for prints turned up anything.

According to the cops, Daniel's positive ID of Kent McRae outside the condo wasn't enough to place him inside. Meanwhile a restraining order was in the works. Apparently, it was the third Mary Elise had taken out on the bastard.

For all the good the others had done her.

Max clapped a hand on Daniel's shoulder. "Anything else you need?"

Answers? "Nah, we're set. I can't thank you enough for this. I already owed you for helping me get the boys out of Rubistan, and now this, too."

"You don't owe me a thing. Just keep your eyes peeled whenever you're flying wingman for Darcy."

"Don't let Wren hear you say that or she'll deck you."

Darcy poked her head through the kitchen bar opening and waggled a fruit roll-up at them. "I heard, anyhow. Wrestling match later, Max. Me and you, *mano a mano*."

"Looking forward to it." Max winked, then thumped Daniel's back. "We'll take good care of them. You just take care of the two of you, and we'll be ready to throw another party by the end of next week."

"I hope so."

"I'll be in touch with you via the secure line 24/7 with updates about the boys and…anything else that comes through."

Daniel nodded.

"Hey, Darce," Max called, hitching his Technicolor swim trunks higher on his hips as he strode toward the kitchenette, "don't forget to pack some of those juice box things, grape-blaster flavor. Baker here has gotten me hooked on them."

Max rounded the corner, dodging Trey ducking back into the living room. Trey clutched a fistful of red licorice in his hands, eyes broadcasting more questions with each step toward the sofa. Damn, but he owed Trey a boatload of eggplant for keeping his little brother occupied today.

Daniel scrubbed a hand over his face, prepping himself for Trey's next round of questions. He wanted to be up-front with him. But as much as Trey put on that hoo-ya brave face, he was still just a kid.

A persistent kid. Interrogations in the Air Force training mock POW camp were a cakewalk compared to the inquisition of two little boys.

Plunking down on the leather couch, Trey waited, his eyes demanding answers with the same imperious right-to-know their old man had mastered well.

Daniel dropped to sit beside him. ''Trey, I'm sorry about all of this.''

''It's okay.''

''No, big guy. It's not. But I'm going to do my best to make it okay again.''

Trey peeled a strand of licorice off. ''Is Mary Elise in trouble?''

''She didn't do anything wrong, if that's what you're asking.'' Other than not come to him in the first place, but then that was as much his fault for closing the door between them years ago. ''But yes, things are a mess for her right now, and she needs a friend.''

Trey unraveled another strand, slowly, then another. ''My dad was trying to help her, wasn't he?''

My dad? Daniel wondered why the kid had the power to rile him with one little freaking pronoun. ''Yeah, Trey,'' Franklin Baker the third, ''your dad was trying to help her.''

''Help her with what?''

His brother couldn't be bought off with a video-game promise. Honesty worked for a reason. He just hoped the kid could understand something that damn well bemused him. ''Her ex-husband isn't a nice guy. He wants to hurt her, and I can't let that happen.''

''Kind of like how you kept me and Austin away from Uncle Ammar back in Rubistan.''

And to think he'd worried about the boy understanding. Life had given Trey a crash course in life's injustices. "Exactly like that."

One day, when he'd ensured the boys' safety, he looked forward to making sure they saw the beauty of their mother's heritage, as well. Man this parenting gig was a complex bag. But he didn't want his brothers' view of a part of themselves to be tainted by experiences with their uncle.

Trey nibbled the end off a strand of licorice. "Well then, I think it's probably a good idea for me and Austin to go to North Carolina."

Daniel let the pride build inside him. Yeah, the kid had to make it seem like his own decision, but no problem. He could live with that. He clapped Trey on the shoulder. "Thank you. I'm trusting you to take care of Austin. It'll hurt Mary Elise to think he's popping out those tears."

Trey rolled his eyes. "Yeah, two of those big fat leaky ones and Mary Elise was crawling inside the crate with us."

The enormity of her sacrifice nailed him dead center like an on-target missile, no warning. He'd respected her bravery before, but he'd been clueless on how difficult it must have been for her to risk a return to the States, to expose her sanctuary with the call for help in the first place. Anonymous or no, the trail was there.

Her call. His father's call. His father's death.

Pieces of information jostled in Daniel's head, searching for edges to make a clean fit. Except connector pieces were missing.

"Danny?"

He startled back out of his pensive trance. "Yeah, kid?"

"Who were you named for?" A simple question with a weight of importance reflected in the boy's eyes.

"For Great-grandpa Baker."

"Our father's grandfather?"

Our. "Yes."

"Cool."

Silence descended. Trey peeled the last strands of licorice apart, sorting them into two piles on the leather sofa. He clutched one stack, leaving the other beside Daniel.

And then his little brother was hugging him. So quick Daniel almost missed the chance to hug those bony shoulders back.

Trey stepped away, stubborn chin jutting just like their father. Like his older brother. "I still hate peanut butter."

"Oo-rah."

"Hoo-ya."

Daniel scooped up the pile of licorice Trey had left behind. *Love you, too, bro.*

Who knew red licorice had such a distinctive scent?

Of course, after an hour alone in the car with Danny, Mary Elise feared she would soon keel over from sensory overload from the different facets of him bombarding her.

Daniel's aftershave drifting with each gust of the vent.

Danny's licorice disappearing strand by strand.

The captain's military paraphernalia wafting an odd hydraulic fluid scent she'd come to realize permeated Air Force gear. Even a well-washed flight suit carried the air.

She lowered the window on the SUV, Daniel's truck having been traded for Bronco's vehicle on base after her doctor visit. After a quick trip to the BX, where Daniel bought the most bizarre assortment of supplies, they'd hit the road. Two dozen plastic buckets rattled around in the back with a bag of twenty-penny nails and heaven only knew what else.

Moss-draped oaks arched over the narrow road, the marshy coastline peeking through on her right out the open window. Reeds bowed a welcome in the breeze.

Mary Elise wriggled in the seat to get comfortable. At least her medicines would be kicking in soon, throwing her body chemistry back in sync, hopefully lightening her mood. This was worse than that day by the pool years ago. At least then Danny had been her friend. She vowed if he offered her boatloads of chocolate, she'd deck him.

Or hug him.

It was a close contest.

She adjusted the angle of the seat.

Daniel tore off another bite of licorice. "Why the hell didn't you let me know you're in pain this week?"

"What did Kathleen Bennett tell you?"

"Nothing." And he didn't look too happy about it.

"But you asked her."

"Hell, yeah, I asked her. And she got her flight suit all in a twist over rules."

Three cheers for patient confidentiality. "Danny, I'm fine, and feeling better by the minute thanks to Kathleen. By tomorrow I'll be a hundred percent, and your chocolate will be safe from me."

"Funny. Not. Why the hell are you so sensitive over a flipping trip to the doctor?"

Boggy wind whipped between them while she searched for a simple answer that would bring the fewest questions. "I didn't want to draw any undue attention to myself that might tip off Kent."

For all the good that had done her. If that False Unicorn plant had been intentionally placed, which she firmly believed, Kent had known about her return within hours of her landing. She shuddered.

''There are a thousand ways around that and you know it. Not to mention we've been to the doctor, and you're still so flipping prickly on the subject you have cactus written all over you. Why?''

Because her mother's calendar carried nothing but doctor's appointments. Because she didn't want to be a burden to anyone. Because Kent had parked her in more doctor offices during three years than most people saw in a lifetime.

She pitched those thoughts out the window with the salty breeze. Hadn't she resolved only a few hours ago to reclaim her strength? She'd had enough morbidity for one day. Real worries would close in soon enough, and for now she just wanted to enjoy her time with Danny. ''Like I said before, women have lived with this since the beginning of time, and the last thing we want is to discuss it with men who wince.''

The big brave warrior threw back his shoulders. ''I did not wince.''

''Oh, really?'' She jabbed him in the side with a teasing poke. ''You wouldn't turn green over the mere mention of a shopping expedition for feminine hygiene products?''

She had to give him credit. He didn't turn green. However, he *was* giving pale a run for its money.

''Okay, maybe you have a point. But I think I could have handled buying you a bottle of Motrin or a request for Kathleen to give you a checkup after she finished with Trey. I'm a modern guy. What's the big deal?''

She snorted and snitched a piece of licorice from his hand. ''Liar.''

''Aw, now cut it out. Be fair. Like you wouldn't wince

over shopping for...for—'' he paused, then snapped his fingers ''—for a jock strap.''

A laugh bubbled. God she missed laughing with him.

''And just think of the poor sales clerk at the sporting store if you had to quiz him on what size you should buy.''

''I remember your size just fine, Danny.''

Had she said that?

His eyes widened, focused on crossing a low rail bridge with exaggerated care.

Oh, yeah. She sure had said it.

''Uh, thank you?''

''No problem.'' Well, actually it was starting to be a problem as need snapped along the air between them.

And they would be spending an indeterminate amount of time alone. No tiny chaperones. No secrets. And a teenage need that had matured into an adult hunger. Now all those memories swirled through the car, the medicine buzz not unlike the champagne buzz all those years ago that had led her to pitch her clothes off.

She sagged back against the headrest. With the lulling pass of each mossy oak, she fought the sensory overload draw of Daniel's smile and bay-rum-tinged hydraulic fluid riding the ocean breeze....

She didn't want to be pregnant. Mary Elise touched a bare foot to the ground and launched her old tire swing into motion under the ancient oak while watching Danny's back door. He'd just pulled into the driveway, home for the summer, and she knew he wouldn't wait long to see her.

To find out if their night together—long, hot hours—had left her pregnant.

Who wanted to be pregnant and unmarried at nineteen with three years of college left to finish? And it wasn't like she even loved the baby's father. Well, she loved *him. She just wasn't* in *love with him. Like, geez, it was Danny. Her best friend.*

Her best friend who really knew how to do it.

Well, as best she could tell then, from her limited—okay, nonexistent—experience. Now she had a weekend of experience under her tightening belt, along with a growing baby. No Air Force Academy graduation for Danny. No journalism degree and crime-beat-reporter job for her.

And the part that sucked most was she hurt more over Danny losing his dreams than she did over losing her own.

She knew without a doubt he would offer to marry her. Would insist on marrying her. She wanted to tell him no, but the thing was, as much as she didn't want to be pregnant, she was. And it was Danny's baby, which made the kid already cute and special and deserving of the best she could manage.

So yeah, if he pushed, she'd marry him. Maybe they could work out one of those married-for-a-year deals so the baby would have his name.

But he'd still be booted out of the Air Force Academy. Would still lose his dream. And an ache started low in the pit of her belly at even the thought of pushing him out of her life in something so harsh sounding as a divorce.

Geez. They should be making plans to go to the beach, not wedding plans.

Then there he was. Danny, striding across the glass-enclosed back porch, through the screen door.

The military precision slipped into his walk a little more with each year at the Air Force Academy. He could wear wrinkled clothes all he wanted. The walk gave him away.

Pushing up from the swing, she made her way past a blooming dogwood tree, through the ivy-covered gate. He looked older, too. His parents' split hit him hard. He kept saying it didn't matter, since he was grown. She knew better. Senator Baker's trophy marriage shrieked cliché to a son who personified uniqueness.

That had to be the reason worry lines creased Danny's face. Not because they both knew they'd been stupid, stupid, stupid not to use birth control.

"Hey, Mary 'Lise." His smile pulled tight as he drew her in for a hug. Are you?

She could feel his unspoken question reach to her. His arms wrapped around her with the familiarity of a hundred other hugs. The awareness tinged with fear, however, was all new.

Are you pregnant? *Again, the silent question pulsed from him.*

Mary Elise swallowed and forced the words out. "I am."

She didn't have to say anything else. He would know what she meant. That damned unspoken connection between them was working just fine. She'd prepped herself for his proposal, knew Danny well enough to understand his sense of honor wouldn't let him do anything else.

But please, please, please, with her hormones in an ungodly tangle she wasn't sure she could handle seeing disappointment in his eyes, even though he had every right.

He held so still, unmoving for four deep breaths of her own. With their connection in total working order, she felt it all rock through his motionless body—the shock, frustration, anger…the resolution.

Finally he stepped back. She opened her eyes, slowly, in no great hurry to face him just yet, and found… Danny's smile at its most kick-ass vibrant.

"Well, Mary Elise, then I guess there's no reason we can't go lock ourselves in the pool house, tear off all our

clothes and have out-of-control screaming sex.'' Scooping her up into his arms, Danny planted a deep kiss on her lips and made fast tracks past the diving board.

Mary Elise laughed, tension easing at least a bit. Her hand snuck up to play with the close-cropped hair at the nape of his neck. Yeah, she knew the proposal would come once their clothes lay in a pile by their sweaty, sated bodies. But he understood her enough to realize she couldn't hear those words yet.

And in that moment she fell a little in *love with Danny after all.*

Daniel scooped up sleeping Mary Elise and kicked the car door closed. Softly. Keeping his motions quiet, steady, although Mary Elise slept like the dead.

Dead.

Not his favorite word today. Pine straw muffled the thud of his boots toward the rectangular cabin—a shotgun-style house, one room deep, long and thin. Nowhere for anyone to hide inside.

He hitched his hold on her, his survival vest and belt dangling from the crook of his arm. He'd unload the rest of the gear once he had her inside, but not a chance would he let his gun out of his reach.

His eyes scanned, assessing for vulnerability with each step closer to the clapboard fishing retreat on stilts. He would have to put trip wires around the open underway to stop anyone from lurking beneath.

Shallow tides bordered the house on three sides, rotting marsh grass emitting a methane scent into the air. At least they would have prior warning of ''visitors'' on those three fronts from the water.

A single road in. Two minor paths. Manageable to defend with traps positioned to disable intruders.

Daniel ducked to avoid the drape of Spanish moss trailing from the limbs of an ancient oak, sidestepped a hammock blowing in the salty breeze.

What a haven this would be any other time, with its uninterrupted view of the water, dock stretching into the reedy surf rippling out into the main ocean way. Max had chosen his retreat well for peace…and safety.

Thudding up the wooden steps, Daniel shifted Mary Elise in his arms, the late-afternoon sun casting pasty shadows across the hollows in her cheeks. He cursed Kent McRae for at least the fiftieth time. Bending at the knees, Daniel flipped open the metal box by the door and punched in the security code he'd memorized from Max, before opening the dead bolt.

She could talk all damned day about how she would be fine, and that didn't change the fact that she should be putting her feet up until her medicines took effect.

Daniel toed open the door and stepped inside the rustic one-room cabin with nothing more than a few pieces of sparse furniture and a walk-in closet bathroom/shower stall. A man's dream retreat. And the least romantic getaway he could think of to offer a woman in need of pampering and R&R.

If he even knew what to do for her in the first place.

Kathleen Bennett and her damn rule book. Screw patient confidentiality. The best she'd given him was directions to check out the Internet, since he already knew Mary Elise had endometriosis and fertility problems. The most freaking unfair thing he could imagine, this woman not having her arms and heart full of babies.

Daniel shut down the image he'd carried for years, a mental picture of what Mary Elise might have looked like holding their kid. Focus on the here and now. He made tracks through the efficiency kitchen with a small counter and two bar stools, past the single sofa in front of a stone fireplace to the quilt-covered bed tucked against the back wall.

Not that Mary Elise would voice a complaint about their accommodations. Of course he appreciated her grit, but only to a point. And if he tried to discuss her medical needs with her again, who knew where she'd flip the conversation this time. The jock-strap-size discussion still had him swallowing his damned tongue.

He grinned.

Yeah, he liked her grit, all wrapped up in a subtle package and gentle smile, which gave the surprise wallop all the more punch. He hated like hell what had brought them here, but couldn't stop the surge of excitement over having her all to himself.

He was one messed-up dude. No doubt.

Daniel lowered her to the bed, surprised at the give under his hands. A water bed. He fixed his eyes on her face for the least sign of stirring. The gentle roll of enclosed waves welcomed her in a lulling embrace.

Unable to resist, a given around Mary Elise lately, he slid his survival vest and belt to the floor and pressed a kiss to her forehead. Lingered. He inhaled the honeysuckle scent of her shampoo like some infatuated adolescent. Except, the powerful tangle of frustration, anger, protectiveness pounding through him had little to do with tender teen emotions.

"I swear I won't let that bastard ever hurt you again," he whispered against her skin.

Her hand glided up to his chest. "Danny?"

She lay so still he missed the motion until he felt the warm weight of her palm seep through his uniform. He stared down into eyes the green of deep summer. And damned if it wasn't just the two of them. Completely alone for the first time in eleven years.

Chapter 13

Water bed rolling lightly beneath her, Mary Elise struggled to shake off the fuzzy dream remnants of long ago riding in Danny's warm embrace. A tough proposition when she could still feel the imprint of his strong arms banded around her after he carried her from the car.

The roar of the ocean outside lulled her, but she fought sleep's call. She brushed the pads of her fingers against the raspy texture of Daniel's flight suit. The whole darkwood cabin decor and dim light through thick panes offered an ends-of-the-earth solitude her sleep-mussed brain couldn't seem to recall why she should resist. ''Were you going to tell me we're here?''

She flicked his zipper tab with one finger.

Daniel jumped back as if burned. ''Were you going to tell me you're awake? I damn near threw my back out carrying you.''

Angling up on her elbow, she started to bristle, the thrown-out-back comment coming mighty damn close on the heels of his pale-hag remark. She looked deeper, found an edgy tension in him that she might have attributed to their dangerous position, except with her own eyes opening and her defenses lowering, she recognized the glint well.

Desire. He wanted her. Bad. Or rather, oh-so-good.

A trill of feminine power sounded through her. It had been so long since she'd felt attractive. She and Danny may have kissed, but only when either she'd come on to him or when they'd been in a full-body press with her leg nestled between his. Against *him.*

Oh yeah, she remembered *him* very well.

"Put your back out? Liar." She sat the rest of the way up and tucked her legs to the side, the gentle glide of the enclosed waves of the water bed undulating against her suddenly sensitive skin. "I think you got a he-man kick out of carrying me in here."

He snagged his survival vest from the floor beside the bed. "Why don't you try to sleep? I should be through before you wake up."

Through? Encroaching panic edged out desire. "Where are you going?"

"To scope the area. Set some warning devices in place."

Warning devices. Her throat closed. She'd just assumed the distant locale and Danny's weaponry would be enough protection, and that she and Danny could use this rustic-haven time to sort through past feelings.

Present feelings.

She wasn't sure whether to be reassured or scared spitless that he saw the need for more security.

Mary Elise swung her legs off the side of the bed. "Tell me what to do."

"Sleep."

"Get real."

"I mean it." He jerked on the green mesh vest, the knife sheathed in black leather attached to his shoulder a harsh reminder of real-world worries. "Rest. You're no good to me dead on your feet."

"Sleep can come later. I may be a little groggy." Understatement. She wished Kathleen had been less pushy with the muscle relaxants. "But I'm far from passing out. The sooner we have this place secured, the sooner I can get that rest you keep insisting I need. Do you really think I could just kick back now?"

"You did in the car."

"That was different. There was nothing I could do."

He buckled a gear belt around his waist with canteens—a gun holster. He pulled free the 9 mm, tugged out the magazine, checked, clicked it in place again before returning the weapon to the holster with clean efficiency. "How about whip up something to eat."

No way was she playing Betty Crocker to his John Wayne. "Oh, yeah, that's really a pressing survival issue right now after the two Big Macs and order of supersize fries you banged back in the car."

The first signs of a grin creased the corners of his eyes. "Well, I'm still hungry. You know me. Never full, jaws just get tired of chewing."

"Great. If Kent finds us, I'll toss up a smoke screen by burning some fried Spam."

Mary Elise shadowed him around the tiny cabin, staying smack dab in his peripheral line of sight. Danny swung his foot up onto the arm of the brown plaid sofa and tucked a second knife inside his boot.

Suppressing a shiver over just the thought of him having to use it, she stepped closer. "Give me something constructive to do or I'm going to follow you around and be a real pain in the butt. You should know from our growing-up years, I can do it.''

''You're already doing it right now,'' he mumbled without glancing her way.

''Good. Now give me a job that doesn't involve a spatula.'' Her hand fell to his forearm. Gripped. Held with a determination she infused in her voice as well. ''Danny, I won't be relegated to a passive role ever again.''

He dropped his foot to hardwood floor, a sigh riding a long trip out his lungs. ''Do you know how to shoot?''

''I took lessons after I arrived in Rubistan.'' Never again would she be caught unprepared. And as much as she wanted to find a peaceful middle ground with Danny, she would battle him to the end for her right to defend herself.

Daniel recognized well the dogged glint in Mary Elise's steady gaze. The woman was in full fighting form.

At least she wasn't gliding those soft hands up his body with a distraction he couldn't afford. Security came first.

And after?

He'd face that later. And pray that by then he could remember all the reasons why he shouldn't lay her back on that water bed and rediscover every inch of her.

First priority, arm Mary Elise with a weapon.

Hooking his hands under the end of the sofa, Daniel hefted the far edge a couple feet to the right. He flipped back the edge of the brown braid rug and knelt, working his fingers down the ridges in the boarded floor.

''Danny?''

''Shhh.'' He waved her silent as he concentrated on finding…bull's eye.

He pried three loose boards up, revealing, just as Max promised, a small gun safe. Spinning up the combination, Daniel opened the door. A gasp sounded from behind him.

He glanced over his shoulder. ''What?''

''I just didn't expect to see that.''

He tracked her wide-eyed gaze down to the two handguns—a Browning M9 and a .45 automatic—surrounded by stacks of ammunition. ''What do you think we do for a living?''

''You fly planes. Spike investigates. I mean, well, I figured you took a gun with you on missions or assignments, like the one in your closet. I just didn't expect to see all of this here, too.''

''Maybe Spike packs a little more firepower than some of us. But like a cop, a military serviceman is never off duty.'' He dug out ammo and tossed it on the sofa. Sitting on the couch, he checked and began loading both weapons.

She eased down beside him. ''Never off duty?''

''Back when you were working for the paper,'' he answered without taking his eyes off his task, ''if you got a three-day weekend, you could hop a plane and go anywhere you wanted as long as you were back at work on time.''

''Yeah. So?''

''If I travel outside the area, I have to apply for official leave and let admin know where I'll be at all times. Even on a weekend.''

''Why?''

''We may not sit alert anymore, but we're always on call, 24/7.'' He pressed bullets into the magazine. Click. Click. Click against the spring action. ''If the world goes to hell, we have to be ready to roll.''

She sank down beside him. ''How can you live that way?''

''How can I not?'' With the heel of his palm, he jammed the magazine home on the 9 mm.

That she even had to ask the question offered a great big reason why he should reconsider a mattress dance with this woman.

"Darcy said you have…connections."

"She did?" His fingers paused in loading the .45, a damned big gun with even bigger stopping power.

"What kind of connections?"

He didn't answer. Couldn't. More reasons to avoid sleeping with anyone he genuinely cared about.

Whoa. Back up. Echoes of *emotionally unavailable* ricocheted like an out-of-control bullet in his skull.

"Danny?"

"I fly airplanes."

She waited.

He rolled a bullet between two fingers. "There's a lot more to being in the military than fighting wars, and that includes things we can't talk about. At times we walk out the door with no indication of where we're going or when we'll be home. Some of those missions bring connections."

End of discussion. He had more current concerns, anyway. Like keeping her alive.

And deciphering why he felt anything but emotionally unavailable at the moment.

He placed the 9 mm in her hands before she could press him to talk anymore. "Don't aim unless you're willing to follow through." Daniel tucked the .45 into his survival vest and strode toward the door.

She followed. "If you have problems with me pitching in once we step through the door, you're just going to have to get over yourself."

The pounding of her determined steps echoed behind him.

An all-out smile pulled free, so damned incongruous at

the moment that he smiled even more. For better or worse, emotionally unavailable was never an option around Mary Elise. A low chuckle rode up and out. "That's my girl."

"What?"

He stopped her in the open doorway, palming the metal frame over her head. And it hit him, full force like the power of the so-damned-pretty green eyes staring back at him. He knew just what had him smiling in the middle of the worst day of his life. "You're back."

"Pardon me?"

Grazing his knuckles along her cheek, over skin still a shade too pale but the woman beneath humming with renewed vitality that had nothing to do with medications. "Before, you were half here, holding pieces away from me."

"I thought we already covered why I felt I couldn't tell you—"

With one finger to her lips, he silenced her. "That's not what I meant. You were holding pieces of *yourself* back, but not anymore. You're here and in my face, and, yeah, it can be annoying as hell, but I'm so damned glad to see *you* again, I can't bring myself to do anything more than…"

Screw wise decisions. He'd have to deal with enough of those after he finished securing the perimeter and locked himself inside alone with Mary Elise who deserved a helluva lot more than what he had to offer.

He kissed her, hard, fast and on the mouth before pulling back. His hand still cupped her head, fingers in tangled red curls that would cling to his memory.

"Welcome home, Mary Elise. I missed you."

Eyes fixed on the purples and mauves of the darkening skyline as she jogged down the cabin steps, Mary Elise wondered how the world could look so level when surely the ground under her feet tipped decidedly to the left. Right when she had her feet steady under her, purpose set… Bam! Danny shook things up again.

Welcome home, Mary Elise.

She followed Daniel, hand on the wooden rail just to be safe from the rocking-world problem, and tried to reconcile the conflicting images. The man who'd stroked such a gentle caress down her face was the same man who'd dug out an arsenal from under the floorboards. And both fascinated her.

I missed you.

Shadowed by the graceful arch of an oak, Daniel popped the hatch on the SUV and reached inside, providing too tempting a view. Sheesh. She might as well be nineteen again given the way her hormones were acting.

From deep inside, he pulled a stack of buckets. "Before you get your knickers in knot, I'm not asking you to mop a floor." He glanced back over his shoulder.

Busted. Scavenger birds squawked a mocking call from the shoreline. A grin teased her lips as she gave him a wide-eyed look of innocence so overplayed she knew she hadn't fooled him for a second.

How bizarre to feel lighthearted with the worst of threats looming. Not unlike that moment years ago when Daniel had scooped her up in his arms, and while she knew they were both in a mess, somehow his smile made it okay.

A tickle of unease fluttered in her stomach.

She didn't want to depend on anyone for her happiness. And most of all, she did *not* want to be a little in love with Daniel Baker again.

He hefted out another bag, a jingling sounding inside. She peered inside to find…

''Twenty-penny nails.''

Large. Spike-size. Well there was a hefty dose of reality for a girl. ''What am I supposed to do with these?''

''Hang tough and watch. You'll need to do this with twenty-three more buckets.''

Daniel sat on the back bumper, a handful of the metal spikes beside him. One by one he shoved three through the plastic on one side, then three more on the other. An industrial-size roll of duct tape in his hand, he encircled the outside to secure the nail heads so the points angled slightly down on the inside.

He passed her the bag of nails. ''Do this with the other buckets while I fan out and work on the first line of protection. This will be our second ring of defense.''

''I'm still not understanding.''

''We'll dig holes around the cabin at the most logical places where someone might approach. Drop these inside, cover each hole with a layer of pine needles and leaves over thin twigs. When a foot goes in, it's not coming back out—at least not without a lengthy process and a lot of pain. Even if he works free before we get there, he'll be slowed from the injury.''

We. Funny how one word could speed that tickle in her stomach. ''Amazing.''

''Untwisted bed springs work as spikes, too.'' He tore the duct tape with his teeth. A hank of hair fell over his brow, and he could have been the boy building a rocket out of his mama's Corning Ware.

She started to reach to brush aside his stray lock of hair.

He jammed the completed bucket trap in her hand as if he wanted space between them. ''Here. You try now.''

Why was he being so brusque? Hadn't he spent the past

days trying to convince her to stay? Of course that was before he found out what she'd been hiding.

She would have known how to break the tension eleven years ago. Now she wasn't so certain.

Mary Elise hopped up to sit in the back of the SUV. She set to work on a second bucket while Daniel hefted out rope, fishing wire and a bag of electronics that looked as if they should have been gifts for the boys.

Wind rustled through the trees, shaking loose a shower of pine needles in the widening silence between them. Where had the guy gone who'd kissed her on the porch? She should be relieved. This Daniel offered fewer complications.

"Where did you learn all of this?"

"Survival training. Study. It's…wise to stay up-to-date." He kept his eyes off her and on the unloading. "There are countless options. Chinese Chopper, Cuban Water Trap, Sheepeaters' Rockfall. But we have to adapt to the situation and means available. The traditional pit takes forever to dig and then you've wasted time on one line of defense."

The reality of it all washed over her again. He was arming for battle when he should be swimming or breaking in the new Zelda game with the boys, prepping for Thanksgiving.

"We're going to use the Malaysian Hawk on the main path in. A log strung high, attached to a trip wire. On the two minor trails in, I'll string Jivaro Catapults using this."

He slid a canoe paddle out of the back. One swift move brought it down on his knee to snap off the handle. "The paddle will be fixed inside a twisted-tight rope tied to a tree limb. Foliage and moss is thick enough here to cover. A stick trigger sets this sucker to spin fast and hard enough to crack ribs. If he finds us before we can nail him with traditional evidence, we'll be ready."

That *we* word again. Strange how it stirred the same strange mix of hope and trepidation as the traps.

No more passive roles, she reminded herself. Except, thinking about all those maybes with Danny scared her hair straight.

Danny's determined strides down the main road took him farther away from her. No surprise, her eyes devoured the look of him. She accepted the attraction, yet in a day full of revelations a final realization settled.

She might not know about tomorrow. And while she felt safer, she knew better than ever to underestimate Kent again.

All she could control were her decisions in the here and now. She was through running from experiencing life, and she damn well intended to make full use of that water bed at the first opportunity.

Sunrise fingering through the bulletproof panes, Danny hooked a foot on the rung of the bar stool. He clicked through computer keys, logging on to the green screen that signified secured communications with Max.

Reaching for his coffee mug, Daniel kept his back to Mary Elise. A power nap, cold shower and two PBJs had recharged him, not enough to face Mary Elise just yet, however. Watching her sleep was a torturous hell, and he wasn't interested in incineration.

Well, maybe he was interested.

But he couldn't afford the distraction, and no question, the woman was one endless distraction. At least the security preparations had worked her into an exhausted sleep through the night. Guilt nicked, but Mary Elise at her pit bull most persistent hadn't been budging. Of course she'd been right in asserting they would work faster together.

He glanced at the second laptop sitting alongside, this one set up with security monitors. He'd rigged two video cameras on opposite corners of the cabin, as well as setting alarms on his three major traps, alarms sending radio pulses back to his computer.

His credit card bill would be hell next month, but when it came to Mary Elise, his peace of mind was priceless.

"Come on, come on, come on, Max." Daniel watched for incoming mail. He'd passed along seven possibilities for underworld types who worked the Savannah area. All fit the profile and description in Mary Elise's initial police report.

The fact that no one followed the too-damned-easy trail a year ago turned his vision red. And why the hell had no one questioned the number of McRaes in the Savannah PD signing off on Mary Elise's reports?

Red turned scarlet.

Daniel channeled his anger into productivity, best line of defense for Mary Elise. Any second now he hoped Max would fill in the next block with his feedback on McRae's overseas bank accounts.

The mail icon flashed. Anticipation chugged. "Thanks, Spike."

Daniel opened the file and scrolled through Max's notations, lists of suspicious bank transfers from an overseas account, crossing multiple state and country lines. McRae would burn for this once Max turned the findings over to the FBI.

Scanning, his eye snagging on a line item. A transfer that routed through three accounts before finally ending…in the Middle East four weeks ago.

McRae had tracked her to Rubistan. She'd been that

close to death. Could that have been why his father had called? Because of a heightened threat level to Mary Elise?

Unable to resist looking at her, hungry for reassurance that she still breathed, lived, Daniel kicked his heel to spin the revolving bar stool to face her.

Protectiveness fired into afterburners. Thank God she slept deeply and he didn't have to hide anything for once. While waiting for Max's response earlier, Daniel had cruised the Internet for information on endometriosis—a painful, chronic disease he now knew affected at least ten percent of all women.

Had he invaded her privacy? Maybe. No doubt Mary Elise would be pissed. But he needed to reassure himself the stubborn woman wasn't pushing herself.

And yeah, being locked up with Mary Elise made him think of sex and he wanted to be certain he didn't make a lame-ass mistake that would hurt her. Heaven knew the woman went out of her way to downplay her medical needs.

So now he knew. Discomfort during sex could be a side effect for some. Talk about a splash of cold water. And how exactly would he bring that up if the situation arose where they happened to find themselves naked together?

An image he did not need but wanted, so much his teeth hurt.

Mary Elise stirred under the patchwork quilt. He turned away from too much temptation arching awake before his eyes. His ears, however, filled in the blanks. The rustle of covers shoved aside to reveal a sleep-mussed Mary Elise. Soft, bare feet hitting the floor. A gentle sigh accompanying a stretch.

He swallowed hard.

Her feet shuffled a groggy path across the floor. The

bathroom door snicked open, then closed. Daniel exhaled long and loud. Then straightened. His ears really didn't need to hear the…

Shower.

The whooshing of water tormented him when his reserves already spiraled in a nosedive. The tenor of the water hitting altered with the intrusion of a body.

He had earplugs in his flight suit.

Fliers carried them to combat flight-line noise and he seriously considered using them now for combating insanity. Except he couldn't afford to miss the warning alarms set on the traps. Not that he expected McRae to track them for at least another twelve hours, if at all.

Just the same, Daniel steeled his ears against the shoosh of the shower beading against Mary Elise's naked body and concentrated on typing a response with feedback for Max.

Ten torturous years—or maybe ten minutes—later she padded into the room, barefoot and smelling so good his mouth watered.

He pulled away from the chair, made tracks for the kitchen. Not near enough space in the cabin.

"I cooked." He unwrapped the paper towel from around the sandwich he'd made for her earlier when he'd slapped together two for himself. "Well, if you call a PBJ cooking."

Silk clung to her damp skin, her shorts and shirt already baring a tempting stretch of arms and legs. "Thank you. Definitely a good sign you've moved out of Cro-Magnon mode."

"Cro-Magnon? Who me?" he asked, although feeling very primal. "Lady, I'm more than willing to let you pull your fair share around here."

"Right after you drag me to your cave by my hair."

He had other ideas of what he'd like to do with all that wet hair. Instead, he nudged the open jar of strawberry preserves toward her on the counter. "Fresh open, canned preserves. I figure we'd better use the bread now and save the military MREs—meals ready to eat—for later."

How long would they be here? He wanted this over and done fast for Mary Elise, but also for his brothers. Trey and Austin didn't need any more disruption in their lives.

Mary Elise tore off a corner of her sandwich and popped it in her mouth. Her eyes widened with surprise before she rushed the sandwich up to her face for another bite. He watched, couldn't take his eyes off her as she savored the simplicity of strawberry preserves with a sensualist's delight.

Damn, but she was a woman after his own heart.

"Happy Thanksgiving, 'Lise. Not exactly a turkey dinner. But actually much better than the chicken à la king MRE." Shuddering, he passed her a bottle of water. "Even I can't stomach that one unless I'm starving."

"Have you ever been…starving, I mean?" Her elegant throat moved with swallows of water, her mouth fitting perfectly around the bottle.

Answer the question, bud. "Survival training was rough for a guy like me who needs a few thousand extra calories a day to burn up all the energy pinging around."

She placed the bottle on the counter and stepped closer. "All the flyers go through this survival training?"

"Yep." He took a step back. "By the end of the course, rabbit eyeballs actually tasted good."

"Eww!" Laughing, she popped the last corner of her sandwich into her mouth, her tongue swiping a hint of strawberry from her lips.

Words fell out but he lost track of them. "Rabbit eyeballs are a great source of iodine."

Remnants of laughter painting her eyes jewel tones, she sucked jelly off the tip of one of her fingers. ''You can't throw me off the track with gross-out stories, Danny Baker. Although I gotta confess, now it's tough to think about kissing your mouth.''

''Did you want to before?''

Crap. Shut the yap, Baker. The woman might have a backbone of steel, but she needed time to get over the hell McRae had put her through. Having to fend off someone who should damn well be protecting her wasn't honorable.

Mary Elise's eyes deepened, darkened with two slow blinks.

Uh-oh.

She dipped two fingers into the strawberry preserves. If she put those fingers in her mouth to taste again, he'd die. Right here. Right now. His obituary would read, ''Toxic case of deadly testosterone overload.''

He had to remember about keeping his distance. For her. And, yeah, for his own freaking sanity.

She placed her fingers...against *his* lips. ''How about a palate cleanser?''

No mistaking her intent. And no way did he intend to die just yet.

Don't do it, Baker.

Too late.

His open mouth closed around her fingers. Mary Elise and sugar. Uh-huh. He was a dead man.

In no hurry, she withdrew her fingers while stepping closer. Maybe he wouldn't be taking advantage of her after all. She obviously knew her own mind.

Yes! His libido shouted while his mind cautioned with logical reasoning—as if logic stood a chance against his need for this woman. He would just control himself while enjoying this torturous-as-hell moment.

Daniel dipped two fingers in the jelly jar still held in her hand. Without once breaking eye contact, he brought his fingers to her mouth.

Oh, yeah.

Her lips closed over him, the subtle suction drawing him inside, deeper. Her tongue circled his fingers.

His vision clouded.

Okay, maybe he didn't need to stay completely away from her. He would just be gentle. Careful. After all, the woman knew her mind and understood her body.

Hell, she'd about decked him over a ''pale'' comment. If he pushed her away… Giving in would be good.

He could almost hear Mary Elise laughing at his reasoning. *Oh, Danny, you are such a man.*

And she would be right. He was feeling very much a man.

Gentle, big guy, he reminded himself. He withdrew his fingers from her mouth, his body throbbing at the moist friction against his skin. He reassured himself that his logic wasn't so far gone that he lost sight of what she'd been through with that bastard.

Take it easy. Take it slow. He hooked his arms low on her waist, eased her to him. Brushed her lips once, twice, found more strawberry preserves on the corner of her lips.

Yeah, slow and tender definitely had its merits.

With a wealth of security surrounding the cabin and at least a few hours' window from detection, Daniel intended to peel every piece of clothing off Mary Elise's body. Worshiping this woman with an attention to detail she deserved.

He would be sensitive, damn it, even if it killed him.

Mary Elise slid her arm from around his neck and

hauled her purse across the counter, just as he reached in his back pocket. Simultaneously they both pulled free… condoms.

Her smile met his. "You know, Danny, since we both remembered contraception this time, there's no reason we can't tear off all our clothes and have out-of-control screaming sex."

Chapter 14

She wanted him. Intense, fast, now, until she forgot everything but him.

Mary Elise arched on her toes to taste fully of Daniel and strawberries and a passion just as vibrantly red. Hers or his? Deepening the kiss, she wasn't sure because that old connection of theirs flowed back and forth and back again until she couldn't ascertain where the need began.

Couldn't imagine its end.

Daniel breezed his fingers down a shivery path over her neck, along her breasts, leaving her aching for more when his hand fell away. Nipping her bottom lip, tracing her ear with growled words about how damned hot he found her, he shucked his vest, hooked it over a chair.

Placed his gun by the bed.

She mentally shoved away that stark image and listened, savored. So what if he was being practical and safe? He was also filling her mind with incredible promises of what he planned to do to her. He dropped the condoms beside the gun, her Daniel never losing sight of his protector role.

She tugged his zipper, yanked his flight suit over his shoulders and down.

"Take it easy, 'Lise. Slow."

Featherlight strokes traveled up and down her back in tantalizing whispers at odds with the bold hands delivering them. She wanted this and more and everything, after so long of nothing. So long wanting just this man.

And if he shoved her away?

"Not a chance," he answered her unspoken thoughts with an ease recaptured from the past.

Relief weakened her knees. Having Danny now meant so damned much to her, almost too much. Something she hadn't realized until she faced his possible rejection.

For a moment she faltered. This was supposed to be about uncomplicated sex, taking charge of what she wanted from life.

Sex with Danny had never been uncomplicated.

Of its own volition and without her permission, the moment became about more, much more. It became about broad hands shaking from restraint. A familiar lock of hair falling over a brow furrowed deep with concentration. On her. The past and the present blended into a combustible need that surpassed just sex.

Her silk shirt glided down her arms, hooked on her elbows before slithering to pool at her feet. A quick snap of the front clasp on her bra bared her.

Would he find her thirty-year-old body less enticing than her nineteen-year-old self?

She didn't have to wonder long. His appreciative eyes burned a slow ride, lingering, moving on to linger and heat again. With an almost worshipful reverence, he reached. Touched. The line of her collarbone. Who'd have expected that to be an erogenous zone?

Mary Elise shivered.

"You're even more beautiful than I remembered."

Such a silly thing, to be pleased over a compliment, yet it wasn't the compliment so much as the desire that accompanied it. For too long, her body had been nothing more than...

She refused to think about any of that now. Not with a rock-solid man in nothing but his boxers and dog tags wanting her every bit as much as she wanted him.

He rested his forehead on hers, his hands hooked low on her waist. "Are you okay with this? I mean physically."

Oh, Danny.

She should have remembered this man had a decidedly earthy, practical side. "Do you think I would come on to you like this if I didn't intend to follow through? And, while I appreciate that you're being careful, I'm finding it rather unromantic to talk about medical conditions right now."

He angled back, pensive Danny in a full-out think mode in direct contrast to an abandon-thought need she could feel hot and hard against her.

"Do you want romantic, 'Lise? Because I'm not much good at that. Never have been. I'm an inside-out-shirt kind of guy. Beer and chips on the beach. Blunt. And, yeah, once I've decided on a course I forget to ask if anyone else has input." He grimaced. "I believe some might even call it intellectual arrogance."

Guilt pinched over having tossed much those same sorts of words at him years ago to push him away. "You're also funny and have a tender heart under all those muscles."

She gave her hands free rein to rove his shoulders, trail forward to skim his dog tags, the light bristle of skin and man. Hard planes and tendons jumped under her fingers.

He rewarded her with a smile. ''You've been checking out my muscles, have you?''

She slugged his shoulder. ''And you're also a jerk sometimes.''

''But you want me?''

Her fist unfurled on his bicep. ''Yes, Danny, I do. Very much.''

Looping her arms around his neck, she fell backward to drag him down with her on the bed. Waves rocked beneath them as the rest of their clothes found their way down, off, into the air.

Daniel eased over her, holding himself away with his elbows, air sliding between them. She wanted more. Forget his slow dictates.

She hooked her leg around his and knocked him off balance with the help of a rogue wave. He bolted from her, rolling to his side. She would have thought he didn't want this if it weren't for the trembling in his arms, muscles bunched from undeniable restraint.

''Danny? What's going on here?''

A broad hand grazed down her damp hair. ''Hon, if you don't know that, then apparently I really didn't have a clue what the hell I was doing back then.''

''You knew just fine.'' Although she had a feeling he knew a lot more now. A tingle of anticipation tripped up her spine, then back down again, sparking lower. Hotter. ''And you're just arrogant enough to realize it. You never held back then, but you're holding back now.''

''It's called self-control.'' With more of that agonizing precision, he untwisted a strand of hair from her hoop earring. ''Something a guy that young doesn't always understand.''

A giggle teased her throat, making her laugh all the more because she was *so* not a giggler. She'd forgotten how fun Danny could be in bed. She wanted that lightness, the ease of being with him.

Still, something wasn't quite right here. ''You made me be honest with you. I expect the same.''

His hand trekked into her hair, gathered up a fistful and cradled her against his chest. ''I don't want to hurt you.''

Her breath hitched in her chest. She'd thought her heart too worn to be hurt again. Could she have been wrong?

The ache of his leaving before crashed back, even when she knew she'd sent him on his way by accusing him of being all his father ever said. Not that she believed any of it. But she'd been so wounded by his obvious relief at freedom. And no matter how much she told herself otherwise, he had that power to hurt her again.

His fingers rubbed a sensuous massage into her scalp. ''You can tell me all day long that you're fine. Kathleen could give me a freaking printout of your records, and that still wouldn't stop me from worrying about you.''

Clarity dawned. He meant physically hurt, minor in comparison to what she'd been imagining. The body—so transient in comparison to the heart. The soul. Her emotions started to scramble her resolve, a mighty inconvenient occurrence with her naked body plastered to his.

She wanted this, damn it. He wanted this. After all they'd been through together, they deserved at least this much. And they deserved to enjoy it to the fullest.

''Do you remember what I said earlier?''

He stroked her hair back with a hand so tender she almost crumbled. ''You said a lot of things, 'Lise.''

Maybe too much. ''I won't be relegated to passive roles.''

Taking advantage of his surprise, she flipped him to his back.

Heat flamed his eyes to smoky black. She draped herself down and over Daniel, blanketing him with her body and hair just before she took his mouth. Searched deep and long, with all the pent-up need she yearned to pour all over him.

Groaning, he gripped her hips. ''You want to be in control?''

She walked her fingers down his chest, lower, counting the ridged flexing of his stomach. ''Do you have a problem with that?''

His heart slammed in his chest against her. ''No, ma'am.''

''I'm not going to break, Danny.'' Her hand dipped lower still until she encircled him, sheathed him in a condom with languorous strokes. ''But I'm thinking it might be incredible to break your restraint.''

His fingers flexed on her hips. ''And I'm thinking you won't have to try very much.''

She lowered herself onto him, took him into her body as once she'd taken him into her heart. Fully, the pressure of his presence within her maybe a bit too much at first until she adjusted to him being there again.

And then so very right she couldn't remember a time he hadn't been a part of her.

His head pressed back into the pillow, eyes closed, jaw clenched tight. She was damned tired of his restraint. She was tired of being half-alive.

She stopped. Waited.

Knees bracketing his hips, she stared down at him, suddenly realizing how much all that restraint cost him, because doing the same was killing her now.

His eyes opened and he stared back up at her. She brought her hands down to his chest, touched him with the same light caresses he'd given her, strokes that at first enticed, then grew progressively more frustrating.

With one teasing finger, she outlined his flat nipple, watching his eyes until… She pulled her hand away, circled her hips once. Stopped again.

His eyes widened then narrowed. Oh, yeah, he was on to her. And who would win? Hopefully both of them.

She could even see him smolder at the challenge. Their battle of wills continued with traded caresses that tempted without satisfying until…

With a growl of surrender that conversely brought his aggressive advance, he sat up. Mary Elise shifted her legs to wrap around his waist, welcome him in further, closer, wrenching another growl from low in his throat. He palmed her back, holding them chest to chest, heart to pounding heart as she glided down while he thrust up.

Restraints fell away. His. Hers. Until everything became *theirs* as they moved together in a frenzied pace of gasping breaths and demands.

His mouth closed over her breast, pulled, drew. The rock of waves beneath them increased the hot friction of skin against skin until she wasn't in control anymore. But then, neither was he.

His dog tags pressed, almost cut into her slick skin. Not that she could think or care, her mind focused totally on Daniel and completion.

Yet also not wanting that end and the afterward that would accompany it when they would have to face each other. Deal with the line they'd crossed that couldn't be retraced. Had she won or lost in demanding his surrender?

And then she couldn't think anymore, just felt the quickening of his pace, his heart, his heated breath against her flesh.

Her memory must have been faulty because no way could she have forgotten this. Knew she never would forget.

"Danny."

His name rode her scream of release. Her name swelled from his hoarse shout against her neck as he buried his face in her shoulder.

And echoing in her head with a resonation that soothed and excited and scared the hell out of her all at once, she heard…

Welcome home.

Daniel sprawled in the hammock, scanning the expanse of ocean in the fading light, his booted foot on the dirt nudging a lulling sway. Mary Elise lounged with her head at the opposite end, keeping watch over the other stretch of ocean. He drew lazy circles along her ankles and wondered when he'd developed a foot fetish. Of course, the woman did have pretty toes in those sandals.

Toes? He was in big trouble here.

As much as he'd enjoyed the hell out of Mary Elise when they'd been younger, this woman flattened him. There was an intensity about her now that demanded more from him than before.

And he didn't just mean in bed.

"I asked you a question, Daniel."

Man she had that schoolteacher tone down pat, and damned if he could remember the question because he'd been busy drooling over her feet.

"Danny?" She scooped up a pinecone and pelted him on the chest, dead center on his survival vest. "I'm tired of talking about me. What have you been doing with your life since finishing the Academy?''

Talk would be good, keep his mind on task rather than on thoughts of taking her back into the cabin.

But once the sun set... He cleared his throat and mind. Talk. ''I started out in a regular flying squadron—then became a test pilot with C-17s out at Edwards Air Force Base in California for a few years. Flew with all the newest cutting-edge gizmos on the planes. Figured out which ones worked, which ones didn't and why.''

''You enjoyed that.'' Her soft affirmation blended with the rustling branches and gushing waves.

''Oh, yeah.'' Almost as much as he would enjoy peeling those copper-colored shorts from her body in another hour.

''Sounds dangerous.''

''Sometimes.'' His thoughts skidded over to less tempting terrain. Would she run screaming from stories of his more-than-one emergency landing? Even a crash landing in the middle of the California desert?

''So you have connections.''

Her question yanked him back to the present. ''So you're a dog with a bone you're not letting go of.''

She toed him in the side. ''You're calling me a dog? First washed-out hag and now dog?''

He grabbed her foot in a firm hold before she could damage a kidney. ''You have the prettiest feet.''

She snorted.

Still, he couldn't unwrap his brain from the notion that his job bothered her, a problem he should have considered before. The stresses of military life had broken up plenty of marriages in the squadron.

Whoa. Marriage?

Wasn't he thinking about trying the dating thing as

grown-ups? Not that they'd ever really dated in the first place, just shot straight from pals to nonstop sex. The next logical step included taking things slow, spending time together, healing old wounds and progressing from there.

But he couldn't stop thinking about her old engagement ring in his flight suit pocket, his permanent reminder not to repeat past mistakes. Couldn't stop remembering what it had once looked like planted on Mary Elise's finger.

She scrunched her toes, drawing him from his haze. "Ouch," she squawked.

His hand jerked away from her foot. "Damn, 'Lise, I'm sorry."

"Gotcha!" She toed him in the side again, her gaze unrelenting. "I told you already. I'm not going to break."

He smiled. God, he loved her spunk, her steely will. This woman was far from breakable.

Memories bombarded him of their hours together, rediscovering each other on the water bed. The floor. The sofa. "I figured that out."

"I'm stronger out of bed, too. I realize there are things about your job you can't tell me. But don't hold back on what you *can* share because you're worried I'll turn all Victorian on you and you'll need smelling salts. Got it?"

He forestalled her lethal toe. "Yes, ma'am."

The ring in his pocket seemed to scorch a brand through the fabric and into his skin. If he even intended to consider those thoughts, then she needed to know more about him before they both landed in way over their heads. "About connections, let's just say once you get a high-security clearance for one mission they tend to tap you for other missions since you're already in the loop."

"And you enjoy that," she answered with understanding and no censure.

"Oh, yeah."

Her fingers trekked inside the leg of his flight suit, scratched along his calf. ‘‘And you enjoy that?’’

‘‘Oh, yeah,’’ he repeated. ‘‘I think I could really get into this shared control gig.’’

Next thing he knew, he had the ring out of his pocket and wasn't sure who was more shocked, him or Mary Elise.

Her hand flew out of his pants leg. ‘‘You kept it.’’

He worked the solitaire between two fingers until the diamond caught the fading sunlight, casting multifaceted sparks. ‘‘So I wouldn't forget what a relationship screw-up I am like my father.’’

‘‘Danny,’’ her fingers slid to his knee, ‘‘you made a single mistake at twenty-one. For God's sake, that doesn't make you like your father.’’

‘‘I don't do relationships well, never have. There are plenty of women besides you who can attest to that. And just look at the mess with my father.’’

‘‘He was proud of you.’’

Daniel jammed the ring back in his pocket where it could brand a reminder he needed before he ended up doing something totally illogical like asking this woman to marry him. ‘‘So damned much he didn't trust me enough to tell me when you came to Rubistan.’’

‘‘I told him not to.’’

‘‘So?’’ If that sounded arrogant, big freaking deal. His father should have called him, anyway.

‘‘I wasn't in a good place right then.’’ She plucked a leaf from a low-hanging branch, crumpled it in her hand.

‘‘I can understand having someone try to kill you must have been rattling as hell. All the more reason extra support and protection should have been a good thing.’’

‘‘Not just that.’’ She studied him for four lazy swishes of the Pawley's hammock, her fist further mangling the leaf. "How much did you learn about endometriosis on the Internet while I was sleeping?"

"What makes you think—" He swung his foot back up on the hammock. "Ah hell, you used to do that when we were kids, too, read my mind and then follow me right into my messes. Yeah, I did some reading, wanted to understand how to help you. Where's the crime in that?"

"You can back off the defensive, Baker. I just wanted to confirm you have a core knowledge here."

He gave her a simple nod. This was obviously tough enough for her. He didn't want to make it worse by shoving his boot in his mouth.

"Then you know the more scar tissue that builds up, the more difficult it is to conceive, which explains how it was easier for me to become pregnant when I younger. But then in some cases with endometriosis, even if pregnancy occurs, the body—" she unfurled her fist and let the wind carry away the shredded leaf "—my body can be a hostile environment. Miscarriage rates are higher."

Hostile environment? He could hear too well the repeat of McRae's propaganda crap.

"After three more miscarriages, I told Kent I'd had enough. Enough of the doctors and hormone injections and surgeries. I just wanted a baby. I really thought he was okay with adoption." Her head fell back against the webbed ropes. "God, he had me fooled."

Her eyes slid away from him for the first time, which should have been a warning to prepare himself. But thinking about himself was the least of his concerns right now. He lifted her cold hand from her side and linked their fingers. A damned paltry offering, but all he could think of at the moment.

"Kent swapped my birth control pills for placebos. I got pregnant." Her flat tones carried on the wind, the hollow tones of a person with no tears left. ''After all those treatments, for some damned reason I finally conceived on my own again. And then I made it past my first trimester. That had never happened before. The hope was...worse than anything else.''

His gut twisted. Tight. Already he could see where this was going. It hurt like hell to breathe just thinking of what she'd been through. Images of their one lost baby had haunted him for a year. How much more had she suffered?

Alone.

''At twenty-four weeks, I gave birth to a stillborn son.''

Her words gut punched him. Even expecting it hadn't prepped him for the silent ache radiating from her. Nothing could have.

Here he'd been arrogant in wondering if she could handle hearing about his freaking job, and he was the one who damn well couldn't breathe. At least he had his head together enough to know she wasn't ready for him to talk or ask questions. She needed him to listen. He could do that much.

He should have been in her life to do so much more, but he'd been too busy staying out of Savannah because he didn't want to run into Mrs. Kent McRae.

''I overheard him with my damn traitorous doctor. Heard what they'd done to me with swapping the birth control pills.'' Her voice faltered for the first time. ''What they intended to try again.'' One shaky breath and she continued, ''I put on my clothes, walked out of the hospital and left Kent. Once the divorce was final, he tried to kill me.''

Rage, barely banked from the day before, exploded within him, riding a silent curse and vow to send Kent McRae straight to hell.

Her fingers tightened around his. ''No, I really wasn't

in very good shape when I arrived in Rubistan. And your father just put his hand on my shoulder and told me it would be okay.''

Waves echoed in the background for five gushes, six, seven and with each one, Daniel thanked his father for giving her that calm acceptance, that quiet strength that he never would have been able to manage. Nothing else mattered.

''He seemed to know the right balance to strike between helping me and urging me to do for myself. Giving me room to heal, room to grow.'' Her thumb brushed his wrist. ''No offense my dear friend, but, Danny, you would have taken over, and I wouldn't have been strong enough to stand up to you then. And maybe I was prideful in not wanting you to see me like that. Weak.''

His fingers tightened around hers. Damn staying quiet. He wouldn't let her buy into any more of McRae's garbage. ''Weak is the last word I would ever apply to you.''

''Thank you.'' She squeezed his hand back. ''I asked your father once why he never told you where I was. He said he'd learned the hard way about letting a person find their own path in the world.''

And in a flash of intuition Daniel had only just begun to acquire from his own brief stint at parenting the boys, he understood. His father had been making amends. Making peace through Mary Elise.

Daniel stopped fighting with his father's shadow long enough to identify his own. ''I'm glad he was there for you.''

And he meant it.

She nodded. Spent.

''Come here.'' He opened his arms.

She smiled one of those gentle Mary Elise smiles he'd

once thought whimsical. Now he knew they held more strength than most combat veterans.

"I'm not about to fall apart, Danny."

"I know. Come here, anyway."

She crawled up the hammock until she tucked in beside him. Her head fell to rest on his shoulder, over his heart that wasn't as numb as he'd thought.

Well, hell. He wasn't emotionally unavailable at all. His emotions were in total and complete working order. They'd just been in deep freeze from the moment he made the mistake of walking away from this woman.

Now he felt it all churn to life inside him. Her pain was his. His heart was hers.

He wouldn't have a second chance with his father, but his father had given him a second chance with Mary Elise. He only had to figure out how to win her back, how to be the man she deserved. Because no way in hell could he lose her again.

Chapter 15

Mary Elise flung her arm over her eyes, even though little light filtered from the moon into the cabin, and tugged the sheet higher. It inched down again.

God, Danny was a covers hog. Except she couldn't remember him going to sleep after they'd made love again.

Hmm. She snuggled deeper under the sheet. Now there was a beautiful thought to savor, the way they'd come together after their discussion on the hammock.

At first she'd been worried he would stomp around, angry at Kent, or push her to talk. Instead he'd just let them both find escape from the roar of emotions through great sex. Awesome sex. Can't-imagine-it-ever-being-that-incredible-again sex.

Wrapped in her memories—if not that darned slippery sheet—Mary Elise mentally listed ways to torment Danny in turn later.

A warm tickle teased along her stomach, whisper thin and…smelling of strawberries?

Her eyes snapped open. Daniel stood over her. Gloriously naked and obviously very happy to see her. Sheet in one hand, jar of preserves in the other, he poured a thin stream of the warmed syrup onto her. Warm?

Danny grinned. "Wonders of the microwave."

Oh, my. Anticipation curled within her. Curious as to how far he would take this, she sank back, even arched into the flow.

He drizzled higher up her body, closer, until with perfect aim, he tipped one breast, then the other. Her nipples tightened under the teasing torment of the heated liquid and Daniel's unrelenting gaze. Her hand drifted up, her body languid.

She swiped a finger through the sugary red thread, traced the hot length of him, tasted.

A growl tore from his throat. Daniel dropped the sheet and straddled her in a clean move. "Good morning."

And it was—for the first time in too long. She tore open a condom with lightning speed and sheathed him. "I sure do like the spin you put on breakfast in bed."

Daniel dipped a finger into the soupy preserves pooled in the hollow of her belly and drew a circle. Then again. Until she tuned in to the pattern of him swirling her initials against her oversensitized skin.

"I may not do romance well, 'Lise, but I do know about thorough, mathematical attention to detail."

"Details. I like your details."

"What else do you like? Maybe I could make a list of all the things I plan to do to you." He continued to write a veritable epistle on her body with bold fingers inking red strokes over her, all of her. "Or maybe you could make a list for me of everything you want, everything you need."

Playfulness lit his eyes, tinged with a deeper intensity,

even an agenda of some kind. Just a byproduct of maturity? The old Danny blending with the new? Visions of him pulling the ring out of his pocket earlier edged into her mind with thoughts of the past and future.

The flicker of nerves tickling her stomach had nothing to do with syrup. While she might be finding her footing in regaining her sense of self, there was only so much a person could handle in a few short days.

And at the moment Danny was giving her all she could handle…and more. She'd faced so many life-changing decisions in the past month, she wanted, needed a brief respite of light, simple.

This.

The rest would have to be faced eventually. If nothing else, she'd learned from the past months a person couldn't run forever. Right now she wanted to embrace Danny's playfulness and ignore the niggling questions in his eyes and her nervous belly.

Daniel watched Mary Elise's eyes slide closed, pleasure flushing her skin almost as rosy as the thin sheen of syrup. Victory chugged through him. He wanted her so hot for him she couldn't remember anything or anyone else. He wanted to drive them both into forgetfulness until he evaded the impending sense of doom dogging his steps. Not so much over McRae. That battle he could fight with strategy and logic and tangible defenses.

But he couldn't shake the fear that had gripped him once he acknowledged his feelings for Mary Elise. The risk of losing her multiplied tenfold without any formula or equation for what he could do to keep her.

This freaking intuitive crap was driving him nuts. And the best he could come up with was a damned heated jar of jelly to mark her.

"Well, 'Lise, my list would include everything I find

totally hot about you.'' With dabs of jelly on his fingertip, he stroked, claimed her as his to touch, taste. Love. ''But I need you to let me know what you want.''

The million-dollar question.

''All of that. I adore it when—'' her words jumbled over themselves in nonsensical affirmations ''—I really like it when you…''

He filled her.

''Yes.'' A purr vibrated her chest against his. ''When you do that.''

He moved again. And again, all the while grappling for self-control, a damned elusive commodity around Mary Elise.

Love wasn't easy and warm like friendship. This gripped him and held him as firmly as her body gliding against his, faster, leaving him no choice but to just move with it, with her, because he'd tried running, only to find she would always be a part of him, anyway.

He gritted his teeth against release, waiting, watching her, touching until he saw, heard her unravel in his arms. Her purr swelled into a cry of pleasure so sweet he waited until the last echoes faded from his head before he cut the bands of control, surrendered to a flat spin fall, ending in an explosion of emotion and raw need.

Each slug of his heart taunted him. No, he wouldn't walk away, but this new Mary Elise had a will of steel he couldn't bend, and this time he could be the one left behind.

Mary Elise perched on a bar stool, monitoring the two laptop computers while Danny took a power nap on the sofa. He'd vowed no way would he be able to drift off in the water bed scented with strawberries and sex.

She smiled. She was officially a strawberry addict.

The computers hummed reassurance beside her with video views of sunrise filtering over the trees, the marshy beach clear except for the occasional pelican or egret scrounging for breakfast. Alarms stayed silent.

Quiet settled, deep and odd after so long on the run with fear roaring in her ears. For the first time since she'd found that hypodermic needle in her bag, she allowed herself to contemplate a future beyond the cabin. She thought…and came up blank. She knew all the logical answers, but taking the last step toward them seemed a bigger stretch than everything that had come before.

Because of everything that had come before with Danny.

Start small. Think about basics. She picked up an ink pen and pad, paused, exchanged the blue ballpoint for a red pen, strawberry red. Surely that was a good omen to use for making a list of the things she would need to do to reestablish her life. Where?

Charleston?

Logically, yes. She loved Danny. Now admitted she always had. How could she not? She loved the boys too. So why the can't-breathe feeling constricting her chest?

The last step stretched further in front of her.

With Kent out of the way, she wouldn't have any more excuses. She would have to face Danny. Face herself. Face risking forever with someone. She should be rejoicing.

Instead she was scared to death.

It was one thing to dream of a future, another to actually live it. Risk it.

And therein lay her core fear—how much it would hurt to fail with him again. Taking Danny's diamond solitaire off her finger had been hell before. This time her emotions went well beyond the teenage swells of first love that had characterized her feelings for him a decade ago.

Her hand slowed on the paper. She glanced down at her list of things to accomplish, things she wanted to tell the boys. Her hand stopped altogether. How strange. Her list had taken on a more conversational tone than a note written in bullet statements.

Slowly she began adding connector phrases, and a letter to Trey and Austin took shape. She let the words flow into a second letter, this time to her parents. Another to Kent that left her hand shaking.

She was writing, certainly not anything like the editorials she'd once written in hope of shaping readers' thoughts and politics. But words poured from her fingers in a healing balm she'd denied herself as if denying the need for a cure negated the ailment.

Time melded into a stack of papers scattering the counter, even the floor around her feet as she wrote to everyone.

Except Daniel.

Words failed her there. She let the half-spent pad of paper fall to her lap and studied him instead. Arms folded tightly over his chest, he didn't seem to be in the least relaxed. She would have thought him awake if it weren't for the soft snore and the quirky twitch of his booted foot propped on the end of the sofa.

That hint of movement spoke of restless dreams. Her fault, no doubt. She considered nudging him, but he needed the sleep, restless though it was, to prep for possible waking nightmares later outside.

Setting the notebook aside, she walked around the edge of the sofa to sit cross-legged on the rug beside him. Her hand lifted, carefully. She smoothed his hair back, and when he didn't stir, stroked again and again until his foot slowed.

Would he have let her soothe him if he'd been awake?

Part of her shouted to quit with the psychobabble self-analysis and grab at this chance for happiness. Once upon a time she would have, except this newer Daniel had reminded her she should expect more from life, herself. Even him.

And if the pushing for more shoved him away again? Her foot twitched this time at even the thought of losing him. If only he would tell her what rumbled around in that thick, dear head of his, maybe then she wouldn't be so afraid of that last step.

Leaning forward on her knees, she brushed her lips to his brow and let the bottled words flow free, an easy enough risk while he slept. "I love you, Danny Baker."

"I love you, Danny Baker."

Daniel forgot to tread, almost choked on a gulp of chlorinated water, before he made his feet move again. "Uh, me, too."

Correct response, right? He was going to be her husband in four days. So, sure, he loved her, too.

Damn. Except he didn't know what the hell he was feeling these days, mostly just putting one foot in front of the other. Marching, focused on the steps like in PT training or cadence calls in formation.

Daniel slid his hands down Mary Elise's slick sides, bared by her bikini, leaned to kiss her so they wouldn't have to talk anymore. Laughing, she ducked away at the last second, diving beneath him. He took chase, both knowing she wouldn't get far, but still enjoying the ritual of their water games. Why did things have to change?

He had his application to the University of Georgia

ready to hand-carry to the dean, with his father's help—a fact that chewed his pride almost as much as leaving the Academy when he'd reached his senior year. Another administrative mess his father would have to smooth over.

Only four more days and it would all be real, marriage, different college…baby on the way.

For now he just wanted to pretend he was home for the summer. Of course his newly invented reality would still include sex with Mary Elise. He sure didn't want to backtrack that far.

But marriage. Kid. Love. That had him cricking his tense neck to the side.

Four days. He kicked through the clear waters, deeper, until there was nowhere left to go, and still he could hear her declaration of love echo in his ears. Same words he'd heard his parents say to each other.

Damned if he'd seen any example of love lasting.

He preferred what he and Mary Elise had and he didn't want to screw it up. Crap. He was acting like a whiny kid rather than an adult. Get it together, Baker.

Daniel kicked upward, snagging Mary Elise and drawing them both to the surface. "Gotcha."

"What do you plan to do with me, Danny?"

"This." He drew her closer, brushed her bikini-clad breasts against his bare chest, eliciting a rewarding purr. He cupped a breast—fuller, more sensitive. The pregnancy thing had definite side benefits, like the visit from the oh-so-generous Breast Fairy.

"Danny," Mary Elise panted against his mouth.

"Pool house, or take a drive and park. Your choice, but make the decision fast." He prayed for the pool house. Closer. Sooner.

She stiffened against him. "Danny, I'm not feeling too good. Something's wrong…"

Daniel struggled to pull himself awake. Awake? But he was in the pool with Mary Elise.

Reality and dreams mussed. He wanted out of the pool or the dream or wherever the hell he was before the rest of the events unfolded: Mary Elise wrapping an arm around her stomach, a drive in the car that hadn't led to parking but instead to the emergency room.

He forced his feet to keep treading water as if that could stave off the end, keep them both from moving to the end of everything. Their baby. Them.

Water churned around them, someone else in the pool, beneath, drawing near Mary Elise to take her, blasting to the surface…

Kent McRae.

Daniel bolted upright on the sofa.

Dragging a hand over his face, he shook off the nightmare fog.

Mary Elise sat cross-legged on the floor beside him, hands in her lap, emerald eyes wide with worry. ''Are you okay?''

He nodded, throat still too tight for talk. Swinging his boots to the floor with a thud, he braced his elbows on his knees and sucked in air, steadied his heartbeat. He kept his hands clasped between his knees rather than gathering Mary Elise hard against his chest to feel her warm and alive against him. ''I'm fine.''

''Bad dreams suck.''

Leave it to Mary Elise not to let him dodge the issue by pretending. ''Yep.''

''You've had a lot on your plate lately, too, not just the boys, but losing your father, not even being able to make the memorial service for closure.''

Death wasn't high on his list of topics for discussion, the word riding too hard on the heels of a time he'd thought Mary Elise might die. The doctor may have called it a routine, first trimester miscarriage. But the doctor hadn't been the one carrying her across the yard to the car while she cried in pain.

Daniel stared at his clenched hands and remembered the weight of Mary Elise in his arms. His father had met him at the emergency room, silent but there. Odd how he'd forgotten that part over the years. "I'll always regret that he and I didn't have a chance to talk."

"Life can change so fast. And when I think of how close I came to being in the car with him that day..."

Daniel's mind raced back to the present. "What?"

"I was supposed to be with your father the day he died. I had a doctor visit in town, but had to cancel it at the last minute because of an emergency teacher's meeting. Your father decided to take his wife along instead, make a day of it and see if they could start working though their problems."

Her words nailed him like relentless mortar rounds. How she should have been in the car. McRae's money transfer to Rubistan shortly before. Daniel blanked his face and prayed she wouldn't draw inferences. He should have known better.

All too soon, dawning horror stained her face. "You don't think? Kent couldn't have been responsible. Could he? Oh, God, Danny, please don't let me have caused your father's death."

Think before opening the yap, Baker.

He forced his mind to work, remember that she needed to be a part of whatever happened. A tough-as-hell thing to do when his instincts blared for him to lock her in the bathroom and barricade her there while he stood between her and the rest of the world.

"Stop looking for trouble, Mary Elise. Ammar makes

the more likely suspect if my father's death wasn't an accident. Killing my father would give Ammar control over the widow, the boys and all their inherited money.'' His conscience kicked him, reminded him of Mary Elise's insistence on no more passive roles. Damn it, he just wanted to keep her safe. His conscience gave him another hefty punt. ''But it's possible he could have been working with McRae.''

''How so?''

''McRae has been funneling money into the Middle East underworld. The FBI has already been alerted.''

''Terrorism?''

''That. And Rubistan is one of the largest suppliers of opium. There are any number of likelihoods. But yes, I think McRae tracked you. And I think it's possible he and Ammar hooked up.'' Daniel paused, ready to pull her close if she fell apart, wondered if he was a sick bastard for wanting the excuse to hold her.

Mary Elise blinked once, tears glinting but not falling, then nodded for him to continue.

''Regardless, I think Ammar was gunning for my father.''

''And Kent would have found help even without Ammar.''

''Exactly.''

The glaze of tears disappeared, replaced by a different glint altogether. Suspicion. ''When did you find out about the overseas transactions?''

Damn. ''Yesterday.''

''Last night?''

Baker, you are so busted. ''Yesterday morning.''

Silently she stood, walked away from him, made a freaking production out of straightening a stack of papers by the computers.

"Go ahead and say it, 'Lise."

"Obviously, I don't need to." The papers slid from her hands in a scattered mess, making lie of her seeming calm.

Not unlike the mess he was making of this conversation. "You'll feel better if you chew me out."

A dry smile twitched as she collected the pages. "I doubt it."

Talk, damn it. Shout. Care enough to fight back so he would have a clue what she was thinking. Then he could plan a counter-defense. Strategize so they wouldn't self-destruct their relationship this time.

He shot to his feet. His boots traced a restless path on the hardwood floor, across the brown braid rug, back and forth in front of the stone fireplace. He needed action. Decisions. All the waiting and inaction left him with too much time to think about the past.

Flashes of his nightmare had him ready to snap like one of those trip wires strung under the cabin. Watching her distance herself from him didn't help. He needed reassurance she wouldn't bolt, not a helluva lot to ask.

Damn it, he wanted to lock her up tight beside him so he wouldn't have to worry about her day and night. "We should probably try to find something in the same school district so the boys aren't uprooted again."

"What?" She tucked the papers in her suitcase.

He paced over to the computers, checked again, found the same uninhabited security picture of sunrise filtering over the deserted beach. Nothing but a pelican and some egrets hunting for breakfast. Alarms stayed silent.

Action. Even a simple e-mail from Max would give him something to do. He would settle for anything that would make him shut up before his rambling mouth pushed her away for good. "A house on the water is out of my price range, but then with Austin around, it wouldn't really be safe or practical long-term, anyway. Buying an older home, we can get more space, but then I don't want you to be stuck dealing with the extra repairs when I'm TDY."

"Daniel."

"Yeah, 'Lise?"

"Slow down." Her hand fell to his arm.

"Oh, yeah, right." He dropped onto a bar stool, his booted foot twitched on the lowest rung. Tap. Tap.

"I didn't mean your pacing."

"Oh." He frowned. What the hell had he been saying anyway? Something about house hunting, an attempt at making something happen to relieve the stretched-taut inaction when what he really wanted was to nail McRae to the wall.

And to make Mary Elise stay. Houses. Duh. His subconscious was having a field day with him. Way to steamroll the woman. "Hang on a second. I think I know what I'm supposed to say here. Uh, what kind of house do *you* want?"

She perched on the other stool beside him, her hands gliding up his thighs in an obvious attempt to distract him. "Danny, this isn't the time to take such a big step with life decisions."

"Why the hell not?" His frustrations swelled to the surface, inconvenient as hell when he knew calm would work better. But his feelings for Mary Elise were anything but placid. "Is it my job? I know the gun safe and the traps freaked you out. Damn, Mary Elise, I realize I'm not offering you much of a deal here, but I'll do my best to make it work for you. I can even back off the secret stuff, stick with more straightforward missions."

He trailed his fingers down a strand of her auburn hair as if he could bind her to him, pull her slim body to him and give her something to do with their mouths so she would quit worrying her rings in circles around her fingers.

"It's not your job. God, I know it's a part of you." She stroked up to his chest, tracing his collar, dipping inside to hook in his dog tags, tug him forward. "And if this past year has taught me anything, I know that life is dangerous no matter what you do. We should live to the fullest."

"Exactly." He manacled her wrist in his grip. "I understand that logic and facts indicate I'm not the best bet for the long haul, but determination can't be gauged, and damn it, I'm hell-bent set on making this work. So why are you holding back from me again?"

Her hand fell to her lap. "Why is it that if someone doesn't go along with your way, then they're holding back?"

Echoes of other arguments pummeled him, nose-to-nose battles with his father, defensive confrontations with the squadron commander. But, damn it, those had been different situations. "Do you love me?"

Where the hell had that come from? His dream.

"Yes."

Say it back, dumb ass. "Then what exactly did I offer up that was so hell-fire terrible? A house?" He fished in his sleeve pocket and pulled out the solitaire. "Or God forbid I should give you a ring."

He held it with two fingers, a silent question between them. Say it back, Baker. His mouth stayed closed.

She folded her hands over his, held his hands in hers without taking the ring. At least she wasn't shoving it in his face. Yet.

"Danny, think. I told you I love you. And I know you love me, too, even if you can't push the words out. I hear you, anyway. I only asked for space.'' She knocked on his forehead. ''Hello? Why does it have to be all or nothing, black or white with you?''

''Seems pretty clear cut to me. Yeah, you're right.'' He said the damn words, ridiculous to hide from them, anyway. ''I love you, too. So either you want to marry me or you don't.''

The words burned his throat, but they were out there like a big purple polka-dot elephant between them they'd been trying to ignore all morning.

''It's not as simple as a ring and love, or everything would have worked out eleven years ago. Why are you just assuming that if my timetable doesn't fit yours I must not want you at all? Maybe I want to take the next two months and go ice fishing.''

''Do you?''

''No. Maybe. I don't know. And that's my whole point. You're pushing too hard, too fast for me right now. I'm not like you, feetfirst jumping in. All I'm asking is that we table this discussion, and then take it slow once we get back to it again. Okay?''

The computer dinged behind him with incoming mail.

Damn. He'd wanted answers from Max, but why couldn't the guy have hit send on the e-mail five minutes prior and saved him from landing in this hellacious conversation? How many times did this woman have to shove the ring back in his face before he got the message?

Daniel jammed the solitaire in his pocket and opened the post from Max.

''Ammar has entered the U.S. Wren and I have the boys locked down and safe.''

Trey and Austin's uncle in the States? Warning bells clanged in his mind, louder, until he realized they were merely an echo of the alarm from the security computer.

Someone had breached the first line of defense.

Chapter 16

Mary Elise stared at the security computer, monitor images of the yard still uninhabited except for gulls. Alarm silent now. Except for in her head where the alarm still blared and the memory of Daniel slipping off into the band of oaks and pines stayed imprinted.

Of course it made sense that she shouldn't go with him. She didn't have the training to move silently enough to stay undetected. She would be a liability to him out in the open.

According to logical Danny, she should stay here, locked down tight behind a dead bolt with her loaded gun. Still, the situation chafed.

Nerves tangled into a snarl that rivaled her hair after a shower. Fear gummed the tangle to near unmanageable levels. Why had she wasted time arguing with Danny? Why couldn't she have waited to make her damned stand for independence—all because she was scared of taking a final step?

Stay calm. The alarm could be nothing worse than a rowdy raccoon setting off a trip wire. Right?

One really heavy raccoon.

If only she could do something besides stare at the freaking computer screen. She hated the inaction.

Well, hell. She was starting to sound like Danny. Part of her wanted to be just like him, able to dive into a situation, completely confident in her judgment. Sure, Danny was a little arrogant. But, doggone him, he was usually right.

And to give him credit, he was trying to include her. Once confronted, he shared more about tracking Kent's finances, working through Ammar's possible connection together when he could have bluffed his way through.

So why the knee-jerk need to pull back from Daniel?

Intellectually she knew he wasn't a threat to her independence. He might get angry and stomp around, but the man eventually listened. He cared.

Danny's words in the car tripped through her mind, his confusion about her reluctance to go for even a simple doctor visit. The answer sidled past her defenses with blinding clarity.

Those doctor visits symbolized weakness to her, and above all she couldn't bear to be weak, dependant. Just as it didn't help denying herself the healing balm of words to negate there was even a problem, staying away from Danny couldn't protect her from the risk of loving him.

The rest of the answer followed in a rush, now that her defenses had been breached. Sharing burdens didn't equate loss of control or weakness, with the right person by her side.

With Danny by her side.

His innate honor, his ever-logical sense of fairness

would make him a man to trust. He might not always agree with her, but he would listen to her. Respect her.

Love her.

How strange that Danny with his black-and-white reasoning helped her see the shades of gray to find the formula for making it all work. She sank back on the stool, exhausted and exhilarated all at once.

A flicker of movement on the screen snagged her attention. Danny?

Nerves drew taut, near to breaking. The figure cleared the trees. Not Danny.

Kent.

Icy pinpricks tingled over her scalp.

Her ex-husband stepped deeper into the clearing. Closer to her hiding place in the cabin. Sunlight played dappled shadows over his blond perfection. She'd once found the dimple in his chin endearing, his classic looks and clean-cut appearance safe.

She'd been so horribly wrong.

Bile roiled up her throat. Swaying, she gripped the edge of the counter. He stared at the cabin, eyes intense, as if he knew.

Of course he knew she was inside.

Oh, God, where was Danny? He couldn't be dead. She refused to believe that. What the hell should she do?

Kent pulled his hand out of his pants pocket, his fingers clenched around a rock-size object. Her methodical, understated ex couldn't have a grenade. Something so overt—so messy—wouldn't be Kent's style.

Still, she winced. Zoomed in with the camera and saw…a piece of paper banded around some kind of weight.

With a gentle underhand toss, Kent lobbed it onto the

porch. Mary Elise heard the thud echo in stereo from outside and through the computer's speaker.

He raised his hand, waved once in a mocking salute and waited.

She shifted on the bar stool, trying like crazy to adopt Daniel's logic and blend it with her own intuition about the madman she'd married. Stepping outside would be reckless, and undoubtedly Danny would be furious with her.

Unless Kent had already—

She sliced that thought away. Damn it, she couldn't even consider that, because then she couldn't think at all.

But what if Daniel had been hurt? Time became crucial. Or worse, what if he hadn't even discovered Kent as of yet and stumbled on him unaware? She knew with a certainty born of both intuition and logic that Kent was well armed in some fashion. Perhaps he had backup lurking in the cover of trees waiting to take her out while he watched.

Certainly a possibility. In which case Daniel would stumble on two people unaware. Which left her with only one choice. She would have to alert Daniel. All she needed was a single warning shout. Or shot.

The past year had taught her she could survive almost anything. But she knew without question, she wouldn't survive seeing Daniel die.

Daniel stared down at the dead body at his feet.

The Javaro paddle dangled from the rope, deactivated. The dead man's unblinking stare made checking for a pulse unnecessary. Problem was, the paddle hadn't killed him. A bullet through the temple from someone else's gun had, someone with a silencer, since he hadn't heard a shot.

All of which meant another armed party lurked out

there. Searching for Mary Elise. And the dead man couldn't help with any information, most likely the reason he'd been silenced once injured.

Daniel shifted the weight of the .45 in his hand. He didn't need to check the man for identification, either. The frozen face below was a direct mirror of one of the mug shots he'd pulled up from intelligence files.

The assassin who'd been hired to kill Mary Elise a year ago.

The dead bastard lying on the ground had been used the way sacrificial troops were run through land mines to clear the field for the next line to march through. Scanning the trees, the path, Daniel found disturbed pine straw continuing down the path. Toward the cabin.

Mary Elise.

A shot split the air.

He flattened to the ground, rolled to the side and steadied his gun in a fluid move. Nothing. Nobody in sight. Crouching, he darted through the trees, dried leaves crunching beneath his feet.

His heart pounded in time with his feet. Damn it, how could things have gone to hell so fast. What could he have done differently? He searched his mind—and came up with zip. Other than the fact he'd been lured out, separated from Mary Elise.

He'd expected McRae to be devious. He hadn't expected tactical savvy.

Of course he should have, if he'd listened to Mary Elise. The commander's warning from only days prior thundered through his head. Every flyer faced the possibility of meeting a missile some day.

His death he could face. Mary Elise's was unacceptable.

Daniel drew closer to the cabin. Voices carried on the

wind. Mary Elise's. Relief hammered him until he almost forgot to make his feet keep moving.

Another voice drifted. Male. The cabin showed through the cover of trees.

Mary Elise eased down the porch steps, gun drawn and steady on the man standing with his back to Daniel.

Good girl. She had McRae cornered, withstanding whatever garbage the bastard was pouring her way in his relentless talking, and holding her own.

Daniel strode closer, sight line clearing. A tie flapped over the man's shoulder, jacket long gone but white shirt a crisp beacon—with the harsh slash of a gun tucked in the waistband out of sight to Mary Elise.

Daniel stopped cold.

He couldn't let her see him now. If Mary Elise called a greeting, thinking she had McRae safely pinned, the bastard would have time to draw.

To shoot. Her.

Daniel blinked as if he could change the hell in front of him. He'd been so damned sure he could protect her. Of course he'd been concerned about injuries, but never, never had he allowed himself to consider that she could die.

Mary Elise dead.

The past and present merged in a blaze of reds—her hair, strawberries, blood. In the middle of the roaring fury, it hit him, why he'd run so hard from her eleven years ago. He hadn't run from commitment, or even from admitting how much she meant to him. Hell, he'd already realized now how damned much he loved her then. How much he loved her now.

He'd run because he was afraid of losing her.

And damned if he hadn't fallen right back into old patterns by picking a fight with her in the cabin. They'd almost replayed the past all over again—the mistakes forgivable in their youth but totally asinine now, given they should know better. Be stronger. Wiser.

Ah, hell. Love wasn't wise, either.

But love did make a person stronger. He just prayed it would make Mary Elise strong enough to stand down a madman until he could come forward with reinforcements.

Training overrode emotions. Crouching low, Daniel made his way around the perimeter of trees, dodging through whatever cover he could to work his way closer. He would have to take out McRae, but it would have to be fast.

Daniel assessed the terrain. Counted steps. Organized the plan of attack in his head.

He inched forward, eyes trained so firmly on McRae he almost missed the flash of movement to his left.

Pivoting, he brought his arm up to defend his face just as a knife came slashing down. Burned. Knocked the gun from his hand. "What the—"

"Where are they?" Ammar asked in heavily accented English, eyes wild with fanaticism. "Where are the boys?"

Mary Elise stepped deeper into the yard, prayed, inched another step, Kent subtly moving toward her every time she did. Closer to the buried bucket trap.

If only she could keep him talking. Good Lord, why had she never realized how much this man liked the sound of his own voice?

"You still haven't unwrapped my gift, Mary Elise. How rude."

Her fingers convulsed around the crystal paperweight

clenched in her fist, the paper crackling around it. No, she hadn't dared do anything after scooping it from the porch.

Was he trying to distract her so he could launch forward?

She locked her gaze with Kent's when she desperately wanted to look down for affirmation on the placement of the submerged spike trap.

God, she hoped her peripheral vision and memory were on target. She needed him disabled, couldn't risk him overpowering her, because heaven help her, she wasn't sure she could actually shoot him. "How about I check it out after you're in jail?"

"That's no fun." He tugged his tie back over his shoulder, tiny pelicans traipsing their pattern across blue silk. "Remember how much you enjoyed seeing me open this for my birthday? The bearer of gifts enjoys watching the receiver unwrap the present almost as much as selecting it." A slow smile crept across his face. "I enjoyed watching you find my other gift, the plant. You knew it was from me, didn't you?"

"You really are a twisted bastard." She willed her feet to adjust closer to the nearest bucket.

"And you're illogical. Old territory. Move on. Did you like the other gifts? The syringe? The fertility clinic flyer in Baker's mail?"

Flyer? Her mind winged back to the stack of junk mail in Daniel's condo on the coffee table, how he'd fidgeted with it after she'd told him about Kent.

Oh, Daniel. Always trying to flipping protect her.

Damn it, she absolutely refused to let Kent anywhere near him. Hatred spiked sarcasm. "As always, Kent, you're too generous."

His smile widened without reaching his eyes. "I do

miss your wit. Now, open your present and I'll tell you whether your lover is alive or dead.''

A frigid fist closed around her heart. She knew Kent was playing with her like a cat tormenting a mouse. And she wouldn't be a mouse. She would play his game and win.

Keeping one hand steady on the gun, and her eyes glued to him, she worked the paper free of the band around the weight. Thicker paper than she'd originally thought. She raised it and glanced at the last thing she would have expected. *Oh, God.*

Her fingers clenched around the funeral mass card for her stillborn child.

Cold hatred iced through her, although she wouldn't give Kent the satisfaction of seeing he'd stabbed her clean through. She thought perhaps she could shoot Kent after all. Fighting back for herself wasn't near as easy as fighting for her child.

Maternal instincts swelled further, encompassing Trey and Austin, demanding retribution for the fear this man had brought down upon *her* boys by working with their uncle. How dare he force Trey and Austin into hiding? Fury clogged her throat.

''It seems only right that you have one, too, since you left everything behind when you ran from me.''

She cleared the haze of emotions and adjusted another inch to the left. *Move, Kent. Move.* ''I didn't run from you. I ran *to* life. Something you could never understand.''

Her finger itched on the trigger until logic teased, reminding her if she gunned him down in cold blood she would be no better than him.

That argument almost swayed her. Almost.

Then logic pushed further that she owed it to Trey,

Austin, Danny to be a stronger person. As much as she wanted vengeance, her life was inexplicably woven with theirs. And that surrender made her all the stronger.

She took a bold step forward toward the trap, placing her within touching distance of pure evil.

Kent lunged.

An explosion of motion from the trees behind him yanked her vision up.

Danny?

Kent grabbed her wrist, twisted, squeezed. Her gun went flying.

She screamed. Jerked, yet was unable to take her eyes off Danny locked in hand-to-hand battle with a knife-wielding foreigner. Blood stained both of them. From which one?

Bodies shifted, revealing a face she'd hoped never again to see outside of Rubistan.

Ammar.

Daniel gripped both of the man's arms, brought his knee up, Ammar twisting to dodge. The man's heavily accented curse floated on the air. ''That McRae bitch should have died in the car, not my sister.''

Mary Elise shuddered. ''Danny,'' she whispered.

Daniel appeared to have the upper hand, but—

Kent's hot breath grazed her face. Adrenaline gave her the strength to break free, powered her back away from Kent and in the direction she'd been trying to lead him earlier. She struggled to orient herself, keep from placing her own foot in a spiked trap. She stumbled, fell to the ground, pine straw offering little cushion.

Panting, she crawled, a gnarled root jamming her knee, her ears filled with harsh curses from Ammar and Danny. Thuds, grunts as fists met flesh.

She grappled for her gun. Kent advanced, foot landing

hard. Slamming through the earth and into the bucket. His scream of agony halted her. He fell to his knees, one leg trapped.

No time to waste.

Mary Elise searched the ground when more than anything she wanted to look at Daniel and reassure herself he was all right. Rustling through the pine needles, her hand grasped, found, closed around her gun.

She rolled to her back just as Kent whipped his hand from behind him. Gun drawn.

''You bitch.''

Death winked in the steady steel barrel.

Heels pushing against dirt, she backed away, her arms outstretched in front of her, 9 mm aimed. ''You might as well give up, Kent.''

''Already have you running again, don't I? Never could stick with anything. Not even a marriage. Now you've ruined my plans. Bet you don't even have the guts to shoot me.''

She wouldn't let him rile her. She kept her eyes trained on him, peripheral vision assuring her Daniel was still on his feet. She couldn't risk shots distracting him.

Let Kent talk. Ignore his words. Daniel would finish Ammar off in seconds. Kent would not win.

Dirt streaked his face, his perfectly groomed facade shot to hell and revealing the monster she knew him to be. ''You believe I don't know what you're thinking, Mary Elise, but I do. I know I'm not going to make it. Ammar is no match for your lover there. And if I shoot you, no doubt Baker will kill me. Oddly enough, you inspire that kind of fanaticism in a man. I should know.''

His twisted logic for love crawled over her like a lethal rash when she wanted more than ever to live. For Daniel. For the boys. For herself. She wanted life with a ferocity she hadn't expected after so long of simply existing. Daniel had brought her back to life.

Kent adjusted his knee, winced at the shift of his foot against the spikes. ''Your leaving hurt me. Did you know that? I loved you and you threw our life together away. If only you'd been more patient, I wouldn't have had to hurt you, too.''

The will to live flamed hotter. ''Kent, you don't have to do this.''

''Oh, but I do.'' Resolution froze his eyes to an icy blue full of certainty. ''And I know the best way to hurt you back.'' Foot anchored in the bucket, he pivoted.

Toward Daniel.

''No!'' The scream echoed in her heart, powering resolve.

She fired.

Kent bucked. Blood bloomed across his chest. Eyes widening with surprise, he fell over backward. His gun skittered from his lifeless hand as he lay, unmoving.

Mary Elise rushed to her feet, ran, toward Daniel, his hands twisted in Ammar's shirt. Daniel hauled back his fist and landed a final, knockout punch.

The boys' uncle crumpled to the ground.

Panting, Daniel barked, ''Rope, from the porch.''

Blood poured from the jagged tear on his flight suit sleeve, but she couldn't waste time thinking about that now. Mary Elise snagged the coil and pitched it to Daniel, her feet suddenly unsteady.

By the time she worked her way back, he'd finished tying Ammar.

Swaying, Daniel flattened a palm to the ground. Extended the other arm to her. Without hesitation or question, she fell forward, into his embrace.

Home.

* * *

Five hours later Daniel hefted his green duffle bag into the back of the SUV. His arm hurt like a son of a bitch from thirty-six freaking stitches, but he'd turned down painkillers.

He wanted a clear head to savor every minute of knowing Mary Elise lived. She had her life back, and damned if he wasn't alive, too.

The cops had already cleared the area, taken statements, hauled Ammar to a holding cell. International laws and extradition would make for a lengthy legal process. If Ammar ever saw the light of day again, at least Daniel would have time to formulate a plan for keeping the boys safe—with Mary Elise's help.

Yeah, he needed a clear head so he didn't screw up this second-chance gift with her. Whatever pace she wanted to set, he could handle, because at least they would be together. He was through running.

After all, she'd given him a gift he'd never received, not even from his father. Total acceptance. Mary Elise didn't want to change him or fix him. Damn, the woman was even okay with his job, a rare-as-hell find. All she asked was that he give her the same consideration in return.

However she wanted to take this, he'd follow and hang in for the long haul. She'd said she loved him. He could hold on to that—especially if she let him keep slathering strawberry preserves and anything else he could scavenge out of the cabinets all over her delicious body.

And he was a mighty damned good scavenger.

Daniel closed the hatch, his gaze skating over the top of the SUV out to the shoreline where Mary Elise stood. God, she was a trooper. McRae's parting "gift" to Mary Elise in the form of that funeral mass card would have leveled just about anyone. No question, if anyone deserved to die, McRae fit the bill, but still, taking a life left an irreparable bruise on a person's soul.

But Mary Elise was stronger than she'd known. His pigtailed buddy who'd needed a defender against playground bullies could bloody noses all on her own now.

She would make a helluva life partner.

Partner. A word he was only just beginning to understand, and he looked forward to a lifetime of learning more with Mary Elise's help.

He skirted the bumper, walking toward the shore. Mary Elise knelt, releasing the card into the tide before standing. He wrapped his arms around her waist and watched with her until it disappeared in the surf. Her head fell back against his chest. With that unspoken connection between them in full working order, he could feel her pain easing into a swelling acceptance.

She tipped her head, looked up at him. "I can't have children, Danny."

"I know."

"You're okay with that?"

He could only think of one reason she would ask him that question. Relief nearly drove him to his knees. Exactly where he wanted to be, on his knees proposing, begging this woman to make their love official. Instead he stayed on his feet and let her find her own pace.

After all, he was a smart guy, and more than his own happiness, he wanted hers. "Yes, I'm okay with that."

Her wise eyes held him. "That's all you have to say? Danny, I've had years to think about this, to accept it. It's more complex than just a single sentence."

Maybe to her. Not to him. But if she needed more words, more—he gulped—emotional analysis, he would dig inside himself for the words and feelings to reassure her. He turned her in his arms to face him.

"Straight-up honest, yeah, it hits me right here—" he thumped the area over his heart "—to think we'll never make a baby together, and I imagine you feel the same." He cupped her face with both hands. "But I also know in that exact same place that I'll love any child we adopt as much as any child we might have made."

Her jaw trembled.

Without a wince she'd risked the retaliation of Rubistanian guards to climb in a box with two frightened boys. No crying, she'd stood down Kent McRae, her worst nightmare, for him.

But now, two big fat tears to rival any from Austin pooled, fell over her eyelids and down her cheeks.

He brushed away the tears with his thumbs. "A child shouldn't be just an extension of me or you, or only my chromosomes and yours mixed up together. A child, our child, is a person."

A watery laugh bubbled free. "I do so love your logical mind."

"You do?" He knew but sure wouldn't mind hearing it again.

Her tears evaporated in the warmth of her smile. "Yes. Of course. I've loved you since you slugged Buddy Davis for me in the third grade."

She traced her hand gingerly over his bandage.

"Buddy's punch back then hurt a helluva lot worse than this." He captured her fingers tracing featherlight paths over his arm as if to heal it. He brought her hand to his lips. "I love you, too."

Whimsy lightened somber emerald eyes to spring grass. "More than Hostess Ho-Hos?"

"Oh, damn, that's a tough one."

She slugged his uninjured arm.

Laughing, he pulled her close, inhaled the scent of honeysuckle shampoo and the promise of forever. He held her while the wind encircled them and could have sworn there was something symbolic in the moment. A damned strange thought for a man more comfortable in the mathematical realm.

He held her closer. "You know I'm not a flowery-words kind of guy. I wish I could tell you how much I love you with the poetry that you deserve. All I can say is that I love you. No measurements. No limits."

Her hands hooked around his neck, she stood in his arms, unmoving while they both watched the fading sunlight stain the sky deeper hues of purple.

One hand slid from his neck to his shoulder, unzipping his sleeve pocket. He smiled, already planning his one-knee proposal once she passed him the ring.

Mary Elise inched away, the solitaire between two fingers. He reached to take it.

She pulled her hand back farther. "Wanna marry me, Danny Baker?"

Surprise nipped and he wasn't complaining at all. He was starting to like the way she assumed the aggressive role. "Yes, I do. Very much."

She placed the ring in his palm and extended her fingers. He slid the engagement diamond in place again. Forever.

He sealed its placement with a kiss on her finger, followed by one on her lips, and knew without question he would be challenged, entranced, in love with this woman for the rest of his life. A strong woman who would, hell yes, demand the best of him.

And would give her best in return.

Pulling back, he stared into eyes a shade of green he'd only ever found on one woman. ''Are you ready to go?''

''Yeah, Danny,'' she answered, her voice echoing with surety along the salty breeze. ''I'm all set.''

He hooked his arm around her shoulders as he'd done a thousand times before with Mary Elise, his best friend, his love. ''Then let's go get the boys and start putting our family together.''

Epilogue

Mary Elise paced around the oval table, spinning each empty chair she passed. Waiting sucked. But the reward for patience would be worth every lap on the industrial carpet in the private hospital waiting room.

"Settle down, boys." Daniel hooked an arm around each brother, immobilizing the hyper kids with a pseudo-wrestling match that landed them on the blue-plaid sofa.

Thank goodness the hospital had provided a small conference room for gathering to meet the newest member of their family. The baby had been born nearly an hour ago, but Daniel had requested they not hear the gender until the infant was brought to them after the doctor finished the exam.

Even though the boys had only arrived a half hour prior, she had been waiting at the hospital with Danny from the minute the call came that the birth mother had gone into labor. Darcy and Max had brought the boys over later, and even now were down in the cafeteria picking up food. Maybe the boys should have gone with them, but she'd been so afraid they would miss "the moment."

Of course Trey and Austin had been more impatient in waiting for their new sibling than she would have expected. The aide from the adoption agency had suggested she and Danny might want to leave the boys home and bring them later.

The boys' crestfallen faces at the mere mention of delay had swayed her.

Danny gave both brothers noogies on the head before releasing them. "Hang tough and we'll go to IHOP soon."

"No chocolate chips," ten-year-old Trey insisted.

"Roger that, bro."

Mary Elise extended her arms for Austin and hitched him on her hip. "How about we check out all the pictures again?"

"Nuh-uh." The wriggling four-year-old slid from her grip back to the floor, seeming more in need of a run to the snack bar than another perusal of a doctor's diplomas.

Snick. The door opened.

Last-minute nerves tangled in her tummy. They knew without question the birth mother was firmly committed to giving up her child. Still, what if the nurse entered empty-handed....

A nurse wearing surgical scrubs backed in, tugging a rolling basinet, the clear sides revealing the wrapped and squirming infant inside.

A newborn with a pink cap.

Mary Elise clutched Danny's arm, endlessly grateful she could share this moment with him. "A girl."

A tide of tender emotion wiped all the traces of nervous butterflies away. At long last, they had their baby.

Smiling, Danny looped an arm around her and drew

her against him for a quick kiss full of joy and even tears. ''Yeah, 'Lise, we have a daughter.''

The past year as Danny's wife had been a gift worth waiting for, like this child. Sure, the path hadn't always been easy with long TDYs, the boys adjusting to their new life, her finding her way as an education columnist. But with Danny at her side again, loving her, she could conquer anything.

He palmed Mary Elise's back, nudging her forward. She almost charged ahead, then changed her mind. This was Danny's child, too. ''Will you bring her to me, please?''

His widening smile, crinkling chocolate-brown eyes, made a hefty reward in exchange for the extra seconds' delay in holding her daughter.

The boys, now stunned silent, stared at the pink blankets with quiet reverence. Mary Elise clutched Trey's and Austin's hands while Danny crossed the small conference room. Stopping in front of the steel-framed wheeled basinet, he slid broad hands beneath the tiny bundle, cradling her like a pro.

Like a father.

He didn't turn right away, instead standing in profile, gazing down at the tiny face and whispering greetings. A boyish lock of hair fell forward over his brow with familiar regularity. As much as Mary Elise wanted to see her baby, she froze, mesmerized by the glow of love warming her husband's eyes as he met their daughter. An image she would always cherish.

And then he pivoted toward Mary Elise, placed their baby girl into the cradle of her arms as she'd imagined him doing so often.

Her arms filled as quickly as her heart.

How amazing that in a simple second, she couldn't remember a time when this precious little one hadn't been in her life. Mary Elise stroked a knuckle over her daughter's tipped nose, chubby cheek, along the softest skin ever.

''Well, hello, Mary Francis,'' she crooned her child's name—Mary Francis, after Daniel's father, Franklin, the man who'd given them all a second chance.

She sank to the sofa, Austin and Trey crawling up beside her, Danny kneeling in front of her. His flight suit stretched across his broad, reliable shoulders, almost pulling out the wrinkles she never could seem to iron free. Not that she really wanted to dispense with those creases. Danny suited her just fine as he was, with his rumpled uniforms and knee-melting kisses.

The nurse backed toward the door. ''I'll leave y'all alone to get acquainted. Just buzz me when you're ready for her to go back to the nursery.''

Mary Elise wasn't sure that time would ever come.

Trey tickled Mary Francis under the chin. ''You're named for my dad, Austin's and your daddy's dad, too.''

Austin leaned over, closer. ''Ooh-rah. Okay? Don't be listening to Trey when he tells ya somethin' else.''

Laughter chimed, then faded, smiles remaining as they became acquainted with tiny Mary Francis—her round face with wide eyes, her sprigs of dark hair and the sweet smell of baby.

Daniel cupped the back of Mary Elise's neck, pulled her forward for a kiss, his forehead falling to rest on hers after. ''Life is good.''

''Yeah, Danny, it sure is.'' Love swelled, flowed in their old connection, but broader now, binding them in a circle through the family they'd built together.

Years ago, Mary Elise had dreamed of filling her arms with Danny Baker's children. But she never could have envisioned anything quite this perfect.

* * * * *

Some Kind of Hero

BRENDA HARLEN

Harlequin Mills & Boon

Intimate

First Published 2003
First Australian Paperback Edition 2003
ISBN 0 733 54849 0

Published by
Harlequin Mills & Boon
3 Gibbes Street
CHATSWOOD NSW 2067
AUSTRALIA

Printed and bound in Australia by
McPherson's Printing Group

BRENDA HARLEN

grew up in a small town surrounded by books and imaginary friends. Although she always dreamed of being a writer, she chose to follow a more traditional career path first. After two years of practicing as an attorney (including an appearance in front of the Supreme Court of Canada), she gave up her "real" job to be a mum and to try her hand at writing books. Three years, five manuscripts and another baby later, she sold her first book—an RWA Golden Heart Winner—to Harlequin.

Brenda lives in Southern Ontario with her real-life husband/hero, two heroes-in-training and two neurotic dogs. She is still surrounded by books ("too many books," according to her children) and imaginary friends, but she also enjoys communicating with "real" people. Readers can contact Brenda by e-mail at brendaharlen@yahoo.com or by snail mail c/o Harlequin Books, 233 Broadway, Suite 1001 New York, NY 10279.

A lot of this book is about family,
and I'd like to dedicate this story to mine.

To my parents—
Diane & John and Dan & Marj—
for giving me such a wonderful example of family.

To Shelly and Jim,
whom I am privileged not just to call
my sister and brother but also my friends.

To Robin & Hazel—
for always accepting me as part of their family.

And, of course, to Neill and Connor and Ryan.

I love you all.

P.S. This book is also dedicated to Ken, who didn't even blink when his wife said three unknown women were coming to invade his cottage for a weeklong writers' retreat. (During which time this story took form in spite of Kate and Sharon and Sheryl. Thanks anyway, ladies.)

Chapter 1

It took Riane Quinlan half a minute to peg the tall, dark-haired man across the room as an out-of-towner, another thirty seconds to figure him for a cop.

She'd spotted him the minute he stepped through the ornately carved double doors of the hotel ballroom where the Fourth Annual Quinlan Camp Charity Ball was in progress. Part of the reason was that his was an unfamiliar face at this type of event. Another part of the reason was much more basic. Whoever he was, he was an incredible specimen of masculinity: broad shoulders, hard muscles, thick dark hair that was just a little too long for the conservative tastes of the social elite.

Not a departmental regulation crew cut, but some guys took pride in breaking the rules. This man, with the chiseled jaw, strong nose and slashing brows, looked like one of them.

From a distance, Riane couldn't determine what color his eyes were, just that they were dark and intense.

He took a slow survey of the room. Deliberately casual. Too casual.

Definitely a cop.

As the daughter of a U.S. senator, Riane had been shadowed often enough to recognize the inherent attributes of those in law enforcement. The sculpted physique, the guarded stance, the constant attentiveness. There were security personnel hovering in the background this evening, but she knew this man wasn't one of them. He wasn't hired muscle—just a cop.

Her lips curved in a small smile. *Just* a cop was hardly an accurate description. He was almost larger than life—a real man's man, the type of man she didn't often have opportunity to cross paths with in her social circles.

As he continued his perusal of the room, his gaze collided with hers. The force of the impact literally took her breath away. His eyes narrowed, skimmed over her in a blatantly masculine assessment. She felt her skin heat, an unavoidably feminine reaction.

He held her gaze a moment longer, then turned his head, dismissing her.

Except that Riane wouldn't be dismissed.

She made her way through the sea of rustling silk and black ties, stopping now and again to speak with someone she hadn't caught up with earlier. She smiled at the secretary of state and tried to ignore the fact that her toes were starting to cramp.

It had been a mistake to wear new shoes when she was going to be on her feet for the better part of the evening, but the sling-back sandals were such a perfect match for the silk crepe dress, she hadn't been able to resist. She'd spent the better part of her twenty-four years in the public eye and knew that image was more important than comfort.

She glanced toward the back of the room again, and her eyes locked with his.

Blue, she realized. His eyes were a startling, stunning shade of blue. And just a little wary.

Her curiosity further piqued, she breached the last few feet that separated them and offered her most winning smile. "I don't believe we've met."

He hesitated a beat before he shifted his untouched champagne glass and offered his hand. "Joel Logan."

His voice was deep and incredibly sensuous, causing her blood to heat in her veins. She disregarded the sensation. She was more than likely overheated from the multitude of lights in the enormous chandeliers, not from hearing this man speak two words to her.

Reassured, she put her hand in his, felt it engulfed by his warm strength. His handshake was firm, his palm wide and slightly callused. There was nothing improper or inappropriate about the contact, and yet she felt a sudden burst of heat arrow straight to her core. She withdrew her hand quickly from his grasp.

"Riane Quinlan," she told him.

"I know."

He said nothing else, offered none of the usual pleasantries.

Riane was intrigued. Her family's wealth and political connections had accustomed her to more deferential treatment. People went out of their way to impress her, never knowing when they might need a personal favor or political ally. But she'd bet every last dollar of the trust fund her grandmother had left her that Joel Logan didn't bow and scrape for anyone, and she couldn't help but admire him for it.

She tried another smile. "What brings you here tonight, Mr. Logan?"

"A desire to support the Quinlan Camp for Underprivileged Children?"

It was more of a question than an answer, and she couldn't decide if he was just unsociable or deliberately trying to annoy her. She should thank him for his support and leave it at that, but there was something about him that made it impossible for her to walk away.

"It must help that your shoulders are so broad," she commented.

He frowned at her. "Excuse me?"

"Your shoulders," she said again. "They must be the reason you can walk upright with the size of that chip you're carrying."

He shifted his champagne glass into his other hand again, his scowl deepening.

Dark, moody, and no sense of humor, Riane decided. She signaled to a nearby waiter, turned to speak with him briefly. When the server disappeared, she plucked the crystal flute from Joel's hand and brought it to her own lips, sipping the cool, bubbly liquid.

"I wasn't finished with that," he said testily.

"I know." Her response was unapologetic.

His mouth opened, then closed again when the waiter returned with a tall pilsner glass filled with amber-colored liquid, a thick foam head skimming the frosty rim.

"Thanks, Jeffrey." Riane took the glass and offered it to Joel. "I thought this might be more to your liking."

For half a second she thought he might refuse the drink, but thirst must have triumphed over obstinacy as he reached for the glass. His fingers brushed against hers and she felt that zing again.

"What makes you think you know what I like?" Joel challenged.

She took another sip of his champagne before responding. "It's something of a hobby of mine—studying people."

"Have you been studying me?"

"I study everyone."

"And what do you think you've learned?"

"You don't like champagne," she said, "and you won't pretend to enjoy it, even though everyone else guzzles it like water at this kind of event."

He tipped the glass of beer to his lips and drank, his eyes still on hers.

"I imagine you suffered through dinner," she continued. "The food and the conversation. You would probably have preferred a nice thick steak, rare, and a discussion about the Yankees' chances at the pennant.''

She saw the corners of his mouth twitch, wondered if he might actually smile. He didn't.

''Medium well,'' was all he said.

''Sorry?''

''My steak,'' he clarified. ''Medium well. I like to be sure it's dead.''

''And the Yankees?'' she prompted.

Now he did smile, and it completely transformed him. With his dark and somber expression, he was dangerously handsome. With those sensual lips curved, he was devastating.

''Absolutely.''

She nodded, but couldn't for the life of her even remember what the question had been. The man had just smiled, and her mind had blanked.

''Is that the end of your analysis?'' he prompted.

''Not quite,'' she said, wondering whether she should pursue the issue or make a tactical retreat. He intrigued her—maybe too much. She was a woman used to being in control of her life and her emotions. But after less than ten minutes in Joel Logan's company, she felt her comfortable world tilting crazily on its axis. It thrilled her. And terrified her.

''What else do you think you know?''

''You're looking for someone. Someone you expected to be here. Whether he is or not, I couldn't say, because I don't know who it is, but I know you haven't found him. Or her,'' she amended quickly.

He pinned her with that deep blue gaze, and she felt as if all the bones in her body had simply melted. When he spoke again, the low, throaty tone was as seductive as a caress. ''Maybe I'm just looking for someone to take home for a quick bout of hot, sweaty sex.''

''I hadn't completely disregarded that possibility,'' she acknowledged, a little breathlessly. ''But I think if that was what you wanted, you would have found her by now.''

"I'm flattered, I think."

"Just an observation, Mr. Logan. So why don't you tell me what it is that brought you to West Virginia?"

"Why do you assume I'm not a local?"

"If you were, we'd have met before now." And she definitely would have remembered. Joel Logan wasn't the type of man any woman would forget.

"I'm here on business," he admitted after a pause.

"What kind of business?"

"You haven't figured that out?"

"I'm still working on it," she said. "But I haven't been able to think of any reason why an out-of-town cop is at my fund-raiser."

"I'm not a cop." He took another sip of his beer.

"Oh." She frowned. Then, in an accusatory tone, she said, "You look like a cop. Standing at the far end of the room, your back to the wall, as if you expect armed gunmen to come charging through the door."

This time his smile seemed to come more easily. "I used to be a cop," he conceded.

"And now?"

He shrugged. "Now I'm not."

Joel tipped his glass to his lips again and drank deeply, wishing for at least the hundredth time since Shaun McIver walked into his office that he'd refused this assignment. It should have been a simple job: to find a child who had been adopted twenty-two years earlier. But four months later Joel had made scant progress.

The few facts he'd managed to uncover so far led him straight to Senator Ellen Rutherford-Quinlan. If the senator had information that would help find Shaun's fiancée's sister, Joel was determined to get it. Which was his reason for coming to West Virginia.

He hadn't counted on crossing paths with Riane Quinlan, though. And he'd been completely unprepared for the quick punch of arousal that struck low in his belly when he'd first set eyes on her.

A smart investigator would turn the situation to his advantage—get whatever information he could from the daughter as the mother was nowhere to be found. But he was having difficulty thinking like an investigator with the subtle scent of Riane's perfume fogging his brain.

Which meant that the wisest thing would be to establish and maintain a safe distance from Riane Quinlan. He needed answers, and he wasn't going to get them if he allowed himself to be distracted. The senator's daughter was quite a distraction.

"Riane, darling—"

Joel exhaled a silent sigh of relief as she was forced to turn her attention to the stocky woman who descended upon them in a cloud of sweet scent and glittering sequins.

"Margaret," Riane said, exchanging air kisses with the older woman. "I'm so pleased you could make it."

The woman looked vaguely familiar to Joel, but it took a moment to search his memory banks for the reference. When it clicked, he wondered that his jaw didn't hit the floor. Margaret Cassidy. The attorney general of the United States.

The upper echelons of political society had turned out for this event—all the way from Washington, even. A reminder of how much political clout the Rutherford-Quinlans wielded. As if he needed any reminders. He'd tangled with them once before, and that encounter had cost Joel his reputation and his career.

He was clearly out of his element here, even if no one else seemed to realize it. He didn't fit in with these people; he didn't want to. He'd attended this gala event because his client was paying all incidental costs—including the thousand-dollar ticket for dinner and the rental of this damn tux—and because he'd been confident he could remain in the background. Riane had taken that option away from him. And he wasn't sure if he should be flattered or annoyed that he'd caught her attention.

While she was preoccupied with the attorney general, Joel scanned the room again, searching for the elusive senator. Ellen Rutherford-Quinlan's name had been on the top of the guest list. This charity camp was her daughter's pet project. So where the hell was she?

His head snapped back to the conversation beside him when the attorney general said, "I'm so sorry I missed your mother."

"She didn't want to miss the ball," Riane told her. "But Daddy convinced her that it was more important to celebrate their thirty-fifth wedding anniversary."

Daddy. Joel fought the urge to roll his eyes. How many grown women referred to their fathers as "daddy"? Then the impact of what she was saying registered and he nearly groaned out loud: the senator wasn't going to make an appearance here tonight.

He accepted the fresh glass of beer the waiter brought to him without question and tipped it to his lips, cursing the fact that he'd wasted his time—and his client's money—in attending this gala event. Hell, his whole trip to West Virginia might turn out to have been a waste of time.

Riane said goodbye to the older woman, turned back to him and smiled. Joel felt that quick punch of desire again and had to remind himself of all the reasons that the senator's daughter was off-limits.

She wasn't his type, anyway. She was too sophisticated and high class. Too everything. He preferred a woman with more simple tastes, more basic desires. And blond, he reminded himself, even as his fingers itched to pull the pins out of Riane's dark silky hair to let it tumble freely down her back.

Joel swallowed, hard. Yeah, he definitely preferred blondes.

Like the one beside the window, tall and slender in body-hugging green velvet. Her hand was on the arm of a short, portly man who looked old enough to be her father, but the hefty chunk of diamond on the woman's hand suggested otherwise.

Despite the ring and the presence of her companion, she caught Joel's eye and sent him a blatantly invitational glance from beneath lowered lashes. There was nothing complicated about that one, Joel thought approvingly. Except that he *never* cut in on another man's territory. It was one of few rules he lived by, and one he'd never consider violating. He knew too well how it felt to be on the other side of that equation.

''Meredith Ashcroft,'' Riane said, close to his ear. ''Of the Boston Ashcrofts—by marriage. Now divorced and currently engaged to Justice Cunningham.''

''The man in the ill-fitting tux?''

''That's the one,'' Riane agreed. ''He hasn't bought a new suit in the past ten years because he won't admit that he's put on forty pounds. He thinks he has the same physique that impressed his first wife. *She* left him more than a dozen years ago and took half his money. He still possesses a sizable fortune and an impressive position on the bench, which is why Ms. Ashcroft is in line to become wife number three.''

''A friend of yours?''

Riane's smile was thin. ''An acquaintance,'' she clarified. ''But I could arrange an introduction, if you wanted.''

''You said she was engaged.''

''Does that matter to you?''

''Yes.''

''A cop with morals,'' she mused.

''I'm not a cop,'' he said again.

''So you said. But you didn't say what you are.''

Not wanting to reveal too much about his reasons for being in West Virginia, he opted to try diversion again. ''Do you dance?''

She tilted her head. ''Is that a hypothetical question or an invitation?''

''An invitation.''

She studied him for another moment, as if considering his motives, then nodded. ''All right.''

Joel led the way to the dance floor, reassuring himself that he'd issued the invitation solely to prevent her from continuing her inquiry. He wasn't ready for her to find out who he was, his real reason for being there. Not until he knew whether or not she was the answer to his questions.

Then Riane put her hand in his, and desire surged through him. Hot and hard. And he knew that however he chose to rationalize the request in his own mind, the simple fact was that he'd wanted to hold her. She was sexy and beautiful and intriguing, and it had been far too long since he'd been with a woman.

The intensity of his own reaction shook him. He was a man of action, in charge of his life, responsible for his own decisions. Yet the moment she turned into his arms, he felt a spiraling sense of panic, a stunning realization that this was out of his control.

He'd only ever felt this way once before—toward the end of the Conroy investigation. Just as all the pieces seemed to be falling into place, he'd known that it had been a little too easy. He'd ignored the instinct, convinced himself it was paranoia.

He'd been wrong.

There was no way he'd make the same mistake again.

Okay, so maybe he was overreacting a little this time. Riane Quinlan was a woman. She might be beautiful, sexy, intriguing, but she was still just a woman.

Yet his instincts warned him that she was dangerous. Very dangerous. Because the scent of her clouded his mind; the subtle curves of her body made him forget his reason for being there; those full, painted lips tempted him to taste. Riane Quinlan made him not just forget, but *want* to forget, that she was off-limits.

Just a woman?

Like hell. This woman was more dangerous than a roomful

of Zane Conroy's trigger-happy minions with fully automatic Mac 10s.

He misstepped, and her hip brushed against his thigh. The fleeting contact jarred him, and he felt his blood begin to migrate southward. He forced himself to concentrate on moving his feet, determined to avoid any more such accidents so that she wouldn't notice how affected he was by her.

Not that his physical response should surprise her. He was, after all, just a man, and she was as warm and soft as the scent that clung to her. And she fit in his arms as if it was where she was meant to be.

Joel gave himself a mental shake. It was ridiculous to even imagine such things. Riane Quinlan might fit in his arms, but she could never fit into his life. Nor he in hers. He knew that opposites could attract. He also knew, from personal experience, that they couldn't coexist for very long.

"How long are you going to be in West Virginia?" Riane asked, breaking the silence that had stretched between them.

"I'm not sure," he responded, then he made the mistake of looking at her. She'd tilted her head upward to speak to him, and her glossy lips were mere inches from his own. He only needed to lower his head a fraction and he could taste her. It was a tempting proposition. Too tempting. Too dangerous.

He tore his gaze from her mouth, saw that she was watching him. Her own eyes were dark, aware. He'd feel much more confident in his ability to do his job if he could keep his distance from Riane Quinlan. And he wouldn't be able to keep his distance if she kept looking at him like that.

Focus, Logan.

Somewhere in the back recesses of his mind this niggling reminder from his conscience registered. He knew he was dangerously close to losing his focus, and he couldn't afford to make any mistakes. Not this time.

"Riane," he said. "That's a rather unusual name, isn't it?"

"It's a feminine form of Ryan, which is my father's name."

His preliminary investigation had revealed that fact, but he didn't know if the similarity was by design or coincidence. That was what he needed to find out, and that was why he needed to talk to the senator.

"Isn't your mother usually a supporter of the Quinlan Camp Charity Ball?"

So much for being discreet, he thought, as the question blurted out of his mouth. But he was more worried about self-preservation than discretion at this point.

If Riane was startled by the abrupt change of topic, she gave no indication of it. "Yes," she admitted. "And I was a little worried that her absence this year would affect attendance, but thankfully it hasn't been a problem."

"She won't be making an appearance tonight?"

"I doubt it." She smiled at him once more, drawing his gaze back to that luscious mouth, tempting him all over again. "She's in Thailand."

"Thailand?"

Riane nodded. "She and my father went on a cruise to celebrate their anniversary."

Joel expected to be annoyed, even angry, at this revelation. His sole purpose in being here this evening was to contact the senator. But it was difficult to be angry when there was a soft, fragrant woman in his arms. Impossible to be annoyed that his source of information had been wrong.

"How long will they be gone?"

"What is your interest in my mother, Mr. Logan?"

"Joel," he said, and smiled.

But she'd homed in on the direction of his questions and wouldn't be deterred. "What is your interest in my mother, *Joel?*"

"I was just hoping, since I was in town anyway, that I might have an opportunity to meet with the senator."

"Are you a Republican supporter?"

He realized, with reluctant admiration, that she was trying

to trip him up. And had he not done his homework thoroughly, she might have done so with that question. Her mother was a Democrat.

"I'm not a card-carrying member of any party," he told her.

He wasn't sure if his response convinced her, but she let it drop. Joel accepted the reprieve, recognizing that he'd have to be a little more subtle if he didn't want to raise Riane's suspicions any further.

Preoccupied with these thoughts, he failed to spot the photographer until the flash of the camera's bulb blinded him. He instinctively stepped away, crushing Riane's toes in his haste.

"Ouch."

"Sorry." He mumbled the apology automatically, concentrated on breathing to slow the rapid beating of his heart as different reminiscences assailed him. Flash after flash. The incessant glare blinding. Reporters shoving, shouting. Microphones thrust at him. Headline after headline. Day after day. Until he dreaded even leaving his home.

"Are you undercover?" Riane asked.

Joel scowled. "I'm *not* a cop."

"Then why did you jump three feet when that flashbulb went off?"

"I don't like having my picture taken."

"Why not?"

"I'm not very photogenic," he said dryly.

Riane laughed, and the soft, sexy sound was a welcome distraction from the recent direction of his thoughts.

"I doubt that," she said.

"I didn't know the press would be here," Joel admitted. But he should have known, and he should have been prepared.

"I would have been disappointed if they weren't," Riane told him. "The more publicity we can generate for the Quinlan Camp, the better. High-level exposure equates to high-level contributions."

He understood that. Just as he understood that Riane was accustomed to living in the spotlight—the last place Joel wanted to be. He'd had his life scrutinized by the media before, and he never wanted to live like that again.

He could only hope that some enterprising young reporter didn't dig deep enough to discover the identity of Riane Quinlan's dance partner. Then as soon as this case was closed, he'd be out of her life forever.

Still, as the song began to wind down, Joel found himself reluctant to let her go. He knew she was a distraction he could ill afford, a complication he wasn't prepared for, but he couldn't deny his attraction to her.

And when the final notes of the song merged into the first bars of the next, he didn't figure it would hurt to hold her just a little while longer.

Then there was a firm tap on his shoulder and a smooth, masculine voice saying, "If you don't mind, I'd like a dance with my fiancée."

Chapter 2

Riane felt the censure in Joel's gaze as he relinquished her hand to Stuart without comment and walked off the dance floor. She wanted to follow him, to explain, but pride prevented her from doing so. He had no right to make judgments about her, and besides, a well-bred lady didn't chase after any man.

Instead she concentrated her attention on her new dance partner, who had already swept her into his arms and was moving smoothly to the strains of the music. Stuart's movements were effortless, each step and turn flawlessly executed. There wasn't anything that he didn't do well, and he was an incredible dancer. But his touch didn't heat her blood the way Joel's had done. Her body didn't yearn to press close to his as it had when she'd been dancing with the mysterious Mr. Logan.

She pushed the traitorous thoughts impatiently aside. She was a twenty-four-year-old woman, not a hormonal adolescent. It wasn't like her to react to a man on such a primal level. Human beings were supposed to be civilized, to have power over their more basic urges.

Still, she couldn't deny that something about Joel Logan appealed to her on a most fundamental level. Unwillingly, her gaze strayed to the back of the room where he'd once again stationed himself.

The formality of his attire failed to disguise the raw power he exuded. He had to be well over six feet—as she'd had to tip her head to meet his gaze despite the three inches her heels added to her five-foot, ten-inch frame—with broad shoulders tapering to a trim waist and long, lean legs. Just the memory of those muscles, solid and unyielding, caused her breath to quicken, her pulse to race.

"You seem lost in thought," Stuart commented lightly.

Riane started, felt her cheeks flush. "Just tired."

"You've had a busy few weeks preparing for tonight."

"Yes," she agreed, grateful for his easy acceptance of her explanation. Still, she was embarrassed to admit, even to herself, that Stuart's absence had gone unnoticed until he'd interrupted her dance with Joel. She'd been so preoccupied with the success of the charity ball she hadn't spared him a single thought.

And then she'd met Joel Logan, and she hadn't thought about anything else.

She felt a twinge of guilt at the realization, but only a slight twinge. After all, she wasn't *really* engaged to Stuart Etherington III. Although they'd talked, in abstract terms, about marriage, she resented his reference to her as his "fiancée," as if their engagement was a fact rather than a possibility. But she wasn't in the mood to take issue with his vocabulary now. It had been a wonderfully successful evening and she wouldn't ruin it by bickering with him.

So she ignored the multitude of recriminations running through her mind and only said, "You were late."

"I'm sorry." His apology was more automatic than sincere. "I got tied up in meetings."

She wasn't surprised. Stuart had a successful corporate law

practice and was often required to work long into the evening and frequently on weekends. She knew his hours would grow longer still when he launched the political career he wanted so much.

"You missed dinner," she told him. "Cream of artichoke soup, warm chicken salad with rosemary dressing, poached salmon with tarragon sauce, champagne sherbet and peppered strawberries."

"That sounds much better than the Italian takeout I had delivered to the office."

"I'm sure it was," she agreed. "But as long as you paid for your ticket, I won't complain about the squandered meal."

"You're a mercenary." There was admiration mingled with amusement in his tone.

"This camp is important to me. And to the kids who visit every summer."

"I know," Stuart placated. "And, yes, I paid for my ticket."

She smiled. "Then I thank you for your support."

"Has it been a successful evening?"

"Very," she told him. "Even more so than last year."

"You have a knack for this sort of thing," Stuart told her. "Organizing, fund-raising, delegating. Valuable qualities in a politician's wife."

Riane's smile was strained. She resented Stuart's implication that tonight's charity ball was an exercise in politics for her; she hated that he couldn't understand how much the camp mattered.

And yet, despite this fundamental difference of opinion, Riane believed that they were well suited for one another. They had similar goals and interests. They'd both been raised in political families, and they both understood the expectations and responsibilities of living in the public eye.

She sometimes wondered if he was more attracted to her political connections than her person, but she could hardly judge him when her own motives were less than ideal. Ultimately she and Stuart wanted the same thing: the White House. He had the ideas and the connections to take him there, and when he did, Riane had no qualms about exploiting her position as his wife and first lady to focus attention on the plight of underprivileged children in this country and around the world.

Yes, her relationship with Stuart was exactly what she wanted. She just sometimes wished he made her feel...

The thought fizzled. She didn't know what was missing; she only knew that she wanted to feel the way she'd felt when Joel had held her in his arms.

She glanced toward the back of the room, searching, seeking.

But he was already gone.

Joel awoke the morning after the charity ball with the mother of all hangovers. He winced against the bright sunlight flooding through the window and cursed himself for not remembering to close the curtains the night before. Slowly he eased his legs over the side of the bed and found the floor. Satisfied that the world was once again solid beneath his feet, he scrubbed a hand over his cheek. It had been a lot of years since he'd drunk himself into a stupor, but he'd done it often enough in the past that he should have known better.

Women, he thought disparagingly. They were all the same. From his mother, who'd abandoned him when he was six, to Jocelyn, who'd dumped him with no hint of remorse when the going got tough, they weren't to be trusted. It was a lesson he should have learned long ago.

Unfortunately, he was a man, and there were times that basic urges couldn't be denied. But sex and love were different things, and he'd managed to avoid emotional entanglements for the most part. Since Jocelyn, anyway. He was smart enough and discerning enough to seek companionship from women who wanted the same thing he did: simple, uncomplicated sex.

Riane Quinlan had almost made him forget that. There was

nothing simple about the way she'd looked at him. Nothing simple about the feelings she'd roused inside him.

He shook his head, then winced at the explosion of pain that resulted from the movement. He'd obviously been too long without a woman if he could be taken in by a pair of dark eyes.

Cursing Shaun McIver for ever asking him to take on this case, everyone with any connection to the name Rutherford, and Riane Quinlan in particular, he stumbled to the bathroom and turned on the faucet. He splashed cold water on his face, then filled a glass and fished a couple of aspirin out of the bottle.

He winced again when the shrill ring of his cell phone echoed in the empty room. He might have been tempted to ignore it, but he knew the only person who would be calling this early on a Sunday morning was his partner. And Mike would only be calling if he had information to share.

"Logan."

"I tracked Felicia Elliott to Flint, Michigan," Mike said without preamble. "She was in a women's shelter there for a few months after she left her husband."

"Have you spoken to her?" Joel was less interested in the trail than he was in the results.

"She moved out several weeks ago."

"Where is she now?"

"The director of the shelter wouldn't give me that information."

Although Joel understood the reasons for such a policy, he was frustrated. Every time he started to make any headway in this case, yet another obstacle was thrown in his path.

"Maybe I should go to Michigan," he suggested. He needed to wrap this case up and move on to something else. Somewhere else. Anywhere but West Virginia.

"I wouldn't bother," Mike told him. "I left our number with the woman at the shelter. She agreed to pass it along to Felicia Elliott if she hears from her again."

Joel knew it was the best they could hope for, which only

frustrated him further. "Do you have any new leads to follow?"

"I could get in touch with Gavin Elliott again, to see if he's remembered any other details that might be helpful."

"Don't bother," Joel said, rubbing absently at the throbbing behind his temple. "It looks like we're just going to have to cool our heels on this one until we hear from Mrs. Elliott."

"You haven't made contact with the senator yet?" Mike asked.

"No," Joel admitted. "Apparently she's in Thailand."

"Thailand?"

"Yeah, that was pretty much my reaction," Joel agreed.

"Do you know when she'll be back?"

"Her daughter wasn't exactly forthcoming with the details."

"You've spoken to the daughter?"

Unbidden, a series of images came to mind. Riane moving toward him. Long legs, short dress, easy smile. Riane in his arms on the dance floor. Creamy skin, subtle curves, intoxicating scent. Riane with her fiancé.

Fiancé.

None of the information Joel had gathered indicated that Riane Quinlan was engaged, and he was certain something like that would have been splashed across all the society pages. Still, he'd recognized the man who'd intruded on their dance. Stuart Etherington III, a corporate lawyer at one of the biggest firms in nearby Huntington and an up-and-comer on the local political scene with big ambitions. Apparently Senator Rutherford-Quinlan's daughter was one of his ambitions.

"Joel?" Mike's voice intruded on his thoughts. "Did you meet with the daughter?"

"Yeah," he said again.

There was a brief silence on the other end of the line, then, "What was your impression?"

Long legs, short dress— Joel severed the thought abruptly this time. "I'd say there's more than a passing resemblance between the two women," he said instead. "And too many other coincidences to ignore."

His years on the police force had taught him to be wary of coincidences, and the scandal that ended his career had given him more than enough reason to distrust anyone with the name Rutherford.

When Joel had first started to examine the potential Rutherford connection in this case, Mike had accused him of letting his personal quest for vengeance interfere with his professional judgment. Joel couldn't deny that his impartiality had been compromised, but regardless of his personal feelings, facts were facts. And all the facts in this case had led him to West Virginia.

"I just can't believe that someone trying to pass off someone else's child as their own wouldn't at least change the name," Mike said.

"The spelling is different," Joel pointed out.

"So is the date of birth," Mike reminded him.

"Do you really think I'm looking for something that isn't there?"

"It would take quite a conspiracy to pull it off."

"Or a lot of money," Joel countered.

There was a long pause, then Mike said, "You know I have the greatest respect for your instincts, but I can't help thinking that your interest in this case is more about digging up dirt on the Rutherfords than finding the woman we're looking for."

"I know what my job is," Joel said coolly. But if he happened to find some dirt in the process of doing that job, he sure as hell wasn't going to wipe it off his hands and pretend it didn't exist.

"Okay," Mike relented.

Joel sighed as he disconnected the call. It looked as if he was going to be stuck in West Virginia for a while after all.

* * *

West Virginia.

He'd known that he'd find her. He hadn't expected it to be so easy. And he hadn't expected it to be in West Virginia.

He was a little disappointed. He'd wanted a challenge. A task worthy of his time and attention. She had rarely been either.

He should forget about her. He knew that was the smart thing to do. But he couldn't forget—or forgive—her betrayal.

She would pay for what she'd done.

But that was only the first part of his plan.

Four days after the charity ball, Riane hadn't stopped thinking about Joel Logan. Even sitting across from Stuart at their usual table at the Casa, where they dined every Wednesday night, she couldn't help but think about the other man.

It was because of Joel that she'd decided to shake up her relationship with Stuart a little. Maybe Stuart wasn't passionate with her, she reasoned, because she didn't inspire him to passion. So she'd bypassed the dark blue Chanel suit in favor of a scarlet silk A-line dress she'd bought several months earlier but hadn't yet found the courage to wear. The dress had a plunging neckline and a back slit that cut more than halfway up her thighs. It was bold, vibrant, daring. Everything she wasn't. Everything she wanted to be.

Stuart hadn't even commented on the dress except to say, as he always did, "You look lovely, Riane."

Not stunning.

Not sexy.

Lovely.

Several hours later, as Stuart pulled through the gates of the Quinlan estate, Riane found herself exhausted and frustrated. Dinner had been delicious, the service impeccable, their conversation monotonous.

It was all she could do not to scream.

When they arrived at the house, Stuart parked his Mercedes in front and came around to open her door. Always the gentleman, she thought, with an unfamiliar hint of resentment.

He walked with her up to the front porch, then touched his lips to hers. She willed herself to feel something, anything, in response to his kiss. But there was no tingle, no warmth, no desire. Nothing.

And then it was over.

"Good night, Riane."

"Good night, Stuart." She held back the sigh until he was in his car again and driving away.

Sophie was waiting for Riane when she stepped into the marble-tiled foyer.

"Good evening, Miss Quinlan."

The housekeeper's presence, as much as the formality she'd used, surprised Riane. "I told you not to wait up, Sophie."

"You have company, miss."

"Company?" Riane frowned.

"A gentleman." Sophie's eyes twinkled mischievously.

Riane's frown deepened.

"He's waiting in the den," Sophie told her.

Riane didn't want to deal with anyone else tonight. Her dinner with Stuart had been an exercise in monotony; his good-night kiss at the front door had left her uninspired. And she mentally damned Joel Logan for showing up at her charity ball and making her feel as though she was missing something.

All she wanted now was to slip into her favorite pair of satin pajamas and climb into bed. But she was a Quinlan, and the responsibilities she bore as such were equal to the rights and privileges. She squared her tired shoulders and turned toward the den.

The unnamed visitor was standing in front of the window, his back to the door. He didn't turn around; he didn't need to. Riane recognized him immediately. She wasn't sure if it was the breadth of his shoulders, the tension in his posture, or maybe just his aura. But she knew it was Joel, and her breath caught in her throat, her heart thudded heavily against her ribs.

She chided herself for the instinctive reaction. She was twenty-four years old, not a law school freshman enamored of the editor of the Law Review. But the feelings he stirred in her weren't so different from those she'd felt the first time she'd set eyes on Cameron Davis. And the first time he'd smiled at her, she'd been halfway in love.

The mental comparison terrified Riane. She didn't want to have these feelings again. She didn't want her emotions to be out of control. She didn't want to be vulnerable.

That niggling fear bolstered her lagging resolve. She wasn't twenty years old anymore—she was a woman. A strong, independent woman, and she could handle this man and her unexpected and inexplicable attraction to him.

"Mr. Logan," she said, in what she hoped was a casually disinterested tone.

He turned slowly, and she realized then that he'd been standing at the window watching for her. That he'd seen her arrive. That, in all likelihood, he'd seen Stuart kiss her good-night.

"Good evening, Ms. Quinlan."

She didn't insist that he call her Riane this time. She'd already decided it would be best to keep this man at a distance—as far a distance as possible. He was too potentially dangerous to her peace of mind to allow him to encroach on her carefully ordered life.

"How did you get in here?" she demanded.

"Your housekeeper, Sophie, let me in."

"I didn't mean into the house—I meant through the security gates."

"Sophie again," he told her.

Riane frowned. "She's not in the habit of opening the gates to strangers."

"But I'm not exactly a stranger, am I?"

"You are to Sophie."

"I told her that we'd met at the charity ball, and that I had something that belongs to you."

"And do you?"

He gestured to the wrap draped carelessly over the back of her father's chair. The velvet wrap that she'd belatedly realized she'd left in the ballroom.

"I didn't realize you worked in lost and found."

One side of his mouth kicked up in a half smile. "Apparently I do."

"Well, thank you for returning it."

"You're welcome."

But instead of moving toward the door, as she expected him to do, he leaned back against the corner of a bookcase and folded his arms over his chest. His pose was deliberately casual, his gaze leisurely as it skimmed over her. His self-confidence bordered on arrogance, the boldness of his stare almost insolent. It unnerved her, and aroused her.

"You look..." Joel paused, his deep blue eyes filled with heat as he sought the appropriate word to complete his thought, "...stunning."

Stunning.

Riane felt her cheeks flush with guilty pleasure. Why did it matter what Joel Logan thought? Why did his reluctant compliment mean so much to her when Stuart's words had only annoyed her?

The answer came quickly, unbidden. Because Joel Logan made her feel like a woman—feminine, attractive, desirable. With Stuart she only ever felt like an accessory—a suitable companion for any press conference or primary.

Uncomfortable with the comparison, with the feelings he stirred inside her, Riane refused to acknowledge the comment. "Was there something else you wanted, Mr. Logan?"

"I expected at least a few minutes of small talk, maybe the offer of a drink."

Riane bit back another sigh, resenting that the manners so carefully ingrained since childhood demanded that she participate in such formalities. But she'd managed to convince herself that Joel Logan had gone back to wherever he'd come from, and his unexpected appearance here—in her home—disconcerted her.

‘‘Forgive my lack of manners, Mr. Logan. It’s been a very long day and I wasn’t expecting company.’’ She didn’t care that her apology sounded more like an accusation. She would go through the motions, but that was all. ‘‘Would you care for a drink?’’

He inclined his head slightly, watching her intently. She stood firm, unflinching beneath his steady gaze.

‘‘I’ll have whatever you’re having,’’ he said at last.

She crossed over to the sideboard, removed the crystal stopper from the Waterford decanter and poured a generous amount of scotch into two highball glasses.

She passed one to him, careful that their fingers not brush in the transfer. She was determined to avoid any and all physical contact with him. She’d let him have his drink, find out what he wanted and send him on his way.

But Joel obviously had other plans, because he set his glass down on the shelf and brushed his fingers over her bare shoulder, down her arm, linking them loosely around her wrist. She felt the jolt of awareness reverberate through her system, sending tingles from the top of her head to the tips of her toes and all the erogenous zones in between. Still, she refused to let him see how he affected her, refused to let him know that her whole system went into overload when he touched her.

She looked at his hand on hers, raised a brow. Most of the men she knew would have taken the not-so-subtle hint and terminated the unwanted contact, but Joel either didn’t understand her signal or simply refused to comply with it. She suspected it was the latter.

‘‘How long have you been engaged?’’ he asked.

The abruptness of the question, as much as the hint of annoyance in his tone, startled her. ‘‘The engagement isn’t official yet,’’ she told him, silently wondering if it ever would be.

‘‘No wedding date set?’’

‘‘No.’’ She tugged out of his grasp and stepped away. She tipped her own glass to her lips and drank deeply, the scotch burning a fiery path down her throat that didn't compare to the heat on her arm where he'd touched her.

He picked up his glass again and sipped. "Nice scotch."

Riane downed the last of her drink, set the glass down with a snap. "Did you come her to discuss my wedding plans, my father's scotch, or was there something else you wanted?"

"Have I said or done something to upset you, Ms. Quinlan?"

Yes, damn it. She wanted to scream the words at him, to let her anger and frustration spill over. She'd been perfectly happy until Joel Logan had come into her life. Okay, maybe that wasn't entirely true. But she'd been content, for the most part, because she hadn't known what she was missing.

She still didn't know, but every time he looked at her, every time he touched her, he made her wonder.

"You're here," she said simply.

"I was thinking if either one of us had a right to be annoyed," he said casually, "it would be me."

"Why?"

"Because a woman who's engaged to be married shouldn't look at another man the way you were looking at me Saturday night."

She dropped her gaze and moved to refill her glass. "I'll apologize for the fact that you obviously misunderstood my intentions."

"I didn't misunderstand anything," Joel said coolly.

Riane lifted a shoulder in a careless shrug, raised the glass. Joel was at her side before it touched her lips, his fingers wrapped around the wrist that held her drink.

Her first thought was that he moved fast.

Her second, he was dangerous.

Her next, she wanted him.

It was irrational, it was insane, but in that instant, she knew it was true. It wasn't the subtle tug of desire she'd felt when she'd danced with him at the ball. There was nothing subtle about this at all. It hit her with the force of a runaway freight train, uncontrollable, unstoppable, undeniable.

Chapter 3

Joel could read the emotions reflected in her eyes.

Surprise. Awareness. Desire.

She wanted him; he wanted her. The attraction between them was simple. Unfortunately, everything else about the situation was not.

Her lips curved slightly and he tightened his grip. He prided himself on having a great deal of control but right now, he was very close to losing it. That sexy little smile almost put him over the top.

Almost.

He dropped Riane's wrist abruptly, unaccountably angry with her for the desire her mere presence stoked inside him. Angrier with himself for not being strong enough to resist. He knew he should back away. Better yet, he should leave—this house, this state. But he stayed where he was, mesmerized by her presence.

Her lips curved again. They were glossy and red, the same tempting shade as her figure-hugging dress and those killer shoes. At the charity ball she'd looked the part of a senator's daughter. Elegant, sophisticated, untouchable. Tonight she didn't look like anybody's daughter. She was all hot, steamy sex appeal in a beckoning package. And if she'd been *his* unofficial fiancée—not that *that* would ever happen—there was no way in hell he'd have said good-night at the door. But the proper Stuart Etherington III had, and his kiss hadn't even smudged Riane's lipstick.

"It's late, Mr. Logan, and I'm too tired for games. So why don't you cut to the chase and tell me why you're here?"

It was a valid question, but he'd forgotten all the reasons he'd contrived for his visit the minute he'd seen her get out of the car. Something about getting answers, he recalled vaguely. He'd decided that the senator's absence didn't have to be a complete roadblock to his investigation, it only required a slight detour. And spending some time with Riane might prove to be a very pleasurable side trip.

But face-to-face with her now, he felt a little uneasy about his agenda. He didn't want to be with Riane under false pretenses; he genuinely wanted to be with her. He wanted to know the woman behind the facade. He wanted to take his time and explore the attraction between them.

But his wants and desires were irrelevant here. His sole purpose for being in West Virginia was to finish the job he'd been hired to do. It was best to remember that, and to remember that a woman like Riane Quinlan was out of his league.

"It looks like I'm going to be in town a while," he said, "and I thought we could spend some time together while I'm here."

"Why?"

He shrugged. "I don't really know anyone else."

Her soft, smoky laugh went straight to his loins, making him again question the wisdom of the course he'd decided to pursue.

"That's the most unique, if not the most appealing, invitation I've ever received," she told him.

"Is that a yes?"

She shook her head. "I don't think so."

Joel nodded, as if her response was what he'd expected. "Your fiancé probably wouldn't approve."

"Stuart's not my fiancé," Riane said again. "And he doesn't dictate how I spend my time."

"Then there's no reason why you can't show me around."

"Except that I don't want to. I'm a busy woman, Mr. Logan."

"I'm sure you are," Joel agreed easily. "I just thought you might enjoy the opportunity to show an outsider the beauty and bounty of your home state."

"There are all kinds of tours you can take if you want to see the sights. You don't need my help for that."

"I was hoping for a more authentic experience."

She smiled again. "Authentic?"

There was something in the mischievous curve of her lips that set off warning bells, something in the gleam of those dark brown eyes that hinted at a secret agenda. Maybe he should back off, reconsider his plan. But he'd never been one to back down from a challenge.

"I'd like to do whatever native West Virginians would do if they had a few days to play."

She studied him for a long moment, considering. "What is it that you really want from me?"

Was she innately suspicious, or had his powers of persuasion been affected by his frustration with this assignment?

Determined to try harder, he smiled. "Just the pleasure of your company."

She raised an eyebrow.

"You're a beautiful woman, Riane. Intelligent, charming—when you want to be. Why do you find it so hard to believe that I want to spend time with you?"

"Most people who seek out my company are more interested in my political connections than sharing conversation," she said candidly.

"Including your fiancé?"

Her eyes narrowed, and her voice, when she responded,

could have frosted the windows. ‘‘My relationship with Stuart is none of your business.’’

‘‘Did I hit a nerve?’’

‘‘Not at all,’’ she denied in the same icy tone.

‘‘I’m sorry,’’ he said. And he was. Although he was curious about her relationship with the other man, he was sorry he’d put that guarded look in her eye.

Riane shrugged stiffly.

‘‘I’d appreciate it if you could find some time to show me the sights.’’

‘‘I’m going to be at the camp all day tomorrow.’’

‘‘What about Friday, then?’’

She hesitated.

‘‘Please.’’

Sighed. ‘‘All right. Where are you staying?’’

‘‘At the Courtland Hotel, downtown.’’

‘‘I’ll pick you up at ten o’clock. Wear something comfortable, casual.’’

‘‘Are you going to tell me where we’re going?’’

‘‘I’m going to show you some of West Virginia’s most impressive sights,’’ she promised.

But Joel didn’t wait until Friday to see her again.

He awoke in the morning determined to move on with his investigation. After all, that was his reason for being in West Virginia, and he was certain there must be other avenues to explore, other possibilities to examine.

According to the travel agent he’d consulted, the only cruise ship currently near Thailand had sailed out of Hong Kong nine days earlier and wouldn’t complete its journey until it reached Singapore in another six days. Which meant that he had six more days to wait—seven, if the senator and her husband stayed an extra night in Singapore. Surely, he could occupy himself for that amount of time.

Yet when he left the hotel late that morning, he found himself stopping at the front desk for directions to the Quinlan Camp—just in case. When he found himself following those directions, he told himself it was simple curiosity. When he pulled through the wrought iron gates, he figured she probably wasn't even there.

There were several cars parked outside a long, low building built of hand-hewn logs. Colorful blooms spilled out of the large clay pots that flanked either side of the wooden stairs.

Joel parked his dusty Explorer beside a shiny red pickup truck and got out to stretch his legs. It was still early in the day, and the breeze was cool, the air crisp and clean and scented with the tangy perfume of cedar from the surrounding woods. Having grown up in the city, he wouldn't consider himself a nature lover, but he couldn't deny the appeal of this place.

He followed the flagstone path to the wide porch that spanned the length of the building. There were three doors at evenly spaced intervals, the one on the far end slightly ajar. He made his way in that direction, and his heart did a slow roll in his chest as he heard Riane's voice coming from inside.

He paused with his hand against the heavy wood. The rational part of his brain reminded him that he shouldn't be here. There was nothing to be gained by pursuing the attraction between them.

Okay, maybe he was hoping that she could give him some of the answers he needed. And he hadn't completely disregarded the possibility that she *was* the answer he was seeking. But he wasn't entirely comfortable using her in such a subversive manner. He was even less comfortable with the feelings that were churning inside him. Feelings that had nothing to do with his reasons for coming to West Virginia and everything to do with the woman who was Riane Quinlan.

There was a pause in the conversation, and he realized that she was on the phone. Then she laughed, and he felt that quick punch of arousal in response.

He should get back in his truck and go.

He pushed open the door.

Riane glanced up, her eyes widening. First with surprise, then pleasure—just a quick, almost imperceptible glimpse of it, immediately supplanted by annoyance. She frowned.

"Someone just came in. Can you call me back later, Adam?"

Adam? Just how many men was Riane juggling in her life? And why was he willing to stand in line to be yet one more?

She nodded and doodled on the legal pad on her desk as she finished up her call. He took a moment to scan the room—utilitarian furnishings, unadorned walls, a few potted plants. It was safer than looking at Riane, at the loose-flowing tresses that framed her delicate features, at the soft pink lips that curved slightly in response to something he couldn't hear, at the close-fitting sweater that seemed to mold to her breasts—

He tore his gaze away.

"I'll talk to you later, then," she agreed.

She hung up the phone, then tilted her head to look up at him again.

"Mr. Logan." It was more of a question than a greeting.

Without waiting for an invitation he knew wouldn't be forthcoming, Joel folded his frame into one of the hard plastic chairs facing her. Riane picked up the mug of coffee on her desk, took a sip and grimaced.

"Do you want to take a break?" he asked. "We could go somewhere to get a hot cup of coffee."

She set the mug back down. "Why don't you tell me why you're really here?"

"I wanted to see you."

When she looked at him again, her deep brown eyes were wary.

"I didn't plan on coming here today," he admitted. "But I was lying alone in my bed last night, thinking about you. Then I woke up this morning thinking about you. And here I am."

"I'm not going to be a distraction for you while you're in town," she said.

"I just want to spend some time with you."

"I agreed to show you around tomorrow."

"I was bored today."

Riane sighed, shaking her head as she pushed her chair back from the desk and stood up. "Come on," she said. "I'll give you a tour of the camp."

It wasn't quite what he wanted from her, but he figured it was a start. So he walked around the grounds with her, listening as she explained the function of the camp, the program, her plans for expansion. She had such passion for the project, such focused enthusiasm. It was obvious the camp meant a lot to her, more than he'd realized during their brief discussion at the charity ball.

"This will be our fourth season," Riane said proudly. "And two of the counselors we've hired for this summer were campers here our first year."

"You must be very proud of what you've accomplished."

"For the most part," she agreed. "But there are still too many kids turned away each year simply because of the limited size of our facility."

"And that's why you're expanding?" he guessed.

"We have the space," Riane told him. "And, thanks to increased contributions this year, we have the funds. By the start of next season, we'll have six new cabins, each one designed to sleep five campers and a counselor."

"How many buildings do you have now?"

"Twelve cabins, a mess hall, an arts and crafts center," she gestured as she explained, "and the stables."

"Stables?"

She nodded and set off toward a fenced paddock he'd passed on the drive in. "We have half a dozen horses the children are taught to care for and ride."

"How many people work here?"

"In addition to the counselors, who are mostly volunteers, there's a registered nurse and child psychologist on staff. Plus

Jared, our horse trainer, year-round groundskeeper, camp supervisor and chef."

"Chef?"

"Someone has to feed the kids."

"How many kids?" Joel wondered aloud.

"We have sixty kids for each of four two-week sessions."

"That's a lot of macaroni and cheese."

"Jared does better than that," Riane assured him.

They stopped at the fence that bordered the paddock, leaning against the rails to watch the horses grazing.

"Have I bored you to death yet with all this stuff?"

Joel shook his head. "I think it's a wonderful thing you're doing."

"Even with the expansion, it won't be enough. We're considering weekend programs in the spring and fall in addition to the summer camp. In the not-too-distant future, I'd like to open another site—maybe in Virginia or Pennsylvania. Somewhere close by, so I can stay involved with both."

She sighed again, a heartfelt expression of frustration and futility. "Let's talk about something else," she suggested.

"Like what?"

"You."

He studied the pair of sleek, chestnut horses grazing contentedly in the paddock. "I'm not very interesting."

Riane clicked her tongue against the roof of her mouth in a sound of disapproval. "That's hardly the kind of statement to impress a woman," she chided.

Joel couldn't help but laugh. "What should I say?"

She shook her head. "I would have thought a guy like you would have figured that out by now."

"And I would think that a woman like you wouldn't be swayed by mere words."

She smiled now, and the curve of those soft, tempting lips did strange things to his heart again.

"You're right," she admitted.

Unable to resist, he reached out and skimmed the pad of his finger over her bottom lip. He heard her breath catch, watched her lips part slightly in response to his touch. When he looked up at her again, her eyes were wide.

"What would sway you, Riane?"

She swallowed, her scrambled brain desperately searching for coherent words to respond to his question. She had to say something, anything, to get him to back off. Anything but the truth. Because the truth was that all it would take to sway her was his touch. He hadn't even kissed her; he'd just brushed his finger over the curve of her lip and her insides had melted.

She'd experienced attraction before but never like this. The jolt of desire, so quick and unexpected, completely debilitated her.

He skimmed his knuckles over her cheek, threaded his fingers into her hair and tilted her head back. She forced herself to meet his gaze, then wished she hadn't done so. Tightly restrained passion simmered in the depths of his blue eyes. A challenge. A promise.

"What would sway you?" he asked again.

She swept her tongue along her bottom lip, unconsciously following the same path as his fingertip.

"Maybe you wouldn't be swayed at all," he murmured, his gaze fixed on her mouth again. "Maybe it would have to be your decision."

"Yes," she agreed breathlessly. Yes, it would be her decision. And yes, she wanted him.

"You're a strong woman," he continued, the low tone of his voice as hypnotic as the desire in his eyes. "Capable. Confident. Passionate."

Her heart melted just a little. No one had ever called her passionate before. No one had ever made her feel so passionate.

"And complicated," he finished, almost reluctantly, before combing his fingers through the ends of her hair and dropping his hand back to his side. "I don't have time for complications."

The desire he'd so effectively stirred up inside of her gave way to hurt and disappointment. She shoved those unwelcome emotions aside in favor of anger.

"What are you looking for, Logan, a quick tumble to satisfy your basic urges?"

"I wasn't looking for someone like you," he admitted.

"Then what are you doing here?"

He looked around, and seemed almost surprised by the setting. "I don't know," he said at last.

"I didn't ask you to come here."

"I know," he admitted. "And I thought I could stay away. But I can't. You've got me all tied up in knots and I don't know what to do about it."

As far as poetry went, it was somewhat lacking, and yet his words touched something inside her. Or maybe it wasn't the words so much as the frustration evident in his voice. He didn't want to want her, but he did. The realization soothed her bruised pride, empowered her fragile heart.

"I'm sorry," he said abruptly. "Why don't we just forget about that little outburst and start over?"

"Sure," Riane agreed, wishing it would be half as easy to forget the unwelcome feelings he'd stirred inside her. She folded her arms against the wooden fence. "Tell me something about yourself."

"What do you want to know?"

Everything. She wanted to know everything there was to know about Joel Logan, especially what it was about him that had her so enthralled. Through her charity work and her parents' political connections, she'd had occasion to dine with millionaires, dance with movie stars, discuss international relations with heads of state. She'd never been flustered by the mere presence of a man—until Joel had shown up at her ball.

But that was hardly an admission she was willing to make, so she opted to start with something more simple. "Where did you grow up?"

He seemed surprised by her question, almost relieved. ''Philadelphia.''

''Is that where you live now?''

He shook his head. ''No. I moved to Fairweather, Pennsylvania, a few years back.''

''Is that where your family is?''

''I don't know that I have any family left.''

''What do you mean—you don't know?''

''I haven't seen my mother since I was six years old. She left me with my grandmother and took off for parts unknown. My grandmother died five years later.''

''Oh,'' she said, feeling unaccountably saddened on his behalf. Her mother often teased that the kids who came to her camp were her surrogate siblings—the brothers and sisters she never had. Riane couldn't deny that there was probably some truth to that. But if she felt there was something missing from her life, she also knew how fortunate she was to have always had the unquestioning love and support of her parents. She couldn't imagine what it would be like to be well and truly alone.

''What about your father?'' she asked.

''I have no idea who my father is.''

''You never knew him?''

''I don't know if my mother knew him,'' he said dryly.

Her brow furrowed; Joel laughed.

''Not everyone has had the life you've had,'' he said.

Riane felt her back go up. ''What's that supposed to mean?''

''You were raised in a perfect little family, in a cozy mansion on the hill. Between your private school education and ballet lessons and horseback riding, you probably never imagined that there were kids who went to bed hungry at night—or kids who had no bed to go to.''

Riane's eyes narrowed on him. ''Do you think I don't realize how lucky I've been? I may gave grown up in a home of wealth and privilege, and I'm grateful that I've never had to worry about my next meal, but I'm not oblivious to what goes on in the rest of the world.

"My parents were in the Foreign Service when I was born. We lived in various places in Central America, Eastern Europe, Africa. It was an incredible opportunity, and it was incredibly disheartening at times. I saw things most people don't want to hear about.

"I went to visit orphanages with my mother—dirty, overcrowded, unsanitary buildings where most of the children weren't just orphans but were sick or dying. There was one little girl—" Even after so many years, her throat tightened at the memory. "She was about three years old, but she weighed no more than fifteen pounds. She wasn't just malnourished, she had AIDS. Both of her parents had died of AIDS a few months earlier, her older sister only days before I met her.

"There was something about her, this child more so than any other I'd seen, that tore at my heart. Maybe it was the way she so simply and quietly accepted her fate. Knowing it was only a matter of time before she died.

"For almost three weeks, I went to that orphanage every day—to see her, to read stories to her. She loved fairy tales. As she listened, she'd smile and get this faraway look in her eyes, as if she was imagining herself inside the story—a life so much better than the one she was living.

"So don't you dare compare my life to yours and say I don't understand. Why don't you stop feeling sorry for yourself for five minutes and compare your life to hers?"

Riane was out of breath by the time she finished, and a little ashamed by her impassioned outburst. It wasn't like her to go off so easily. She was used to people making judgments about her, treating her commitment to the underprivileged like a hobby or, worse, a stage she would outgrow.

Even Stuart had once suggested that she was too involved with the kids, that she needed to detach herself from their problems. He'd only said it once.

Still, Joel couldn't have known the depth of her feelings, and she shouldn't have taken her annoyance out on him.

"You're right," he said at last. "I'm sorry."

"Forget it." She was more embarrassed than angry now.

"I guess I've spent so much time being bitter and resentful about my childhood that I never considered the others who were less fortunate. My grandmother might have bitched and grumbled every time she put a plate in front of me, but she never let me starve."

She felt his hand on her arm, his touch gentle but firm, forcing her attention back to him. "The little girl in the orphanage, is she the reason you have the camp?"

Riane nodded. "She died just a few weeks after we got there. That was when I resolved to do something to help children like her."

"How old were you?" he asked.

She looked away again. "Twelve."

"That's a hell of a commitment for a twelve-year-old to make."

"It's a hell of a way for a three-year-old child to die," she replied sadly. Then she shook her head, shook off the melancholy mood that had stolen over the moment.

"We were talking about your childhood," Riane reminded him.

"I think you got the gist of it."

"Do you have any brothers or sisters?"

He shook his head. "I had a sister. She was a few years older than me, took off on her own when she was fifteen and died on the street of a drug overdose less than a year later."

"I'm sorry," she said, meaning it. As an only child, she couldn't imagine what it was like to grow up with someone, to lose that someone, to be left alone to remember. For so many years she'd wished for a sister—would willingly have settled for a brother—but her parents hadn't been able to have any more children. Riane knew it had to be easier to have never had a sibling than to have shared such a connection and have it ripped away.

He shrugged. "It was a long time ago."

"You were close," she guessed.

"At one time." Then, in a not-so-subtle effort to change the topic, "Will you have dinner with me tonight?"

Riane shook her head. She'd agreed to play tour guide for him to prove that she was her own person—and to prove to herself that she was immune to whatever chemistry she thought existed between them. Her reaction to his unexpected appearance at the camp today proved otherwise. She wasn't immune at all.

She'd never believed in chemistry or destiny or any other such nonsense. But the more time she spent with Joel, the more she found herself questioning her beliefs. Rational or not—and she was pretty sure it was *not*—she was attracted to Joel Logan. Which was why she was determined to keep her distance from him as much as possible. She may have already committed herself to showing him around the following day, but that was going to be the extent of her involvement.

"Do you have other plans for dinner?" Joel's question interrupted her meandering thoughts.

"Yes."

"With the fiancé?" Joel prompted.

"No."

Joel didn't take the hint. "What are you doing?"

"Not that it's any of your business," Riane said, "but I told Sophie I'd be home to eat."

"What's she making?"

"Pot roast."

"Sounds better than anything room service has to offer," Joel said hopefully.

"I'm not inviting you to my house for dinner." Although there was a part of her that wanted to do just that. She was intrigued by this man who'd appeared in her life seemingly from nowhere. She wanted to spend time with him, to get to know him. All she really knew was that he was a former cop who lived in Fairweather, Pennsylvania. These sparse details didn't begin to satisfy her curiosity.

Despite her curiosity, though, she was afraid. Not of Joel, but of her own responses to him. And it was this fear that held her back.

''Please.''

She sighed again. Although she knew it could be dangerous to spend more time with him, they wouldn't be alone together. Sophie would be there.

So she relented, not entirely unwillingly, to his request. ''Dinner will be on the table at seven o'clock.''

Chapter 4

At precisely seven o'clock, Riane found herself seated across from Joel at the gleaming mahogany table in the Quinlan dining room. On her way home from the camp, she'd called Sophie to tell her Joel would be coming for dinner, and Sophie had set the table with the best china, sparkling crystal and gleaming silver. As if that wasn't enough, she'd added long, slender candles in antique holders and opened a bottle of Riane's favorite merlot.

It was obvious, at least to Riane, that Sophie was setting the scene for romance. But Riane wasn't looking for romance—not with anyone, and especially not with Joel Logan.

Still, that wasn't the worst of the housekeeper's betrayal. Worse, far worse, in Riane's mind, was that Sophie had set the table for two. Sophie usually took her meals with the family, but tonight she'd begged off, leaving Riane to dine alone with Joel—the exact scenario Riane had been confident she could avoid by inviting him to the house.

"That was the best pot roast I've ever had," Joel told Sophie when she came to take their empty plates away.

Sophie beamed at him as though he was a favorite child. "Are you sure I can't offer you another helping?"

"I'm sure," Joel said. "I've already had seconds."

"Then I'll leave the two of you to finish up your wine before I bring out dessert," Sophie said, slipping out of the room as quickly and quietly as she'd slipped in.

"I'm glad you invited me for dinner," Joel said to Riane.

"You invited yourself," she reminded him.

"And you very graciously didn't withdraw the invitation."

Riane felt a reluctant smile tugging at her lips. They both knew there had been nothing gracious about her response.

"Don't do that," Joel warned.

The blossoming smile faded. "Don't do what?"

"Smile. If you do, you might have to admit that you don't detest my company as much as you want to, sweetheart."

"If I really disliked your company, I wouldn't be in it."

"But you're not entirely comfortable with me," he noted. "Why is that?"

She sighed and pushed away from the table. He stood, too, and followed her to the enormous arched window that overlooked the backyard.

"Because I don't know anything about you. Every time I ask a question about what you do or why you're in town, you evade or mislead or redirect the conversation. For all I know, you could be a tabloid reporter or a con man or—"

"A private investigator," he interjected.

"What?"

"I'm a private investigator."

"Oh." She took a minute to absorb that tidbit of information. "Why are you in Mapleview?"

He hesitated.

"Are you going to evade, mislead or redirect this time?"

He smiled, and Riane felt her heart skip a beat.

"I'm thinking about how to answer without revealing any confidential information."

She took a sip of wine, waiting.

"I'm looking for someone," he said at last. "A potential witness to a case I'm working on."

"Oh," she said again. "Why couldn't you tell me that the other night?"

His lips curved again and his eyes were dark, intense as they pinned her with a look that caused her blood to heat. "I wasn't thinking about business when I was with you."

It was a smooth response, and evasive. Again. She shook her head. It shouldn't matter. It *didn't* matter. Joel Logan was none of her concern. As soon as he finished whatever business had brought him to town, he would be gone, out of her life forever. Except that she couldn't shake the uneasy feeling that his business would somehow affect her.

"Why were you at the charity ball?"

His hesitation seemed answer enough.

"You're looking for someone I know."

"I'm following a lead," he admitted.

"Is it someone who's involved with my camp?" She sent up a silent but fervent prayer that the answer would be no. She couldn't bear to think of anything negative impacting her camp and the children who so desperately needed it.

"It has nothing to do with your camp," Joel assured her.

Riane wanted to believe him, but—

"I promise." He interrupted her thoughts with his softly spoken vow. "I know I should have told you, but my interest in you seems to have taken precedence over the case I'm working on."

"I thought your interest in me was solely as your tour guide."

"I lied," he said easily.

Riane lifted an eyebrow.

"Would you have agreed to spend tomorrow with me if I'd admitted I had designs on your body?"

"I can still change my mind."

"You won't. You're not the type of woman who would consciously break a promise. Now you'll just have to take your chances with me."

"I thought it was a violation of your personal code to move in on a woman who is otherwise involved."

"It is," he agreed. "But you've convinced me that you and Stuart aren't engaged."

"Not officially."

"Make up your mind, Riane." He took a step closer, and she took an instinctive step back. It was only when she felt the heavy velvet curtains behind her that she realized she'd been retreating. She forced herself to stand her ground; she wouldn't let him intimidate her.

"You can't use your relationship as a shield when it suits your purpose," Joel said, the low timbre of his voice sliding over her like a caress. "Are you engaged...or not?"

Her throat was dry, her heart pounding. Unconsciously she swept her tongue along her bottom lip to moisten it. His gaze dropped to her mouth, lingered.

"No," she admitted breathlessly.

He leaned closer, and when he spoke again she could feel the warmth of his breath on her cheek. "Then I don't have to worry about violating my personal code, do I?"

She didn't know what to say, how to extricate herself from the situation. She only knew that it was what she had to do. What she really wanted to do, however, was to breach the few scant inches that separated them and touch her lips to his. She wanted to—

"I have cheesecake," Sophie said, returning with two dessert plates in hand and effectively cutting off Riane's building fantasy in midstride. "And fresh strawberry sauce."

Joel stepped back, and Riane exhaled slowly. She should be relieved by Sophie's interruption, but she was unaccountably disappointed instead.

"Mr. Logan was just saying that he has to get back to his hotel," Riane said.

"I'm sure I have time for cheesecake," Joel countered.

Riane glared at him; Joel grinned.

And in that moment, Riane knew that he knew exactly how

his almost-kiss had affected her, how much she'd wanted to experience the touch of his mouth against hers.

"Good," Sophie said, apparently oblivious to the undercurrents passing between Riane and Joel. "I'll bring in coffee for you to have with your dessert."

Riane couldn't sleep, and she knew without a doubt that Joel Logan was responsible for her sudden bout of insomnia. Just as she knew it had been a mistake to invite him to come for dinner—even if it had been his suggestion rather than her own. It had been an even bigger mistake to agree to see him tomorrow.

She had so many other things she should be doing—obligations and responsibilities. She didn't have time to play tour guide for some bored, out-of-town P.I. And she wasn't sure she had the willpower to continue to resist the desire inside her.

With a groan of frustration, Riane pushed back the covers and commenced pacing the length of her bedroom. Pacing helped her to think, to get her thoughts in line and clear out her brain. But she knew, on some basic level, that it wasn't her brain that was the problem. It was her heart.

She groaned again, annoyed with herself for such fanciful notions. Whatever was wrong with her had more to do with her hormones than her heart. Hormones that had been stirred by Joel Logan's mere proximity and that continued to churn restlessly.

She sank down on the edge of her four-poster bed. Why was she so attracted to a man who was so obviously wrong for her? Was there something innately masochistic about her that she was destined to fall for men who could only break her heart?

She pushed herself to her feet again and resumed pacing. She didn't believe in destiny, and she was *not* going to fall for Joel Logan. She couldn't deny that she was attracted to him—what living, breathing, heterosexual woman wouldn't be? But feeling an attraction and acting upon it were completely different things. And Riane had no intention of acting upon this insane attraction.

Besides, she was involved with Stuart. Stuart was a good man—solid, stable, dependable. After her disastrous relationship with Cameron Davis, that was all she wanted.

Then why, a nagging voice from deep in her subconscious wondered, was she feeling so unsettled? And why was she pacing the floor of her bedroom at 3:00 a.m.?

Unable to answer either of these questions, Riane found herself reaching above her dressing table and plucking a toy from the shelf. Her action may have seemed random, but the doll she instinctively sought out was the one she'd called Eden for as long as she could remember. The one she'd always found gave her a measure of peace and comfort when nothing else could.

She couldn't recall when she'd started her collection, and she had dolls from various countries around the world, but Eden had always been her favorite. She smiled wryly in the darkness, embarrassed to admit—even to herself—that she still found solace in the tattered old doll.

She turned back toward the bed as a soft knock sounded at the door, immediately contrite that her nocturnal wandering had awakened the housekeeper. "Come in, Sophie."

The door pushed open, light spilling into Riane's bedroom from the hallway. The housekeeper followed, an elegant gold-rimmed cup in her hand.

"You're restless tonight," Sophie commented, offering the drink.

Riane set Eden down on her pillow and cradled the delicate china between her palms. She raised the cup and inhaled the sweet scent of chocolate. Sophie had played a key role in Riane's upbringing. She understood Riane's moods and needs, and she knew there was nothing that worked better than chocolate when she was feeling unsettled.

"I didn't mean to wake you," Riane said. "Please, go back to bed."

"You didn't wake me," Sophie told her, picking up the

doll Riane had set aside. She smoothed back the tangled hair, straightened the faded skirt of her dress. Riane hid a smile behind the cup as she sipped. It was Sophie's nature to want to fix and soothe, even when it wasn't always possible.

"Do you want to talk about it?" Sophie asked.

Riane wasn't sure she could talk about feelings she didn't understand. She was an intelligent, educated woman, yet the intensity of her reaction to Joel Logan continued to baffle her. "I don't know."

"It's Mr. Logan," Sophie guessed.

"It isn't always about a man," Riane chided, trying to deflect Sophie's focus.

"It is when you're pacing in your bedroom at 3:00 a.m."

Riane frowned. Being up in the middle of the night wasn't usual for her. "I've *never* been up pacing at this hour."

Sophie's smile was smug. "Exactly."

"Sophie, you know that I'm going to marry Stuart."

"I know that you *think* you're going to marry Stuart."

Riane took another sip of hot chocolate. "I thought you liked Stuart."

"I like him well enough for a politician."

"Sophie." Such a statement was almost sacrilege in the Quinlan household, but Riane grinned.

"He's not right for you," Sophie insisted.

"He'd make a good husband," Riane said loyally, wondering why she sounded unconvincing even to her own ears.

"You need someone who can put a sparkle in your eye, a flush in your cheek."

"This is reality," Riane said dryly. "Not a fairy tale."

"The flush in your cheeks was real enough when Mr. Logan was here."

And just the memory of the almost-kiss Sophie had interrupted caused Riane's cheeks to flush with color again. She hid behind the heirloom cup, sipped the hot drink.

"I've seen the way he looks at you and the way you look at him," Sophie told her. "There's chemistry there."

"I never was any good at science," Riane said lightly.

''You can joke about it, but you can't deny it.''

Riane sighed. ''Okay—I'm attracted to him.''

''And that scares you,'' Sophie guessed.

''I haven't felt this way since I met Cameron Davis in my first year of law school.'' It was the only time she'd allowed her hormones to overrule her head, and the results had very nearly been disastrous. She refused to make the same mistake again.

''You won't ever be happy if you don't follow your heart.''

''I'm happy with Stuart,'' Riane told her, but even to her own ears she didn't sound very convincing.

Sophie snorted. ''Then why haven't you told Mr. Logan to stop coming around?''

''I did.''

''And then you invited him for dinner.''

''He invited himself,'' Riane felt compelled to point out.

''He wouldn't have been here if you didn't want him to be.''

''He's very persistent.''

Sophie chuckled.

''All right,'' Riane admitted. ''And maybe I enjoy his company.''

''Maybe?''

Riane shrugged, unwilling to make any further admission. Unable to express feelings she didn't understand. The initial attraction had been purely physical. She'd spotted Joel Logan from across the room at the charity ball and had immediately been intrigued. But it was more than that. There was something about him that tugged at her—something even stronger than the self-protective instinct that warned her away.

She finished the creamy chocolate drink in one long swallow, then feigned a yawn. ''I can probably sleep now.''

''All right, then,'' Sophie relented, taking the cup from Riane and exchanging it for the doll she still held in her arms.

''Thank you, Sophie.'' Riane's comment referred to both the hot chocolate and the understanding.

Sophie nodded and kissed her cheek. ''Sweet dreams.''

But when Riane finally fell asleep with her doll in her arms, she dreamed of a little girl crying.

Joel was waiting in front of the Courtland Hotel at precisely ten o'clock Friday morning when Riane pulled up in her snazzy little BMW coupe. It was a gorgeous car, and as he slid into the passenger seat of the vehicle, he noticed the driver was gorgeous, too.

She was wearing a red scoop-necked T-shirt and softly faded jeans. Her hair was tied away from her face today, and he itched to loosen the band around the end of the braid and sift his fingers through the silky tresses.

He heard her speak but had been too preoccupied with his little fantasy to decipher the words.

''Did you say something?'' he asked, buckling his seat belt.

She gave him a strange look, then glanced down at his feet. ''I asked if those were sturdy shoes?''

Joel looked down at the loafers he'd donned with khakis and a golf shirt. ''As long as you don't intend to take me rock climbing, I think they're adequate.''

''All right.'' She pulled away from the curb, merging smoothly into the flow of traffic.

''We're not going rock climbing, are we?'' he prompted.

''No, we're not going rock climbing.''

He waited a beat, but she offered no additional information. ''Where are we going?''

''Caving.''

''Oh.'' It seemed harmless enough, if he could forget that he hated close, dark spaces. If he could forget about the day he'd been lured into Conroy's deserted warehouse and trapped for hours with the dank smell and fetid rats.

He rubbed a hand over the scar on his abdomen and tried to relegate the memories and frustrations to a back corner of his mind. There was no point in thinking about any of that now, nothing to be gained by recalling the sense of futility that had plagued him for so long.

Instead, he concentrated on the scenery as Riane drove toward Charlotte's Corridor.

"So named," she explained, "because the man who discovered the underground caverns, David Charlotte, couldn't believe that such an elaborate system of interconnecting tunnels was a naturally occurring phenomenon. He believed they had to be a corridor to some kind of underground civilization."

Riane pulled into a gravel parking lot. "He passed away before anyone could disprove his theory, and the caves have been known as Charlotte's Corridor ever since."

There were several other vehicles already in the lot, a few people wandering around. There were picnic tables in a shaded area at the far end of the parking lot along with a simple square building that advertised tourist information and public rest rooms. What he didn't see was a ticket booth or concession stand or any other inherent signs of what a city dweller would consider civilization. His sense of apprehension magnified.

"These caves have almost twenty-five miles of mapped passages," Riane told him, pulling a canvas backpack out of the trunk. "It's one of the more elaborate systems in this part of West Virginia."

He had no idea whether he should be impressed or not. He couldn't imagine that they'd be expected to walk twenty-five miles—that would take days.

Riane took a long-handled flashlight out of the bag, flicked the switch, then tucked a spare package of batteries into the back pocket of her jeans.

"Where's the rest of the group?" he asked, following her to the mouth of the cave.

She glanced at him over her shoulder, frowned. "What group?"

Uh-oh. "Isn't this a tour?"

She shook her head. "I thought you wanted to experience West Virginia like a native."

He wasn't entirely comfortable with the note of challenge in her voice. Less so facing the huge, black hole in the wall of rock in front of him. "I've reconsidered," he muttered.

She laughed, and his irrational fear receded. He would walk naked through all twenty-five miles of cave to hear that sound again. She had such an incredible laugh. Low and smoky, unconsciously seductive.

"Don't be such a wimp, Logan. The only way to see the caves properly is to explore them on your own."

Joel plunged into the mouth of the cave behind her. There was no way he was going to let her call him a wimp.

Still, he was unprepared for the sudden and complete darkness. It descended thick and fast, obliterating everything else. Riane had a flashlight but he didn't, and the fragile beam from her light dispersed quickly in the large passageway. He could see nothing but dark, feel nothing but damp, and his breath started to come in short, shallow bursts as the horror of that day in the warehouse ambushed him again.

Focus, Logan. He closed his eyes, inhaled a deep breath. The air was cool and moist, but not foul. He opened his eyes again, took a tentative step forward.

"I think I'd like to try a museum tomorrow," he said.

Riane laughed again. He let the sound envelop him, blocking out the awful memories. There was no one here but Riane and him. The reminder was not only reassuring, it was inspiring. He was alone in the dark with a beautiful woman. Maybe this outing had some potential after all.

It only took a couple of twists and turns for him to realize that Riane was a veteran of caving. She moved easily through the winding chambers while he stumbled along, trying not to think about the fact that he had absolutely no idea of where he was going—or where the men with the guns were hiding.

"Maybe we should have taken one of the guided tours," Joel commented from somewhere behind her, cursing under his breath as he tripped over yet another unseen obstacle protruding from the ground.

She reached behind her to take his hand, and he happily linked his fingers through hers.

Riane continued to move ahead, unhampered by the close confines, navigating the narrow corridors and tight corners without difficulty. Of course, *she* was the one with the flashlight.

He had no idea how long they'd been inside the maze of tunnels when she stopped abruptly. Joel bumped into the back of her, mumbling a quick apology as he stepped back again.

"What's the matter?" he asked.

"Dead end," she said, turning to face him.

"We're lost?" He hated the note of panic in his voice, hoped she didn't recognize it as such.

"No, we're not lost," she chided. "We just have to follow this corridor back the way we came and turn around. All the tunnels are interconnected, like a maze. They twist and turn in all directions. A few are dead ends, but eventually they all lead back to the amphitheater."

"Amphitheater?"

"The big chamber that we started out from."

"Oh." It seemed simple, and she sounded confident enough that his uneasiness abated.

Then she moved forward, as if to step past him, and the side of her breast brushed against his arm. The current of awareness jolted him, and he heard her sharp intake of breath. Obviously, he hadn't been the only one affected.

"We have to follow this, um, corridor back," she said again.

"I heard you the first time. I was just thinking that, since we're not lost, there's really no hurry."

"Yeah." She cleared her throat. "There is."

"Why?"

"It's getting hot in here."

"Yeah," he agreed. "It is." He reached out, his hand

coming into contact with her bare arm. Her skin was soft, but he could feel the tension in her muscles. He trailed his fingers down her arm, felt the goose bumps rise on her flesh. He caught her hand, slid his palm against hers, linked their fingers together.

He knew she had the flashlight in her other hand, but the beam of light was directed at the ground, unseen, forgotten. The darkness didn't seem so ominous now, and in the pitch-blackness of the cave, his other senses were heightened.

He could smell the scent of her perfume. Light and spicy. He could feel the heat from her body and the tension in it. He heard her exhale, slowly, deliberately. And he could hear the beating of her heart, loud and fast. Or maybe it was his own.

''We agreed we weren't going to do this,'' she said, her voice slightly breathless, unsteady.

''Yeah,'' he confirmed, before his mouth touched hers. Softly. Gently. A fleeting caress.

He felt her stiffen, but she didn't pull away.

He brushed his lips against hers again, lingered this time. A low hum sounded deep in her throat, then her lips softened beneath his and she was kissing him back.

Her response was hesitant at first, almost uncertain. He wanted to take it slow, to savor the moment. But when her lips parted willingly beneath the pressure of his, the tenuous thread of his control snapped. His tongue dipped into her mouth, tasting, testing. She met his searching thrusts with her own, and he was lost.

He groaned, helpless to do anything but surrender to the desire. The depth of her passion stunned him. This was a woman who would hold nothing back, who would demand as much as she gave. And right here, right now, he could refuse her nothing.

It was a terrifying realization for a man who not only prided himself on his independence but guarded it fiercely. He had no time for distractions, no interest in complications. Riane Quinlan was both.

She was also soft and warm and she tasted like heaven.

He had decided there was no harm in savoring the kiss a little longer when he was blinded by a sudden flash of light. Riane pulled away abruptly as a voice came through the darkness.

"Sorry, man. We didn't know this one was taken."

The young, masculine voice was followed immediately by a younger, girlish giggle.

The beam of light that had flashed in his face dropped to the ground, illuminating a couple of cigarette butts, a crushed pop can, a discarded condom package.

Then the light was gone, the voices of the lustful teenagers drifted down the corridor, and he and Riane were alone again.

Or rather he was alone.

He'd felt her push past him, but he hadn't realized she'd moved away until he reached for her and she wasn't there.

"Riane?"

There was no response.

Joel felt a first bead of sweat trickle between his shoulder blades. He closed his eyes and took a deep breath, tried to remain calm despite the fact that he couldn't see four inches in front of his face.

"Riane?" he said again.

Chapter 5

Riane leaned back against the hard rock of the cavern wall, taking slow, deep breaths and willing her knees to stop trembling. Her entire body felt flushed, hot, despite the cool air inside the cave.

She started when she heard Joel calling to her, but she couldn't respond. Not yet. She needed a minute to regain her composure. She was still too shaky to face him.

It had been a mistake to bring him here. She knew that now. She should have taken him to the art gallery or the museum of technology or a minor league baseball game. Somewhere bright and noisy and filled with other people. Somewhere he wouldn't have been able to get close enough to kiss her.

But no, she'd had to bring him to Charlotte's Corridor—dark and quiet and isolated. What had she been thinking?

Obviously, she hadn't been. She'd been annoyed by some of the statements he'd made the previous afternoon at the camp—assumptions he'd made about who she was and what she did. He would have expected an art gallery or a museum, and she'd been determined to shatter his expectations.

Now, after the way she'd responded to his kiss, he probably thought she'd led him into that dead-end tunnel on purpose. And maybe subconsciously she had. Ever since that first night, when he'd held her on the dance floor, Riane had been fighting against the attraction growing inside her.

She leaned her head back against the rock and closed her eyes, fighting against the urge to scream out her frustrations. She could just imagine the headlines in tomorrow's paper if she gave in to the impulse: Senator's Daughter Has Episode in Charlotte's Corridor. People would think she was as crazy as David Charlotte himself.

She heard Joel call to her again, a hint of fear evident in his tone. She shouldn't have left him alone, or she should have left him the light. Her decision to bring one flashlight had been deliberate and, yes, petty. But she'd needed to assert herself as the one in control of the situation, because every time she was near Joel Logan she felt completely out of control. Today had been no different despite the instrument in her hand.

She directed the light at the cavern floor and pushed away from the wall. The meager beam helped her navigate her way through the maze of tunnels, but it gave no answers on how she was supposed to deal with Joel.

"I'm here," she called out, hating that her voice didn't sound entirely steady.

"I thought you'd left me."

She stepped closer to the direction from which his voice was emanating. "Sorry. I forgot I had the light."

She wished she had a second flashlight to give him, but because she didn't, she was forced to reach out and take his hand again. His fingers, warm and strong, wrapped around hers. It should have been no more personal than holding the hand of a child, but there was something incredibly sensual about the way his much larger hand engulfed hers, something undeniably seductive about the touch of his palm against hers.

She cleared her throat. "Follow me."

"I'm as anxious to get out of here as you are, sweetheart," Joel said. "But I think we should talk about what happened."

"Not necessary," Riane told him, tugging on his hand.

But he was bigger and stronger and he wouldn't be budged. "Do you want me to apologize for kissing you?"

His voice had dropped to little more than a whisper, the husky cadence doing strange things to her insides. "No," she said simply, hoping he would let the matter drop.

He didn't.

"Good. Because I'm not going to." He traced circles over the inside of her wrist with the pad of his thumb, and she knew he would feel her pulse jolt in response to the lazy caress. "I've been thinking about kissing you for a long time. Probably since that very first night, the first time I held you in my arms."

She'd thought about it, too. Far more than she should have. She'd wondered how it would feel, the pressure of his mouth on hers, the touch of his hands on her. Now she knew, and the reality had far exceeded any of her fantasies.

But she couldn't admit that to him. So she just shrugged, as if the earth-shattering kiss hadn't affected her at all. "It wasn't a big deal."

She repeated those words again and again to herself as she led the way out of the caves. Maybe if she said them often enough, she might actually believe them. Because despite her verbal dismissal, Riane was afraid that it had been a very big deal.

They left the caves and headed to Memorial Park for lunch. Joel made no further mention of the kiss they'd shared, for which Riane was grateful. She was confused enough without trying to put her feelings into words. The only thing she knew for certain was that no one had ever made her feel the way he did.

Not that she had any visions of a future with Joel. They lived in completely different worlds; they had different wants and expectations. Besides, Joel was only going to be in town for a short while. As soon as he finished whatever business he'd come here to do, he'd be gone. And her life would go back to normal again.

The thought wasn't nearly as reassuring as it should have been. Nor was the realization that she knew very little about his business in West Virginia. He'd told her only that he was looking for a witness, and she hadn't even given that fact as much consideration as she should have done. She'd been distracted by his presence and her growing attraction to him. But after he'd gone last night, she'd wondered. And worried. Was it merely a coincidence that he'd hoped to meet with his witness at her charity ball? Or was his witness someone she knew?

The possibility had kept her awake long into the night, and it niggled at her subconscious again. He'd promised that his investigation had nothing to do with her camp, and she believed him. But how was he supposed to track down his witness when he was spending so much time with her?

It was a question she should ask him, but she wasn't entirely sure she wanted the answer. She didn't want to know that Joel's interest in her was motivated by something other than the attraction between them.

She bit back a sigh as she unfolded the thick Mexican blanket. Joel took it from her hands, his fingers brushing hers—deliberately?—in the transfer. Deliberate or not, the casual contact sent that heated awareness zinging through her body again. This time she wasn't quite able to bite back the sigh, and it carried more than a hint of frustration.

Joel sent her a quizzical look, then busied himself spreading the blanket on the grass beneath the widespread branches of an old red maple tree. Riane set the picnic basket on the woven fabric and began unloading the array of food Sophie had packed.

"Why did you become a cop?" Riane asked, determined to channel their conversation toward impersonal matters.

Joel was, understandably, startled by the question. He bit into a fresh buttermilk biscuit and swallowed before responding. "Maxwell Archer."

"Who?"

"He was a cop with the Philadelphia PD."

"How did you meet him?" Riane asked, toying with the potato salad on her plate.

"He arrested me." Joel grinned at the memory and helped himself to a piece of fried chicken. "Caught me with a pocketful of stuff outside a convenience store, took me down to the station. We went through the motions—mug shots, fingerprints, et cetera. The routine wasn't new to either of us.

"At the end of the whole process, he sat me down and talked to me. He didn't lecture, he didn't preach. He looked me in the eye and talked to me. It was weird," he said, shaking his head a little at the memory. "It was the first time in my life I could remember someone talking *to* me instead of at me, and listening to what I had to say.

"Not that I had much to say," he admitted. "I was too tough, too cool, to make any excuses for my behavior. Especially to a cop."

He shook his head. "And then he did something I'll never understand."

"What was that?" Riane uncapped the thermos and poured lemonade into two plastic cups. She passed one to Joel, took a sip of her own.

"He took me home with him. I was a juvenile delinquent on the fast track to a life of crime, and he opened up his home to me like some kind of invited guest. Hell, I could have cleaned the place out while he was sleeping."

"But you didn't."

Joel shook his head again. "No. And I guess he knew I wouldn't. In any event, I only wanted someplace to spend the night. Just until I figured out where I was going the next day."

"How long did you stay?"

He grinned. "Four years."

"And that's why you became a cop."

"He was a great cop. It was never just a job to him. He believed in truth. He fought for justice. He made me believe."

Riane smiled. The way he'd talked about Max, with genuine admiration and reluctant affection, made her realize how important this man had been to him. He'd become, whether Joel realized it or not, the father he'd never known.

"Max was there when I got my badge. It was the happiest day of my life."

Riane smiled. "He must have been very proud of you."

"He was," Joel agreed. He picked up his cup, drank deeply.

She saw the cloud come over his eyes, knew the joyful memory had been supplanted by one less pleasant. She waited silently for him to continue, not willing to pry into his painful memories but wanting him to share the rest of the story with her.

"He was there the day they took away my badge, too," he said at last.

"What happened?"

"I was working undercover in a drug importation and distribution center, compiling the evidence we needed to shut it down. I had the names of suppliers and local dealers, shipment dates. Everything was carefully logged and checked and double-checked. I was careful."

He shook his head. "Not careful enough. We thought we'd zeroed in on all the key players, but we'd missed one. We'd never considered that the game couldn't have gone on as long as it had without somebody on the inside."

"A cop?" The words were blurted out before she could stop them.

"There was a cop," he agreed. "But she'd been under suspicion for a while. My investigation confirmed her involvement. It was the judge we didn't know about.

"I still don't know what they had over him," Joel mused. "He was independently wealthy, from a prominent family in the community. But for some reason, he was in their pocket."

"What happened?" she prompted.

"We went to him for a warrant, after a big heroin shipment had come in from Colombia. I knew exactly what was there; I'd helped unload it. But the judge wasn't convinced of the veracity of the affidavits I'd sworn. He asked to see me personally, to verify the information.

"Of course, he'd already notified Zane Conroy. Conroy was—is—the head honcho of the syndicate. And although the judge eventually signed the warrants, by the time they were executed, everything was gone. Every single shred of evidence was gone. We didn't find so much as an empty baggie."

Riane flinched at the barely suppressed anger in his tone.

"And that wasn't the worst of it," Joel told her. "Somehow the media got wind of the investigation, the screwups, and focused on my role in it. Undercover Cop Turncoat the headlines claimed. It was all crap, of course, but it created enough of a ruckus that I was suspended pending investigation into the matter."

"Is that when you quit?"

"No. I waited until the investigation was complete, until internal affairs had concluded that I'd been a victim as much as anyone, and then I quit.

"Through all of it, Max stood by me. He never believed any of the accusations made against me. He was the only one. His confidence meant a lot to me, and I needed to prove that it wasn't misplaced." He dropped his gaze, set aside his empty plate. "Max died a few weeks before the investigation was complete."

"I'm sorry," Riane said gently.

Joel just shrugged.

"What happened to the judge who compromised your case?"

His eyes darkened, his mouth thinned. "Nothing."

"He's still on the bench?"

"No. He retired shortly after the investigation fell apart."

"And that one case destroyed your confidence in the system," she guessed.

"It made me realize that there isn't one system," he told her. "We pretend there is. We promote the ideal of 'justice for all.' But the truth is that the laws are applied and interpreted differently for different members of society."

Riane frowned, but didn't dispute his statement.

Joel finished his glass of lemonade in one long swallow. "Now it's your turn," he said.

"My turn for what?"

"To share the events that decided you upon your course in life."

"I'm not sure I know what that course is," Riane admitted. "I'm supposed to start work at my father's law firm in September, but I can't seem to envision myself drafting partnership agreements and corporate memos for the rest of my life."

"What do you want to do?" he prompted.

She sighed and began packaging up the leftovers. "I want to concentrate on the camp. Increasing our funding, expanding our capacity, improving our programs."

"Then why are you considering anything else?"

"I don't know. Maybe I feel I owe it to my parents to use the education they gave me. Which is ironic, when I think about it, because they've never pressured me to do anything I didn't want to do."

"No suggestion to follow your mother's footsteps into politics?"

Riane shook her head.

"I imagine you'd be well suited for the role, though," Joel said. "After all, you grew up in the public eye."

"Mostly I grew up in unknown countries. I was thirteen when my parents left the Foreign Service to come back to the States. That's when my dad opened his law practice and my mother ran for office. It was hard at first," she admitted.

"I was used to being with her almost all the time, and suddenly there were all these other demands on her. But it got easier as I got older, when I started to understand the importance of what she does."

"What about your father? Does he ever feel like he's in her shadow?"

Riane was genuinely surprised by the question. "Of course not. He's always been supportive of her career."

"It sounds like they have a good relationship."

"The best," Riane agreed. "She wouldn't be half as successful as she is without his support."

"Is that what you're looking for with Stuart—a husband who will support your career ambitions?"

"It's a valid consideration," she said, hating that she sounded so defensive. She snapped the lid back on a salad container, set it inside the basket. She reached for the plate of cookies, but Joel's hand on hers halted the motion, forced her attention back to the intensity of his deep blue gaze.

"What about passion?" The heat in his eyes, the low timbre of his voice, were enough to heat her blood without any discussion of passion.

She tugged her hand away, covered the plate of cookies. "What about it?"

"Was it a consideration?"

"I don't see how that's any business of yours."

His lips curved in a slow smile. "I've seen you together," he reminded her. "You generate about as much heat between you as a subzero freezer."

"It's difficult to be demonstrative when your every move might be recorded by the media," she responded coolly.

Joel seemed to consider her statement for a moment, then he shook his head. "I might buy that explanation…except that I've kissed you."

Damn it, she did *not* want to be reminded of that kiss. "What is *that* supposed to mean?"

His eyes glinted with challenge. "You're a passionate

woman, Riane. You need a man who can elicit your passion, share your desire.''

Until she'd met Joel, she'd always believed herself to be rather dispassionate. Even with Cameron, she'd wanted to want him more than she really did want him. Frowning at the memory, she put the plate of cookies in the basket, picked up the bowl of strawberries. Joel deftly plucked a ripe berry from the top, popped it in his mouth.

''Mmm. These are fabulous,'' he said.

Riane tried to focus her attention on gathering up the remnants of their lunch, but the unadulterated pleasure in his voice stirred something inside her. Passion? she wondered, feeling a little bewildered and a lot intimidated by the depth of her reactions to this man.

''I used to want to fall in love,'' she told him, surprising herself with the admission. ''I wanted to know the deep, abiding, forever kind of love my parents share.''

''Why are you using the past tense? You can't have given up already.''

She shrugged. ''Love isn't always what it's cracked up to be.''

''That's a rather cynical statement for a woman of twenty-five years.''

''Twenty-four,'' she corrected stiffly.

Joel grinned, and Riane's pulse leaped.

''Respect and affection are more important, more enduring, than some elusive emotion glorified through Saint Valentine.'' She had respect and affection with Stuart, and if their relationship lacked the passion she'd sampled with Joel—well, there were more important things than passion.

''I can't disagree with you,'' Joel said. He reached for another berry, but this time, instead of biting into the juicy fruit himself, he offered it to her.

Riane shook her head.

He skimmed the deep red berry over the curve of her bottom lip. It was cool and fragrant and she had to clamp her lips together to prevent herself from accepting his offering.

She refused to be drawn into whatever seductive game he was playing.

"But don't you think it's possible to have it all?" he asked, the warmth of his breath caressing her cheek. "Respect, affection and passion?"

She averted her gaze, unable to respond. Unwilling to say anything that might betray the longing in her heart.

"Does your passion scare you, Riane?"

She cleared her throat. "I'm not..."

Whatever words she'd intended to utter in protest strangled in her throat when his lips touched the pulse beating erratically at the base of her jaw. It was a feather-soft caress, not even a kiss, but the brief contact jolted her heart as effectively as a fully charged defibrillator.

"You're not what?" he prompted, his breath warm on her cheek. "Were you going to deny your passion—or your fear?"

She swallowed, struggled to find the words she'd lost, but he nipped at her earlobe. She couldn't deny that she was afraid. In fact, she was terrified. Not of Joel, but of the feelings he evoked. Feelings she didn't know how to respond to, didn't dare even acknowledge. It was the acknowledgment of this fear, however, that mobilized her. She pulled away abruptly, away from the tempting lure of his lips, away from her own desires.

"You need an outlet for all the passion churning inside you," Joel said. "And Stuart isn't it."

"And I suppose you are?" she asked coolly.

"We connect on a very basic level, sweetheart. You can't deny that."

"Maybe not," she admitted. "But I'm not going to throw away my future for a few nights in your bed."

"It would be a mistake to marry Stuart."

"Why do you care?" she demanded.

"Because I care about you."

"I'm not naive enough to believe I'm anything more than a diversion for you while you're in West Virginia."

He was silent for a long minute, then he said, "That might have been true at first. It isn't true anymore. I do care about you, Riane."

His words, as much as the emotion evident in his tone when he spoke them, unnerved her. She'd deflected a lot of masculine overtures in the past several years, although substantially fewer since her involvement with Stuart had become public knowledge. But one thing she'd learned in averting such advances was that it was easier to do when there weren't emotions involved. And in that moment she knew that her emotions were already involved. To what extent she wasn't certain, but she wasn't about to risk having her heart broken.

"I'm not going to sleep with you, Joel."

That slow, sexy smile spread over his face again, and her heart practically melted into a puddle at his feet. "If I had you in my bed, I wouldn't waste a single minute of the time sleeping," he promised her.

"Well then..." She felt her cheeks flush as her mind immediately conjured all-too-vivid images of what they might be doing rather than sleeping. And the warmth in her face quickly spread to other parts of her body. "You should know that I have no intention of ending up in your bed, either."

"It's going to happen, Riane."

The unwavering confidence in his voice annoyed her. Taunted her. Terrified her.

"That kiss we shared was—"

"It was a mistake," she interjected quickly. Frantically.

"Maybe it was," he agreed. "It was also like dropping a match in a pool of gasoline—fiery, explosive, irreversible."

"My mother always warned me not to play with matches," she said lightly as she resumed packing up the rest of their dishes.

"Do you think she'd warn you about me?"

She managed a smile. "Aren't you the kind of guy *all* mothers warn their daughters about?"

Joel grinned. "Do you always listen to your mother?"

"Always."

"And yet, you were just as much a part of that kiss as I was."

"It won't happen again," she assured him.

He linked his fingers with hers, tugged her a little closer. "It would be easy enough to prove you wrong," he taunted softly, his mouth hovering mere inches above hers.

Riane was mesmerized by the intensity in his eyes. She blinked, forced herself to look away. "I should be getting home."

He smiled, as if her response was exactly what he'd expected.

"Soon," he agreed. Then he pulled her braid over her shoulder and started to unfasten the elastic at its end.

"What are you doing?"

"I like your hair loose."

"I like it tied back," she countered.

"Too bad," he said, already unwinding the interwoven strands.

There was something strangely intimate about his fingers sifting through her hair, something incredibly erotic about the touch of his fingertips against her scalp. Then he slid his hand to her nape and clutched a handful of hair in his fist, tilting her head back. "Yeah," he said softly. "This is just how I pictured it."

"Wh-what?"

"How you'd look when I kissed you." Then his mouth came down and took possession of hers.

His kiss stole what little breath she had left, silenced her soft sigh of pleasure. Her eyelids fluttered, closed; her hands moved instinctively to his shoulders, held on. His tongue touched her lips, and they parted willingly, eagerly. The heat that he'd stoked with that first kiss continued to build inside her, filling her with a sense of warmth and anticipation she'd never felt before.

Then he stroked her tongue with his, and the fire flamed hotter. She tried to breathe, but his scent filled the air, intoxicating her. His fingers untangled from her hair, traced slowly down her spine to the bottom of her T-shirt. When his hand dipped beneath the fabric and his palm splayed against her bare flesh, her skin felt seared by the touch.

She gasped, shocked by the flood of sensations coursing through her. She leaned into him, needing his strength to keep her upright as the world tilted. She arched as his fingers skimmed over her rib cage, the curve of her breast. She felt her nipple pebble, straining against the lacy fabric of her bra. Tremors coursed through her, hot, pulsing. When his thumb brushed over the aching peak, she gasped with shock, with pleasure.

She made no protest as he laid her back on the blanket, covering the length of her body with his own. She could feel the throbbing of his arousal between her thighs and the answering, aching heat that pooled inside her.

Joel had said she needed a man who could elicit her passion. What he didn't know was that he was the only man who ever had. And whatever resolutions she'd made earlier about not becoming involved with him scattered like so many remnants of last year's dried leaves in the brisk spring breeze.

Then the snap of a branch echoed in the stillness like a gunshot, shattering their idyllic paradise. Riane pushed him away, gasped for breath.

"I seem to have a knack for choosing all the wrong places," Joel commented wryly as he dragged a hand through his own hair.

"Maybe it's a sign."

"Of what?"

"A reminder that we shouldn't be doing this."

"Are you still going to deny that you want this?"

She shook her head. "No. But wanting something and getting it are two separate issues."

He grinned. "I won't put up much of a fight."

"If it was just sex, it would be easy," she said. "But as much as I'd like to, I can't fall into bed with a man I barely know."

"So get to know me."

She laughed softly. "I'm not your type of woman, Logan. I'm looking for more than a night or a week."

"I won't make you any promises I can't keep, sweetheart."

She knew that, and maybe that's why she wanted so desperately just to be with him. Just for now. "We should head back."

Joel sighed, then nodded. "Let's go."

Joel made his way through the lobby of the hotel toward the elevator. *Alone.* He'd considered inviting Riane up to his room, was confident that if he got her there he could have her naked and horizontal in short order. But he hadn't issued the invitation because he hadn't wanted to pressure her.

She wanted him, but she didn't want to want him, and he'd sensed that confusion within her. He wanted her—period. His own doubts about the wisdom of becoming involved with Riane had been supplanted by the fierce desire that swept through him whenever he was near her. But his conscience wouldn't let him take advantage of her uncertainty. It wasn't often difficult to silence his morals, but two factors held him back: Riane's unspecified relationship with Stuart and the fact that Joel really did care about her.

It had been a long time since he'd cared about anyone, and he wasn't entirely comfortable with the feelings he had for Riane. He couldn't have found a woman who was more wrong for him if he tried. And yet, knowing they were so completely ill suited did nothing to tame his libido.

Maybe the promise of forbidden fruit had made him want her more. That was exactly what had happened with Jocelyn. He'd known her father disapproved of their relationship from the outset. He hadn't known that his disapproval was the greatest part of the attraction for Jocelyn.

This bitter reminder should have been more than enough to make him rethink the insane attraction he felt for Riane, but hadn't she already proven she was different from Jocelyn? At the charity ball Riane had even referred to the waiter by name. Jocelyn hadn't seen the servants who hovered around except to scream at them when something wasn't exactly as she'd thought it should be. Then again, just because their methods differed didn't mean their attitudes did. After all, Riane was the daughter of a politician—and even a servant had a vote.

He scrubbed his hand over his jaw. He'd tried to keep things in perspective, to remain objective, but it was already too late for that. He wanted to believe Riane was different; he wanted her to be different. Because he wanted her.

The shrill ring of his cell phone was a welcome intrusion. He didn't want to think about Riane Quinlan anymore. He didn't want to remember how close he'd come to laying her down on the grass and—

"Logan," he barked into the phone.

"You okay?" Mike asked. "You sound like you're having trouble breathing."

"Bad connection," Joel grumbled, in no way prepared to admit to his friend that he'd become aroused by his own prurient fantasies. "You better share whatever you've got before we get cut off."

"I spoke with the director of social services in Tucson," Mike said. "And I'm beginning to think I was wrong to ever doubt your instincts."

The infamous instincts went on high alert. "What did you find out?"

"She remembered the child's name."

"Are you sure?"

"She was adamant. She said she remembered because the name was uncommon. I gave her the approximate time frame we were looking at, and she dug out her old telephone logs. Sure enough, she found a notation about a call regarding Rheanne Elliott."

"Did she follow up?"

"She referred the matter to another worker," Mike said.

"A Camille Michaud. Ms. Michaud, however, denied any involvement with the child."

"Yet another futile lead," Joel surmised, not entirely dissatisfied. Despite his earlier conviction that Riane was the woman he was looking for, he was now willing to be convinced otherwise. He wanted to be free to pursue a relationship with her without the threat of secret agendas or hidden pasts to come between them.

Mike's next words annihilated that possibility.

"I think she was lying."

Joel frowned. "Why would she lie?"

"That's what I was wondering," Mike admitted. "But I found it strange that a woman who never met the child remembered the name after so many years while another, who apparently was sent to investigate the complaint, claimed never to have heard the name."

"Is that what she said?"

"Not in those words," Mike told him. "In fact, she seemed very careful about the information she disclosed. What she said was that the name didn't sound familiar and that if she'd had any contact with the family she would have made a note of it. If there's no file, obviously there was no reason for social services to get involved."

"How does this help us?"

"After I spoke with Ms. Michaud, I did some digging—to see if there was any connection between her and Samuel Rutherford, the attorney who handled the adoption. I didn't find anything. But I did find a connection between Camille Michaud and Ellen Rutherford."

"Now Ellen Rutherford-Quinlan, the Democratic senate representative from West Virginia?" Joel guessed.

"Bingo."

Joel shook his head, impressed by the information his partner had managed to uncover, perplexed by the increasing facets and layers of the case, and disturbed by what this meant for his developing relationship with Riane.

''There's more,'' Mike told him.

Joel waited.

''According to the baptismal records of St. Jacob's Church, Camille Michaud is Riane Quinlan's godmother.''

Chapter 6

He adjusted the knot of the tie at his throat. The silk was smooth beneath his fingers. He brushed his hands over his trousers. The pleats fell in perfect alignment to the tops of his polished loafers. He'd always taken pride in his appearance. It was important to make a good first impression.

It had never been more important than today.

He didn't have a mirror. He wouldn't have believed the reflection in the glass, anyway. He'd lost weight over the past few months, added some lines to his face. But he was still handsome. Still charismatic. And he still knew how to play the game.

He would be earnest, contrite, acquiescent.

Then he would be free.

Free to implement his plan. Free to seek his revenge.

Riane convinced herself that she'd done the right thing by ending her day with Joel early. She needed some time to think and she couldn't do that while he was around. But even now, she was having a difficult time concentrating on anything but the kisses they'd shared that afternoon. Hardly the most appropriate thing to think about as she was getting ready for dinner with the man she planned to marry.

She wished her mother was home. There was nothing she couldn't talk to her about. Ellen Rutherford-Quinlan might be in her second term in the Senate, but first and foremost, she was Riane's mother. No matter how pressing her schedule, she always found time for her daughter.

Riane missed her terribly. She knew that she could contact the ship, but she didn't think her personal crisis was an emergency that warranted interrupting her parents' second honeymoon. They deserved this time away together, and Riane was thrilled that they'd finally decided to take the trip they'd put off for so long. Still, she missed both of them.

When the phone rang, she pounced on it, appreciative of any reprieve from her confused hormones.

"Mom." Grateful desperation gave way to genuine delight as she heard Ellen Rutherford-Quinlan's voice on the other end of the line. "Where are you?"

"We've just docked at Brunei and are getting ready to venture into the city."

There was something in her mother's voice, even over the long-distance connection, that concerned Riane. "What's the matter?"

"What do you mean?"

Riane could almost see the false smile plastered on her mother's face. The smile that never failed to fool political allies and adversaries but had never worked on Riane or Ryan. They knew her too well.

"You're tense, Mom. Is everything all right? Is Daddy okay?"

"We're both fine, honey. I guess I was just missing you. We both miss you."

"You're on a second honeymoon. Neither of you should be thinking about anything but each other," Riane admonished.

Her mother laughed, as Riane had hoped she would. ''How is everything with you?''

''Good.''

''Have you met any interesting people lately?''

Riane frowned, wondered—briefly—where that question had come from. ''What has Sophie been telling you about Joel Logan?''

''Logan?'' Ellen sounded genuinely surprised. ''I haven't heard anything. Is there something I should know?''

''No,'' Riane denied quickly. Then she added, ''I don't know.''

''Oh, baby.'' Ellen managed a laugh. ''It's not like you to sound confused about anything, much less a man.''

''I've never met anyone like him,'' Riane admitted.

''Where did you meet him?''

''At the charity ball last weekend.''

''He can't be all bad if he supported your camp,'' Ellen teased.

Riane smiled. She was so glad her mom had called, but somehow hearing her voice and knowing she was so far away only made her miss her more. ''I wish you were here,'' she said softly.

''We can fly out of Muara if you want.''

Riane laughed. ''No. You can't cut short your vacation to try and sort out my messed-up life.''

''We'd do anything for you, Riane.''

''I know, Mom. But you'll be home soon enough.''

There was a pause. ''Will you do me a favor?''

''Anything,'' Riane promised.

''Give me a call—day or night—if you're contacted by a Michael Courtland.''

''Who?''

''Michael Courtland,'' Ellen repeated.

''Who is he? And why will he be contacting me?''

''I'm not sure that he will,'' Ellen answered, ignoring her daughter's first question. ''But call me if he does.''

Riane frowned, wanting to press for further details, but the chime of the doorbell from downstairs alerted her to Stuart's arrival. "Okay."

"Thanks, honey. I've got to go now. Your father's looking at his watch."

"Give him my love."

"I will. And ours to you."

Riane hung up the phone, her conversation with her mother only adding to her confusion. She couldn't make any sense of her mother's request—or her own feelings about anything right now. She wished, for once, she could just crawl into bed and shut out the world. Instead she put a smile on her face and went downstairs to greet her future husband.

When Stuart drove Riane home after their habitual Saturday meal at LeJardin, he asked if he could come in to talk to her. His request was unexpected, a break in their pattern, and it concerned Riane. Stuart didn't like anything to upset his carefully structured routine.

He turned off the ignition and climbed out of the car, then he came around to open her door. It was an action performed more out of convention than consideration, but she respected the habitual gestures that were such an integral part of their relationship. They gave her a sense of security and stability she'd only started to appreciate after spending time with Joel. She didn't want her world shaken—not when it left her heart pounding and her knees trembling. Not when it made her feel so completely out of control.

So resolved, she pushed the lingering thoughts of Joel from her mind and focused on Stuart. She led him into the den, feeling unaccountably apprehensive about this unexpected turn of events.

"Can I get you a drink?" she offered.

"Please."

She uncapped the decanter and splashed a generous amount of scotch in a glass for him, then poured another drink for herself.

"What did you want to talk about?" Riane asked.

"A couple of things." Stuart set his glass down and reached for the Louis Vuitton briefcase on the floor by his feet. She was so accustomed to seeing Stuart with it in hand that it hadn't struck her as odd when he'd brought it into the house with him.

He set the case on the table and flipped open the locks, then withdrew his date book. "I have a meeting with the arts committee next Saturday afternoon, but my morning is open. If your schedule is clear, I thought we could go to the jewelers."

"Jewelers?" she echoed blankly.

"To get your engagement ring."

"Engagement ring," she echoed again, wondering where was the burst of joy, the rising anticipation she'd always thought she'd feel at this moment.

"Is your schedule clear?" he asked, his voice tinged with impatience.

"Um…yes…I think so," Riane admitted. "But, Stuart, you haven't actually asked me to marry you."

"I didn't think I needed to get down on one knee," he said, making the idea sound ridiculous.

Riane washed down the lump of disappointment with a mouthful of scotch. Maybe she was old-fashioned, maybe she had high expectations, but she'd heard the story of her parents' engagement a hundred times—a tale of candlelight and wine and soft music, culminating with her father on bended knee offering more than a ring—offering his heart and his love and his devotion. Was it so unreasonable to want more than an appointment to pick out a piece of jewelry?

"You don't have to do anything," she said softly. "I just…never mind."

Stuart gave her a strange look, then penciled "jeweler" into his agenda for the following weekend. He snapped the book shut, smiled. "Good. That's settled then."

Riane forced her lips to curve, wondering why she suddenly felt so *un*settled.

"The other matter I wanted to discuss," Stuart said, forging ahead with absolutely no clue as to his "fiancée's" feelings, "is your inappropriate association with this Mr. Logan."

Inappropriate association? It was all Riane could do not to roll her eyes.

"There is nothing inappropriate about my association with Joel Logan." Okay, maybe those kisses hadn't been entirely appropriate, but she wasn't going to think about those now. She wasn't going to think about those ever again.

Stuart looked decidedly annoyed by her contradiction. "I know you've been spending time with him."

"How?"

He smiled thinly. "It's a small town, Riane. Surely you didn't think I wouldn't find out."

"I wasn't hiding anything," she said, feeling guilty nonetheless. "He's in town for a short while and wanted someone to show him around."

"Why is he in town?"

She sipped at her scotch again, uncomfortable with his scrutiny. "I don't know."

"Riane," he chided gently, shaking his head. "What do you know about the man?"

"I know he's a private investigator," she said, uncertain why she felt compelled to justify her association with Joel.

"Who used to be a cop," Stuart said.

Riane frowned. "How do you know that?"

"I did a background check on him."

"What? Why?"

"Because I thought it was important for at least one of us to know something about the man you've…befriended. And because he seemed a little too focused on you the night of the charity ball."

"Is it so hard to imagine that another man might be interested in me?"

"Of course not," Stuart denied.

"But you immediately assumed he had ulterior motives."

"He does."

Riane set her glass carefully down on the desktop, hating that his statement came so close to her own suppositions about Joel that first night and determined not to exhibit any of the frustration churning inside her.

"I've dealt with this my whole life," she said softly. "People either seek out my company or turn away from it depending on their ambitions and their politics, and we both know that you're not any different."

"I care about you, Riane."

She sighed, because she knew he did. Still, she didn't understand why he was making an issue of her spending time with Joel. She wanted to believe his reaction was emotional—that he was concerned he might lose her affection to the other man. Unfortunately, she knew his actions were fueled by an interest in self-preservation. Investigators and reporters were often useful tools in furthering political aspirations; they could also be dangerous enemies.

"Don't you want to know what my investigation revealed?"

"No. You had no reason to dig into his life."

Stuart smiled thinly. "His life is digging into other people's," he reminded her. "And if you weren't so blinded by your attraction to him, you'd agree that my actions were completely reasonable."

She decided it was best not to respond to that comment, because she couldn't deny that she was attracted to Joel, not after the way she'd responded to his kiss. Not after the way her body had heated and quivered in response to his touch. Just the memory of that stolen interlude brought a warm flush to her cheeks and made her wish, even if just for a minute, that she could know what it was like to make love with Joel Logan.

No other man, Stuart included, had ever made her feel the way she'd felt when she was in Joel's arms. No other man had inspired the kind of erotic fantasies she'd succumbed to since she'd met him. Would his lovemaking be as awesome and passionate as his kiss had been? Would the aching emptiness inside her be filled by the physical union of their bodies? Would the overwhelming desire she could scarcely even comprehend be satisfied by this man?

Stuart was right. It was entirely possible that her attraction to Joel Logan was clouding her judgment.

"Have you slept with him?" Stuart asked.

"No!" Riane was indignant. She couldn't believe he would even ask such a question. Whatever erotic fantasies she might have were just that—fantasies. She would never become physically intimate with one man while involved with another.

"Why not?"

"Why not?" she echoed, stunned.

He shrugged. "If you're attracted to him, why not just sleep with him and get it over with?"

Disbelief turned to shock. "You *want* me to sleep with this man?"

"I'm merely suggesting that sex with him might help purge the attraction from your system. As long as you're discreet about it, of course."

Riane folded her arms across her chest as she stared at the man she'd been involved with for the past three years. "I can't believe we're having this conversation."

"I'm only being practical, Riane. I don't expect you to take a vow of chastity when we're not sleeping together."

"Obviously, *you* haven't," she said, feeling unaccountably bitter.

Stuart sighed. "Why are you making an issue out of this?"

"Because it should be an issue. Damn it, Stuart, not five minutes ago we were talking about getting engaged. I thought that meant, on some basic level, you cared about and respected me."

"I do," he said solemnly.

"But you're sleeping with other women."

"I'm hardly being promiscuous."

"One other woman is too many," Riane said.

He sighed again. "I want to marry *you.*"

She shook her head sadly as all her hopes and dreams for the future tumbled like a house of cards around her. "I want to be with someone who wants to be with me. Not because I fit his image of the woman he wants as his wife, but because of the person I am."

"Is that why you think Logan is with you?"

"This doesn't have anything to do with Joel."

Stuart slipped a manila folder out of his briefcase and offered it to her.

Riane eyed it suspiciously. "What's that?"

"It's the information my sources uncovered about Logan," he said. "Take a look at this, and then tell me he doesn't have an ulterior motive for wanting to be with you."

She took the folder and tossed it onto the desk. "Why are you so preoccupied with Joel?"

Stuart nodded toward the discarded folder. "Read it," he said again. "After you've checked it out, you'll reevaluate your position."

She tucked the file into the desk drawer without opening the cover. She couldn't deny a certain amount of curiosity, especially since Stuart seemed convinced that the information he'd obtained would alter her feelings for Joel. She wouldn't play those games. If there was something she needed to know, she'd wait for Joel to tell her.

Joel had never before suffered pangs of conscience. Then again, he'd never before made the mistake of mixing business with pleasure. And he was starting to feel uneasy about his deception; starting to acknowledge that his feelings for Riane were growing.

It would be smart, he knew, to call in his partner—to have Mike take over this part of the investigation. But he didn't want to be smart, he wanted to be with Riane. Which meant that he needed to tell her the truth about his trip to West Virginia.

And he couldn't put it off any longer.

When he'd returned to his room after his picnic with Riane, he'd found a complimentary copy of the local weekly paper, the *Mapleview Mirror,* on the table in his room. It had given a fair amount of coverage to last weekend's charity ball, including several photos. Joel cringed when he saw the picture of him and Riane, although the caption beneath the photo referred to him only as an "unknown guest."

Still, the picture was clear and it reminded him that spending time with Riane was detrimental to his anonymity. He didn't want to live in a media circus again, but he also didn't want Riane finding out about his investigation from anyone else.

So it was that he found himself standing back on her doorstep several hours after he'd left her there. He'd passed Stuart's car on its way out, so it was safe to assume that Riane was still up. And alone.

"It's after eleven o'clock," Riane said when she opened the door. "What are you doing here?"

"I wanted to see you."

"Can't it wait until tomorrow? I was on my way to bed."

"Don't let me stop you."

"Funny, Logan."

He grinned. "Can't blame a guy for trying."

"Right now you're trying my patience."

"Give me ten minutes, sweetheart," he cajoled.

She sighed. "Ten minutes," she agreed, stepping away from the door so he could enter. "As long as you promise to leave when your time's up."

"Scout's honor."

She lifted an eyebrow. "You were a Scout?"

"No." He followed her into the den, enjoying the gentle sway of her hips in the clingy yellow dress she was wearing. "But I do keep my promises."

She turned to face him, folding her arms across her chest. She probably didn't realize how the movement thrust her breasts together, providing a delectable view of cleavage above the low V-neckline of her dress. "The clock's ticking," she said.

He'd been rehearsing the words throughout the ride across town. But now he was nervous. He knew she would be angry, she might even hate him, but he couldn't continue to deceive her.

Before he could tell her what had driven him to her door, however, the ring of a cell phone intruded. Hers this time.

Frowning, Riane dug the device out of her purse.

"Is this going to cut into my ten minutes?" Joel asked.

Riane ignored him and connected the call. "Hello?"

He turned away to give her some privacy for her conversation. He moved over to the bookcase, studying the photos aligned on the top shelf. Riane as a child in her school uniform, her lips curved in a mischievous smile, her deep brown eyes sparkling at the camera. Riane in a prom dress, several years later, absolutely stunning in the shimmering gold gown that only hinted at curves she now possessed. Riane graduating from Harvard, proud and happy and breathtaking. Riane and her parents, all formally attired, a beautiful and cohesive family unit.

Or were they?

Uneasiness stirred as he reviewed his conversation with Mike. He had so many questions, too few answers.

"Okay. Wait right there, Adam, I'm on my way."

She disconnected the call, already moving toward the door, as if she'd forgotten Joel was even in the room. Her easy dismissal annoyed him, probably more so because he now knew she'd been summoned away by another man.

He stepped into her path. "Who's Adam?"

"I don't have time for this, Joel. I have to go."

"It's after eleven o'clock," he reminded her. "I'm not letting you run off in the middle of the night with no idea where you're going."

"Then you can come with me," she offered.

Riane was grateful for Joel's company on what she knew could only be an ill-fated mission. She'd been to Adam's neighborhood once before, in the middle of the day, and that had been a scary enough experience. She'd have to be insane to venture there alone in the darkness of night.

She was also grateful for Joel's silence. He said little as they made their way across the city to the impoverished east end, and most of the questions he asked were in the nature of directions. While Joel was driving, Riane made a few phone calls.

"Turn right at the next light."

"Are you going to tell me what's going on?" Joel asked.

"As soon as I know," she told him. "There." She gestured to a run-down apartment building in front of which a crowd of spectators had gathered along with three police cruisers, a paramedics truck and an ambulance.

Joel's car wasn't completely stopped at the curb when Riane unfastened her seat belt and pushed open the door. She plunged into the crowd and up the broken sidewalk that led to the entranceway of the building. She didn't see the faded and chipped brick, the boarded-up windows, the peeling paint on the trim. She was only thinking about Adam.

The exterior door was propped open by a rock, the narrow hallway inside dimly lit and thick with the scents of old garbage and—she felt her stomach lurch—something even less pleasant that she was probably better off not trying to identify.

Her heels clicked loudly on the metal stairs as she made her way up to the third floor. With each step, the air grew thicker, the nauseating scent stronger. She heard Joel's footsteps behind her, but didn't wait.

The door to apartment 3A was open and—she exhaled a shaky sigh of relief—Adam was still there. Staring at her mutinously through the tears in his eyes, but there. Handcuffed, she noted with shocked disbelief, to the leg of a scarred coffee table.

She turned to the uniformed officer seated on the battered sofa, idly thumbing through an outdated fashion magazine. "You cuffed him?"

He glanced up, shrugged unapologetically. "It was the only way I could be sure to hold on to him."

"He's a *child*." Joel's voice came from directly behind her now, and he sounded equally stunned.

"He's slippery and he's fast and he's got a helluva kick," the officer said defensively, rubbing a hand over his shin.

Riane turned her attention to the child. "You kicked him?"

Adam didn't give any indication that he'd even heard her. She knew that he viewed her phone call to the police as a betrayal. He didn't trust anyone in uniform, and although she knew he had valid reasons for this distrust, she thought he at least trusted *her* enough to know that she'd never put him in any danger.

"Ever heard of assaulting an officer?" she tried again.

Adam continued to ignore her.

"You Quinlan?" the cop asked Riane.

She nodded, her attention still focused on Adam, and dug into her purse for identification. She passed him her driver's license.

"The lady from social services is on her way with some papers," he said, returning her ID. "Do you think you can handle him until she gets here?"

Riane nodded again.

The cop bent over to unlock the cuffs. As soon as he was freed, Adam backed away, into the corner of the room, rubbing the red mark around one slender wrist where he'd strained against the metal enclosure. His gaze darted from Riane to Joel and back again.

"You called the cops," the child said accusingly.

Riane knelt down in front of him, mindless of the skirt of her Carolina Herrera dress. "I had to, Adam."

"Why?"

"Because if there was any chance that your mom was still alive—" she'd seen the body bag they'd loaded into the back of the ambulance, so she knew she wasn't "—I had to get someone here fast to help her."

"But you said *you* were coming."

"And I did."

"Who's that?" he demanded, glancing warily at Joel again.

"He's a—" Riane hesitated, not sure how to answer the question "—a friend," she said at last.

"Another cop," Adam said derisively.

Riane had to hold back a smile. She should have guessed that Adam would peg Joel so quickly, probably even more quickly than she herself had done. "He says he's not," she confided.

Adam snorted.

"I'm a private investigator," Joel said, stepping farther into the room.

Adam instinctively moved closer to Riane. "What's he doing here?"

"He's not here to take you away," Riane promised the child.

She could tell he wanted to stay angry with her, but there were too many emotions competing inside him. Too much horror and heartbreak for a six-year-old to handle. He blinked, fighting for control, but the first tear spilled over, tracked its way slowly down his cheek.

Riane held her arms open, and after a brief hesitation Adam launched himself at her, desperate for contact, for comfort. She folded her arms around him, her own eyes filling with moisture as his rail-thin shoulders trembled against her. She lifted him off the ground effortlessly—he didn't weigh half as much as a six-year-old should—and moved to the dirty sofa the cop had abandoned, cradling the child in her lap.

Joel felt his heart lodge somewhere in the vicinity of his throat as he watched Riane settle back into the old sofa with Adam, oblivious to the fact that his tears and snot were staining the front of her designer dress. And in that moment he finally understood how dedicated she was. Not to the ideology of her camp, but to the children who needed it—and her—so desperately. And he realized how truly incredible she was.

He took an instinctive step back, as if to protect himself from the unwanted feelings that stirred to life inside him.

"What's going to happen to me?"

The child's tentative question reminded Joel that there were more immediate problems than his conflicting emotions about Riane.

"Don't worry about that right now," Riane said gently.

"Are they going to take me away again?" He looked at her, eyes wide, terrified.

Again? Joel wondered.

"They won't take you away," she said firmly.

"But now that my mom's—"

"They won't take you away," she said again. "I promise."

And that promise was enough for the child, apparently, because he nodded his head, snuggled against Riane's shoulder, and promptly fell asleep.

"You have no business making promises you can't keep," Joel told her, careful to keep his voice low enough so as not to disturb the sleeping child.

"I don't."

"The cop said social services has already been contacted."

"I know. *I* contacted them."

"There's a procedure they have to follow in these situations," Joel told her. He'd thought, because of her work through the camp, that she'd have some kind of understanding of the system. Apparently not. "The procedure generally involves placement in a group or foster home pending review—"

"I'm aware of the procedure," Riane interrupted. "I also know that Adam's mother has a sister. He'll stay with me until she can be found."

"You're going to take the kid home with you?" He couldn't keep the skepticism from his voice.

"I'm going to take him home," Riane confirmed.

Joel just shook his head, certain she was in for a wake-up call when the authorities got there.

He was wrong.

Chapter 7

As Joel watched Riane tuck the child into bed in one of the numerous spare rooms of the Quinlan mansion, he knew he should have expected that she would somehow manage to skirt the rules that applied to the rest of the world. She was, after all, a Rutherford.

Strangely, though, the thought didn't bother him as much as it might have a week earlier. Oh, there was no doubt that Riane had used her political connections to get her own way in this case, but how could he resent that when she'd obviously done so to help this child?

He glanced at his watch as he followed Riane down the stairs. It was nearly 4:00 a.m. "I need to get some sleep."

"I can make up another one of the guest rooms," Riane offered.

Tempted as he was to stay close at hand—to ensure she didn't run off on any other crazy missions—her proximity wreaked havoc on his hormones. He was exhausted, both mentally and physically, and still he wanted nothing more than to take her in his arms and spend hours making slow, sweet love with her. Which, considering the frightened child sleeping upstairs, wasn't likely to happen anytime soon.

So he shook his head in response to her invitation. They'd both be better off if he went back to his hotel, far out of reach of temptation.

Yet he was reluctant to go. "How long have you known Adam?"

"Long enough to know that he's better off here than in an emergency intake shelter."

He didn't blame her for sounding defensive. He'd made it clear that he doubted the wisdom of her actions tonight, but he was curious about her relationship with this child. "I wasn't questioning your motives..."

Her raised eyebrow effectively communicated her disbelief. Joel managed a wry grin.

"I'm just trying to understand your connection to him."

"He's been coming to my camp for the past three years," she told him. "That makes him my responsibility."

"Three years? But he's only six."

Riane nodded. "We usually don't take children younger than five, but we make exceptions when circumstances warrant it."

"What were his circumstances?"

"Adam's social worker contacted me after reading an article about the camp," she explained. "She was desperate for anything to get him out of his home for a few weeks. A lot of children who go there are abused—physically, emotionally, sexually. Adam wasn't abused in any traditional sense, but he was horribly neglected.

"At three years of age he was still confined to a playpen for most of the day. He didn't walk, he could barely speak. He was undernourished, understimulated, barely functioning."

"Why the hell didn't the social worker put him in a foster home?"

"She wanted to. But it's hard to prove neglect, harder still when the parent knows her social assistance will be cut off if she loses the child. Every time the worker visited the home, the mother was there. She might not have been feeding Adam three meals a day, but there was food in the refrigerator. He was clothed, if not always adequately.''

''Why did the mother let him come to the camp?''

''Because it was only supposed to be for two weeks, and it wouldn't affect her assistance. But when the two week period was over, his mother couldn't be found.''

''So he stayed,'' Joel guessed.

Riane nodded. ''For almost two months.''

''Is that when she finally came for him?''

''She didn't come for him. Near the end of Adam's third week there, the police picked her up on Queen Street, already higher than a kite, trying to score more drugs.''

''What happened?''

''We got her into rehab.''

''There's usually an extensive waiting list for beds in the publicly funded facilities,'' Joel commented. ''You were lucky to find one available.''

Riane glanced away. ''I sent her to Newhaven,'' she admitted, naming an exclusive private clinic.

''And you paid for it.''

''I did it for Adam. To give him a chance.''

And Joel would bet he wasn't the first child she'd done something like that for. The realization caused something inside his heart to shift, settle. ''Is Adam the youngest child you've had at the camp?''

Riane shook her head. ''He was the first, but not the youngest. We had two-year-old twin girls last summer.''

''And your heart breaks for every one of them,'' he guessed. ''Not just the little ones, but every single kid who walks through the gates of that camp.''

''Am I that transparent?''

''You're that devoted,'' he said. ''I've never known anyone who gives so much for so little in return.''

She shook her head again. ''I get so much more than I give. Every day I spend with those kids is a gift.''

"Ah. The lonely, only child syndrome."

"Maybe." She shrugged. "I've always wanted a sibling, or a dozen siblings. A sister was my first choice, but I would gladly have settled for a brother."

Her admission, and the undisguised yearning in her voice, tugged at something inside Joel. It might very well be within his power to give her what she'd always wanted, but at what cost? If Riane really was Arden Doherty's sister, that revelation would tear the rest of her family apart.

Would she thank him—or hate him—for the part he would play in bringing that fact to light? He couldn't know. He only knew that he didn't have the energy to tackle any more truths with her tonight.

"I really should be on my way," he said. "So you can get some sleep."

If she thought the change of topic abrupt, she didn't comment on it. She just walked him to the front door. "Thank you for coming with me tonight. I'm glad you were there."

Unable to resist, he cupped her cheek in his hand, rubbed his thumb gently over the fullness of her bottom lip. How was it, he wondered, that this woman who was so obviously unsuited for him could nevertheless have come to mean so much so soon?

"Me, too."

She smiled, a slow curving of the lips that did strange things to his insides.

And before he knew what he was doing, before he could remember any one of the dozen reasons that it was a bad idea to get more involved with her, he lowered his head and touched his mouth to hers.

Her lips were soft and warm, and he sank into the kiss. He tried to keep it simple, to maintain some distance. But then her tongue slipped inside his mouth, searching, tasting, teasing, and he was lost. With a groan Joel slid his hands down her slender torso to her hips, pulling her more fully against him. Soft curves molded to hard angles, joining them together as completely as two pieces of a puzzle.

Oh, man, he was obviously in big trouble if he was starting to think in terms of romantic clichés. He wasn't ready for this, he didn't want this, but he was damned if he could do anything about it. His attraction to Riane was one thing—he could dismiss that as purely instinctive, nothing more than a natural physical reaction. But the sweetness of her kiss, the yielding of her body, were doing strange things to his heart. He didn't want to get emotionally involved. He couldn't.

His mind screamed at him to retreat; his body urged him to advance. Since he feared his body might collapse from sheer exhaustion, and since he knew he couldn't take their relationship to the next level until he'd clarified the reasons for his presence in West Virginia, he opted for retreat.

Slowly, regretfully, he eased his lips from hers.

Riane opened her eyes. Then she ran her tongue over her bottom lip, as if to savor the taste of him there. The unconsciously seductive gesture only aroused him further. He forced himself to take a step back.

''I'll call you tomorrow. Later,'' he amended.

And he made a hasty retreat.

He didn't call, Riane thought with more than a little annoyance when she walked into the kitchen later that morning. If he'd called, she could have prepared herself. Instead he'd just shown up, and she was helpless to prevent the silly flip-flops her heart was doing in her chest when she found him at the table enjoying a breakfast of pancakes and bacon.

''You said you would call,'' she said by way of greeting.

Joel's head swiveled toward her, his eyes skimming over her short, silky robe with obvious approval.

''Good morning,'' he said. ''And I did call. Sophie said you were sleeping and invited me to come for breakfast.''

''I didn't think you'd mind,'' Sophie said, flipping more pancakes on the griddle. ''Especially considering how helpful Mr. Logan was last night.''

Riane took a mug from the cupboard. ''I thanked Mr. Logan for his assistance. I'm sure breakfast wasn't necessary.''

"Not necessary," Joel agreed. "But appreciated. These are great pancakes, Sophie."

Sophie beamed and refilled his plate, then set another plate at the table for Riane.

"Sit," Sophie directed.

"I'm not hungry," Riane said.

"Eat."

Riane sighed and sat. Sophie continued to watch until Riane picked up the fork.

"Where's Adam?" Joel asked, not bothering to hide his smirk.

"Still sleeping." He'd been restless and whimpering, so Riane had sat beside his bed throughout the night, his hand secure in hers. She didn't mind—she hadn't been able to sleep anyway as the memory of that bone-melting, skin-tingling kiss she'd shared with Joel had kept her body stimulated long past the hour when her brain was more than ready to shut down.

"You should be sleeping, too," Sophie told her.

"I'm okay," Riane said, stifling a yawn.

Sophie's look was one of patent disbelief but she made no further argument. "I'll go see if he's ready for breakfast," she said, dropping a fresh stack of pancakes on the platter before ducking out of the room.

"Actually, I'm glad you're here," Riane said to Joel.

"Why's that?"

"Because I want to hire you."

"Sorry?"

"You are a private investigator, aren't you?"

"Yes," he agreed slowly.

She nodded. "I've been thinking about this all night. As much as I want Adam to stay here, I know his aunt needs to be found."

"Social services will track her down," Joel said.

"I know. Eventually. But you could do it faster."

"I could," he agreed. "Why are you so anxious to find her?"

"Because Adam has a right to know what's going to happen to him. He's had enough upheaval in his life lately, and I don't want him to get settled here only to be torn away again."

"What if the aunt can't take him?"

"Then at least we'll know, and we'll deal with it."

He hesitated. "I'm not sure I should get involved in this."

Riane shrugged. "If you can't do it, I'll find someone else. I just thought, since you were here, with so much time on your hands..."

"Ahh. You're trying to keep me occupied—away from you."

"I'm offering you a legitimate job. Take it or leave it."

And that was how Joel found himself driving through the streets of Woodburn, Pennsylvania, on Monday morning. It had been remarkably easy to find Lois Ryder. A phone call to a friend at the Department of Motor Vehicles and he had her address—1314 Paradise Avenue.

If it wasn't really paradise, it was a hell of a lot closer to it than the run-down apartment complex where Adam had lived with his mother. The neighborhood was postcard pretty, with well-kept houses and neatly manicured lawns littered with bicycles and toys. Number 1314 was a large two-story with blue siding and white gingerbread trim.

Joel parked his vehicle across the street and picked up his digital camera, snapping a few quick shots.

If only his search for Rheanne Elliott had been half as successful.

Rheanne. Riane.

He knew it wasn't just a coincidence. His gut didn't believe in coincidences.

Unfortunately, his gut was a little short on facts.

He tossed the camera back onto the empty passenger seat and pulled away from the curb, unable to shake the feeling that the woman he'd been hired to find was right in front of him.

* * *

After his trip to Woodburn, Joel decided to return to Fairweather to check in with his client, and they agreed to meet for coffee at the courthouse café.

"I'm glad you could meet me on such short notice," Joel said, as Shaun McIver pulled out the empty chair across from him.

"I'm anxious for an update," Shaun told him.

"I don't have much to tell you," Joel warned. "It's almost as if the child ceased to exist when she was taken out of her parents' home."

"Gavin Elliott wasn't any help?" Shaun prompted.

"Not much." In his brief meeting with Rheanne's biological father, Joel had got the impression the man was holding something back, but he didn't share that feeling. "He did lead me to a Samuel J. Rutherford, the attorney who handled the adoption."

"Well, that's something," Shaun said.

"It's a dead end," Joel said dryly. He waited for the waitress who'd refilled their coffee cups to move out of earshot before continuing. "Sam Rutherford passed away three years ago.

"His secretary still works at the firm and she found an old file labeled Elliott-Adoption. But the only documentation in it was a copy of Rheanne Elliott's birth certificate, which we already had from the registrar's office.

"We really don't have anything else," Joel admitted. "By all accounts, Rheanne seemed to drop off the face of the earth before her second birthday. But in August of that year, another child's birth was registered through the American Consulate in Tavaria. Her name is also Riane, spelled *R-I-A-N-E.*"

"But she would be two years younger than the woman we're looking for," Shaun pointed out.

Joel shook his head. "The child's birth wasn't registered until she was two years old."

"You think the people who adopted Arden's sister took her out of the country and registered her as their own child?"

"I think that's a possibility," Joel agreed.

"Do you have any other evidence?"

"It's all circumstantial," Joel warned.

"I'm not worried about it holding up in court," Shaun said dryly. "I just want to find my fiancée's sister."

"Okay." Joel summarized the few facts he and Mike had managed to compile: "The lawyer who handled the adoption of Rheanne Elliott is a distant relative of the other Riane's mother, and the caseworker assigned to investigate the complaint is her godmother."

Shaun considered this information. "Don't you think they would have changed her name, not just the spelling?"

"That bothered me at first," Joel admitted. "But the child was almost two years old. It would have been traumatic enough for her to be removed from her home and sent to a new family in a new country without changing her identity as well."

"Where is this Riane now?" Shaun asked.

"Mapleview, West Virginia."

"You've seen her? Met with her?"

"Yes, on both counts."

"When can I meet her?" Shaun said.

Joel hesitated. "If this woman is Arden's sister, she has no idea she was adopted."

"I hadn't considered that possibility," Shaun admitted.

"There's something else you need to consider."

"What's that?"

"If I'm right—and I still can't be one hundred percent certain—the adoptive mother is Ellen Rutherford-Quinlan."

Shaun frowned. "Rutherford-Quinlan? As in *Senator* Rutherford-Quinlan?"

"Yeah."

"Christ."

Joel just nodded.

"I know it would mean the world to Arden to find her

sister,'' Shaun said. ''But I'm not sure she'd want to turn Rheanne's whole world upside down in the process.''

''Arden still doesn't know you're looking for her?''

Shaun shook his head. ''I wanted to wait until we knew something definite.''

''The senator and her husband have been out of town,'' Joel told him. ''They should be back on Friday.''

''Do you think you'll get anything out of her?''

''I can only hope.'' Without any concrete evidence that the senator and her husband had adopted a child, there was little else he could do.

''If she won't cooperate, what about DNA testing?''

''It's something we could consider,'' Joel agreed. ''As a last resort. There are a few problems with that approach, however.''

''Such as?''

''Primarily the fact that Arden and Rheanne are only half sisters. Without a comparative sample from the mother, the results wouldn't be one hundred percent conclusive. Plus, the labs are so backed up with DNA testing for criminal trials and paternity cases, it could be months before we got any results.''

''I can't wait months.''

''Are we working on a deadline?''

''Not really.'' Shaun raked a hand through his hair. ''I just want this to be over for Arden. She hasn't seen her sister in more than twenty-two years, but I know not a day has gone by in all that time that she hasn't felt the void in her life.

''I see her looking at that picture sometimes—the same picture you have a copy of—and I know she's wondering, worrying. She needs to know. She wants to move on with her life, to put the past behind her, but I don't think she'll ever be able to do that until she knows what happened to her sister.''

''Then you want me to follow up on this?''

Shaun nodded, giving him the green light to go back to West Virginia.

Joel wished he could be making the trip for any reason other than to destroy Riane's beliefs about her perfect family.

On Tuesday, Riane received Joel's report on Lois and David Ryder. By courier. She sat at her father's desk in the den and thumbed through the pages, wondering what it meant that Joel had chosen to send the file rather than deliver it himself.

Maybe he'd found the witness he'd come to Mapleview in search of. Maybe he'd finished his business in West Virginia and had gone back to Pennsylvania. Maybe he'd found someone else to show him around—a woman who might be willing to play tour guide in the bedroom.

Riane groaned and shook her head. She'd hired Joel to find Adam's aunt, and he'd done that. Anything else he did or didn't do wasn't any of her business.

So, resolved, she focused her attention on the information in front of her. Lois Ryder, thirty-seven years of age, high school physics teacher. Married twelve years to David Ryder, an electrical engineer and Little League coach. Lois and David were the proud parents of two boys, Matthew and Michael, ages ten and eight. Photos of their home, a four-bedroom in Woodburn, Pennsylvania, were in the file, as was a telephone number.

Tuesday night Riane called Lois Ryder. Wednesday Lois came to pick up her nephew. Her easy and immediate acceptance of the child she'd never known reassured Riane. He was going to a good home, a good family. And he'd been so thrilled to meet his cousins he didn't even look back as they drove away.

It was a positive resolution, and Riane was confident that the security of a new family would help Adam adjust—as much as possible—to the loss of his mother. She was thrilled that he would finally have a future to look forward to.

Why then, she wondered as she watched the van disappear, was she crying?

* * *

Twenty-four hours.

In twenty-four hours Ellen and Ryan Quinlan would be home and he could get answers to the questions that had plagued him for the past several weeks. That was the first thought on Joel's mind when he awoke two days later.

Two excruciatingly long days in which he'd focused his attention on one goal: staying away from Riane. The realization that his feelings had grown so quickly out of control scared the hell out of him, and he knew his only hope was to keep his distance and forget about Riane in any context except how she might be the answer to his investigation.

He grabbed his keys and headed for the door. He needed to get out of this room, to stop thinking about Riane. He told himself he was going out for a bite to eat. Yet somehow he found himself pulling into the long winding drive that led to the Quinlan mansion.

"I thought you'd skipped town," Riane said, when she came downstairs and found him waiting in the den.

He managed a smile, wondering if he'd ever get used to her stunning beauty, wondering if he'd ever see her again after he finished the job he'd come here to do. "I wouldn't go without saying goodbye."

"Is that why you're here?"

"No. I was just thinking about you and somehow this is where I ended up." He glanced around the room. "Is Adam gone?"

She nodded, blinked away a hint of moisture in her eyes. "Yesterday."

He knew there was nothing he could say to make her feel better, so he just put his arms around her. After a brief hesitation, she leaned into him, accepting his comfort.

"Have dinner with me tonight," he said, his earlier resolution to avoid spending time with her pushed aside by a more basic need just to be with her.

Time was running out. He knew the end of the charade was inevitable, but he wasn't yet ready to let her go. He didn't know if he ever would be. There could be no future for them—the senator's daughter and the reclusive P.I. But the logic of the mind couldn't suppress the yearnings of his heart.

"I can't." Riane pulled out of his arms with obvious reluctance. "There's a charity auction at the country club that I promised to attend."

"With Stuart?" he guessed, feeling oddly annoyed.

She nodded.

"Tomorrow, then?" He was begging for scraps of her time, and he didn't care.

But she shook her head. "My parents are coming home tomorrow."

Somehow, the return of the senator and her husband lost all significance when he was with their daughter.

"Maybe I'll stop by to meet them." He was only half teasing. After all, making contact with the senator was his reason for coming to West Virginia in the first place.

"You could," Riane said. "I'm sure they'd like that."

Her confidence only made him feel more guilty. "They wouldn't worry that I was trying to corrupt their daughter?"

"They trust my judgment," she told him.

"Only because they haven't met me."

Riane smiled. "You think your tough-guy persona will intimidate them? We've known people—some were friends, some not so friendly—who make you look like the Boy Scout you never were."

"Did they even have Boy Scouts in Tavaria?" he asked.

As soon as the words were out of his mouth, he recognized his mistake. He'd been drawn into the easy banter, had forgotten to be cautious, but the silence that greeted his question let him know how thoroughly he'd blown it. Just as he knew he'd never have made such a stupid mistake if he hadn't let himself become personally involved with the subject of an investigation.

"How did you know I was in Tavaria?" she asked.

He hoped it wasn't too late for damage control. "You must have mentioned it," he said lamely, unable to meet her gaze.

"I didn't."

"Then I must have, uh, read it somewhere."

"You've investigated me," she said, hurt and anger mingled in her tone.

He wanted to deny it, but he couldn't. He felt guilty enough about his deceptions without adding to his list of sins.

"I should have expected this. I'm used to people prying into my past—it's part and parcel of who I am. But I thought you were different. I *wanted* you to be different."

She laughed, but it was without humor. "The most ironic part of all of this is that I would have told you whatever you wanted to know."

He didn't know what to say. He wasn't sure there was anything he could say that wouldn't make the situation worse.

"Why?" she demanded. "Why were you digging into my past? What did you expect to find?"

"You weren't the focus of my investigation," Joel said. That, at least, was the truth. Initially, anyway.

"The fact that I spent the first six years of my life in Tavaria isn't common knowledge. The only way you could have found that out was if you were researching me..." Her voice trailed off as another thought occurred to her. Her eyes widened in shock, disbelief, anguish. "Or my parents."

He should never have left his hotel room.

"Why? What's going on, Joel? What haven't you told me?"

"I can't talk about this. I'm sorry, but I can't."

"You can and you will," she insisted. "I'm not going to let you use me to hurt my family."

"I'm not trying to hurt anyone," Joel told her.

She laughed, bitterly. "It's an election year—I should have expected this."

"Expected what?"

"Someone trying to sabotage my mother's career. What was the plan? Were you supposed to seduce me and get compromising pictures to discredit her stance on family values?"

Joel was stunned, not just by the accusation but by the hostility in her tone. ''You can't really believe I'd do something like that.''

''What am I supposed to believe?'' she challenged. ''You pretended to be interested in me, all the while digging into my life without my knowledge or consent.''

''I didn't have to pretend to be interested in you,'' Joel told her.

''Then why have you been with me?''

''Because I *want* to be with you.'' He turned away, raked his hands through his hair. ''Damn it, I knew this was a bad idea.''

''What was a bad idea—investigating me, using me, or lying about everything?''

''You were never part of my plan.''

''Oh, that's reassuring,'' she said sarcastically. ''So nice to know you just used me because it was convenient.''

''I never used you.''

''What am I supposed to think? What am I supposed to believe?''

''Just trust me, Riane. Please.''

She laughed. ''You want me to trust you? You've lied to me since the day we met.''

''I've never lied to you.''

''A lie of omission is still a lie.''

Client privilege be damned, Joel decided. He couldn't let Riane continue to believe the worst. ''I came to West Virginia to see your mother.''

''Why?''

''Because I thought she might be able to help with a case I'm working on.''

''What kind of case?''

''I have a client who's trying to find someone.''

Some of Riane's anger seemed to dissipate, her brow furrowed. ''A missing person?''

''Not missing, exactly,'' Joel hedged.

''Then what—exactly?''

"The woman I'm looking for was adopted twenty-two years ago."

"Why do you think my mother can help?"

"The child was adopted privately. The lawyer who handled it was Samuel Rutherford, your mother's second cousin. He died a few years ago, and the file pertaining to the adoption has either disappeared or been destroyed. In any event, I haven't been able to access the relevant information. I can't find the child's biological mother, and the father hasn't exactly been forthcoming with any details."

"What does any of this have to do with my mother?" she asked again, clearly starting to lose patience with him.

He hesitated, reluctant to state the conclusion that would crumble all of Riane's conceptions about her life. But the fierce determination in her eyes forced his hand. She wouldn't let him continue to evade. More compelling than that, however, was the realization he owed her the truth.

"I think you're the woman I'm looking for."

She took an instinctive step back. "I'm not adopted."

"I think you might have been."

"Th-that's ridiculous." Her words were disdainful, but he heard the tremor in her voice, the uncertainty. He saw the questions, the confusion, the panic that swirled in the depths of her eyes.

He stepped toward her, softened his tone, as if it might somehow soften the impact of what he was saying. "Your birth wasn't registered until almost two years after you were born."

"I was born in T-Tavaria," she reminded him. "When the country was on the verge of civil war." She wrapped her arms around herself. "I'm sure my parents had more important things to worry about than registering my birth with the appropriate authorities."

"Or maybe they didn't adopt you until you were two years old."

She shook her head.

"Why won't you even consider the possibility?"

"Because it's ludicrous."

"Just listen to me. Please."

"No. I refuse to waste any more—"

"Your name is the same," he interrupted.

She shook her head. "Is that the basis for your claim? The fact that I have the same name as someone who was adopted more than two decades ago?"

"It's an unusual name," Joel pointed out.

"Unusual, not unique."

"Your birth dates are close—"

"Close?" Riane cut off his explanation. "This is unbelievable. You expect me to accept your asinine theory on the basis of a name and a birth date that isn't even the same?"

"And the fact that the case worker assigned to the missing child was Camille Michaud."

"My—" she swallowed "—my aunt Camille?"

He nodded. He could tell this piece of information surprised her, but she recovered quickly.

"Are you suggesting that Camille just took this baby from its home and gave it to my parents?"

He had to admit it sounded a little far-fetched when she put it in those terms. "I have some questions about her involvement in this situation, and some questions for your parents."

"Maybe Camille knows something about this person you're looking for," she allowed. "But I know my parents aren't involved. They wouldn't lie to me about something like this."

"Are you absolutely certain?" he asked gently.

She stared at him, stunned, hurt, bewildered. And he wished—for the hundredth time—that he'd never accepted this assignment.

"I have pictures," she said at last, seeming to seize that thought with both hands.

"Pictures?"

"Baby pictures."

He frowned. "Baby pictures?"

She crossed to the bookcase and pulled down an old, worn-leather photo album and opened the cover. She pointed to the first page, to the picture of a sleeping infant.

Joel took the book from her. He was hardly an expert on children, but he knew the baby in the picture wasn't more than a few weeks old. Definitely not two years old. He flipped through several pages, his frown deepening as he viewed photographs depicting stages of the baby's growth. First smile, first tooth, first steps.

He'd been so sure his instincts were right this time. He'd been wrong. He closed the cover of the album and met Riane's gaze.

"This might be where you apologize for being a complete ass." Her tone was stiff with anger, her eyes filled with pain.

His heart felt as if it was overflowing with grief and regret. The last thing he'd wanted was to cause her any pain. "I'm sorry, Riane."

"You should be. And maybe this whole incident could have been avoided if you'd been honest about why you wanted to see my mother in the first place."

"Maybe it could have," he admitted.

She snatched the book from his hands, her eyes bright with unshed tears. She turned away and stuffed it back onto the shelf. "I think you should go now."

"Riane, please—"

"No. I want you to leave. *Now.*"

"It was a possibility I couldn't ignore," he told her.

"A possibility," she scoffed. She faced him again, almost defiantly. "If you were as lousy a cop as you are a private investigator, it's no wonder you had to find another job."

Chapter 8

She hated to do it. She hated to admit that it even mattered to her. But after the accusations Joel had made that afternoon, Riane still had too many questions unanswered. So she dug out the file Stuart had given to her—the information *his* investigator had compiled on Joel Logan.

There were newspaper clippings regarding the case he'd told her about—the investigation that had gone bad, ending his career as a cop. Reading through the reports, she could understand why he hadn't wanted to go back to working for the system that had turned on him.

She also got details he hadn't shared with her. The fact that the judge who'd blown the case was named Marcus Rutherford. Seeing the name in black-and-white had given her pause, made her wonder if that was the real reason for Joel's visit to West Virginia. Was there a missing person, or was that another story he'd made up? Was it possible he was pursuing some personal vendetta against her family for the actions of a distant relative she'd never even met?

She read further into the article, learned about the injury

he'd sustained. A near-fatal gunshot wound that had required emergency surgery to remove the bullet lodged in his abdomen. Just the thought made her skin go cold. He could have been killed. She told herself it didn't matter, she didn't care. But she did.

Then she saw the picture. The clipping was dated several years earlier than the rest, but there was no mistaking the nature of the photo or the man in it. It was a wedding picture—Joel's wedding picture.

The pain sliced into her, so sharp and deep it took her breath away. Still she couldn't tear her eyes from the image, painfully clear even through the sheen of her tears. After the initial shock passed, she forced herself to close the cover of the folder. She didn't read any more. She didn't want any more details about his betrayal. She didn't need any more proof to know what an idiot she'd been.

It was time to get ready for her dinner with Stuart, anyway.

In a cheap motel room outside Wheeling, West Virginia, he was also getting ready.

He sat alone in the darkness. Oblivious to the bright sun beyond the drawn curtains. Oblivious to everything but his own agenda.

It was almost time. His plans had been made, each and every detail carefully plotted and scrutinized. The scenario had played out in his mind so many times he didn't doubt that everything would go exactly as he'd envisioned. He closed his eyes, let himself watch the events unfold once more.

She was surprised to see him. That was her first mistake.

She should never have underestimated him, never challenged his domination. He had the power. He was in control. She was helpless. Crying. Begging for mercy.

She didn't deserve mercy. Not after the way she'd betrayed him. But he let her plead. He listened as she cried. Her tears and pleas were proof of his power. He became aroused by the imaginary cries and whimpers.

He wouldn't need to imagine them very much longer.

She thought she'd gotten away. That she was safe. It was just one more illusion to be shattered.

Soon. Very soon.

"What's the matter, honey?"

Riane lowered herself onto the edge of her parents' bed and forced a smile in response to her mother's question. "Nothing."

"Riane," Ellen said patiently.

She sighed, thinking it both a curse and a blessing to have a mother who knew her so well. They'd been home from the airport less than an hour. Her father had already been called into the office to deal with some kind of crisis, signaling that his vacation was well and truly over, which left her mother to zero in on Riane's discontent. "I don't want to talk about it."

"Problems with Stuart?"

"Yes," she admitted, although she'd relegated those problems to the furthest recesses of her mind in response to more immediate concerns.

"Do you want to tell me about it?"

"There's not much to say," Riane said. "I'm not—I can't marry him." She'd always known Stuart didn't love her, but his lack of genuine affection didn't bother her half as much as his admitted unfaithfulness. And after the charity auction they'd attended together the previous evening, she'd told him in no uncertain terms that their relationship was over.

The senator sat on the edge of the bed beside her and put an arm across her shoulders. "Are you okay?"

"It was my decision."

"That doesn't mean you can't be hurting."

"I'm okay," Riane assured her. At least she was confident that the decision she'd made regarding her relationship with Stuart had been the right one. Her feelings for Joel were a lot less clear, the pain of his betrayal more intense.

"I must admit, I'm a little relieved."

Riane turned to her mother, startled. "You are?"

"I like Stuart," Ellen said. "I just never felt that he was the right man for you."

"You never said anything."

"I wasn't dating him," her mother said simply.

"You've always let me make my own decisions—and my own mistakes." Riane sighed, rubbed a hand over the ache in her chest. "I made a big one."

"So this isn't about Stuart?"

"No," Riane admitted.

"Is it Joel?"

Riane wasn't surprised that her mother remembered the name. She nodded.

"What happened?"

Riane just shook her head. She couldn't bear to give her mother all the details, to admit what a fool she'd been. Again. After her disastrous relationship with Cameron Davis, she'd been understandably cautious. Her decision to get involved with Stuart had been a practical one, based on logical reasoning. With Joel she'd followed her heart. And had it broken all over again.

"I'm so sorry, honey."

Riane forced a smile. "Me, too."

"And I'm sorry I wasn't here for you."

"You're here now." Riane's smile came more easily this time. "And I want to hear all the details of your trip. Right now, though, I have to get over to the campground."

"But we just got home," Ellen protested.

"And Daddy's already dealing with yet another crisis at the office," Riane pointed out.

"All the more reason for you not to abandon me, too."

"I won't be long," Riane promised. "I just want to go over the changes the architect has suggested before the construction crew comes back in the morning."

It could have waited until the next day, but she was still feeling a little raw about the whole situation with Joel and she needed some time alone.

"Riane?"

She turned back to her mother.

"I love you, baby."

Riane's eyes filled with tears as she went into her mother's arms. The rest of her life might be a mess, but she knew she could always count on her parents. Her family was everything to her—her safe harbor through any storm—and she would never forgive Joel for trying to take that way from her. "I love you, too."

Joel could hardly believe that his whole theory had been blown to pieces by baby pictures.

But the photos Riane had pulled out were tangible and undeniable proof of his mistake. If the senator and her husband had adopted Rheanne Elliot when she was almost two years old, they wouldn't have pictures of her as an infant.

So now that Joel knew Riane Quinlan wasn't Rheanne Elliott, there was just one reason for him to stay in Mapleview: Ellen Rutherford-Quinlan. She was still his only connection between the parties involved, so he reverted to Strategy B—hanging around West Virginia to speak with the senator.

Still, having a contingency plan didn't make him feel like any less an idiot. His instincts had let him down again. The first time they'd failed, he'd lost his job—and nearly his life. This time, he'd followed his gut and he'd lost the woman he…

Joel wasn't sure how to complete the thought.

How did he feel about Riane?

He cared about her, more than he'd expected to in such a short period of time. And he hated that his deception and speculation had hurt her. Which was the main reason he wished he could just skip town—as if distance might somehow assuage his guilt.

Besides, Riane had made it clear that she didn't want to have anything more to do with him. It was his own fault, he knew. He should have been honest with her from the outset.

All he could do now was track down the real missing child

and put this whole situation behind him. And the only hope he had of doing that was to talk to Senator Rutherford-Quinlan. So instead of heading back to Pennsylvania the next morning, as he wanted to do, Joel found himself driving toward the Quinlan mansion.

He'd followed the same route so many times in the past few days that his car could probably negotiate the course on its own. As he pulled up in front of the house he was grateful that Riane's car was absent from its usual parking space. Not only did he want to spare her the discomfort of another confrontation, he was certain she would do everything she could to prevent him from talking to her mother.

Yes, Riane's absence was a good thing.

Why, then, did he feel so empty inside?

He pressed the doorbell, expecting it would be Sophie who responded to the summons. Expecting to have a few more minutes to prepare his speech before he had to see the senator.

But the woman who opened the door could be none other than Ellen Rutherford-Quinlan herself. He'd seen pictures of her, of course, and clips on the news. She wasn't a blend-into-the-background politician. She had strong views and never missed an opportunity to express them. But nothing he'd read or heard had prepared him for this face-to-face meeting.

She was attractive, tall, although not as tall as Riane, and quite slender. Almost delicate. He reminded himself that there was a sharp mind and steely determination behind the delicate facade. And if he misstepped on this assignment again, she could—and very likely would—squash him like a bug.

''Senator Rutherford-Quinlan.''

Ellen smiled, and in the half second it took her lips to curve, his assessment changed from ''attractive'' to ''stunning.'' She extended a hand. ''Can I help you?''

''Joel Logan.'' He accepted the proffered hand. ''I'm a

private investigator. If you have a few moments, I'd like to speak with you regarding a case I've been working on.''

Her smile dimmed, her gaze sharpened. ''What kind of case?''

''Could I come inside to discuss this?''

She hesitated a second, then nodded and stepped back. She gestured to the French doors that led into the den, the room he'd waited in the first night he'd come here to see Riane. It seemed like a lifetime ago rather than the ten days he knew it to be.

''I'll have Sophie bring in coffee,'' she said, continuing down the hall toward the kitchen.

She returned a few minutes later, Sophie behind her with a gleaming silver coffee service on some kind of antique cart. Sophie acknowledged his presence with a brief nod of greeting and none of her usual warmth. Was her reserved demeanor a result of the senator's presence or a reflection of Riane's animosity?

''Tell me about this case you're working on,'' the senator said when Sophie had left the cart and exited the room.

Joel forced his thoughts away from Riane. ''I'm trying to find a child who was adopted twenty-two years ago.''

If she was surprised, she didn't show it. Which made Joel consider that his visit might not have been completely unexpected. Had Riane warned her mother about the nature of his investigation—or had Mike's discussion with Camille Michaud somehow come to the attention of the senator?

''How do you think I can help you do that, Mr. Logan?''

''I believe the adoption of this child was handled by Samuel Rutherford.''

There wasn't the slightest flicker of recognition. Of course, she was a politician—she was accustomed to public scrutiny, to hiding her personal feelings behind the party line.

''He was your cousin?'' Joel prompted.

''Second cousin, actually.'' She moved to the cart Sophie had left, filled two cups with the fragrant hot brew. She passed one to him. "I believe Sam's specialty was criminal law."

"It was," Joel agreed. "Which is probably why his secretary remembered this particular case."

Her hand trembled, very slightly, as she added a splash of cream to her cup. She seemed to pull herself together again, faced him. "Why do you think any of this concerns me?"

"Camille Michaud," Joel said simply.

The senator met his gaze levelly, unflinching.

"She was your roommate at Vassar."

"She was," Ellen agreed.

"Are you still in contact with her?"

She hesitated briefly, then nodded. She obviously knew he could check her phone records if he wanted to.

"She was the social worker assigned to the case. My partner has been in contact with Ms. Michaud, but she claims not to remember the child."

The senator finished stirring her coffee, took a sip.

Stalling for time, Joel guessed. Considering her strategy.

"Who's paying you to find this child?" she asked at last.

"Why does that matter? Are you going to offer a larger fee not to find her?"

"If you want my cooperation, Mr. Logan, it would be wise not to insult me."

She was right, of course, and he had no reason to make such an accusation. Except that the senator was a Rutherford, and Rutherfords were notorious for bending the rules to suit their own purposes. But he forced down his irritation, unwilling to let his quick temper blow his only lead. "Are you going to cooperate?"

"I want to know who's looking for this child."

"Her sister."

Her cup clattered in her saucer. She set both onto the glossy tabletop and lowered herself to the edge of the sofa, smoothing her hands over her skirt. "Sister?"

He nodded, intrigued by this hint of nerves, the first genuine evidence of any emotion. "The child who was adopted had a half sister, older by about eight years."

"Why would only one child have been taken away?" she wondered aloud.

"The older sister was taken out of the home by a relative. An aunt on her father's side," he explained. "The biological mother of the girls wouldn't consent to this aunt taking the younger child, since there was no blood between them."

"But she let her children be separated?" The senator seemed genuinely shocked, distressed even, by this possibility.

"Apparently."

Before either of them could say anything else, the front door slammed shut and Riane stormed into the room, eyes flashing with venom and fury.

"What the hell are you doing here?"

The senator rose to her feet, obviously shocked by her daughter's outburst.

At that moment the resemblance between the two women struck Joel. It wasn't so much their looks, although they were both tall and both had dark hair. It was the way they carried themselves. With confidence and grace. Although right now every inch of Riane's graceful form was practically vibrating with tightly suppressed anger.

"Riane, honey—"

Riane paid no attention to the warning note of her mother's voice or the restraining hand the older woman laid on her arm. She didn't so much as spare a glance in her direction, but aimed all of her fury at Joel. "Get out!"

"I need to talk to—"

"Haven't you done enough damage without insulting my parents with your neophyte theories?"

"Your mother might be the only person who can help me find the child."

"That isn't her problem, it's yours."

"Riane—"

She shook her head, tears glistening in her eyes. ''Get out.''

He couldn't give up when he was so close to getting through to the senator. He also knew he couldn't stay now, not when he could see how much Riane was hurting. Not when he was the one responsible for her pain.

He took a business card out of his pocket, passed it to the senator. ''If you think of anything at all that might help me, I'd appreciate hearing from you.''

The senator took the card from his hand but didn't glance at it. Her gaze seemed to dart from her daughter to him and back again, concerned, wary and all too understanding.

Joel decided to make an exit while he still could.

It was a long moment after she'd watched Joel's truck disappear before Riane felt composed enough to face her mother again. She was embarrassed by her outburst. It wasn't like her to give free rein to her emotions, but when she'd pulled into the driveway and seen his vehicle parked in front of the house, something inside her had snapped. And all the hurt and anger and frustration she'd kept bottled up inside had burst forth.

''I'm sorry,'' she said at last, turning to her mother. ''I didn't really believe he had the nerve to come back here or I would have warned you.''

Ellen glanced down at the business card in her hand, brushed her thumb over the simple black lettering. ''Courtland & Logan Investigations,'' she murmured. ''I should have guessed.''

''Courtland,'' Riane repeated, feeling an unaccountable chill despite the sunny warmth of the room. ''Is that the same Courtland you asked me about?''

''I would guess so.''

''Then you knew…about Joel's investigation?''

Ellen shook her head. ''Not enough, apparently.''

Riane felt the pressure building at her temples. ''How could you know?''

"Camille contacted us on the ship."

"Then she is...involved in this?"

When Ellen looked at her, Riane noticed that her mother's face had gone white beneath her tan, and her eyes were wide, wary. "I didn't want it to come out like this."

"What? You didn't want *what* to come out like this?" Riane asked, a heavy emptiness settling in the pit of her stomach.

"Ryan and I have talked about almost nothing else since Camille's phone call," Ellen admitted. "And we still hadn't come to any decisions about what to do. But now, after what Mr. Logan said..."

"Now *what?*" Riane demanded impatiently. "What is Camille involved in?"

"It isn't just Camille," Ellen admitted, a single tear sliding slowly down one pale cheek.

Riane had never seen her mother like this—so flustered and obviously upset. She didn't know how to respond. Nor was she certain she wanted any of the answers she'd demanded.

"Camille arranged a private adoption without the knowledge or consent of social services. She could have lost her job, she might have faced criminal charges, but she did it because she knew the child needed a good home and she knew a family who desperately wanted a child."

"Is this the child Joel is looking for?"

Ellen nodded, heedless of the tears that now streamed down her face. "We did what we thought was best. We never knew..."

The "we" scared Riane even more than her mother's tears. It confirmed what she'd suspected, even though she'd refused to admit it: somehow her parents were involved. The throbbing at her temples escalated. She ignored the pounding and put an arm across her mother's shoulders, wanting to comfort her and yet feeling hopelessly inadequate at the task.

"Forget about it, Mom. No one needs to know what happened. Joel doesn't have any evidence. If he did, he wouldn't have come here on a fishing expedition.''

But Ellen shook her head sadly. ''I can't keep this secret anymore.''

The sick feeling inside Riane intensified along with an almost desperate need to halt her mother's next words. She shook her head. ''Forget it. Forget he was ever here.''

''I'm sorry, Riane.''

''Sorry? Why?'' Riane didn't realize her own cheeks were wet.

Ellen looked at her, her soft green eyes filled with regret and sadness. ''The child he's looking for is you.''

Chapter 9

Riane stepped away, stunned. Even though she'd somehow known, in her heart, that it was true, hearing the words hit her with the force of a physical blow. She leaned against the edge of the desk, gulping in lungfuls of air, desperately trying to stop the room from spinning.

Slowly she turned back and faced the woman she'd always believed was her mother. "I was adopted?"

Ellen nodded.

"Why?"

"Because we were desperate to have a child, and the doctors said I wouldn't ever be able to have one of my own."

It was a valid explanation, but it wasn't what Riane wanted to know. "Why did you hide the truth? Why didn't you tell me?"

Ellen dropped her gaze, folded her hands together in front of her. "We couldn't."

"What do you mean—you couldn't? Why couldn't you?"

"Do the details really matter?"

Riane was stunned, infuriated. "Of course they matter. This is my *life* we're talking about."

"We gave you a good life," Ellen reminded her. "We gave you everything."

"Except the truth."

"We did what we thought was best at the time."

"Best for who?"

"For all of us, I like to think." Ellen sighed. "But mostly for me. It was so hard for me to admit that I'd failed."

"Failed how?"

"By not being able to have a child of my own."

"There are lots of women who can't have children."

"I'm not saying my situation was unique, I'm only trying to make you understand how *I* felt."

"Try harder," Riane said bluntly. "Because so far I'm not understanding any of this."

"I was an only child, and my father had been making noises for years about wanting to be a grandfather. I'd always felt that he was disappointed in me, because I hadn't been the son he wanted. I couldn't bear to let him down again."

"So you secretly adopted a child and passed it off as your own to placate your father?" Whatever explanation Riane had expected, this was not it. "Did you even *want* a child? Or was having a baby a calculated maneuver to ensure your inheritance?"

Blinded by tears, she didn't see Ellen's hand swing toward her. But she felt the sting of the palm against her cheek, heard the slap resound in the tense silence of the room. Never, in her entire life had her mother—*Ellen,* she mentally amended—hit her.

Riane gingerly touched her fingertips to her hot cheek. "Was I hitting a little too close to the truth?"

"No!" Ellen's eyes were wide, horrified. "Oh, God, Riane. I'm sorry. So sorry."

She reached out a hand, as if to comfort, but Riane recoiled from the gesture. "Are you sorry for hitting me? Or because it's true?"

"It's not true." Ellen shook her head from side to side vehemently. "Of course I wanted a child. For years Ryan and I tried desperately to have one of our own."

"And when you couldn't, it was easy enough to take someone else's." She didn't try to keep the bitterness from her tone; she couldn't stop the anger and resentment building inside her.

"None of this was easy."

"For twenty-two years you raised me as your own and never gave any indication otherwise." Everything she'd ever believed about herself and her family had been a lie. A whole series of lies, one piled on top of another, until the truth had been buried so deep it should never have been discovered. And it wouldn't have been, if Joel Logan hadn't started digging.

"As far as we were concerned, you were our child." Ellen wiped at the tears sliding down her cheeks. "You *are* our child."

Riane had basked in that knowledge over the years. Now, faced with the realization that Ellen and Ryan weren't really her mother and father, that none of the past twenty-two years had been real, she didn't know how to feel. She was hurt and angry, but overriding all else was an aching emptiness deep inside. A void that obliterated any sense of self she'd ever possessed.

"From the moment you came to us, I believed you were meant to be ours. That God sent you to us—"

"God?" Riane interrupted, her tone derisive. "Are you suggesting that Camille was on His payroll?"

"The Lord works in mysterious ways," Ellen said evenly.

Riane shook her head. "How dare you claim divine intervention as justification for your actions?"

"Whether you believe it or not, *I* believed it. I believed you were given to us because you needed a family to love you as much as we needed a child to love."

"I hope that helps you sleep at night."

"And when *you* go to sleep at night, it's in the home we provided for you," Ellen reminded her tersely.

Riane fell silent.

"You have a right to be angry," Ellen continued, "but I am still your mother and I deserve your respect."

Riane bit back the sharp retort that sprang to her lips, because despite the fact that Ellen hadn't given birth to her, she had been her mother in every way that mattered. And that was why her betrayal struck so deeply. "Did you—" She swallowed around the lump in her throat. "Did you ever really love me?"

The tight lines around Ellen's mouth relaxed a little. "Always. And so much more than I ever would have thought possible."

The unwavering certainty in Ellen's voice sliced through Riane's anger, tore at her heart. She swallowed. "Then why did you have to ruin everything by telling me the truth now?"

It was a ridiculous question, of course. But as furious as Riane was that the truth about her parentage had been hidden for the past twenty-two years, she couldn't deny there was a part of her that wished the lie had continued. So long as she'd been Ellen and Ryan Quinlan's daughter, she'd been someone. Now she didn't know who she was, what was expected of her.

"Do you remember the Christmas when you were four years old?"

Riane frowned. "No."

"I do." Ellen smiled, almost wistfully. "You asked for only two things from Santa that year: a ballerina doll and a sister."

"What does that have to do with anything?" Riane demanded impatiently.

"Have you ever wondered why you wanted a sister so desperately?"

"Only-child syndrome," she guessed, unconsciously echoing the label Joel had used a few days earlier.

"Maybe. Or maybe it went deeper than that."

The throbbing in Riane's head grew faster, stronger.

"Maybe you didn't want *a* sister," Ellen continued, "you wanted *your* sister."

"What—" she swallowed "—what are you getting at?"

"According to Mr. Logan, you have a sister. She's the one who hired him to find you."

"No." She shook her head furiously, refusing to believe it. "You're lying."

"Do you really think I'd lie about something like that?"

"You've lied about everything else!"

Ellen blanched. "You're right. I'm not going to make excuses, because a lie of omission is still a lie." She stepped toward her daughter; Riane stepped back. "I'm not lying about this."

"I would remember if I had a sister," Riane insisted, desperately needing to believe it.

But what if she was wrong?

"You weren't even two years old when you came to us," Ellen reminded her gently.

"If I have a sister, then you took me away from her."

"No! We didn't know. Camille never mentioned another child."

"Would it have made a difference?"

Ellen was silent for a long moment. "I like to think so, but I'm not sure. I'd had four miscarriages in the three years before we went to Tavaria, and each one was more devastating than the last."

Riane didn't want to feel any sympathy. Her emotions were chaotic enough without the tug of empathy that responded to this admission.

"It was one of the reasons we decided to go overseas," Ellen continued. "But I still couldn't escape the sense of failure I felt. And when Camille called and said she'd found a child we could adopt—well, I probably didn't ask as many questions as I should have."

"Then you believe it's true—I have a sister?"

"I don't think Mr. Logan would have made such an allegation if he didn't have the evidence to back it up."

"Evidence," Riane scoffed. "He didn't even have my correct date of birth."

"October second," Ellen said softly.

"October second?" Riane echoed. "But my birthday is August twenty-fourth."

"We changed your birth date to coincide with the date we adopted you," Ellen admitted. "To celebrate the day you came to us."

Riane shook her head. She couldn't believe this was happening, that her whole life was unraveling before her very eyes. Not even her birthday was really hers, but an arbitrary date her parents had chosen.

How many more secrets would be uncovered before this nightmare was over? How many lies had been manufactured to cover the truth? How many deceptions had she unquestioningly accepted?

The questions swirled through her mind now. She wanted to demand answers, but she was afraid to know. She wanted to demand the truth, but she wasn't prepared to accept what it might be.

Instead, blinded by a haze of confusion and tears, she simply walked away.

Not long after he'd left the Quinlan mansion, Joel received the call that he'd started to think would never come. From Felicia Elliott—or Reynolds, as she now called herself—the biological mother of Rheanne Elliott.

After he spent no less than ten minutes assuring the woman he hadn't been hired by her ex-husband to track her down, she finally agreed to meet him.

It was ironic, he thought, that he'd chased this woman from Arizona to California to Michigan, only to find that she was now in Wheeling, West Virginia. Another bizarre coincidence in a case that seemed to be full of them.

He checked out of the hotel and met her at a public coffee

shop. Despite the assurances about his reasons for tracking her down, the former Felicia Elliott was obviously still wary. It was apparent in the way she jumped every time the bell above the door rang, the way her eyes darted around the room, and in the way she was dressed.

There was no doubt that Felicia had once been a beautiful woman, but her thick dark hair was threaded with gray and chopped short, her deep brown eyes were shadowed and bare of makeup, her slender figure hidden beneath baggy pants and an unfashionable sweater. Considering the abuse she'd suffered for so many years at the hands of her second husband, none of this surprised Joel. What surprised—and disturbed—him was her careless habit of referring to the child she'd given birth to and given away as "the kid."

And although he didn't think she was deliberately withholding any information, her recollection about the events of twenty-two years ago was unclear. Joel took a sip of the bitter coffee and reworded his question. "Did you want to give up your baby, Ms. Reynolds?"

She shrugged her thin shoulders. "The kid was difficult. Cried all the time. Always hungry, fussing. I couldn't handle her. My husband couldn't handle her. We did what was best."

"But you hadn't considered adoption until you were approached by this woman?"

"Never thought about it," she admitted. "What are you looking for, Mr. Logan? Do you want me to say that we felt pressured by this woman? That she forced us to give up the kid?" She shrugged again. "Maybe we did feel pressured, but we also felt relieved. Once she was gone, I didn't regret my decision. I don't regret it now."

"Do you remember the name of the people who adopted your child?"

"I don't recall that we were ever told."

He pushed his cup aside, not sure if it was the caffeine eating a hole in his stomach lining or this woman's blatant disregard for the child she'd borne. "It didn't bother you, not knowing who would raise your child?"

"I had other things to worry about. And Gavin never really wanted the kid, anyway."

No matter how many questions he asked, no matter how many times they went over the facts that she did remember, nothing changed. Desperate to jog her memory, Joel pulled a picture out of his wallet. "Do you remember when this was taken?"

A trembling finger traced the faces of the two young girls in the photo. "It was Arden's ninth birthday. Rheanne was about eighteen months old."

It was the first time she'd mentioned either of the girls by name, and the wistfulness in her voice made Joel realize that she had, at least at one time, loved her children. And if she had cared about them, she might have kept some mementos.

"Would you happen to have any other pictures of Rheanne?" Joel asked. He knew he was grasping at straws, but if he could get a better photo, he might be able to have it enhanced and computer aged. He needed something more than what he had in order to continue his search for Arden's sister.

But Felicia shook her head. "We gave away the pictures with the kid."

Riane kicked the tire of her BMW coupe, as if it was somehow the fault of the vehicle that she'd run out of gas. She knew it was her own stupidity. She'd been driving for hours since she'd left home, following the same path in and around Mapleview, never once looking at the gas gauge. But she wasn't feeling very rational or logical at the moment. She didn't know how or what to feel. Hell, she didn't even know who she was anymore.

Except that she was alone. Completely and utterly alone, and stranded on the side of a road going to God only knew where.

She reached into her purse for her cell phone, resigned to

calling the automobile club and admitting that she'd been a scatterbrain. It would probably make the papers: Senator's Daughter Runs Out of Gas on Roadside. She gave a half laugh. Except that she wasn't the senator's daughter, not really.

Well, running out of gas wasn't so bad. It could be worse—such as her cell phone battery being dead.

Riane threw the phone onto the passenger seat in disgust.

Damn Joel Logan, anyway. If he hadn't started digging around, prying into her past, she'd be at home right now in her nice warm bed.

She glanced around, could see nothing but thick trees lining either side of the gravel road. The sun was starting to go down, which meant it would be dark in about an hour. Riane sighed and looked down at her attire. She was still wearing the silk dress and high-heeled pumps she'd put on to pick her parents up from the airport. Now she was going to have to trudge down this dusty road in search of a phone.

But who was she going to call when she found one? The auto club was the obvious choice. They could tow the car or take her to a gas station. Then what was she going to do? She wasn't ready to go home, but she had nowhere else to go.

She closed her eyes, irritated when her thoughts strayed to Joel once again. No. There was no way she'd turn to him for help. Not when he was the one responsible for this whole mess.

Joel was on his way back to Mapleview when he found Riane's car, apparently abandoned, on the side of the road.

Riane, however, was nowhere in sight, and the night was dark and heavy. He drove along a little farther, but the street was deserted. He called the house, even though he knew she wouldn't be there if her car was here. The senator reluctantly confirmed that Riane had left a few hours earlier, upset after a discussion they'd had.

He didn't need to be told that Riane Quinlan was Rheanne

Elliott, nor did he get any satisfaction from the fact. The only thing that mattered now was finding Riane.

He couldn't begin to imagine how she'd felt when she'd realized that everything she'd believed in had been a lie. She was probably still angry with him, too, and he knew she had reason to be. It didn't make him feel any better to know that he'd finally succeeded in doing the job he'd been hired to do. Which reminded him that he should contact his client to share the news, but not yet. Not until he found Riane and knew she was okay.

After several more miles had passed with no sign of Riane or any kind of dwelling, he turned around and went back in the other direction. He slowed his vehicle as Rusty's Tavern came into sight. He couldn't imagine that Riane would ever set foot in such an establishment, but he couldn't disregard the possibility. She wasn't the kind of woman who was easily overlooked, and maybe someone inside would remember seeing her.

He felt responsible, at least in part, for Riane's disappearance. He wanted to blame her parents—the senator and her husband. After all, they were the ones who had lied to Riane for twenty-two years. But he knew it wasn't that simple. And it had been his investigation that had precipitated the crumbling of the foundation of her whole world.

Was it some kind of white knight syndrome that made him want to lift her up from that crumbling foundation? Or had he really fallen for the senator's daughter?

The strains of a mellow country-western tune drifted out the open windows of the tavern. He pushed open the door of the bar and stepped into the dimly lit interior.

A quick scan revealed most of the tables around the perimeter of the dance floor were occupied, as well as a majority of the stools that lined the scarred expanse of bar. And that was where he found her.

She was sandwiched between two men, her long dark hair falling straight down the back of the same peach-colored dress she'd been wearing earlier. She turned her head to respond to something the man beside her said, and her eyes locked with his.

He didn't believe in déjà vu, but the sensation that curled in the pit of his stomach when she saw him was reminiscent of the night they'd first met at the charity ball. Unlike that first night, however, she didn't smile. She didn't make a move toward him. She just turned her head away, tossing her hair over her shoulder, dismissing him.

Joel moved purposefully across the room, leaning down to brush a quick kiss on her lips before she could avert her face. It was a tactical move, yet it gave him enough of a taste of her that he craved more. He knew that if he tried to take it, though, she'd probably deck him. So he smiled. "Sorry I'm late, sweetheart."

When she turned to glare at him, he sent a meaningful look at the cowboy seated beside her. The other man took the nonverbal hint and pushed back his stool, moving on to search for other company.

"Clint and I were in the middle of a conversation," Riane said coolly, picking up the glass of beer in front of her.

"Your parents are worried about you," he said.

"Is that why you're here?"

"Partly." He straddled the now-vacant stool beside her, ordered a draft beer. "I was worried about you, too."

"Well, as you can see, I'm fine."

"You're drinking watered-down beer in a country-western bar," Joel said mildly. "I don't think you're fine."

"I like this place," Riane told him. "The people are friendly, the mood is mellow, the beer is cold."

"How much of that beer have you had?" he asked, passing a few bills to the bartender for the glass set in front of him.

"Not enough," she said.

"Drinking yourself into oblivion isn't the answer, Riane."

"It's a start."

"Why don't we go somewhere to talk about this?"

"I don't want to talk about it. And I *definitely* don't want to talk to you."

"You can't blame me for something that happened more than twenty years ago."

"Maybe not," she acknowledged. "But I can, and I do, blame you for what's happening now."

"I was only doing my job, Riane."

"I hope that helps you sleep at night." Then she slid off her stool, not looking entirely steady on her feet, and moved to the other end of the bar where the cowboy she'd been speaking to earlier had relocated.

Joel sipped his own beer. He'd be damned if he'd chase after her. He *had* only been doing his job. This wasn't his fault; she wasn't his responsibility. And yet he knew he couldn't leave her here. It had taken only one glimpse into those dark eyes of hers to see that she was feeling alone and vulnerable. And the cowboy was looking decidedly encouraged that Riane had sought out his company again.

Resigned to settling in for the night, Joel finished his beer and went outside to make a phone call.

Riane wasn't sure whether she was relieved or disappointed that she'd managed to brush Joel off so easily. She didn't want him here; she didn't need him. And yet, even in the crowded room, she felt alone.

And she felt like a coward. It wasn't in her nature to run away from something just because it was unpleasant. Her parents had taught her to take a stance, adhere to her principles. People had often commented that she was a lot like her mother—strong and determined—and she'd always been proud of that fact. But Ellen Rutherford-Quinlan wasn't really her mother.

She sighed and finished the last few drops of beer in her glass, still stunned by the realization that the truth about her parentage had been hidden from her for so many years.

The song on the jukebox changed to something softer, slower.

"Dance with me," Clint said, rising to his feet.

It wasn't really an invitation, but Riane didn't care. Maybe dancing would help get her mind off other things. That's really all she wanted right now—to forget. Forget that everything she'd thought and believed about herself and her life had been a lie.

The cowboy pulled her into his arms, a little too close for comfort, but she didn't protest. She laid her cheek against his shoulder, closed her eyes. It was nice to feel his arms around her, to lean on his strength. He wasn't Joel, but—

She pushed aside the thought. She didn't want to be with Joel. If she should be thinking about anyone right now, it was the man who was holding her. The man whose hand was inching lower, from her waist to her hip, from her hip to the curve of her behind, lower still, until he was cupping her buttock. He pulled her closer, tighter against him, until she could feel the evidence of his arousal. Panic began to rise inside her, slowly, steadily, as he ground his pelvis against her.

He dipped his head to skim his lips over her ear. His breath was hot against her neck. He was an attractive man; she should be attracted to him. But she wasn't. Because he wasn't Joel. And she mentally cursed Joel Logan again for being the first thought on her mind. It wasn't fair that he'd gotten to her so effortlessly, turned her entire life upside down and walked out again.

She forced her attention back to the cowboy. Clint, that was his name. He was sweet and attentive. Okay, he was a little too free with his hands, but maybe what she really needed to forget this whole mess that was her life, was a night of mindless sex. It always seemed to work in the movies, anyway. And cowboys always had starring roles in romance novels. She wondered if they made love with their boots on, and giggled at the thought.

Giggled?

Riane *didn't* giggle. Ever.

She giggled again.

Maybe she'd had more to drink than she'd thought. She couldn't really remember how many times the bartender had set a new glass in front of her.

The hand that was on her butt squeezed lightly again, the other moved along her side, skimmed the side of her breast. Riane felt her stomach lurch, and she pushed away from him.

"Hey," Clint protested, grabbing for her again. "What's the matter?"

Riane shook her head. "I'm sorry. I can't— I...I have to go."

He didn't let go of her. "You're not going anywhere, honey. Your car's broken down on the side of the road, remember?"

She closed her eyes, groaning softly. She had forgotten. She was well and truly stranded.

"Why don't you come home with me, honey? We'll come back out here in the morning and take a look at your car."

She knew it was a bad idea, although her brain seemed pretty foggy right now and she wasn't sure exactly *why* it was a bad idea. "Can't you look at my car now?" she asked.

"It's too dark out there to see what's wrong," he told her.

"I think I just ran out of gas." Yes, she was sure she remembered now. She'd been driving a long time and had forgotten to monitor the gas gauge.

"Then we'll come back in the morning with a can of gas," he said. "You're in no shape to drive home tonight, anyway."

She nodded, then wished she hadn't when the room started to spin. He was right, of course. It would be better to find someplace to sleep, then reevaluate the situation in the morning.

"Are you ready to go?"

She started to nod again, thought better of it. "Yes," she said instead.

Chapter 10

Joel had been in his share of scrapes in his life, and he'd always held his own well enough. But he'd never been in a bar fight, he'd never fought over a woman, and he didn't intend to start now. He also didn't intend to let Riane leave with the cowboy who was currently directing her toward the door.

Joel stepped into their path, pasted what he hoped was a friendly smile on his face. "Thanks, pal," he said to the man at Riane's side. "But I can take it from here."

The man might have backed off easily enough before, but he wasn't inclined to do so now. Of course, Riane had given him additional encouragement on the dance floor, allowing him to grope her in public. Which was when Joel realized, without a doubt, that she was drunk. Not tipsy, not happy, not just a little uninhibited. She was completely, stinking drunk, and she probably had no idea that the man beside her was mentally ticking off the minutes until he could have her out of the sexy little dress and on her back.

"I don't think so," the cowboy drawled, tightening his

arm around Riane's shoulders. "The lady's coming home with me tonight."

"The lady's not going anywhere with you," Joel denied.

"Take it outside, boys," the bartender called over, obviously anxious to avoid any brawling in his establishment.

Joel looked at Riane, concerned, as her face seemed to go from flushed to pale in half a second. "Are you okay, Riane?"

"She's fine," the cowboy responded for her.

"Riane," Joel said again, trying to appeal to reason.

"I think I'm going to be sick," she said, pulling away from the cowboy and pushing through the front door.

The cowboy backed away so fast he almost created a draft. He didn't seem to mind taking advantage of an intoxicated woman, but he didn't want to have to clean up after her.

Joel shook his head and followed Riane out the door.

She was leaning against the side of the building, her cheeks still pale, her lips trembling, a fine sheen of perspiration on her forehead.

"Are you okay?" he asked gently.

She started to shake her head, then apparently thought better of it. "I think I'm drunk," she told him.

His lips twitched. "You're wasted, sweetheart."

"I can't be. I don't get drunk. Ever."

"There's a first time for everything," he said.

She started to shake her head again, then bent at the waist and threw up.

Joel caught her hair and pulled it back, holding it behind her head and out of the line of fire as she continued to retch. Apparently, she'd consumed quite a bit of alcohol, more than he'd have thought she'd be able to hold inside and still stand up. It almost made him admire her tenacity, even though he had no idea what he was going to do with her now.

"Do you feel better?" he asked, after the bout of vomiting had finally stopped.

"No." She straightened and shook off his hand. "But I don't think I have anything left inside me."

She didn't protest when he led her over to his truck. Or when he opened the passenger side and helped her inside. "I'll be right back," he told her.

"Wait." She put her hand on the door and looked up at him with watery eyes. "Don't leave me here."

"I'm just going inside to get you some paper towels."

Still she hesitated.

"I'll be gone half a minute," he told her. "I promise."

"Okay," she relented.

He was gone only as long as promised, returning with a handful of paper towels he'd moistened in the bathroom. He opened the passenger door again and gently wiped her face. The cool water must have helped revive her, because she took the towels from him and finished the task herself.

"Why are you here, Joel? Why did you come back?"

"I needed to see you again. I want to try and explain."

She closed her eyes, leaned her head back against the seat. "Do you think anything you have to say will make a difference at this point?" Her voice was sad, resigned, and he hated that he'd had any part in bringing this misery upon her.

"Probably not," he admitted. "But I didn't want you to think that you didn't matter to me, because you do."

She opened her eyes, looking at him with a combination of wariness and sadness.

"Are you ready to go home now?"

"No." Her response was immediate and vehement.

"You can't run away from this forever," he said.

"I know. I just can't face them tonight." She closed her eyes again. "Not like this."

"Okay," he relented, already knowing he would regret it.

Riane was mortified. Completely and utterly mortified. She wasn't sure if she'd really puked all of the alcohol out of her system, but she'd sobered up enough to be thoroughly embarrassed by her own behavior. She'd *never* done anything like this; she never would have dared. But the Riane Quinlan who'd been raised to always be on her best behavior, who was conscious that any wrong step could be exploited by the scandal-hungry media, hadn't been inside Rusty's Tavern. The woman at the bar, desperately and ineffectually trying to drown her misery in watered-down beer, had little in common with the senator's daughter. She didn't even know who she was.

Now, she was at some two-bit motel off the side of the highway with a man she barely knew. Well, at least she knew Joel better than she knew Clint, and she'd almost been ready to go home with him. *That* would have been a mistake of monumental proportions.

Maybe she should have allowed Joel to take her home. It probably would have been the smartest thing to do. But she just wasn't ready to deal with any of this right now. She wasn't ready to face her own feelings about everything.

Did that make her a coward?

Maybe.

She was leaning against the hood of his truck, taking deep breaths of the cool night air. Her head was still spinning, and her stomach was a little unsettled, but she thought the worst of it had passed. Now she was just waiting for Joel to come back with their room keys, then she could drown herself in the shower.

"They only had one vacancy," Joel told her, holding up the single key on a square plastic holder.

Riane scanned the sad exterior of the building. The faded orange brick, the peeling paint around the dingy windows, the rusted numbers nailed into scarred doors. But sure enough, there were vehicles parked outside of almost every unit. Except for the second one from the end.

"Number 9," Joel said. "It has two beds."

"That's fine." Riane knew she was in no position to object.

"There was a little general store attached to the office," he told her, passing her a small brown paper bag. "So I picked up a few things I thought you might want."

Riane opened the bag as he went around to the trunk to

get his suitcase. He was obviously a little more prepared than she for this roadside adventure. She knew it was silly to be annoyed by the fact that he would have a change of underwear and she wouldn't, and any hint of resentment was forgotten when she dipped into the bag and found a toothbrush and toothpaste, a travel-size bottle of shampoo, and a bag of corn chips. She almost wept with gratitude. "Thanks."

He shrugged, as if it was no big deal, but it was. At least to her. She was hot and sweaty and embarrassed, but maybe she wouldn't need to drown herself in the shower, after all. If she could just wash her hair and brush her teeth, she might actually feel human again.

"I thought you might be hungry," he said, then grinned as her stomach growled in response to his statement.

"Starved," she admitted, only now realizing she hadn't eaten since breakfast. She hadn't even given a thought to food. But she did so now, taking out the bag of corn chips and tearing it open.

"Well, you can start with those," he said, gesturing to the bag. "And we can always order a pizza if you're still hungry."

"Pizza?" She perked up immediately. Joel laughed.

Riane followed him into the room. It wasn't much more than he'd said—two twin beds, each with horrid orange floral covers. She wondered if the decorator had consciously tried to match the interior decor with the exterior facade. What other reason could there be for such a particularly putrid shade?

She continued her cursory survey of the room. A single table with a lamp sat between them. On the other wall was a long dresser with a television on top of it and a paper card advertising several triple-X movie options. Past the dresser was a closed door. Riane pushed it open and flipped on the light. The bathroom was as sparse as the bedroom—a shower stall, toilet and pedestal sink. But it looked relatively clean, and the towels were neatly folded.

"I'm going to take a shower," Riane told him.

"I'll order pizza," Joel said.

She offered him a tired smile. "Thanks. Sun-dried tomatoes, artichoke hearts and hot peppers."

She didn't see the face Joel made as she closed the door.

The pizza delivery boy had just left when Riane stepped out of the bathroom.

Joel did a double take. She stepped out of the bathroom wearing only a silky camisole with tiny straps and a matching pair of high-cut underwear. Her skin glowed, her hair was damp, and her nipples pushed against the fabric of her top. What was she trying to do to him?

He snapped his jaw shut, unstuck his tongue from the roof of his mouth, and somehow managed to speak. "Where's your dress?"

"I hung it up in the bathroom."

"I think you should put it back on."

She frowned. "I can't sleep in it."

"You're going to sleep in *that?*"

"I left my pajamas in the bar," she said dryly.

He'd never even thought about what she was going to sleep in. He had his suitcase because he'd checked out of the hotel after his meeting with the senator, but Riane had been stranded on the side of the road with nothing but whatever she carried in that little purse. Obviously, a pair of pajamas wasn't an option.

"I have a T-shirt you could put on," he offered.

"This is fine," she said.

"No, it's not," he grumbled, wondering how the hell he was supposed to get any sleep knowing that she was in the bed beside him in a couple of scraps of tantalizing silk, thinking about how easy it would be to strip them from her body and get his hands on her naked flesh. He lowered the pizza box to hide the evidence of his wayward thoughts, and only then remembered it was there.

"Pizza's here," he said.

"Great. I'm starving."

So was he. But he had no interest in the pizza anymore.

He passed the box to Riane and picked up the remote for the television. He needed a distraction, any kind of distraction, to get his mind off all that tempting skin Riane was displaying. He pressed the power button.

Panting and moaning filled the room as a tangle of naked limbs appeared on the screen. It took Joel less than three seconds to realize that it was a pornographic movie—two seconds longer than it would have if all the blood hadn't already drained from his head into his lap when Riane came out of the bathroom practically naked. He hit the power button again to shut off the television and dropped the remote onto the table with a clatter.

Riane glanced at him strangely. "What was that?"

He shook his head. "Nothing you'd want to watch."

"What was it?" she asked again.

"It wasn't the Disney channel," he said dryly.

"Porn?" She sounded more curious than offended. "I've never seen a pornographic movie before."

"And you're not going to see one now."

"Why not?"

"Give me a break, Riane."

"What's wrong with wanting to expand my horizons?" she demanded.

He tapped the pizza box. "Eat."

She frowned as she flipped open the lid on the box. Her frown deepened as she inspected the contents. "This doesn't look like sun-dried tomatoes and artichoke hearts."

"Expand your horizons."

"You expect me to eat this?" she asked, looking at the pepperoni and sausage with distaste.

"You will if you're hungry," he said easily.

"I'm not sure I'm *that* hungry."

He reached across for a slice. "It has hot peppers."

She still looked skeptical.

Joel bit into his slice, unconcerned. He was hungry, and there was no way he was going to order—much less eat—

something that had no meat on it. He was reaching for his second slice when he heard Riane's stomach growl.

She was eyeing the pizza more wistfully than skeptically now. He offered the slice to her. After a brief hesitation, she took it from his hands.

Joel indicated the two cans of ginger ale on the table. "I found a vending machine outside," he said. "You're probably thirsty."

She nodded, her mouth full of pizza. "Thanks," she said, after she'd swallowed.

He concentrated on his own slice, determined to look anywhere but at her, at all that tempting flesh exposed by her skimpy attire.

"I owe you an apology," Riane said softy.

"For criticizing my pizza?"

She managed a smile. "For calling you a lousy investigator. I guess you were closer to the truth than I wanted to admit."

Joel shrugged. "Forget it."

"I wish I could." She took another bite of pizza, then, "Why didn't you tell me you were married?"

He stiffened instinctively. "I'm not."

"Stuart did some investigating of his own," she admitted. "Trying to find out who you were and why you were interested in me—"

"If Stuart couldn't figure out why I was interested in you," Joel interrupted, "then he's a bigger idiot than I thought."

"He was right to be suspicious, though, wasn't he?"

Joel didn't respond.

"Anyway," Riane continued. "He gave me the file he'd compiled, including a copy of your wedding photo."

"Apparently the file wasn't up-to-date."

"What do you mean?"

"I'm divorced."

"Oh," she said again, a slight furrow marring her brow as she reached for another slice of pizza. "What happened?"

"My wife didn't like my being a cop," he told her. "She kept trying to convince me to go to work for her uncle, who had a security consulting business."

"I can understand why she wouldn't be thrilled by your choice of career," Riane told him. "But I'd have thought, if she loved you, she would have supported you in whatever you wanted to do."

"Obviously she didn't love me." He'd realized that fact soon after they were married. Too late to undo the damage that had already been done, and too soon to understand that they would hurt each other a lot more before they were through.

She'd married him, she admitted later, because her father had forbidden her to do so. It shouldn't have hurt him. It shouldn't have surprised him. It did both.

He wasn't sure he'd loved her, either, but he'd been awed that a woman of such class and sophistication would want him. And he'd cared for her, believing that their marriage would last, that their vows were forever.

"The irony of the whole situation," Joel admitted, "is that we split up when my career with the police department fell apart. We've been divorced for several years now."

Afterward, after the divorce was final and he was alone again, he'd realized he preferred it that way. None of the women who'd moved through his life had brought him anything but heartache and grief.

"Oh," was all Riane said.

"I should have realized it was doomed from the start."

"Why?"

He shrugged. "I was a cop—a bad boy in uniform. She was a college professor's daughter—wealthy, privileged, sheltered."

"You don't think class differences can be overcome?" she asked.

"I don't think we even tried," he admitted. "She wanted the grisly details of my cases to shock her high-society friends, but she never considered how my job affected me."

"I'm sorry," Riane said softly.

He shrugged again, wondering why he was even talking to her about his ex-wife. He'd never shared the details of his ill-fated marriage with anyone, and Riane hardly seemed a logical choice of confidante. Especially since she came from the same kind of wealthy, privileged background as his ex-wife.

On the other hand, maybe Riane was exactly the right person with whom to unburden his soul. After all, he knew everything there was to know about her, it only seemed fair that she be given some inside information about the man who'd destroyed her fairy-tale existence.

He gave himself a mental shake, as if to shake off the guilt that weighed heavily on his shoulders. He shouldn't feel guilty—he wasn't the one who'd lied to her for twenty-two years. But he hadn't been completely honest with her, either, and he refused to hide behind any more half truths. He needed her to know that she was more than a case to him.

"Despite the problems in my marriage—" and there were more than a few "—I never cheated on my wife. And I wouldn't have kissed you if I'd been involved with someone else."

She dropped her eyes, a faint blush staining her cheeks. He would like to think just the memory of those kisses caused her body to heat, but he couldn't rule out the residual effects of alcohol.

"Did you have any children?" she asked, reaching for her can of ginger ale.

"Thankfully, no."

"You don't like kids?"

"I don't have enough experience with them to really say one way or the other. I only meant that I'm glad we never had any. I hate to see what happens to them when a marriage falls apart."

She nodded and took another slice of pizza from the box. It was her third, and she'd devoured the previous two without a single additional complaint about the lack of artichoke hearts.

"Why didn't you leave me at the bar with Clint?" Riane asked, after the last of the pizza had been consumed and the empty box tossed aside.

"Because I didn't want to be responsible for you doing something I knew you'd regret."

"No one's responsible for me but me," she told him.

"You weren't yourself, sweetheart."

"You don't know me."

"Yes," he insisted. "I do. I know the kind of person you are, and I know it's not a habit of yours to go home with men you meet at bars."

"Is this something your investigation revealed?"

"No." He might have dug deeper into her background, he realized, except that he'd felt guilty for intruding as much as he already had. He wanted to know so much about her, but he wanted her to share the information. "I just know it's not you."

She laughed, bitterly. "How can you know the kind of person I am? I don't even know *who* I am."

"Finding out that your mother didn't give birth to you doesn't change the basic facts of who you are."

"It changes everything," she insisted. "Everything I've believed for more than twenty years has been a lie. I'm a fiction—a child they created. They even changed my date of birth."

"Why?" Joel was still puzzled by that bit of information.

"My mother said it was because they wanted to celebrate the day I came to them." Riane didn't sound convinced.

"You don't believe her?"

Riane shrugged. "She seems to have a ready answer for everything. How am I supposed to know what's fact and what's fantasy?"

"I'm not going to pretend I agree with, or even understand, what your parents did," Joel said. "But after talking to your mother today, the one thing I am sure of is that she loves you.''

Riane shrugged again, but he noticed the sheen of tears in her eyes. ''We've always been close. We never went through the usual mother-daughter difficulties. She's always been unquestioningly supportive, unfailingly understanding.''

''Because she loves you,'' Joel said again.

''If she really loved me, how could she lie to me?''

''She told you the truth now,'' Joel pointed out. ''Doesn't that count for something?''

''Maybe she just knew she couldn't keep it a secret much longer.''

''Do you really think that's what prompted her confession?''

Riane sighed. ''No,'' she admitted. ''I think she's genuinely sorry about what happened. The way it happened. But I don't know. I'm not sure I can trust my own feelings about any of this.''

''It's going to take some time to get used to,'' Joel agreed.

''I have a sister I know nothing about,'' she said, speaking almost to herself. ''Someone who apparently cared enough about me to want to find me all these years later, and I don't even remember her. What does that say about me?''

''It doesn't say anything about you. You weren't even two years old when you were adopted.''

''But shouldn't I have known? Shouldn't I have remembered something about the family I'd left behind?''

''You were a child,'' Joel said again. ''You can't take responsibility for everything upon yourself.''

Riane wanted to believe what Joel said was true. Logically, she knew that most people didn't have memories of anything prior to the age of five. But in her heart she felt as if she'd let her sister down by forgetting her. Especially when her sister obviously hadn't forgotten Riane.

She rubbed her fingers against her temple, trying to assuage the throbbing ache as she contemplated the complete upheaval of the past several hours. It was hard to believe that she'd only picked her parents up from the airport that morning. She felt as if she'd lived a lifetime in the interim.

Her parents. Ryan and Ellen. She knew they were probably worried about her, but she couldn't deal with them just yet. She didn't know what to say to them; she didn't know how any of them would handle the disclosures that had been made today. But she did know that if the truth about her parentage ever came to light, if the public ever found out that her mother had sworn false affidavits regarding Riane's birth, Ellen's political career would be over.

Somehow, thinking of her mother's political career brought to mind her own ambitions. And reminded her that the fairy-tale life she'd once envisioned with Stuart was no longer an option. It didn't matter that she'd already decided she couldn't marry him. Her concerns about their partnership were irrelevant now. There was no way Stuart would marry her with the lies of her past ticking like a time bomb, liable to blow up in all their faces at any moment. The truth hit her with the force of a prizefighter's blow. *She was alone.*

"Riane?"

She started when Joel's hand came down on her shoulder. She'd been so preoccupied with her thoughts, her own misery, that she'd forgotten for a moment that he was there. And she needed him now, she needed the comfort of his presence more than she'd needed anything else in her life.

"Are you okay?" he asked, his hand dropping off her shoulder to gently stroke her bare arm. The physical contact banished all other thoughts from her mind, and she turned her head to look at him. She could see the concern in his eyes. Concern…and something else she wasn't sure she recognized. Awareness, maybe. Desire.

Acting purely on instinct, she breached the scant distance that separated them and touched her lips to his. She couldn't have said which of them was more surprised by the boldness of her action. She'd never initiated a kiss with Joel before—

she'd always let him take the lead, as if doing so absolved her of responsibility. Because she'd been afraid.

The realization almost made her pull away. She was afraid of so many things: the emptiness inside her, the uncertainty of her future, the desires she'd never felt before she met Joel. And she was especially afraid that he'd walk out of her life tomorrow and she'd never know what it was like to make love with him.

It was that fear which bolstered her courage. She stroked her tongue over the seam of his lips, slipped inside the warmth of his mouth. He tasted spicy and hot, dangerously tempting.

She heard a low groan rumble in his throat, then she was on her back on the bed, Joel sprawled on top of her. He took control now, his kiss neither coaxing nor gentle this time. Instead he was insistent, demanding. Riane wrapped her arms around him and responded with a passion she hadn't known she possessed.

His hand inched upward along her thigh, his fingers burning a path against her skin.

She felt his hand slip under the edge of her camisole, glide over the skin of her abdomen. Then his hand was on her breast, his thumb teasing the nipple. She arched toward him, her hips rising off the mattress, her pelvis moving against his.

She heard him groan, felt the insistent thrust of his erection against the soft cleft between her thighs, and heat flooded her body. His mouth trailed hot, hungry kisses down her throat. She had never been kissed like this before. She'd never felt so desperately wanted, so desperately needed. She'd never wanted so much that she actually ached inside.

Then his mouth was on her breast, through the silky fabric of her top. His teeth grazed the nipple, sending sharp, hot currents to the very center of her being.

"Oh, Joel, please."

He pushed up her top, eliminating the barrier, and covered her breast with his mouth again. Riane couldn't think, she couldn't breathe. She was assaulted by sensations. Overwhelmed. Out of control. And yet, she wasn't afraid, because it was Joel.

She tugged his shirt out of his pants, wanting to touch him, taste him, explore. She ran her hands eagerly over the taut muscles of his abdomen, the wide, hard planes of his chest, the strong breadth of his shoulders. His skin was hot and damp. She pressed her lips to his shoulder, let her tongue savor the salty warmth of his skin. His low groan of pleasure encouraged her, and she skimmed her lips along the curve of his collarbone, nibbled at the base of his throat.

She let her hands skim down his torso, over the bulge at the front of his jeans. He groaned again. She stroked him through the denim, felt the pulsing response of his erection even through the fabric. She fumbled with the button of his jeans, slid her hand beneath the waistband of his briefs and wrapped her fingers around the hard length of him.

Joel groaned and removed her hand. He rolled onto his back, away from her, his breathing shallow and labored.

It wasn't quite the reaction Riane had hoped for.

She sat up, stunned and aching from his sudden withdrawal. "What's wrong?"

"We can't do this."

"Why not?"

"Why not?" he echoed, scrubbing his hands over his face. "I can think of a hundred reasons."

She straightened the front of her camisole, stung by his rejection, then pushed herself off the bed and walked over to the window. Tears burned her eyes, but she held them back. She wouldn't let him see her cry.

She jolted when his hands settled on her shoulders, hated that she had to fight the urge to lean into him as he stroked down her arms. How could she want him still? Was she so pathetically needy that she would turn to this man again, after he'd already turned her away?

"Your whole life has been turned upside down today," he said gently. "This isn't a good idea."

"Thanks for your input," she said shortly. "But I've been making my own decisions for a while now."

"I don't want to be something you'll regret."

She laughed, but there was no humor in it. "Don't worry about it, Logan."

"I care about you, Riane."

"Is that supposed to let me down easily?"

"You're completely misreading this situation."

"I don't think so."

He turned her to face him, his expression guarded and somehow dangerous. "Do you think I don't want you?"

"I'd think that's pretty obvious."

He hauled her into his arms again, banded his arms around her and covered her lips in a kiss that screamed of anger and frustration. This time she didn't question the desire. She couldn't. It was strong and fierce and all consuming.

But as quickly as he'd pulled her into his arms, he pushed her away. "I want you, Riane, but I don't want it to be like this."

Before she could respond, he was out the door.

And she was alone again.

Chapter 11

She was working at the café. It was exactly where he'd been told she'd be, and he was relieved that his information was accurate. Relieved to see that his wife was okay. And distressed to see her like this. Her beautiful long, dark hair chopped off. Her face pale and bare of makeup. Her slender figure clad in a short black skirt and a low-cut shirt. Serving meals. Cleaning dishes. Flirting with men who were looking down her top.

He felt the rage stir inside him.

Wantonness. Lust. Infidelity. He added to the list of sins for which she would have to atone.

Soon.

For now it was enough to watch. To know that she knew he was watching. And she did. In her heart, in her soul, she knew.

They were linked, after all. Inextricably bound by vows spoken in front of God. Vows that no package of papers delivered by a process server could eradicate.

She turned suddenly toward the window. Her dark eyes

wide, searching. She didn't see him. And she wouldn't recognize him if she did. Still, the coffeepot trembled in her hand.

His lips curved in a satisfied smile as he turned away.

She knew she was being watched.

For now that was enough.

Two days had passed since Riane had found out about her adoption. Two long days in which an uneasy tension had hovered over the Quinlan household like a storm cloud. Her relationship with her parents was strained. Maybe that was understandable, considering recent revelations, but it was unusual.

Would things ever return to the sense of normalcy that had existed before? Or would their family forever be tainted by the lies of the past? Riane had no answers to these questions and no one with whom to share her thoughts and her feelings. No one she could trust with such a secret.

She might have talked to Joel about the situation, but he'd hightailed it back to Pennsylvania after the night they'd spent in the motel. Or the night *she'd* spent in the motel. She still didn't know where, or even *if,* Joel had slept that night, and the short trip from the motel back to her home the following morning had been difficult, the unresolved sexual tension straining through the veneer of polite conversation.

She still blamed him for the upheaval in her life, but she missed him, anyway. He was the one person who knew the truth about her, the one person who hadn't seemed to care that she wasn't who she'd always believed herself to be.

Not knowing where else to turn or what else to do, she kept herself busy at the camp, watching over the construction, catching up on paperwork and doing anything else that would occupy her time. Unfortunately, it wasn't enough to occupy her mind.

So when she came in late on that second night and found her parents together, she shared with them the decision she'd made: "I'm going to Fairweather tomorrow."

"Good," Ryan said. Ellen just nodded.

"I don't know how long I'll be gone," Riane told them.

"Will you call?" Ellen asked.

Riane wanted to refuse, but she knew it would be petty to do so. Instead she nodded.

Ellen forced a smile. "I'm glad you're going."

"Are you?" Riane asked, a deliberate note of challenge in her voice.

"Of course."

"Why?"

Ellen slipped her hand inside her husband's larger one, linking their fingers together. It was a subtle but unmistakable gesture of solidarity, and Riane didn't so much resent it as she resented no longer feeling as if she was a part of that cohesive unit. Since the truth about her parentage had come to light, she'd felt more isolated and alone than ever.

"Because we know you won't stop wondering until you've met your sister," Ryan told her.

"Aren't you worried that I might find something with her that's been missing from my life?"

Riane got no satisfaction from seeing the pain she'd deliberately sought to inflict reflected in her parents' eyes.

"We've thought about almost nothing else since we found out you had a sister," Ellen confessed.

"Then why do you want me to go?"

"Because we've been incredibly selfish for twenty-two years. Because we believe this is something you need to do for you."

"For me?" Riane challenged. "Or for you? Won't it assuage some of your own guilt if I reconnect with the sister I lost?"

"Maybe," the senator acknowledged. "And maybe you've been so dissatisfied your whole life because there's a part of you that hasn't forgotten her."

Riane wanted to believe that could be true, but she'd racked her brain searching for some memory—anything—

that would give her a hint about her sister. Always without success.

"What about my biological parents?" Riane taunted. "Maybe I should look them up, too. We could have a real family reunion."

Ellen paled noticeably, but it was Ryan who responded. "That's enough, Riane." His tone was sharp, commanding. "We know you're hurt and angry, but you don't ever speak to your mother that way."

It was on the tip of Riane's tongue to snap back that Ellen wasn't her mother, but she was tired of the fighting and she knew that hurting her parents wouldn't resolve anything.

Ellen put her other hand on her husband's arm. "If you want to find your biological parents, that's your choice."

Riane sighed wearily. "I don't know what I want anymore."

"Do you want us to go to Fairweather with you?"

The offer shouldn't have surprised her. It did. And what surprised her even more was the urge to accept the offer, to let her parents take control and make everything better—as they always had when she was a child. But she wasn't a child anymore, and this was a journey she had to make on her own.

"Thanks, but I think I need to do this alone."

Ellen nodded, as if she understood. And she probably did. She'd always known what was in her daughter's heart—sometimes before Riane did herself. The realization made Riane feel both petty and ungrateful. She'd been difficult and confrontational since she'd learned of her adoption; her parents had continued to be loving and supportive.

So why couldn't she just forget that she had another family somewhere? Why was she so preoccupied with finding a sister she didn't even remember?

She wasn't sure of the answers to these questions, she only knew that she had to go to Fairweather.

* * *

Now that she was in Fairweather, Riane had no idea how to take the next step.

She drove through the town, propelled by curiosity and indecision, and she was amazed at how much the town reminded her of Mapleview. The tree-lined streets, the classic architecture, the tidy little shops, the friendliness of passersby. Despite the fact that it was more than twice the size of her hometown, it had a similar, welcoming feel. It unnerved her, that someplace she'd never been could feel so much like home.

She parked in front of the Fairweather Courthouse—a beautiful building highlighted with towering white pillars and gleaming, multifaceted windows. Still, she knew it wasn't the architecture that had drawn her to the location, but the possibility that Arden might be inside.

Joel had told her that Arden was a family law attorney, engaged to a criminal defense attorney. She didn't know much more than that, and she wasn't sure where to look or even if she was ready to find Arden. She probably wouldn't recognize her, anyway. The only picture she had of her sister was the one Joel had given to her—a picture taken almost twenty-two years earlier. But she ventured inside and wandered through the halls.

She followed a group of people as they filed back into one of the courtrooms. When the proceedings resumed, Riane quickly realized that Arden was one of the lawyers at the front of the room. The judge never called her by name; the woman never turned around. But somehow Riane knew, and she found it a little disconcerting that she'd happened into this particular room, almost as if drawn by a will stronger than her own.

Determined to banish such nonsensical thoughts from her mind, Riane slipped out before the arguments were finished. The halls were quieter now, and she leaned back against the stone wall and wondered at the fate that had sent her into that courtroom—and the cowardice that had sent her out again.

"Riane?"

She turned, then chastised herself for doing so. She didn't know anyone in this town. The man who had spoken must have been speaking to someone else. But Riane wasn't a very common name, and the speaker was coming straight toward her.

"Riane Quinlan?"

She hesitated briefly. "Yes."

"Shaun McIver." He held his hand out to her, and she accepted it automatically.

It took her a minute to place the name. Shaun McIver was the man who was engaged to marry Arden. The man who had sent Joel to find her. "How did you know who I was?"

"You're kidding, right?"

She frowned.

"The resemblance between you and Arden is unmistakable."

Riane wasn't comfortable knowing she looked so much like the sister she couldn't remember that this stranger had picked her out of a crowd. Okay, so it was a small crowd, but a crowd nonetheless.

"Did you see her?" Shaun asked.

"No. I mean, I think she was in the courtroom, but I didn't talk to her."

"Isn't that why you're here?"

"No, um, I was just passing through."

"Oh." He made no effort to mask his disappointment. "I thought—I hoped—that you'd come to see her. Us."

Riane sighed. "I'm not really sure why I'm here."

"Oh." This time he smiled, as if he understood. "Do you have time for a cup of coffee?"

She glanced at her watch, desperately scrambling for an excuse as to why she didn't have the time, but her brain seemed to have shut down.

"All right," she agreed.

Joel replaced the receiver in its cradle, staring at it warily for several long seconds after he'd terminated the connection.

His instincts were in overdrive again, and he wasn't sure if it was a result of the phone call he'd just completed or because that phone call had brought Riane to mind again.

Again. As if he'd ever stopped thinking about her.

He hadn't seen or heard from her since the morning after the night they'd spent in that dreary little motel room. The night they hadn't made love. The night he'd wished he could go back to ever since and play things differently.

He still believed he'd done the right thing. She'd been vulnerable, half-drunk, and almost engaged to Stuart Etherington III. But he was damn tired of doing the right thing. What he'd wanted to do, what he still wanted to do, was hold her in his arms and spend hours making love with her.

But that wasn't a likely scenario. He'd done his job. His client was satisfied, and Joel had other cases to focus on. But Riane was never far from his thoughts.

Which was why that telephone call bothered him. What possible information could Gavin Elliott have that would be relevant to an assignment already completed?

Still, Joel hated to think that he might have left any stone unturned. Ever since the fiasco that had ended his career with the police department, he'd been diligent in crossing every *t* and dotting every *i*. So he would attend the proposed meeting, and he would find out what the hell was going on.

He made some notes in another file, reviewed the report on a domestic surveillance case and kept himself busy until the sun was finally setting. Mike had left hours ago, but Joel wasn't in a hurry to return to his empty home.

He'd been content with his life before he'd met Riane. After the time he'd spent with her in West Virginia, his life seemed empty somehow. Rationally, he knew nothing had changed. Everything was exactly the way it had been before he'd ever taken that trip. His office was the same. His house was the same—although his houseplants had been in desperate need of watering, his lawn in need of mowing…

The thoughts trailed off as a knock sounded at his door.

He glanced up, surprised that anyone would stop by at this hour. His surprise turned to disbelieving pleasure when he saw Riane in the doorway. He blinked, not certain if she was really there or if his mind had conjured up her image. And what an image: she was wearing a dark purple dress of some clingy fabric that molded to the curve of her breasts—soft, creamy breasts that had filled his palms, centered with luscious pink nipples that responded eagerly to his touch—

"Hello, Joel."

The sound of her voice yanked him out of his reverie, but the blood continued to hum in his veins. "Hi."

"I wasn't sure if you'd still be here," she admitted.

"I had some things to finish up," he said inanely. He wanted to go to her, touch her, but he wasn't sure how she'd respond. Things had been awkward between them the morning after the night at the motel. And he didn't know why she was here, what she was doing in Fairweather.

Riane just nodded.

The silence stretched between them. Tense and uneasy.

"What are you doing here?" he asked at last.

"I was in town." She shrugged, as if her being in town was a usual occurrence. "I thought, if you didn't have other plans, maybe we could have dinner together."

"Tonight?"

She nodded.

"No plans." He closed the file he'd been studying, shoved it on top of the pile on his desk. If he'd had any plans, they were forgotten the moment she appeared in his doorway.

"There's a great Italian restaurant just a few blocks down," Joel told her, finally rising from behind his desk and moving toward her. "We could walk from here."

"That sounds good," Riane decided.

"Okay." He indulged his need to touch her by taking her elbow and guiding her out of the office. He locked up the building.

She walked quietly beside him as he turned onto Queen

Street. "I wasn't sure I'd ever hear from you again," Joel said. "You didn't even say goodbye the last time I saw you."

She smiled wryly. "I suppose I owe you an apology for that. I was hurt and I was angry, and I shouldn't have taken it out on you." She twisted the strap of her purse around her hand, not looking at him.

"I needed you that night. You made me feel things I'd never felt before. Want things I'd never wanted. And when I realized you didn't want me…" Her words trailed off, she lifted a shoulder in a half shrug. "I was hurt. I felt as though I'd been rejected all over again."

"Wait a minute, sweetheart." Joel took hold of her elbow again, forcing her to stop and look at him. "What do you mean, I didn't want you?"

Riane shrugged. "I thought it was pretty self-explanatory."

"How could you possibly think I didn't want you?"

"You wouldn't make love with me. You walked away."

"I walked away because I had to, and it sure as hell wasn't easy. You were engaged to another man."

"I told you that was over," she said, frowning.

"But you hadn't told *him.*"

"So you walked out on me because you were concerned about Stuart's feelings?"

He didn't give a damn about Stuart Etherington III, he never had. "I was concerned about yours. Your life had just been turned upside down. You didn't know what you wanted."

"I wanted *you,*" she said again.

Just the words heated his blood. "You didn't want to be alone," Joel corrected gently, "and I was there."

"Do you think I would have made love with just anyone that night?"

"I didn't know. And I hated to think that you would regret it in the morning."

She shrugged again and continued walking. "It doesn't

matter now, anyway. Nothing happened. There's no reason for either of us to regret anything."

"I have regrets," Joel admitted, falling into step beside her again.

"About what?"

"About not making love with you."

Riane turned her head, her dark eyes wide. Surprised. Questioning.

"Every night since then, I've lain alone in my bed, thinking about you. Thinking about what might have happened. Wondering why my conscience suddenly decided to make an appearance when I wanted nothing more than to be with you."

"If you'd really wished things were different, you could have called," she reminded him.

"I wanted to call," he told her. "I can't tell you how many times I picked up the phone. But I didn't think you'd want to hear from me."

"Why?"

"Because I was responsible for all the upheaval in your life."

"I can't argue with that."

"As long as you're not still holding a grudge," Joel said dryly.

Riane smiled. "I'm not."

Their conversation paused when they entered the restaurant and waited to be escorted to their table. Riane ordered the angel-hair primavera, Joel the chicken parmigiana.

"I'm glad you came by," Joel said, after the waiter had delivered their drinks.

"Me, too. And I'm glad we cleared the air…about that night."

"Did we?" Joel wondered. He wasn't sure they'd accomplished anything except to stir up already vivid memories. Memories of Riane stretched out beneath him on that narrow bed, her skin soft and warm beneath his hands, her body writhing in response to his touch.

Riane picked up her glass of wine. "I thought so."

"What's the situation with you and Stuart?" he asked, needing to know, even if the answer wasn't what he wanted to hear.

"It's over."

He studied her for a moment, wondering about the complete lack of emotion in her response. She didn't sound heartbroken, but maybe she was just hiding her emotions. "Are you sorry?"

"No. Sad, a little, that our relationship didn't mean more to either one of us. He didn't want to accept it at first, but when I hinted that I might be a political liability, he didn't ask any more questions."

The man was an even bigger idiot than Joel had given him credit for being. Regardless of her parentage, Riane was an incredible woman, and Stuart Etherington III obviously wasn't worthy of her. Of course, a bastard child from the wrong side of town could never be worthy of her, either, but Joel wasn't going to think about that now.

"What did your parents say about it?" he asked instead.

"Not too much," she admitted. "They try not to interfere in my personal life, although I know my mother was relieved. She's always been fond of Stuart, but she knew—maybe even before I did—that I wasn't in love with him. She wanted more for me than a political alliance."

"She really does love you."

She nodded. "I know."

"Then you've come to terms with everything?"

"I'm starting to. That's one of the reasons I'm here. I think I want to meet my…" The words trailed off, as if she had trouble saying *sister,* acknowledging the relationship she had with a woman she couldn't remember. "I want to meet Arden."

"Have you contacted her yet?"

"No." She sipped her wine. "But I met her fiancé today."

"How did that happen?"

"Unintentionally."

"And?" he prompted.

"He invited us to dinner tomorrow night."

"Us?"

"Well, me," she admitted. "But he said I could bring a friend. I'm hoping you'll come with me. I-I'm not sure I can go…alone."

"You can," he assured her. "But I'll go with you, if you really want me to."

"Thank you."

Then their dinner arrived, and conversation moved to more neutral topics while they ate. They both refused dessert but accepted the offer of coffee.

"How do you know Shaun?" Riane stirred cream into her cup.

"I've done some investigative work for his law firm in the past," Joel admitted. "Including trying to find the man who was stalking Arden."

"When? What happened?"

"It started just about a year ago. She was getting threatening letters. Then her apartment was torched and a bomb was planted in her office."

"Did you find whoever was responsible?"

"I confirmed who it was. Shaun saved her. Actually, they saved each other. It's a long story," he said. "You'll have to ask her if you want the details."

"And the stalker?"

"A guest at the Lakewood Psychiatric Facility."

Riane shook her head. "I think maybe I should be grateful for my nice boring life."

"I don't think anyone would consider your life boring," Joel mused. "But if you wanted to shake it up a little…"

He let his words trail off, deliberately enticing her.

"What did you have in mind?"

"There's a new country-western bar that we passed on the way here. It just opened a few weeks ago."

Riane grimaced. "Country-western wouldn't be my first choice."

''I don't know,'' he teased. ''It brings back pretty good memories for me.''

''My memories of that night are definitely mixed.''

''Then let's make some better ones,'' he said, pushing his chair away from the table.

Chapter 12

The only thing country-western about the bar Joel took Riane to was the music. There were no horns mounted on the walls, no Stetsons, no cowboy boots. Most of the patrons appeared to be white-collar businessmen just wanting to unwind with a drink or two after a long day at the office, or women in search of such men.

They found a small table on the perimeter of the dance floor and nursed their drinks and watched the crowd mingle. The volume of music made conversation difficult, but Riane didn't mind. She was just grateful for his presence. Grateful for the fact that she wasn't staring at the walls of her hotel room and contemplating the mysteries of her life.

Joel leaned closer. So close she could practically feel the heat radiating from his body. She could still remember the texture of his skin beneath her palms, the warm, musky scent of it. She swallowed, her throat suddenly dry.

''Shall we dance?'' he asked.

His voice was low, his breath warm on her cheek.

Riane nodded, even while her heart warned her that it

would be a mistake. But she couldn't resist the opportunity to get closer, to feel his arms around her.

She should have heeded the warning from her subconscious. As soon as he touched her, she was lost. His hand scorched her skin through the fabric of her dress, bringing to mind all-too-vivid memories of the feel of those hard, wide palms on her bare flesh. His thighs, solid and strong, brushed against her, reminding her how they'd clamped down on either side of her hips, holding her immobile while he'd done all kinds of delicious things to her body.

"Relax, sweetheart." He murmured the words gently, his warm breath fluttering the wisps of hair at her temple.

She was trying to relax, but with every second, every movement, her awareness heightened. Her heart was pounding so loudly she couldn't hear the song being played. It was different from the first time they'd danced. So much had happened since that first night. So much had changed. The desire she'd felt from the very beginning was still there, but stronger now. Fueled by the knowledge of his kiss, the memory of his touch.

Still, despite her own yearning, she felt safe in his arms. Protected. She wasn't exactly sure why she felt that way, or why she welcomed the feeling. She'd always prided herself on her independence. She needed to know that she could stand on her own. But his hold didn't restrain, it supported. His strength didn't make her feel weak, only cherished.

She tilted her head to look up at him. His eyes held hers for a long moment, intent, searching, then his gaze dropped to her lips. Riane's breath caught in her throat. Excitement tingled inside her as she waited for his kiss. Waited with breathless anticipation, mounting desire.

But he didn't kiss her.

He pulled back abruptly. "I think we should be going."

"Oh. Okay," she agreed, trying to mask her disappointment.

He took her hand to guide her through the maze of patrons as they exited the bar. The air had cooled a little since they'd first left the hotel, but it was a pleasant evening to walk. Still she shivered when Joel let go of her hand, acutely conscious of the loss of warmth from his touch.

She folded her arms over her chest. "Thank you for tonight," she said.

"I had a good time," Joel said.

Riane nodded. "I wasn't sure if I should stop by your office today. I know it was last minute. You might have had other plans." She knew she was babbling, but she didn't seem able to stop. She didn't know what it was about Joel that unnerved her so much.

"Other plans? You mean a date?" He chuckled.

"Why is that funny?"

He shook his head. "To be honest, tonight is the closest I've come to a date in a long time."

"Oh." She was surprised by this revelation, and strangely pleased. "Why?"

"I don't know. Lack of interest, maybe."

"Still mourning the failure of your marriage?" she suggested.

"Hardly. My marriage was over long before the divorce papers were signed."

"Because of your job?" she prompted.

"Because my wife was sleeping with my partner's husband."

Riane stopped in the middle of the sidewalk and turned to stare at him. "You're kidding?"

"Unfortunately, I'm not." He stuffed his hands into the pockets of his jeans and resumed walking.

"Is that the reason you're so adamant about not becoming involved with anyone who's otherwise committed?"

"One of the reasons," he agreed. "Unfortunate personal experience and a general belief that extramarital affairs are in poor taste. If a relationship is that bad, get out of it."

"Would you…" She hesitated, knowing she had no right to ask the question, but curious anyway.

"Would I what?"

"Would you ever get married again?"

He was silent for a long minute. "I didn't used to think so," he admitted, then shrugged. "But maybe."

Riane wasn't sure what she expected him to say, and she couldn't have said why she was disappointed by his response. But she was, and that unnerved her enough that she decided not to pursue the topic any further.

"Here's your hotel," Joel said.

"Oh." Riane just stood there, staring up at the building and feeling awkward. She could feel Joel shift on his feet beside her, knew he was probably anxious to get back to his own place, but she didn't want to be alone. Not yet.

"Do you want to come in for a drink? Or a cup of coffee?"

Joel shook his head. "I don't think that's a good idea."

"Oh. Okay." She nodded.

He started to step away, hesitated. "Are you going to be okay?"

She forced a smile. Strong and independent, she reminded herself. "Sure."

Joel sighed, wondering why he wasn't able to walk away from her when he knew it was the smart thing to do. "Did you want me to come up for a while?"

Riane turned back to him, her deep brown eyes pleading. God, he was such a sucker for her eyes. "Would you?"

No. *Absolutely not.* The last thing he needed was further stimulation of his fantasies by accompanying Riane to her hotel room. As if the night they'd spent in that shabby motel wasn't torture enough on his libido. But when he opened his mouth, the response that came out was "Sure."

She fell silent again on the ride up to the seventh floor in the elevator. She was probably having second thoughts about inviting him up to her room. And she should be. He'd told her he had regrets about not making love with her before; she had to know how much he still wanted her.

"I know this is going to sound ridiculous," Riane admitted, stepping through the door of her hotel room. "But I don't like being alone. Since I found out about my childhood, I..."

Her words trailed off, her cheeks flushed.

Joel closed the door behind him and moved toward her. He cupped her cheek in his hand, tilted her head so that she had to meet his eyes. "Tell me," he said softly.

"I've been having nightmares," she confessed. "I wake up in a panic, not knowing where I am, who I am."

"I'm sure that's a natural reaction, considering everything you've been through."

"Maybe. And as soon as I open my eyes and recognize my surroundings, I'm okay. But..."

"But nothing's familiar here," he guessed.

She nodded.

"Do you want me to stay with you?" If he'd thought about it, he never would have made such an offer. But the words were out of his mouth before his brain had clicked into gear, and when Riane turned those big brown eyes on him and nodded in gratitude, he was lost.

"Come on," he said, taking her by the hand.

"Where?"

"To bed."

Her eyes widened.

Joel chuckled, even while his hormones were raging at his insanity. "I'm going to lie down with you, not attack you," he told her.

"Oh."

He led her over to the king-size bed that dominated the room. The bed that had been the focus of his attention since he'd walked through the door behind Riane and laid eyes on it. Now, as she willingly followed him, his treacherous mind conjured erotic images of Riane and him rolling over on that mattress, naked, sweaty, panting. He nearly groaned aloud as he desperately tried to banish the images. But his body was on full alert and he didn't know how he was going to get through this night.

"Can I put my pajamas on?" Riane asked as he pulled back the covers.

Joel hesitated, remembering the skimpy camisole top and high-cut panties she'd worn at the budget motel. But that was because she didn't have anything else, and the word *pajamas* brought to mind images of warm, bulky flannel.

"Sure," he agreed, feeling magnanimous. Pajamas had to cover more skin than the dress she was wearing. And he intended to tuck her safely away under the covers, anyway. For his own sanity and self-preservation, he'd sleep on top.

She tugged something out of her suitcase and disappeared into the bathroom.

Joel stretched out on top of the bed and stared at the ceiling, waiting for her to return, envisioning a more enjoyable end to the evening than Riane sleeping peacefully beside him. The images came back with a vengeance: naked, sweaty, panting.

Unfortunately, Riane had made it clear that her interest in him was in the past tense. *I wanted you,* she'd said. Not *want,* but *wanted.* And she'd assured him she had no regrets about that night, about not making love.

He'd never regretted anything more. To hell with his own moral code—she hadn't really been engaged to Stuart. To hell with the rules of consent—she may have been drunk, but she wasn't too drunk to throw herself at him.

Joel sighed and scrubbed a hand over his face, razor stubble rasping against his palm. Yes, he had regrets. He also knew that if he could go back to that night, he'd walk away again. Because he cared about her too much to take advantage of the situation. And that, he knew, would be his downfall. Caring was a weakness; caring for someone like Riane was complete folly. He'd learned that lesson from his ex-wife.

He'd been attracted to Jocelyn, flattered that she'd reciprocated his interest. But when the passion had waned, there had been nothing left. Nothing but bitterness and regrets.

He pushed the memories aside. It was easier to do now.

Jocelyn was part of a past he didn't care to remember, and time and distance had healed the wounds—or most of them, anyway. The pain of those that remained had dulled enough to be tolerable.

He heard the click of the door as Riane stepped out of the bathroom, and all thoughts of his ex-wife were vanquished from his mind.

Maybe, technically, what she was wearing were pajamas, but they were neither bulky nor flannel. The top was less than a camisole, the neckline plunging, the thin straps crossing over her bare back. The bottoms were long, but they sat low on her hips, exposing a tantalizing few inches of creamy skin and the darker hollow of her navel. He wasn't sure what the outfit was made of, except that the material was flimsy and silky and clung enticingly to her curves.

He forced his jaw shut, swallowed. "All set?"

Riane nodded.

"Okay, then." He patted the empty space on the bed beside him. "Let's get some sleep."

Thankfully, it didn't seem to take her long to drift off. But when she rolled over and pillowed her head on his chest, Joel's hopes of getting any shut-eye diminished. It was torture to have her in his arms and not be able to touch her, to watch the rise and fall of her breasts beneath that skimpy top and remember the weight of them in his palms, to listen to her soft, even breathing and recall her throaty moans and whimpers.

He tried to move away, hoping that a little physical distance might cool the heat raging through his body, but the hand she'd tucked under her cheek fisted in his shirt, as if to hold on to him. And Joel resigned himself to staying awake—and aroused—for the duration of the night.

He considered reneging on his promise and just getting the hell out of her hotel room, but he couldn't forget the way she'd looked at him. The embarrassment when she'd admitted to the nightmares. The undisguised gratitude when he'd offered to stay. No one had ever looked at him like that—like he was some kind of hero.

He'd never wanted anyone to look at him like that; he'd never wanted anyone to need him. But he wanted to be there for Riane. He wanted her to know that she could depend on him. He wanted a lot of things where Riane was concerned, and they were all out of his reach.

The circumstances of her adoption had brought them together, but there was nothing to hold them there. She was the cherished daughter in a family of wealth and privilege; he'd grown up in a loveless and impoverished home. She thrived in the spotlight; he abhorred it. There was no way their pasts could be reconciled, no hope for a future together.

He should get out of here—out of her hotel room, out of her life. So what if he'd promised to go to her sister's with her tomorrow? So what if she was depending on him for moral support? He needed to start thinking about self-preservation, because he knew if he spent any more time with Riane, he could fall in love with her. Hell, he was already halfway there.

No, there was no way he could allow that to happen. He had to step back, step away, and never look back. And he would.

Tomorrow.

Riane was relieved when they arrived at Shaun and Arden's house the following afternoon and found there were others in attendance for the barbecue. Arden's cousin, Nikki, and Nikki's husband, Colin—who also happened to be Shaun's brother. And Nikki and Colin's children: Carly, a darling six-and-a-half year old girl, and Justin, a chubby-cheeked little boy who wasn't yet six weeks old.

The boisterous interaction awed Riane just a little. It had been just herself and her parents for so long that she didn't know what to say or do. She felt confident that she could hold her own in any discussion about global politics, but she didn't know the first thing about family dynamics.

Still, everyone made an effort to draw her into the conversation, and Joel was careful not to venture too far from her side. She hated that she needed the reassurance of his presence, and yet she found such immense comfort in his nearness. She'd been working crowds at political functions for years, accustomed to mixing with acquaintances or strangers. But these were people she should know; this was her family.

Carly was a blessing. The child took to Riane immediately, and Riane enjoyed listening to her animated chatter. It was easy to relate to her because she wasn't worried about the little girl's preconceptions and expectations.

Arden, on the other hand, baffled her completely. The elegant professional woman she'd witnessed in court the previous day had dissolved into tears when she'd seen Riane and Joel on the doorstep. Riane had backed away instinctively, having no idea how to respond.

Arden had excused herself tearfully.

"She wasn't sure you'd really come," Shaun said by way of explanation.

And then he'd taken Riane's hands in both of his and kissed her on the cheek. "Thank you."

And that simply, Riane had felt herself drawn—willingly or not—into the chaos that was the McIver family.

A family barbecue, Riane quickly realized, was nothing like a formal evening at the country club. There was plenty of laughter, an abundance of food and a ton of chaos. Conversation flowed as freely as the wine and left Riane equally dizzy. She was glad she'd agreed to come, and relieved that Joel was with her. His was the only familiar face within this group of strangers, and she was comforted by his presence. At least until his thigh brushed against hers under the table, and comfort shifted to awareness to desire.

When Carly piped up from the other end of the table asking for a Popsicle, Riane was quick to offer to get it for her. She'd just sent the child back outside with her coveted cherry treat when Arden came in. It was a decidedly awkward moment as the two sisters faced each other without interference.

Riane cleared her throat, searching for something to say. Something that might, perhaps, break through the polite facade that had governed their interaction.

"Dinner was great," she ventured at last, unable to come up with anything more substantial.

"Good. I mean, I'm glad you enjoyed it. Shaun picked up the steaks, but I know a lot of health-conscious people avoid red meat these days, although try to explain that to a meat-and-potatoes kind of man."

It was while listening to Arden babble about the meal they'd already consumed that Riane considered something she hadn't before: Arden was just as nervous about this meeting as she was. While the realization didn't alleviate any of her own apprehension, it did, at least, level the playing field a little. And it gave her the courage to cut through the polite distance they'd respected throughout the afternoon.

"This is awkward, isn't it?" she asked.

Arden nodded. "I expected it would be, and yet I hoped it wouldn't."

"I'm not sure I understand why you were looking for me, what you expected," Riane admitted.

"I don't know what I expected, either," Arden told her. "I mean, twenty-two years is a long time, and you were little more than a baby the last time I saw you."

"I don't remember you," Riane confessed.

Arden's smile was obviously strained. "The logical part of my brain knows you couldn't. The emotional part wishes you did."

"Why were you looking for me? Why now?"

"That was Shaun's doing," Arden admitted. "Not that I didn't want to find you. But I was afraid."

"Of what?"

Arden folded her hands in front of her, toyed with the large square-cut-solitaire diamond ring on the third finger of her left hand. "I was afraid you'd hate me."

This revelation stunned Riane. Whatever she'd expected, it hadn't been that Arden would be haunted by any of the same doubts and insecurities that plagued her. "Why would I hate you?"

"Because I left you."

"I don't understand," Riane said. "I thought I was the one who was adopted."

Arden nodded. "I guess you don't know as much about everything as I thought you did."

"My parents—my adoptive parents," she amended, "have answered all my questions. But maybe I haven't been asking all of the right ones."

"We share the same mother," Arden told her. "My father died when I was four, and our mother married your father about a year later.

"Our family life wasn't very pleasant. Gavin—your father—was abusive. Verbally at first, but it soon escalated to physical violence. It got worse when our mother got pregnant with you. There's no need to go into all the details," Arden said, "but my aunt—Nikki's mother, my father's sister—came to visit for my ninth birthday. She recognized that it wasn't a healthy environment, and she convinced our mother to let me go live with her.

"She wanted to take you, too," Arden said. "Although I didn't know that at the time. I only remember her telling me that I was going to live with her from now on, and I cried and cried. I didn't want to leave you. I didn't want him to do to you what he'd done—" She shook her head, as if to dislodge the memory, and Riane's stomach churned as her mind thought of countless ways to finish the incomplete thought—none of them pleasant.

"Anyway," Arden continued, her lips curving slightly in response to a happier memory, "I had this doll. It was the last gift my father ever gave me. A beautiful doll with long dark curls and big blue eyes. She was my most prized possession, and you used to look at her and say 'pwetty.'"

Riane shifted, a little embarrassed to hear stories of her

childhood from a woman she didn't remember. Memories she couldn't share.

"When I left, I gave that doll to you. I wanted you to have something to remember me by."

"Ohmygod." Riane clapped her hand over her mouth, stunned. "Eden."

Arden looked at her strangely. "Eden?"

"That's what I called her—I must have been trying to say 'Arden,' but everyone thought it was 'Eden.' I called the doll Eden."

Arden smiled. "You remember it?"

"I still have it."

Riane watched her sister's eyes fill with tears and felt her own throat tighten. She'd been so sure there was nothing left between them, no connection. But she was no longer so certain. The doll she was referring to was old and worn, but she'd still held on to it. After all these years she still had that doll—the doll her sister had given to her.

"I'm glad you kept it," Arden told her.

"I never understood why I was so attached to it," she admitted. "I remember packing up my room as I was getting ready to go away to law school and thinking that maybe it was time to give her up. But I just couldn't do it."

"You went to law school, too?"

Riane shrugged. "It seems to be a family tradition."

"Your parents must be really proud of you."

"Yeah, I think they are." She hesitated, then finally asked the question she hadn't been able to bring herself to ask of anyone else. "Do you have any contact with my biological parents?"

Arden shook her head. "No. Not since—no."

Riane nodded.

"Ask."

"Ask what?"

"Whatever's on your mind but you think you shouldn't."

Riane smiled. "You're very perceptive."

"Being able to read people is an important part of my job."

"You're very good at your job," Riane said.

Arden looked startled.

"I saw you in court yesterday," she explained.

"It's easy when you're always on the side of truth and justice." She grinned. "It's something Shaun and I often disagree about."

Riane laughed, starting to feel a little less awkward.

"You haven't asked yet," Arden reminded her.

"I'm not sure I want to know."

"About our family," Arden guessed.

Riane nodded. "I feel disloyal to my parents—my adoptive parents—"

Arden waved off the proviso. "They are your parents in every way that counts."

"I'm curious," Riane admitted. "About the people who contributed to my DNA. On the other hand, I know I wouldn't have been taken out of their home if they'd been good parents."

"I don't know why they did the things they did, why they made the choices they made. All I can tell you is that I was relieved to know that you didn't have to grow up with them."

"When I first learned I'd been adopted, I just wanted to pretend it wasn't true," Riane confessed. "I was happy with the life I have in West Virginia, with my parents."

"I'm glad you're happy," Arden said sincerely.

"I'm glad you found me," Riane told her.

Arden's smile was luminous. "Me, too."

Somehow Joel found himself back in Riane's hotel room after driving her home from the barbecue. He had every intention of dropping her at the door, but when she'd looked at him with those big, dark eyes and asked if he wanted to come up for coffee—well, he suddenly had an undeniable craving for coffee.

Just coffee, he promised himself as Riane dumped the prepackaged grounds into the coffee filter. One cup and then he was out of there. No way could his body survive another night like the last one.

"Did you have a good time at Arden and Shaun's?" Joel asked.

Riane flicked the switch, set the coffee brewing, and nodded. "Thank you."

"I enjoyed myself," he told her. And he had, despite the flak he'd taken from Shaun about being the "friend" Riane had invited. Even if he'd known that Shaun would question the relationship between his investigator and his soon-to-be sister-in-law, as he should have, he wouldn't have refused to go. Riane had needed a friend, and he'd needed to be there for her.

"The whole family seems very well integrated," she said.

Integrated. Joel smiled. "You fit in well with them, too."

She seemed surprised, but pleased by his observation. "I liked them. All of them."

"Why does that surprise you?"

"I've never made friends easily."

"You didn't seem to have any trouble making the rounds at your charity ball," he pointed out.

"That's different," she explained. "Most of those people aren't friends, they're acquaintances. It's superficial interaction. It's harder with people who could really matter."

"Why?"

She turned away as the coffee finished brewing. She poured two cups, passed one to him.

"I've led a pretty sheltered life. It's not just that my parents were protective, which they were, but I didn't have much privacy. Every family outing was a media event. As a child I didn't mind, really, because I didn't know any different. But as I got older, it made it difficult to cultivate any kind of personal relationships. So I didn't date much through high school, and never anyone exclusively.

"I didn't get my first real taste of freedom until law school.

I met Cameron Davis in my first year. He was a year ahead of me—smart, popular, incredibly sexy."

"Feel free to edit out any unnecessary details," Joel interrupted dryly.

Riane smiled. "Well, he was. He was the kind of guy every girl wanted to date—and he wanted to date me. I was twenty years old at the time—probably the oldest living American virgin, and determined to change that status.

"And then I found out...I'm still not sure whether or not it was deliberate, but my roommate let it slip that Cameron wanted to get naked pictures of me to sell to the tabloids."

Joel felt all the protective instincts he'd never known he had stir to life inside him.

"He'd never really been interested in me." Riane plunged ahead with the story, but he could tell she was still hurt by this betrayal. "He just wanted to take advantage of who I was to make a quick buck."

"He didn't deserve you," Joel told her.

"I know that now," she agreed. "At the time, though, I was hurt. Angry. Humiliated. I couldn't believe that I'd been so naive. And I was horrified to think how devastating that could have been to my mother's career. I decided, then and there, that if I was ever going to become involved with someone else, it would have to be someone with a similar background and similar interests.

"That same year, when I came home for Christmas vacation, I met Stuart. He was everything Cameron wasn't. He didn't sweep me off my feet or fulfill any kind of romantic fantasies, but I wasn't looking for anything like that after my recent relationship disaster."

Joel shifted uncomfortably. He didn't want to hear the details of her relationship with Stuart Etherington III, but for some reason she felt compelled to share them.

"We started dating. Stuart took me to the finest restaurants and private showings at art galleries and opening nights at the theater. We had a lot in common despite the age difference, and there were no sloppy kisses, no groping, no pressure. There was also no excitement or spontaneity, but I didn't mind.

"And then I met you," Riane said. "And I realized that kisses didn't have to be sloppy, touching wasn't always groping, and I knew that I wanted something more than what I'd previously been willing to settle for."

She lifted her cup to her lips, sipped. "In some ways, finding out that I'm not the biological daughter of Ryan and Ellen Quinlan has been liberating. It's given me the courage and freedom to think about what I want instead of worrying about how my actions will affect anyone else. I want something for me."

He nodded, still not certain where she was going with this conversation.

"I want to make love with you."

He was glad he was already sitting down, because he was pretty sure that statement would have knocked him over.

"If you're not interested," she continued hurriedly, "that's okay. But you indicated that you might be, so I thought that if you were…interested, that is, maybe we could…you know."

Oh, yeah. He knew. He'd spent far too much time over the past few days fantasizing about what it would be like to make love with Riane. Wishing he'd never walked out of that motel room.

Now he was in her hotel room, and she was looking at him with those deep brown eyes, telling him he didn't have to walk away. She was offering him everything he wanted. And still something made him hesitate.

"It's not that I'm not interested, Riane."

"But?"

"But you've just come out of a long-term relationship and—"

"Stuart and I never had sex."

"You—what?" He couldn't believe what she was saying. He knew that she and Stuart had dated for more than three years, they'd talked about getting married. How was it possible that he'd—that they'd—never?

Christ, what was wrong with the guy? He cleared his throat. "Why not?"

She shrugged. "He said he was willing to wait until we were married, if that's what I wanted."

"Is that what you wanted?"

She shrugged again. "I didn't have strong feelings one way or the other." She hesitated, then said, "He didn't make me feel the way you make me feel."

It was her unflinching honesty that undid him. "Don't tell me things like that, sweetheart," Joel practically groaned.

"Why not?"

"Because I'm trying very hard to be noble here, to do the right thing, and you're not making that easy for me."

"What do you think is the right thing?"

"Getting out of here before I take you up on that offer."

"I know what I want, Joel. And I want to make love with you."

She'd said she wanted to get rid of her virginity with Cameron, although she hadn't followed through with it. And she said she'd never slept with Stuart. Somehow he didn't think she'd been having sex with anyone other than her boyfriend, but he needed to know for sure.

"Have you ever, um, been with a man before?"

Her cheeks flushed with color; she shook her head.

A virgin.

He couldn't get his mind past those two words. His brain simply refused to compute anything else. He didn't believe it.

She was twenty-four years old, sexy, sophisticated. There was no way— And yet, he knew it was true. In fact, it explained a lot of things. The intriguing contrast between her hesitation and eagerness, the honesty and uncertainty in her responses to his touch. But there was still one question unanswered.

"Why me?"

''Because I thought if I was finally going to be with someone, it should be someone I trust. You know me, Joel. You know everything there is to know about me, and you're not impressed by who I am or appalled by the details of my life.''

She lifted her chin, met his gaze directly. ''So the only question now is, do you want me?''

Chapter 13

It took every ounce of willpower Riane had to stand her ground and meet Joel's gaze as she asked him that question. Or maybe she was just too paralyzed with fear to move. What if he said no? What if he turned her away—again?

She couldn't bear another rejection. Not from Joel. Not when she wanted him with a depth of desire that seemed to obliterate all else. She didn't quite understand how it was that her body could so desperately crave something it had never known, all she knew was that when she was with Joel, she wanted him.

''Do I want you?'' Joel repeated the question slowly. Then he set his coffee down and stood up.

Riane was rooted to the floor. He took a step toward her. Her breath backed up in her lungs. He reached out and pried her mug from nervous fingers, set it aside. Then he cupped her cheek in his palm, stroked his thumb over the curve of her lips.

''Only more than I want to breathe,'' he said softly.

Riane let out the breath she hadn't realized she was holding and managed a tremulous smile.

"I want you so much it scares me," he admitted. "Especially now, knowing that you've never been with anyone else. I want to touch you, every inch of you, but I'm so afraid of hurting you."

"I'm not afraid," she told him. And she wasn't. Somehow she knew that everything would be okay because she was with Joel.

But Joel still looked as if he needed some convincing, so she rose onto her toes and touched her lips to his.

She wasn't prepared for the wealth of emotions she felt as he took control of the kiss, his mouth moving over hers with masterful purpose, his hands stroking over her body in lazy seduction. No one had ever touched her the way Joel touched her. With every brush of his lips, every caress of his fingertips, she felt cherished.

She didn't really have any expectations about making love. When she'd lived in the dorm, she'd heard other women compare horror stories about their "first time." The one common thread was that it was painful and generally quick. She was prepared for that.

And she thought that once the decision had been made, they'd take off their clothes and go to it. Joel had other ideas.

He did take off her clothes, but there was no haste. Instead, he stripped her garments away with painstaking slowness. First her blouse, lingering over each button, drawing out her anticipation, his eyes never leaving hers. His so dark and intense it made her breath catch in her throat. But breathing didn't seem to matter anymore. Nothing mattered but experiencing the moment, being with this man.

When all the buttons were undone, he slid his hands inside. His fingers skimmed over her collarbone, sending tingles of awareness, currents of desire, through her veins. Anticipation continued to build inside her, crowding out the last remnants of anxiety, any lingering vestige of uncertainty.

He pushed the blouse off her shoulders, slid it slowly down

her arms. Then he lowered his head and captured her mouth in a kiss that she wished would just go on and on forever. His lips were firm and warm, moving over hers with seductive expertise. Her own parted on a sigh, and his tongue slipped inside and mingled with hers. Riane threaded her fingers through the thick silky hair at the nape of his neck, holding him close, closer.

So captivated was she by his kiss that she didn't realized he'd unfastened the clip of her bra until she felt his palm skim up her rib cage to the curve of her breast. Instinctively she arched toward him. His thumb brushed over the distended nipple, and she gasped at the shock of pleasure.

He found the zipper at the back of her pants and slid it down slowly, his fingertips skimming over her buttocks. Then the fabric pooled at her feet and his hands were on the backs of her thighs, moving upward again in a teasing caress that simply melted her bones.

As if sensing her complete and unconditional surrender, he picked her up and carried her over to the bed. He laid her on top of the mattress and disposed of her panties.

Suddenly she was aware of her nakedness, self-conscious. She tried to pull the spread to cover her, but Joel stopped her. His eyes raked over her, appraising, approving. ''You're so beautiful.''

The husky tone of his voice convinced her that he believed it. And she felt beautiful. Desirable. Desired.

She lifted her arms in silent invitation, and he lowered himself onto the bed. His mouth found hers again, his kiss deeper now, hungrier. She shifted her hips, positioning him at the juncture of her thighs. Joel groaned against her lips, and his hands found her hips, stilling their instinctive movements.

''I'm trying to take my time.''

''I don't want you to take your time. I want to feel you inside me.''

''We'll get there,'' he promised her. ''Eventually.''

''Now.'' She wasn't sure how much longer she could endure the torturous teasing. She was assailed by so many sensations she thought her system was just going to explode. There was an unfamiliar tightness coiling in the pit of her belly, seeking release, demanding fulfillment.

He chuckled softly. ''Let's do this my way, this time.''

This time.

She liked the sound of that. She wanted to believe that they would be together like this again. That they could have more than one night.

So she let him have his way, and she had absolutely no regrets. His hands were relentless on her body, stoking the fire that burned inside her. He left no inch of her skin untouched, his lips following the path that his fingertips had traced on her skin until she practically wept with the urgent need to mate her body with his. When Joel's teeth closed over her nipple, his tongue swirling around it, her release came. Hot and fast, it left her gasping and breathless and completely confused. She hadn't expected this. Hadn't expected anything like it. And already the anticipation was building inside her again, and she wanted more.

''Joel. Please.'' She could feel the wet heat between her thighs, the throbbing ache. The emptiness she needed him to fill, the pressure only he could release.

But he wouldn't be hurried, and she was stunned to realize how much more he could coax from her body. How much more she could give. It seemed like an eternity before he stripped off the rest of his clothes. He took a condom out of his wallet and sheathed himself. Riane had given absolutely no thought to protection and was grateful that he'd done so.

When she felt him part her thighs with his knee, she thought, *Now. Finally now.*

But he didn't immediately rise over her, thrust into her. Instead he drove her up again, higher even than before, and she was still quivering with the aftershocks of her climax when he slipped inside her. Her body was more than ready for the intrusion, aching for the fulfillment. There was a brief—almost imperceptible—stab of pain. She tightened instinctively, and Joel stopped moving, but the pain was already gone, the pleasure overwhelming all else.

''Are you okay?'' he asked, holding himself immobile over her.

She lifted her hips off the mattress, pulling him deeper inside, and heard him groan. She smiled. ''Much better than okay.''

Then he was moving inside her, long, steady strokes that seemed to touch the very center of her soul. And as her body stretched to accommodate his movements, she felt her heart expanding, too, and taking him inside.

The simple beauty of their joining stunned her, and she wished she could just hold on to the moment forever. Then his movements quickened and his thrusts came harder, deeper, faster. Tension coiled inside her; sensation layered upon sensation. And suddenly everything exploded in a shower of heat and light and so much pleasure she wasn't sure she could stand it.

She screamed out with her release, shocked less by the wanton cry emanating from her throat than by the violent shudders that racked her body. Joel's mouth fused with hers, swallowing her cries. And he leaped with her.

When their lovemaking was completed, she *was* afraid. Afraid of feeling so much more than she ever thought she could; afraid of losing her heart to this man who she couldn't ever hope to hold on to.

Joel eased his body slowly from hers and back onto the mattress, tucking her close to his side. ''Are you okay?'' he asked again.

She nodded and snuggled contentedly against him, determined not to think about anything but the here and now. ''I never expected…so much.''

''I wanted to make sure there was pleasure before the pain,'' he told her.

She smiled. There had been so much pleasure she couldn't remember anything else.

''Is it always like that?'' she asked, still awed by the whole experience.

He laid his hand on her cheek, gently stroked his thumb over her skin. His eyes were dark, serious. ''No.''

She frowned, uncertain how to interpret his response.

''But sometimes, if you're very lucky, it can be that good.''

Her relief must have shown, because he chuckled softly.

''Of course, that might have been an anomaly. The only way we'll know for certain is if we try it again.''

Then he proceeded to prove to her that it wasn't an anomaly at all.

Having accepted his departure from the police force and the failure of his marriage, Joel had built a new life for himself. A new career in a new city. And he'd been content. He hadn't thought anything was missing—until he'd met Riane.

When he awoke in Riane's bed, her body nestled close to his, he felt his heart swell with a feeling of such profound contentment and inexplicable happiness it stunned him for a moment. And that was when he realized he'd done something he thought he'd never do: he'd fallen in love.

The realization almost sent him into a full-scale panic because regardless of the depth of his feelings for her, he knew there was no future for them. She was a Rutherford—that should have been more than enough incentive to keep him the hell away from her. Okay, so maybe it wasn't Rutherford blood running through her veins, but she'd grown up in their world, with all the attendant rights and privileges. He was a Logan—paternity unknown. There was no way her parents would ever approve of him.

Not that he wanted their approval. He'd be damned before he'd try to fit in with the Rutherford-Quinlans of this world. He'd tried to be what Jocelyn wanted, and his failure had hurt them both. He wouldn't do that to Riane. He wouldn't make her promises he couldn't keep. He wouldn't ask for anything she didn't want to give. Which meant that he couldn't hope for anything more with Riane than what they had now.

Despite the warm presence of her sleeping beside him, he suddenly felt alone. Having experienced the joy and fulfillment of making love with Riane, how could he live the rest of his life without her?

There was no easy answer to the question, but he knew that it was what he'd have to do. But not yet. For now she was here. And he intended to enjoy every single minute they had together.

He skimmed a hand over her torso, his fingertips trailing over the silky softness of her skin. Riane murmured in her sleep and snuggled closer, one of her legs sliding between his, her breasts pressing against his chest. He touched his lips to her throat, nibbled gently. Her eyes opened; her lips curved.

''Hi,'' she said softly.

''Hi.'' He cupped the fullness of her breast in his hand, stroked his thumb over the pebbled nipple. Her breath caught, her eyes darkened. ''Any regrets?''

''Only that I wasted so much time sleeping.''

He kissed her, a tender soul-stirring kiss to express the feelings he couldn't put into words. Despite his intention to take things slowly, to spend hours cherishing every inch of her body, their passion escalated quickly.

Her hands roamed over him, boldly, freely. Whatever inhibitions Riane might have had before they'd made love last night had been quickly shed. She was eager and curious and—his eyes crossed when she wrapped her fingers around him—a very fast learner.

She stroked him slowly, teasingly, until his breath grew ragged and he had to remove her hand or risk disappointing both of them. But Riane wasn't deterred. She continued her leisurely exploration of his body, halting only when her fingers found the scar low on his abdomen.

He wondered if it would bother her, this tangible evidence

of his failed career. She traced the puckered flesh slowly, her touch gentle. "Is this where you were shot?"

"Yeah," he admitted.

"Does it hurt?"

"Most of the time I don't even remember it's there."

Her eyes were dark with concern. "Can you tell me what happened?"

He shrugged, as if every second of the incident wasn't permanently etched in his memory. "I got an anonymous tip that there were videotapes in the building. The police had gone over every square inch of the warehouse looking for evidence, but they'd missed the tapes because they were hidden inside a hollow door. On those tapes was evidence of executions that Conroy had ordered. Evidence he kept to ensure the continued loyalty of his executioners and—some members of his inner circle believed—for his own viewing pleasure."

"That's sick."

Joel didn't disagree. "I knew the tip might be nothing more than a trap, an attempt to get rid of me because I'd come too close to exposing the truth about Conroy. But I wanted so badly to make the case against him, and I needed those tapes to do it."

"Did you find them?"

"I found them," he admitted. "They were in my hand when I was shot. But when I came to, hours later in the hospital, no one seemed to know anything about the videotapes."

She rubbed her fingertips gently over the scar again. "I read the newspaper account of your injury. And even though I was furious with you at the time, it terrified me to think how close you'd come to being killed."

"I wasn't."

"Thank God for that." She looked up at him and smiled. "If I'd never met you, I'd still be a virgin."

Joel chuckled, surprised that he could find humor in anything when his body was wound up so tightly with wanting her. But Riane was constantly surprising him, as she did when she slid down his body and touched her lips to the scar. Then she moved lower.

He sucked in a breath and hauled her back up, flipping her onto her back and pinning her to the mattress with his own body.

He paused only long enough to protect her, then slipped into the welcoming wet heat of her body. They moved together, falling into a comfortable rhythm as if they'd been making love for years. He'd never felt as complete as he felt when his body was joined with Riane's, and he never wanted to let her go.

Later that morning Joel convinced Riane to check out of the hotel and go back to his house. Not that it had taken much convincing. It was as if they both knew their time together was limited and didn't want to spend a single minute apart unless it was absolutely necessary. Not that she'd made any mention of leaving, but he knew it was inevitable.

He'd never managed to keep a woman in his life for very long. Not even his mother had stuck around. He and Jocelyn had maintained the illusion of their marriage for almost four years, but the relationship had deteriorated long before their vows were dissolved. So he resolved to enjoy the time he had with Riane and treasure the memories when she was gone.

They spent the day together, wandering through the market and the shops of downtown. They had lunch at a little café overlooking the water, then walked through the botanical gardens and bought ice cream from a street vendor. They held hands and shared kisses on the sidewalk, oblivious to the passersby, oblivious to everyone but each other. Joel couldn't remember the last day he'd spent like this—doing nothing and having the time of his life.

They stopped at a Chinese takeout place on the way home and forgot about the food the minute they stepped through the door. It was a long time later before they bothered to reheat their dinner, and much later still when they finally fell asleep, their bodies tangled together.

When Joel finished his shower Monday morning and stepped back into the bedroom to get dressed, he was disappointed to find that Riane was already out of bed. Not that he had time to slide between the covers with her again, but simply because he liked to see her there.

He found her in the kitchen sipping from a mug of coffee. She was wearing one of his T-shirts and, he could tell by the way the soft cotton molded to her curves, absolutely nothing else. He felt his system snap to attention without the necessity of caffeine.

"I have a meeting this morning," Joel said, after a long, lingering kiss. "But I'm hoping it won't take too long."

"I'll be here whenever you get back," she assured him.

He kissed her again, more tempted than ever to blow off his scheduled appointment. The whole meeting would probably be an exercise in futility, anyway. He couldn't imagine anything that Gavin Elliott might tell him that was more important than taking Riane back upstairs and making love with her again.

He slid his hands beneath the hem of the T-shirt, confirming his earlier supposition that she was naked beneath the garment. She sighed as his fingers skimmed over her skin, pressed herself closer to him, and he completely forgot that he even had an appointment.

It was Riane who finally pulled away. Her cheeks were flushed and her breath came in shallow gasps, but she put her hands on his chest and pushed him toward the door. "You have a meeting."

He glanced at his watch and swore. He was already late. Still, he brushed one last kiss on her lips. "I'll be back soon."

It would be soon, he promised.

He held the society page closer. Studied the picture. It was a poor quality photograph, but it was her. The last piece of the puzzle.

This meeting would confirm it. Eliminate any residual doubt. As soon as he was certain, he could set his plan in motion.

The door of the diner opened.

He tucked the paper out of sight.

Joel pushed aside his lingering apprehension as he pushed open the glass door. He wasn't convinced that Gavin Elliott had anything of interest to tell him, but he couldn't forget about the phone call. He couldn't stop wondering about the information Elliott claimed Joel would want.

The only thing Joel wanted right now was to go home—to Riane. But he knew that she wouldn't be able to move ahead with her life until she'd dealt with all the ghosts of her past. Unfortunately, Gavin Elliott was one of those ghosts.

The breakfast crowd had long since gone, and only a couple of tables were occupied when Joel stepped into the diner. The scents of burned grease and stale smoke permeated the air. A female voice crooned from the ancient jukebox in the corner about love gone bad.

Joel spotted Elliott immediately. He was seated at one of the green vinyl booths near the back of the restaurant. He looked better than he had in prison. He was clean shaven and dressed in a suit. His hair was neatly combed, his eyes clear, purposeful, the hint of a smile on his lips.

His demeanor unnerved Joel. What did a man recently released from prison have to look so damn pleased about?

He slid into the seat across from Elliott.

"Coffee?" Elliott asked, as pleasantly as if he was entertaining in his own home.

Joel wanted to refuse, but Elliott was already waving the waitress over to their table.

She was young, probably not much more than twenty, Joel guessed, and her faded pink uniform stretched tightly across her very pregnant belly. She flipped over the cup in front of Joel and filled it from the carafe she carried in her hand.

"Can I get you a menu?" she asked, offering a tired but pleasant smile.

"No, thanks." Joel wanted to get this meeting over as quickly as possible.

"I'll have the special," Elliott said. "Eggs scrambled with sausage."

The waitress nodded and retreated to the kitchen to place his order.

"Pretty little thing, isn't she?" Elliott commented, watching the woman's retreating form.

Joel sipped at his coffee.

"She'd be about my daughter's age, wouldn't she?"

"I wouldn't know," Joel said.

"You've found her though." It was more a statement than a question, as if Elliott already knew the answer.

"I'm not at liberty to discuss the details of my investigation with you."

"'Not at liberty,'" Elliott mocked, then smiled. "I gave you useful information, didn't I?"

"You gave me the name of a lawyer who passed away several years ago," Joel told him.

"Lawyers keep files," Elliott said.

"Usually they do," Joel agreed, wondering if Elliott had brought him here to seek rather than impart information.

Elliott shook his head. "I thought there was something unusual about the way things were handled."

"What do you mean?"

Elliott turned to the waitress as she set his plate in front of him. "Thank you, darling."

She offered another tired smile. "Enjoy your breakfast."

"I'm sure I will," Elliott responded pleasantly, and proceeded to dig his fork into the mound of eggs.

"Why did you think there was something unusual about the adoption?" Joel demanded.

Elliott sprinkled pepper onto his eggs, slathered grape jelly onto a triangle of toast.

Joel sat back, his fingers clamped tightly around the ceramic mug in his hand. The man was playing him. He knew it. He just didn't know how to end the game. He could walk away, of course, but he couldn't shake the feeling that Elliott was holding back some crucial piece of evidence. And that this meeting was his only chance to get it.

"They took good care of her, didn't they?" Elliott asked, slicing through a sausage link.

Joel was surprised by the question. The last time he'd spoken to Elliott, the other man had shown no interest in the daughter he'd given up more than twenty years earlier.

"Bet she grew up in a big house, with lots of fancy clothes and expensive toys." Elliott continued to eat, not bothered by Joel's lack of response. "The atmosphere in this place leaves a lot to be desired, but the food is phenomenal."

Joel accepted a refill on his coffee. It was strong and a little stale, but he imagined it was better than whatever they served in prison.

"Was there a reason you requested this meeting, Mr. Elliott, or did you just want company over breakfast?"

"Of course there was a reason," Elliott assured him. "I don't believe in wasting time—mine or anyone else's."

"Are you going to share that reason with me?" Joel asked, his patience rapidly dissipating.

"It's about my daughter," he said. "Rheanne."

Joel waited while Elliott dabbed his mouth with his napkin and pushed his empty plate aside.

"I thought you might want to know that they paid us to give up our baby."

Chapter 14

After his meeting with Gavin Elliott, Joel's urgency to return to Riane was superseded by a combination of guilt and confusion. He didn't want any more lies between them, so how could he not tell her what he'd learned? And yet sharing the information without verifying it first would only hurt her more. Intentionally or not, he'd already caused her enough pain.

He couldn't tell her. Not until he knew for certain whether or not what Gavin Elliott had told him was true. There had been a time when he'd wanted, more than anything, to dig up some kind of dirt on the Rutherfords. Riane had changed things for him. But if Ellen and Ryan had paid to adopt her, their actions were very definitely illegal, and Joel would have all the ammunition he needed. He just wasn't sure that he wanted it anymore.

He stopped by the office, hoping to discuss the latest revelation with his partner. Mike was waiting for him, with a copy of the *Fairweather Tribune* in hand.

Wordlessly he passed the paper across the desk. Joel recognized the picture immediately—it was the same one that had been printed in the *Mapleview Mirror* after the charity ball. The caption, however, was new:

> Professional Acquaintance or Personal Vendetta?
>
> No one knows why local P.I. Joel Logan has been spending so much time with West Virginia Senator Ellen Rutherford-Quinlan's daughter recently, but speculation is that Logan has finally found a way to avenge his dismissal from the Philadelphia PD. Marcus Rutherford—yes, a relative of the lovely Ms. Riane Quinlan—was the presiding judge in a case that ended Logan's career in Philadelphia. Logan was charged with, although never convicted of, leaking investigative information to the Conroy crime syndicate.

Joel didn't read any further.

"Is this today's paper?" he asked.

Mike nodded. "We could sue for libel. The reporter whose name is on the article obviously didn't even check his facts."

"They'll print a retraction tomorrow," Joel guessed. "A tiny little 'oops' buried somewhere on the back of the last page." He didn't care, really. He didn't believe the article could hurt the business, but he was concerned that it might hurt Riane.

"Does she know about the Rutherford connection in the Conroy case?" Mike asked, somehow following Joel's train of thought.

"Not from me."

"Then maybe you should tell her," Mike advised. "Before she sees it in print."

Joel was surprised by his friend's advice, especially since Mike had made no secret of the fact he disapproved of Joel's personal involvement with Riane. He nodded. "I'll be at home if you need me."

He was almost out the door before his partner spoke again.

"I'll cover for you tomorrow," Mike said, then grinned. "In case you have some extra groveling to do."

"I hope she gives me the chance."

Joel made several stops on the way home, arming himself with the groveling essentials: a bottle of Riane's favorite merlot, a large pizza with extra cheese, pepperoni and hot peppers, and a huge bouquet of fresh spring flowers. Still, as he turned on to his street, he breathed an audible sigh of relief when he found her car still parked in the driveway.

And then he found Riane—in the bathtub. Her hair was piled loosely on top of her head, her body hidden beneath a thick layer of scented bubbles. She had a glass of white wine in her hand, a second glass and the bottle were on the apron of the tub along with about half a dozen flickering candles.

Somewhere in the back of his mind it registered that she must have taken a trip into town, because he was sure she wouldn't have found those romantic trappings around his house. Thankfully, she hadn't picked up a newspaper.

He cleared his throat and she opened her eyes, her lips curving in a slow sensual smile.

"I was hoping you'd be home before the water got cold," she told him.

"I was hoping you'd be naked when I got home."

"I'm not naked."

He took a few steps into the bathroom. "What are you wearing?"

She stood up, her body rosy and glistening from the heat of the water, ribbons of foam adorning her satiny skin. "Bubbles."

All the blood in his head quickly migrated south. "I must be dreaming."

He didn't realize he'd spoken the words aloud until Riane's tentative smile widened.

"I wanted to seduce you this time," she admitted shyly.

"You've succeeded." He dropped the pizza box on the counter, the flowers and wine beside it.

"I haven't even started." She picked up a glass of wine and offered it to him.

Joel stepped forward to take the glass from her fingers and set it back down. Then he lifted Riane out of the tub and into his arms, mindless of the water soaking through his clothes and dripping on the floor as he moved purposefully to the bedroom.

"I'm wet," Riane protested.

Joel grinned down at her. "I hope so."

She laughed softly when he dropped her on the mattress. The humor in her brown eyes quickly turned to desire as she watched him strip off his clothing. He lowered himself onto the bed beside her, muscles quivering, straining. He forced himself to rein in his escalating passion. Less than forty-eight hours earlier he'd taken her virginity—and he'd taken her several times again since then. Both her actions and her words proved that she shared his desire, but he figured her body would be aching, tender.

He touched his mouth to hers, softly. He stroked his tongue over the fullness of her bottom lip, savoring. He trailed kisses over her jaw, nipped at her earlobe, nibbled his way down the slender column of her throat.

He worked his way down to her breasts and lingered. Milky flesh, rosy nipples, dusky peaks. He tasted and teased, tormenting them both before he moved on. His tongue trailed a path to the center of her belly, and lower still.

She squirmed, and he knew he was again leading her into new territory. The realization only heightened his need to explore.

He skimmed his hands over the length of her torso, under her hips, lifting her off the mattress slightly. He felt her hands on his shoulders, her short nails digging into the flesh.

To restrain or encourage?

He didn't know. He only knew that he had to taste her.

He dipped his head between her thighs, heard her gasp, felt her jolt when his tongue plunged into her. And he feasted.

Riane's body quivered and bucked as the climax ripped through her, her passionate reaction causing his own desire to spiral out of control. No, it was more than desire. It was stronger, deeper, undeniable.

He *needed* Riane. He needed her like he'd never needed anyone before. He needed her more than he needed to breathe. With no regard for his earlier thoughts of care and patience, pausing only long enough to protect her, he plunged into her.

She didn't balk at the primitiveness of his possession but rose up to meet him, taking him deeper and harder with each thrust. Her hands raced over him greedily, her fingers burning his flesh, each frantic touch driving him closer to the edge. He captured her mouth, swallowed her trembling sighs and throaty moans. Then her muscles contracted around him, and he plunged into the abyss of pleasure right along with her.

"Not that I have any complaints," Joel assured her later. "But was there any particular reason you wanted to seduce me?"

"I wanted to see if I could," Riane admitted.

"Anytime."

She smiled, but he detected a hint of worry in the endless depths of her dark eyes. "And because I wanted to take your mind off things."

"What things?"

She slid from the bed and pulled a folded newspaper out of the side pocket of her suitcase. "Have you seen this?"

He closed his eyes and silently cursed his hormones for overruling his head. It had been his intention to talk to her about the article as soon as he got home, but then Riane had been naked and he hadn't thought about anything but burying himself inside her.

"Yes, I've seen it." He tensed, waiting for her to vent her outrage and accusations.

But she climbed back onto the bed and wrapped her arms around him. "I'm sorry."

He was speechless for a moment. "Why are you apologizing?"

"Because I have a pretty good idea who leaked this story to the press."

"Stuart," Joel guessed.

"Probably," she admitted. "He blames you for the end of our relationship."

"And this is his way of trying to make you question my involvement with you."

"After three years, I would have thought he'd know me better than that."

"You're not angry?" Joel asked. "That I didn't tell you who the judge was?"

"No. I wish you had told me. But the information was in the file Stuart gave me last week."

"Why didn't you ask me about it?"

She shrugged. "Because I don't believe that our relationship is about anything or anyone but you and me."

He was stunned. Jocelyn would have ranted and raved and likely destroyed something expensive. Riane's calm and unquestioning acceptance forced Joel to acknowledge how different from his ex-wife Riane really was, and how extraordinarily lucky he was.

He cupped her face in his hands. "You are an incredible woman."

Riane smiled. "Of course, if I find out I'm wrong, I'll have to really hurt you," she teased.

Joel grinned and dropped a light kiss on her lips. Was it any wonder that he'd fallen in love with this woman?

He pulled back, as if a few inches of physical distance might give him a better perspective. But he could no longer deny the truth of what was in his heart. He did love her. He wasn't sure exactly how or when it had happened, but somewhere along the line, he'd fallen in love with Riane Quinlan.

Unfortunately, loving her didn't change anything: she was still the daughter of a senator, a Rutherford-Quinlan by upbringing if not by blood; he was a kid from the wrong side of town who didn't have a clue who his father was. He'd be a fool to think they could have a future together; he'd be even more of a fool to spoil what they had right now by wishing for something that could never be.

And right now he was starving.

"How does pizza sound?"

Riane lingered in bed while Joel went downstairs to reheat the pizza. She stretched, feeling aches in muscles she didn't even know she had, but she smiled. They were the aches of a woman who had been well and truly loved, and she wished she could hold on to the feeling forever.

Of course, they both knew this wasn't forever. Joel's life was here in Pennsylvania; hers was in West Virginia. Okay, maybe the geographical distance wasn't insurmountable, but it was significant.

She had to go back to Mapleview. She *wanted* to go home. Meeting with Arden and learning more of the details about her biological family had cleared up some of her confusion. She might never understand why her parents had lied about her adoption, but she would be forever grateful for their unconditional love and support.

But the issue with her parents aside, why couldn't she have a future with Joel? She knew he had doubts about whether her parents could accept him, but she didn't. Her parents would love Joel because she did.

She sat up straight, stunned by the revelation that had come so easily from her heart. She loved Joel.

She clutched the bed sheet against her chest, considering. Maybe she wasn't really in love. Maybe she was confusing sex with love. She'd never been intimate with a man before, she'd never experienced the kind of physical connection she'd shared with Joel. Maybe what she was really feeling was just…gratitude, she decided, for his initiation into the rites of lovemaking.

She shook her head, wondering why she was so determined to discount her emotions. She'd given up on falling in love; she'd made a conscious decision to marry for practical reasons rather than emotional ones. Then Joel had walked into the charity ball and her entire life had changed.

And she had no intention of letting go of the best thing that had ever happened to her.

Resolved, Riane pushed herself off the bed. She grabbed a softly worn denim shirt from Joel's closet and hastily fastened the buttons. Now that she'd acknowledged her feelings, she wanted to share them. She wanted to spend the rest of her life with Joel, and she wanted to start now.

The thought brought a smile to her lips and her step was light as she headed downstairs to the kitchen. She could smell the pizza in the oven, the spicy aroma teased her nostrils, caused her stomach to rumble. But Joel wasn't in the kitchen.

There was a light on in the den, so she stepped through the family room and into the open doorway. He wasn't there, either, but something—an instinct she would later wish she could have ignored—propelled her closer to the desk. His agenda was lying open on top of the blotter and beneath the current date was a notation:

Sam's Diner
9:30
re: Rheanne

She felt a sudden hollowness in her gut that had nothing to do with her want for food. She backed away from the desk, her eyes still glued to the page.

"There you are," Joel came into the room, offering her the glass of wine she'd abandoned earlier.

"Rheanne," she said, surprised that her voice sounded so steady. "R-H-E-A-N-N-E. Is that the name on my original birth certificate?"

Joel hesitated, his gaze dropping to the book on his desk and the easy smile slipping from his face before he answered with a short nod.

''Why is that name in your agenda for today? Did you have an appointment with someone about me?''

''Yes,'' he admitted.

''Who?''

''I can't talk to you about it right now.''

''If it's about me, why can't you discuss it?''

''Because I don't know if there's any truth to the information I was given.''

''Does it matter?'' she asked. ''Your job was to find me. You found me.''

''It's not that simple.''

''It can be. If you could just let it go.'' Then she laughed, bitterly. ''You're still a cop, aren't you? You just won't stop digging until you have all the answers. Even if it ruins my life.''

''It isn't just about you,'' Joel said gently. ''It's about right and wrong.''

''It is about me,'' she insisted. ''And if you cared about me at all, you wouldn't do this.''

''Damn it, Riane, I'm doing this because I care about you. If we're going to have any kind of relationship, we can't start with lies or deception between us.''

''I haven't lied to you about anything.''

''Don't you want to know the truth?''

''No.'' She didn't care that she sounded unreasonable. She wasn't feeling very reasonable at the moment. ''Not if it's going to hurt the people who mean the most to me.''

''You know I can't walk away from this.''

''Well, I can.'' She walked past him and up the stairs again.

She pulled on a pair of jeans and shoved the rest of her clothes into her suitcase. Not half an hour earlier she'd been euphoric to discover she'd fallen in love. Now she knew that the man she loved was continuing to pursue a personal vendetta against her family, and she couldn't be a part of that. She had to leave, and it was tearing her heart out.

If this really was love, she decided as she wiped a single tear off her cheek, she didn't want any part of it.

Joel stood at the bottom of the stairs, looking stunned and hurt when she came down with her suitcase in hand. "Don't go, Riane. Please."

"You've made your choices. I have to make mine."

She scooped up her purse and keys off the coffee table and walked out the door.

Chapter 15

He walked into the apartment as if he had every right to be there. Which, of course, he did. He was her husband, after all.

''Hi, honey. I'm home.''

The magazine slipped from her fingers. She glanced up, her dark eyes wide and haunted. She rose from the chair, stepped behind it. ''H-how did you find me?''

''I told you I would.''

''You sh-shouldn't be here,'' she said. Her fingers dug into the back of the chair. Ragged nails on faded upholstery. ''They'll send you b-back. To jail. For vi-violating your p-parole.''

''Only if they know I'm here.''

''P-please, Gav.'' She swallowed. ''You have to go.''

''I don't think so, honey. Not until we've settled a few things.''

''P-please.''

He smiled at the tremor in her voice. Yes, this was going

exactly as planned. She was begging already. Her eyes swimming with tears.

"You let them put me in a cage." He crossed the room to where she stood.

She shook her head in denial. Tears spilled onto her pasty cheeks. "I n-never wanted you to g-go to jail—"

"It doesn't matter what you wanted." His tone was cold. "That's what happened. You stole four months of our life."

"I-I'm s-sorry. I'm s-so s-sorry."

He cupped her chin in his hand. His fingers bit into the flesh. Forced her to meet his gaze. "You were always sorry, Felicia. And I always forgave you. Maybe that was my mistake."

"I am s-sorry."

"Words. Just words." He shrugged.

"Wh-what are you g-going to do?"

"I'm going to make you sorry."

She shook her head again. "N-no. P-please."

Her pleading was more annoying than satisfying now. She was ruining the whole scene with her pathetic whimpering, and that really pissed him off. He lifted his arm and lashed out with a backhand. It sent her flying. Adrenaline surged through him again.

She crashed against the dining room table. Crumpled to the floor. She didn't cover her face or cower. She didn't move at all.

"Get up," he demanded.

She didn't respond.

He bent over, grabbed her by the shoulder.

And saw the blood.

It was already pooling on the linoleum. Spilling out of the side of her head. He stepped back. Stared in disbelief at the smear of red. His wife's blood. On his hand.

Panic trickled into him. A slow and steady stream. This wasn't part of his plan. This wasn't supposed to happen.

She was just lying there.

Lifeless.

Almost like she was dead.

Damn it, this wasn't supposed to happen!

Was she dead?

Had he killed her?

He hadn't intended to kill her. He'd only wanted to hurt her—to make her suffer as he'd suffered.

He scrubbed his hands through his hair. Tried to order his chaotic thoughts. He needed to think. He needed a new plan. Whatever happened, he wouldn't go back to jail.

He'd have to leave the country. He'd go far away. Somewhere that had never even heard of extradition. But to do that he'd need money. A lot of it.

It was close to midnight by the time Riane arrived home. She'd managed to hold back the tears throughout the three-hour drive, but as she sat in her car in the driveway, the sheer relief of being home overwhelmed her and she was no longer able to do so.

She leaned her forehead against the steering wheel and wept. She couldn't believe she'd been such an idiot. *Again.* It had been one thing to make a fool of herself with Cameron Davis, but she wasn't twenty years old anymore. She should have known better. This time, not only had she let her hormones overrule her head, she'd let her heart get involved, too. She'd fallen in love with Joel Logan, and he'd betrayed her.

She sat up straight and swiped impatiently at the tears streaming down her cheeks. She'd managed perfectly well before he walked into her life and she'd do so again. She had her family—both the parents who'd raised her and loved her, and the sister she'd rediscovered—and her responsibilities at the camp. She didn't need anything else.

So why did her heart ache at the thought of never seeing him again?

She was angry with Joel, angrier with herself. He'd never made her any promises. What right did she have to be upset now simply because she'd learned he wasn't the man she'd wanted him to be?

She climbed out of the car and made her way up to the front door. She hadn't even put her key in the lock when the door opened. Ellen Rutherford-Quinlan stood on the other side, wearing a long, silky robe and a hesitant smile. Her hair was tousled, her deep green eyes shadowed.

"How is it that you always know I'm home even before I've opened the door?" Riane asked.

"Mother's intuition." Ellen stepped back so that Riane could enter, her eyes anxiously searching her daughter's face. "I've missed you."

"I missed you, too."

"Any particular reason you chose the middle of the night to venture home?" There was no censure in her voice, just concern.

"We can talk in the morning, Mom. You should get back to bed before Daddy starts wandering around looking for you."

"I'm not worried about your dad, I'm worried about you." And she gently but firmly took Riane's arm and guided her into the den. "Do you want something to drink—a glass of water, a cup of tea, something stronger?"

Riane shook her head. "No, thanks."

Ellen propelled her toward the sofa, sat down beside her. "Tell me."

Those two words were all it took for the last of Riane's resolve to crumble. "I found out that Joel's still digging for information about my adoption." And the tears started all over again.

Ellen held her while she cried, as she'd done so many times in the past. And, as always, her quiet comfort and reassurance soothed Riane. Eventually the sobs subsided, the tears dried, but the ache in her heart remained.

"He's only doing his job," Ellen said gently.

"Why aren't you angry about this?"

"I was never entirely comfortable with the way things

were handled,'' Ellen admitted. ''And I've never stopped worrying that somehow, someday, this would all come back to haunt us. It's almost a relief to know it's going to happen.''

''I know my adoption wasn't handled through all the proper channels,'' Riane said. ''If that information comes out, it could ruin your career.''

''Do you really think that matters to me now?''

''It should.''

''The only thing that matters is you. I made some bad choices, a lot of mistakes, and I regret a lot of them. But I'd do it all again if it was the only way I could have you.''

Riane's tears spilled over again. She'd been so hurt and angry when she found out about her adoption, she hadn't paid enough attention to her parents' feelings. She hadn't really considered how difficult the whole situation was for them, how they must have agonized over the choices they'd made.

Ellen cradled her daughter's face in her palms and brushed away the tears. ''I appreciate your concern,'' she said. ''But somehow I don't think all these tears are for me.''

''I'm tired. I'm confused. I'm not sure what I'm feeling right now,'' Riane told her.

Her mother smiled sympathetically. ''You're in love with him, aren't you?''

Riane hadn't even wanted to admit the truth to herself, to acknowledge that she'd fallen in love with a man who'd used and betrayed her. But she couldn't lie to her mother; she didn't want to. ''Yes,'' she admitted.

''How does he feel about you?''

Riane laughed, bitterly. ''I have no idea. He says he cares about me.''

''You don't believe him.''

''He wouldn't be doing this if he really cared.''

''Love isn't always that simple,'' Ellen told her.

''It should be,'' Riane said, then sighed. ''Why couldn't I have fallen in love with Stuart?''

''Do you think that would have been easier?''

"I don't know. Maybe. All I want is someone to share my life and my dreams. Someone with whom I can share the kind of connection that you and Daddy have."

Ellen smiled. "Do you think it was love at first sight for your father and me?"

"Wasn't it?"

"I didn't even *like* him when I first met him."

"Why not?" Riane felt strangely insulted on her father's behalf.

"Because he was arrogant and rude and much too sexy for his own good."

The explanation appeased Riane somewhat. "What changed your mind?"

Ellen considered. "It wasn't any one thing, really. But we were at law school together—we had classes in common and group assignments to complete, so we were forced to spend a fair amount of time together. And eventually I realized that there was more to him—more substance, more heart—than I'd wanted to believe. And when he first kissed me," she smiled a little at the memory, "I felt as though the ground was actually trembling beneath my feet."

Riane sighed. She knew that feeling all too well. "Is that when you knew you were in love?"

"No, that's when she decided not to speak to me for the next six months."

Riane turned to see her father leaning nonchalantly against the door frame. "I didn't realize you were up, too."

"I didn't want to miss out on all the girl talk," he said, moving into the room to brush a kiss on Riane's temple. "When did you get home?"

"Just a little while ago." But Riane didn't want to rehash her reasons yet again. "Why didn't Mom talk to you for six months?"

"Because as soon as he stopped kissing me, he opened his mouth and reminded me what an arrogant ass he was," Ellen told her.

"Because I told her I was going to marry her," Ryan offered an alternate explanation.

"After that very first kiss?" Riane asked.

"I knew even before then," Ryan admitted. "For me, it *was* love at first sight."

"You're a hopeless romantic," Ellen chided, but she was smiling with genuine love and affection at the man who'd been her husband for thirty-five years.

"And you're practical enough for the both of us," Ryan told her.

And in that moment, Riane realized that her mother was right. Love wasn't easy—it wasn't supposed to be. It was about affection and caring and compromise. And although the realization didn't ease her own heartache, her parents' relationship affirmed for her the power and endurance of love.

"Go back to bed," she told them. "I didn't mean to disturb you."

"Are you going to get some sleep?" Ellen asked.

Riane didn't know if she could with the jumble of chaotic thoughts swirling around in her mind, but she nodded and feigned a yawn to appease her mother. "I'll see you in the morning."

Ryan kissed her again. "I love you, baby."

She blinked away the moisture behind her eyes. "I love you, too. Both of you."

Ellen squeezed her daughter's hand in a silent show of support before letting her husband drag her out of the room.

Riane didn't sleep much, but she felt somewhat better in the morning. Her late-night conversation with her parents the previous evening had reassured her of the constancy of their love despite the uncertainty of everything else at this point in her life. And it had alleviated the strain they'd all been living under since she'd learned of her adoption. Life was pretty much back to normal in the Quinlan household, which allowed Riane to focus her attention on her other concern—the camp.

It was her work at the camp that gave her life direction and purpose, and she desperately needed both right now. So, after a quick breakfast with Sophie, she headed over to the site.

She wandered through the drizzle, mindless of the cold and wet, inspecting the progress on the new cabins. She was excited about the program that already existed and her short- and long-term plans for the camp, and she was proud that her fund-raising efforts had made this current expansion possible. If the progress continued on schedule, and she had every reason to believe that it would, the Quinlan Camp for Underprivileged Children would double its capacity within the next three years.

Why had she felt so compelled to focus on the needs of underprivileged children? It was a question that had been asked of her numerous times over the past few years. Her explanation had always been the same as the one she'd given Joel: that witnessing the plight of impoverished children through her parents' work in the foreign service had motivated her to find a way to help. While she still believed there was validity in that response, she wondered if there wasn't more to it.

Was it possible that her own experiences as a child, experiences that she couldn't even recollect—the neglect by her biological parents, the trauma of being separated from her sister—had subconsciously instilled in her an empathy for children in similar situations? And if there was any truth at all in that supposition, maybe she and Joel had more in common than she'd realized.

She shook her head. Regardless of their similarities or differences, she couldn't get past the fact that she'd been so wrong about him. She'd thought he cared about her. Damn it, he'd made her believe he cared. But it had all been a facade. The whole time he'd been luring her toward his bed, he'd been digging for dirt on her family.

Okay, if she was honest, she had to admit he hadn't lured her into his bed. She'd wanted to be there. In fact, she'd practically pushed him there. But that didn't make his betrayal hurt any less.

"Ms. Quinlan?"

Riane started at the sound of the unfamiliar masculine voice close behind her and hastily wiped the tears from her cheeks. She'd been certain she was alone, that all the workers had left the site for the day because of the inclement weather. Obviously she was wrong. She blinked the remaining traces of moisture out of her eyes before she turned.

And found herself staring into the snub-nosed barrel of a gun.

Chapter 16

It wasn't in Riane's nature to give in to a bully, and she couldn't think of any better way to describe the man who was holding her at gunpoint. Still, she kept her chin up and her resolve firm.

Her resolve faltered just a little when he directed her to his car and ordered her to get in. Even with her rudimentary knowledge of self-defense, Riane knew a victim was never supposed to get into an assailant's vehicle. But he'd seemed ready, even eager, to use the gun he'd waved in her face, and she hated to think that her blood could be spilled on the grounds of her camp. She wouldn't let some madman tarnish the project she'd put so much of her heart and soul into.

So she'd ignored her self-preservation instincts and gone with him. She wasn't exactly sure where, since he'd tied her hands behind her back and blindfolded her when they got to his car. A green midsize vehicle with Michigan plates, she noted. She knew it would be important to give as much information as she could to the police, if she managed to get out of this in one piece.

Her abductor removed the blindfold when they arrived at their destination. It was, Riane realized with a bizarre sense of irony, the same motel where she and Joel had stayed the night she'd run out of gas on Highway 27. It had to be the same motel. She couldn't imagine two different establishments choosing the same horrid shade of orange for their decor.

Still, it didn't do her any good to know where she was unless he let her use the phone to call someone. And she didn't think that was likely.

So she was surprised when he pushed her onto one of the twin beds and said, "I want you to make a phone call.

"You're not going to talk," he continued, eliminating her quick burst of hope. "You're just going to dial. I'll handle the rest."

"Who am I supposed to call?" she asked, forcing her voice to remain level. His request had calmed some of the panic that had been escalating inside her. Whatever this man wanted, it wasn't sexual in nature, and for that she was infinitely grateful.

"You're supposed to be a smart woman," the man taunted. "I'm sure you can figure it out."

"Why don't you enlighten me?" she suggested, unaccountably angered by his smug tone.

"I'm the kidnapper, you're the hostage. The only thing you need to know is that if you don't do exactly what I tell you, I'm going to put a bullet through you."

She was helpless to prevent the instinctive shudder that rippled through her at the threat. He seemed to look forward to the possibility of doing just that.

"If I'm a hostage, it means you think someone is willing to give you something you want in exchange for me. I won't be much good as a bargaining chip if I'm dead," she pointed out.

He smiled menacingly. "Only if they know you're dead."

Okay, he had a point there. "What do you want?"

"Money."

''Why?''

''Why?'' He laughed. ''Because money makes the world go round.''

''Why me?'' she asked. ''What makes you think anyone would be willing to pay anything for me?''

''I've seen that fancy house on the hill you live in, the car you drive, the jewels you wear.'' He flicked a grimy finger against the sapphire stud in her ear. ''And I figured if they were willing to pay a hundred thousand dollars for you before, who knows how much they'll pay now?''

His lips curved in a sick smile. ''I think I'll ask for a million. Yes, that's a nice round number. It'll be enough to get me out of this hick town, out of this stinking country.''

Riane was no longer paying attention to his tirade. ''What do you mean—they paid before?''

''Your parents,'' he said. ''I don't imagine a hotshot senator will have any trouble finding a lousy million bucks.''

''Who did they pay? Why?'' She didn't know why she felt compelled to ask the questions; she was certain she wouldn't want to know the answers.

''They paid *me,*'' he told her, and the slow, obscene curving of his lips made her skin crawl. ''Because I'm your father.''

Joel's attention was riveted on the side of Felicia Reynolds's face, on the menacing-looking bruise visible just beneath the peak of her baseball cap. ''What happened to you?''

She dropped her gaze again and folded her trembling fingers together. ''I fell.''

He'd heard it before—he'd heard all the excuses before. ''He found you, didn't he?''

''I don't know what you're talking about.'' But her response was belied by the tremor in her voice.

Joel swore viciously under his breath, and Felicia flinched as if struck by a physical blow. He forced himself to rein in his anger. She'd obviously seen enough evidence of temper recently. "Have you been to the hospital?" he asked more gently.

She nodded and pushed her hat back slightly, revealing a neat little row of stitches that disappeared into her hairline.

"How about the police?"

She pulled the cap back down, her eyes wide, terrified. "The cops don't need to know that I'm clumsy."

"They need to know if Elliott was here."

"He wasn't," she insisted.

"Ms. Reynolds, any contact with you is a violation of his parole—he would go back to jail and you'd be safe."

"Only until he got out again," she said bitterly.

"You need to go to the po—"

"No," she interrupted, no longer denying Elliott's involvement. "I'm safe now."

"How can you be sure?"

She hesitated, folding her fingers together again so tightly that her knuckles turned white. "B-because...because Gavin thinks...I'm dead."

"You could have been," Joel agreed, studying the swelling and discoloration on the side of her face more carefully.

"If he goes back to prison, I will be."

"You can't let him get away with this."

"I thought you came here to talk about Rheanne," she reminded him.

Joel nodded. He had, and he knew better than to insist on helping someone who didn't want help.

"Your ex-husband told me the adoptive parents paid for your child," he said at last.

She hesitated for a second, then nodded.

"How much?" The amount didn't matter nearly so much as Felicia Reynolds's admission that she and her husband had signed away their rights to their child in exchange for a sum of money, but he'd gone too far to turn back now.

She didn't look up. "A hundred thousand dollars."

He'd seen and heard a lot in his thirty-three years, but he was still shocked. Not by the figure she'd recited but by the fact that this woman had, without any indication of regret or remorse, sold her two-year-old child. "Whose idea was it to sell her?"

"We didn't sell the kid," she denied. "That's illegal."

Not to mention immoral and unethical and abhorrent.

"What would you call it when you give up your child in exchange for a sum of money?" he challenged, unable to mask his disgust.

She looked up now, lifting her chin in a gesture of defiance. "We were entitled to be, um, reimbursed, Mr. Rutherford said, for our expenses."

He had the truth now, but he still didn't know what he was going to do with it. Mike had been right when he'd accused Joel of using the connection in Arden's sister's case to pursue a more personal agenda. When Judge Rutherford had destroyed his career, Joel had vowed that he would someday have his revenge against the privileged classes who thought their money could buy them anything.

Now he knew without a doubt that Ellen Rutherford-Quinlan had used her money to buy a child, and it was within his power to reveal the truth and bring her down. After five seemingly endless years, revenge was finally within his grasp. He should have been ecstatic. Instead, he felt only growing despair and aching emptiness, because every step he took closer to exposing the secret was a step further away from Riane. There was no way she'd ever forgive him if he used this information against her mother.

He tried to tell himself that it didn't matter. Riane had already walked out of his life, just as he'd known she would. She was a woman, after all, and every woman he'd ever cared about had abandoned him.

Why, then, did her leaving hurt so much? And why did finding a way to win her back suddenly seem so much more important than the revenge he'd sought for so long? So much more important than anything else?

As he reached for his cell phone to call Riane, it started to ring.

* * *

Both Ellen and Ryan Quinlan were in the living room when Joel arrived. Ryan sat on the edge of the couch, his concentration focused intently on the phone, as if he might will it to ring. The senator was pacing. Her usually immaculate hair looked as though she'd repeatedly run her fingers through it, her face was bare of makeup, her eyes red rimmed and filled with anxiety.

Until that moment Joel hadn't been convinced of the gravity of the situation. All Ellen Rutherford-Quinlan had said on the phone was that she needed him to come to the house right away. Joel had sensed the urgency and hadn't asked any questions.

"Thank you for coming, Mr. Logan." It was Ryan who spoke to him, his voice shaky, as if he was holding on to the little control he had by a fraying thread.

It was Joel's first meeting with Riane's father, and not at all the circumstances under which he might have wished the introduction to take place.

"Our daughter's been kidnapped," the older man continued.

Joel felt his heart drop like a stone into the bottom of an empty well. But he shook his head, refusing to believe it. She'd probably just gone for a drive. Or maybe she'd gone to the camp. There were a million possibilities, but kidnapped was not one of them.

"We got a telephone call," Ryan told him. "Just before we called you, from the man who's taken her."

Joel had come right away. Still, the drive from the diner had taken more than an hour, and every minute of it seemed interminable. "You haven't heard anything since then?"

"No."

"Do you have any idea who's taken her? Why?"

Ryan just shook his head. "He only told us that he has Riane."

"Did you speak to Riane at all?"

"He wouldn't let me."

"Then maybe he doesn't have her," Joel suggested, wanting desperately to believe it himself. "Maybe this is some kind of hoax."

That was a better alternative than to believe some nut really had Riane, because even in the movies kidnappers made their hostages say a few words. Proof of life, it was called. If the kidnapper wouldn't give it, the hostage was as good as dead. He shook off the thought. Riane was going to be fine. She had to be.

"We wouldn't have bothered you if we thought this was a hoax, Mr. Logan." The senator's voice whipped across the room like a physical slap. "My daughter is missing. She went to the camp this morning. Her car is still there. She isn't."

"The grounds are pretty extensive," Joel reminded her. "If Riane decided to take a walk or—"

"She didn't take a walk. She was kidnapped. Jared, the camp supervisor, went out there this afternoon to tend to the horses. He found—"

Her voice broke and she turned away, as if ashamed for him to see any hint of her suffering. "He found her Harvard ring on the ground beside her car."

She turned to face him again, her eyes flashing with annoyance, "And before you suggest that it might have slipped off her finger, I can assure you that it didn't. We gave her that ring after law school graduation, and she has never taken it off. She did so now to tell us she didn't go willingly."

"Forgive me for being blunt," Joel said. "But I know that Riane has had a lot to deal with in the past few weeks. Can you really be certain that she didn't just go off somewhere for some time alone?"

"We're certain," Ryan said, slipping his arm across his wife's shoulders in a visible sign of support. "When Riane came home last night, we resolved a lot of things. She wasn't angry or upset when she left here this morning."

Joel scrubbed his hands over his face, surprised by the rasp of stubble against his palm. He'd forgotten to shave this morning. Hell, since Riane had walked out on him last night he hadn't even slept. He felt grossly unprepared to deal with this latest crisis, but he knew he couldn't be anywhere else right now.

Focus, Logan.

He wouldn't be any help to Riane if he didn't keep his mind on the present situation. So, unthinkable as it was to believe that she'd actually been kidnapped, he forced his mind to accept the possibility and gather all the details.

"Did the kidnapper ask for money?"

Again Ryan shook his head. "He said he'd call back. He had some details to take care of first."

Christ, Joel thought with disgust. It was like whoever had kidnapped Riane didn't know any of the rules. There was nothing worse—or more dangerous—than an amateur.

"You need to speak to Riane," Joel said. "Don't agree to anything until you talk to her."

"We'll do anything to get our daughter back," Ellen told him.

And so would he, Joel vowed silently. "I understand that," he told her. "But I don't want the kidnapper to know that until we've heard from Riane."

She looked at her husband, wordlessly seeking his agreement. Ryan nodded.

"Okay," the senator agreed.

"Depending on his reasons for targeting your daughter," Joel said, and he was afraid to even speculate on what those reasons might be, "the kidnapper may want some kind of media exposure."

"No," Ryan said immediately. "We want this kept out of the press."

"Shouldn't your priority be getting Riane back?" Joel asked, his tone cool.

"Riane is, and always has been, our priority," Ellen told him. "That's why we don't want the press getting wind of this. Wackos get ideas—"

"Not to mention the damage to your political career if the details of recent revelations came to light," Joel said.

The senator turned to him, her eyes hot with anger. ''Is that what you think—that I'm trying to cover my own ass?''

''Aren't you?''

She gasped. ''No. We—''

''Regardless of what you may think of us,'' Ryan interrupted his wife's outburst, ''the only thing that matters here is getting Riane back safely. I agreed to call you because Ellen thought you cared about Riane. If she was wrong, if our daughter doesn't matter to you, then we'll find someone else to track her down and bring her home.''

''No,'' Joel said. ''I'll do this.''

The senator nodded stiffly. ''Then do it.''

So Joel made some phone calls and pulled strings with a buddy in the FBI. With the political clout of the senator to back him up, he had the Quinlan telephone lines tapped within twenty minutes without the necessity of any official Bureau involvement.

When the phone finally rang, another agonizingly slow thirty minutes later, he was waiting on the extension.

''Hello?'' Ellen's usually controlled voice wavered.

''Mom, it's me.''

Ellen closed her eyes, silent tears sliding down her pasty cheeks. Joel's own sense of relief was so overwhelming he had to lower himself into the nearest chair or risk falling down.

''Are you okay, honey?''

''I'd feel better after a few slices of sausage pizza, but I'm fine.'' Her voice trembled a little, but she sounded strong.

''We'll get you a dozen pizzas,'' Ellen promised. ''Just tell us what we need to do. Whatever it takes, we'll get you home.''

Joel should have been annoyed that the senator had so blatantly disregarded his instructions, but he couldn't blame her for promising anything. Right now, he was so anxious to see Riane, to touch her—to know she was alive and well and safe, he would have promised the moon and the stars to bring her home.

''He wants a million dollars,'' Riane said. ''If you don't have the money ready within the next two hours, the price is going up by half a million.''

''We'll have the money,'' the senator promised, heedless of the tears that continued to fall. ''Just tell us where to deliver it. We'll make sure it's there.''

''He hasn't told me where he wants it dropped off,'' Riane said.

The next voice over the line wasn't Riane's, but Joel recognized it anyway.

Gavin Elliott.

''I'll call you in half an hour with more details,'' Elliott said, then disconnected.

Joel's stomach clenched. He was responsible for this. For everything. He'd gone to see Elliott, he'd started asking questions about Riane, he'd set this whole thing in motion. And if anything happened to Riane, he'd never forgive himself.

Joel dropped the receiver back into its cradle and looked at the tracing equipment. He shook his head. He hadn't expected the call would be long enough, but he'd had to give it a shot.

''I don't understand Riane's comment about pizza,'' the senator said, wiping at the wet streaks on her face. ''Why wouldn't he feed her if she's hungry? Aren't kidnappers supposed to show good faith or something like that?''

''I don't think she was saying she was hungry,'' Joel admitted. ''I think she was trying to tell us something.''

''What?''

''That I'm not sure.'' He stood up and paced the length of the room, trying to kick-start his brain. He couldn't think straight. He was so tied up in knots worrying about Riane that he was barely functioning. But he knew she was depending on him. Her comment about the pizza proved that. She, at least, seemed to be thinking clearly.

She must have known her parents would contact him after

they received the first call. She had to know he'd be listening in to the conversation. But still, her comment didn't make any sense to him. She didn't even *like* sausage pizza.

And that suddenly, he knew what she was trying to tell him. Riane was at the motel where they'd stayed the night he'd found her at the country-western bar. The night she'd eaten, with a reluctance exceeded only by hunger, three slices of sausage pizza.

Clever girl, he thought, his heart swelling with pride. She'd given him an invaluable clue about her location without tipping off Elliott to the fact that she knew where she was. She was beautiful and brilliant and brave, and if he hadn't already been head over heels in love with her, he would have fallen right then.

"I think I know where she is," Joel said.

"Where?" Ellen and Ryan demanded in unison.

He glanced at his watch. Elliott said he'd call back in half an hour. If he remembered the location of the motel correctly, it would take him almost that long to get there. And if he was wrong—

No. Riane had definitely been telling him that she was at that motel. In fact, he should have suspected Elliott would take her there. It was off the beaten path, yet close enough to facilitate a quick exchange of money for hostage. Elliott certainly wouldn't expect that Riane had ever been there before. She was a senator's daughter; it was one step above a fleabag motel.

"I'm not positive," Joel cautioned them. "But there's someplace I need to check out."

"I want to go with you," Ellen said.

"No."

"She's my daughter."

"And if she's there, you could blow everything by rushing in."

"I want to be there. I need to see her. To know that she's okay."

"I'll bring her home," Joel promised.

"But—"

Again, it was her husband's wordless communication—a simple touch of his hand on her arm—that silenced the senator's further protests. "Let him go," Ryan said. "We have to get the money together and we need to be here when Riane calls back."

Ellen nodded reluctantly.

Ryan exchanged a look with Joel. A plea. A promise.

Then Joel was gone.

He tied her up. He bound her wrists and stuffed a washcloth in her mouth. To keep her quiet and out of the way. He wouldn't let another woman screw this up for him.

Rheanne had always factored into his plans. Anyone who'd paid a hundred grand to buy a baby would pay again—and pay dearly—to keep that secret. And the woman who'd bought his baby was now a bona fide U.S. senator. It was almost too perfect. Any scent of a scandal would ruin her career, shame her family. He never doubted that she would pay.

The money he'd get from the senator would have given Felicia and him a new start. Felicia had ruined that part of his plan. And he'd been forced to take immediate action. To upgrade his strategy from blackmail to kidnapping.

He glanced at the woman on the floor. She was restrained, helpless. But she glared at him with fire in her eyes. He almost smiled. She had spirit—like her mother and her sister. He felt a pang of sorrow over losing Felicia. Fury for Arden's role in all of this. She'd been the one to turn her mother against him.

But maybe he should thank Arden. Her desire to be reunited with her little sister had led Joel Logan to Rheanne. And Rheanne was his ticket out of this whole mess.

The senator hadn't even balked at the million-dollar price tag. He should have asked for more. Two million. Five million. She would have paid anything.

He smiled. Maybe next time.

* * *

When it came down to the crunch, it was almost too easy. That realization sent a fresh wave of panic through Joel. It was the same thought he'd had before he'd taken a bullet in the gut, before his life had unraveled in front of his eyes. This time there was so much more at stake. This time it was the woman he loved.

He recognized the car as soon as he pulled into the parking lot. The dirty green Malibu with a patch of rust on the rear fender and Michigan plates. Joel swore and checked the clip in his gun. Gavin Elliott was a smart man, but taking Riane had obviously been an act of desperation, and that made him much more dangerous.

Joel picked up the empty pizza box he'd tossed onto the passenger seat. It was a prop—a reason to knock on the door. He hadn't planned any further than to get inside. He needed to know that Riane was okay. God help Gavin Elliott if she wasn't.

He pulled his Yankees baseball cap lower over his forehead and marched up to the door of room six. He'd already verified Elliott's registration with the desk clerk. He'd given a false name—John Smith—and paid cash, but he'd noted his license plate number on the registration card. That was proof enough for Joel.

Snatching Riane had obviously been an impulse, or Elliott wouldn't have used his own car in the act. Which made Joel realize that Felicia Reynolds was right: Elliott thought he'd killed her. No doubt he needed the ransom money from Riane's kidnapping to get him out of the country. And it was further proof of how far gone the man was that he actually thought he would get away with it.

Joel knocked boldly, as if he was expected. As someone delivering a pizza would be. He saw the curtains flutter, heard the slide of the chain being drawn back. Then Gavin Elliott was at the door.

"I didn't order any pizza," he rasped, his eyes shifting

from the flat cardboard box to Joel's face, widening in recognition and alarm. ''What the hell are you doing here?''

Joel's only response was to plow his fist solidly into Elliott's jaw. The older man staggered backward and crumpled into a heap on the orange shag carpet. Joel was almost disappointed that he didn't get to throw more punches. But as much as he would have enjoyed going a few rounds with Elliott, his concern was for Riane. He flexed his fingers, his eyes desperately searching the shabby room for any sign of the woman he loved.

He found her, kneeling on the floor behind the dresser. Her wrists tied together in front of her, a rag of some kind stuffed into her mouth. Her hair was tangled and her eyes were smudged with shadows of fatigue, but she was there. And despite the way they'd parted at their last meeting, he could tell she was relieved to see him.

He knelt beside her, carefully removing the cloth from her mouth, murmuring softly to her as he brushed away the tears of relief and gratitude that tracked slowly down her cheeks. ''Are you okay, sweetheart?''

She nodded, although she couldn't seem to stop trembling—or crying. ''B-better now.''

There was so much he wanted to say to her, so many feelings warring for expression inside him. But the most important thing right now was to get her out of there. ''Let's get you home.''

He started to fumble with the knot binding her wrists together, stunned to see that his own hands were shaking. In all his years as a cop, even in that final showdown, he'd never been as terrified as he'd been when he'd learned of the danger Riane was in. God, he loved this woman, and if he hadn't already screwed things up too badly, he was going to spend every day of the rest of his life showing her how much he loved her.

''He's g-got a gun,'' Riane said, her voice shaky, frantic.

So preoccupied was he with Riane that it took a moment for her words to register, and that moment—probably not more than a fraction of a second, was a fraction of a second too long. He turned just as the gunshot exploded.

He never saw how Riane managed to launch herself from her position on the floor and throw herself in front of him. But he did see, as if in slow motion, her body jerk back as the bullet slammed into her.

Chapter 17

Joel's response was automatic. He wasn't aware of his own gun in his hand, his finger on the trigger. He didn't hear the discharge; he didn't feel the recoil; he didn't see Elliott fall.

He only saw Riane—and he watched in horror as she fell back against the wall, slid slowly to the floor.

"Christ, Riane." Blood was seeping from her shoulder, the dark crimson stain spreading over the shirt, soaking it. "What the hell were you thinking?"

It was easier to be angry than to think that she could be dying. The rational part of his brain knew it wasn't likely. The bullet didn't seem to have hit any major arteries and a .22 caliber handgun didn't have a lot of firepower. But her skin was clammy, those beautiful dark brown eyes wide and glazed, and she was losing a lot of blood.

He propped her up a little higher, trying to keep the injured shoulder above her heart. He knew he should get a towel to stanch the flow of blood, but he'd have to go into the bathroom for that and he couldn't bear to leave her. Not even for a few seconds. So he pulled his own T-shirt over his head and pressed it into the wound. She didn't wince, and he knew then that she probably couldn't even feel the bullet hole in her shoulder. But the blood continued to flow.

She licked her lips, blinked several times. He knew she was going to lose consciousness, and he couldn't stand the thought of her slipping away, even for a moment. He dug his cell phone out of his pocket and managed to dial 911, tersely explaining the situation and requesting immediate ambulance assistance.

Then he disconnected the call and began to pray. He'd never been a particularly devout man, but he found himself seeking divine assistance now. The words and pleas and promises tripped over one another, jumbled together in his head, with only one consistent thought: *Please, God. Let her live.*

He cradled her in his arms, still applying pressure to the wound. "Stay with me, sweetheart. Please, stay with me. The ambulance is on the way. Just hold on a little longer."

Riane managed a slight nod, then closed her eyes.

"Come on, Riane. Talk to me."

Her eyes flickered open slowly, and she blinked, as if trying to bring his face into focus. "Sorry about your shirt."

Riane spent four days in the hospital. Four torturously long days. As if the pain in her shoulder wasn't excruciating enough every time she moved, her parents never seemed to leave her room. She knew they'd been worried about her, and she appreciated their concern, but she was starting to feel smothered by their love.

And forgotten by the man she loved.

She had a vague recollection of Joel riding in the ambulance with her, holding her hand on the way to the hospital. She'd found comfort in his presence and the steady reassuring murmur of his voice. She wasn't sure she clearly remembered anything he said, but she thought—or maybe she just hoped—he'd told her he loved her.

It was those words—real or imagined—that had given her

hope. But since she'd regained consciousness, she hadn't so much as caught a glimpse of him. When she finally gathered up the courage to ask about him, her mother admitted that he'd gone back to Pennsylvania.

His apparent indifference hurt so much more than the residual pain in her shoulder. The scar from the bullet was insignificant compared to the scars on her heart.

She didn't really blame Joel for not wanting to stick around. They'd each understood that their relationship wasn't for the long term, and she'd reiterated that statement, clearly and finally, by walking out on him. So she shouldn't have been surprised that he hadn't stayed; she had no right to feel hurt. They lived in different worlds, wanted different things. Or so she'd honestly believed. Right now all she wanted was Joel.

She was released from the hospital on Thursday, with strict instructions from her doctor to get plenty of rest. Ellen and Ryan continued to hover over her bed, as if afraid to let Riane out of their sight. Sophie fluffed pillows and baked cookies and brought magazines Riane never got a chance to read.

News of the abduction, the shooting, and the death of her abductor, had been plastered all over the news. For three days it was the lead story on the local stations—things like that just didn't happen in Mapleview. The incident even garnered national coverage because the victim was Senator Ellen Rutherford-Quinlan's daughter. Despite the media frenzy, no one seemed to have made the connection between Riane and Gavin Elliott, which was at least something for which she could feel grateful.

Arden and Shaun came to visit the day after she arrived home from the hospital. The second reunion between the two sisters had been more natural, and more emotional, than the first.

"I was so afraid I'd found you only to lose you again," Arden said tearfully.

Riane had cried, too, feeling incredibly blessed despite recent events. It wasn't so hard, she realized, to open up her heart to this extended family that she'd never known she had. And both Ellen and Ryan had seemed genuinely pleased to meet their daughter's older sister and Arden's fiancé.

Still, Riane couldn't help feeling as though there was something left unfinished.

Three days later she was in the solarium, stretched out on a wicker chaise lounge with both sets of French doors open to allow the cool breeze and the scent of spring flowers into the room. Her arm was still in a sling, and although the pain had lessened somewhat, her sense of restlessness had not.

Sophie brought her a glass of fresh-squeezed lemonade and a plate of oatmeal-raisin cookies. "I can't just sit around eating all day," Riane complained. "I'll get fat."

"You need to put on a few pounds," Sophie told her, fluffing the pillow from the end of the lounger, replacing it beneath Riane's feet. "If that wind picks up any, it'll blow you away."

"I hardly think that's likely."

Sophie huffed. "You haven't eaten a decent meal since you've been home. Since Mr. Logan left town."

"My lack of appetite has nothing to do with him," Riane said firmly.

"And he calls here every day for a report on the local weather," Sophie muttered sarcastically.

"He called?" Riane asked, annoyed at the sudden flutter of excitement in her belly.

"Every day since you've been home."

Riane paused with the glass of lemonade halfway to her lips. "Why?"

Sophie shook her head. "Why do you think? Because the man's in love with you."

"If he loves me, why hasn't he come to see me?"

"Because men are idiots. Men in love are even worse. And that's just what I told him, too."

Riane couldn't help but smile at the assessment. Sophie had strong opinions, strong emotions, and she never hesitated to express either one. She didn't doubt that Sophie had told

Joel exactly that. Riane's smile faltered. Regardless of what Sophie might have said, Joel was still in Pennsylvania and she was here.

"He nearly wore a hole through the floor in the waiting room while you were in surgery," Sophie said, shaking her head. "As if we didn't know that you could survive a little gunshot wound."

"Little gunshot wound?" Riane said indignantly. "I could have been killed."

Sophie shook her head again. "Not my girl. She's tough. Too stubborn to let a bullet take her down."

Riane laughed. It felt good to return to some sense of normalcy after the craziness of the past couple of weeks.

"Now that's a sound I haven't heard around here in far too long," Ryan said, coming into the solarium from the family room.

"What are you doing home in the middle of the day?" Riane demanded.

"Just came by to check on my favorite girl," he said, bending to kiss her cheek. "How's the arm?"

"Stiff."

Sophie snorted. "How much longer are you going to let her play up that scratch?"

Ryan grinned and sat on the lounger beside his daughter, taking her uninjured hand and squeezing gently. "As long as she wants."

Sophie retreated into the main part of the house, shaking her head the whole way.

"What *I* want," Riane told him, "is my files from the camp. I'm going crazy just sitting around here day after day."

"Everything's on schedule," Ryan assured her. "You have a very capable staff who are finally getting a chance to prove themselves because you're not around to do everything."

"I like doing everything," Riane said mutinously.

"I know. You're a control freak, just like your mother." Ryan's tone was affectionate.

"I'm not a control freak," Ellen denied, following her husband's path into the room.

Ryan chuckled.

Riane turned to her mother, eyed the red silk dress and jacket Ellen was wearing. The suit Riane knew she wore whenever she was about to tackle a controversial issue in the Senate or just generally needed to boost her self-confidence. "Where have you been?"

"I had a press conference this morning."

"Why? Why didn't you tell me?"

"Because I didn't want you to worry."

"Control freak," Ryan said again.

But this time Ellen smiled at him, and in her eyes was a wealth of emotion—gratitude, affection, relief.

"I resigned my seat in the Senate."

Riane sat up abruptly, winced at the resultant pain that lanced through her shoulder like a hot blade. She swore under her breath and sank back into the thick cushion. "Because of me," she said weakly.

"No," both Ellen and Ryan denied in unison.

Riane wasn't convinced.

Ellen sat down on the end of her husband's lounge chair. "Because it was what I needed to do."

"You think Joel will take the information about my adoption to the press?"

"My decision had nothing to do with Mr. Logan."

"But you love your job," Riane protested.

Ellen shrugged. "Now I'll find another job to love."

Riane couldn't help looking skeptical.

"I happen to know of a law firm that has an opening," Ryan said. "There's even a corner office with a pretty good view."

"*My* office?" Riane asked.

Ryan smiled. "It's not *your* office until you take the job, and we both know you're not going to."

"But—"

"No 'buts,'" her father interrupted. "I've already given your job—and your office—away."

Riane blew out a frustrated breath.

Ellen reached over to take Riane's hand, cradling it between both of her own. "You have to decide what *you* want to do," she said gently. "Not what you think *we* want you to do."

"I don't know what I want," Riane admitted.

"Do you want Joel?"

Riane looked down at their joined hands, drawing strength from the unquestioning support of her family. Even now, after everything that had happened, neither of her parents was trying to influence her decision. Whatever mistakes she'd make in her life would be her own, but she knew they would always stand by her. And it was that knowledge that gave her the courage to answer her mother's question.

"Yes."

"Then go get him."

"Why should *I* have to go after *him?*" Riane demanded sulkily.

"Because you're the one who walked out," Ellen reminded her.

"He's the one who hightailed it back to Pennsylvania."

"I think he blames himself for what happened," Ryan said. "And believing that, he wouldn't think he was welcome to stay."

It was something Riane hadn't considered but realized she should have. Joel had been instrumental in uncovering the truth about her adoption, and in doing so he'd brought Gavin Elliott into her life. Rational or not, she knew him well enough to know he'd feel responsible for the events that had followed.

The realization gave her hope. Maybe he wasn't staying away because he didn't want her but because he felt guilty about what had happened in that motel room. And he wouldn't feel guilty if he didn't care about her.

"Do you love him?" Ellen asked gently.

Now Riane smiled. "The first time he kissed me, I felt as though the ground was actually trembling beneath my feet."

Ryan shook his head. "I don't need to hear these things about my little girl."

Ellen only smiled back at her. "Go get him."

"Now?" Riane asked, startled.

"Why not? If you sit and think about it, you'll think of a hundred reasons why you shouldn't go. Follow your heart."

"You're really okay with this?"

"I think the one thing I've learned over the past couple of weeks is that I have an incredible daughter. She's beautiful and strong and exactly the kind of woman I hoped she'd be someday." Ellen leaned forward and took both of her daughter's hands in hers—a gesture of support, a symbol of unity. "It takes a very special man to appreciate a woman like you, and I think you've found him."

So Riane went to Pennsylvania to find him.

Eight days had passed since the incident in the motel room. Eight nights in which Joel watched over and over again as Riane threw herself in front of the gun. He awoke from those dreams with the warm stickiness of her blood on his hands.

In a futile attempt to banish the torturous memory, he worked harder and longer and slept less. But he couldn't forget the image of Riane on that stretcher. Pale, almost lifeless, the blood continuing to spill out of the hole in her shoulder.

When the doctor had come out after the surgery to tell Riane's parents that she was going to be okay, he'd done something he couldn't ever remember having done before. He'd put his head in his hands and he'd wept.

He'd experienced loss before. His mother, his grandmother, his sister. His career. His wife. Max. He'd never felt the heart-wrenching agony he'd experienced every single moment that Riane was behind the closed doors of that operating room.

Even when they'd told him that she'd be okay, he wasn't convinced. He wouldn't believe it until he saw her with his own eyes. And so he'd waited until visiting hours were long over, and he'd sneaked into her room.

She'd been sleeping—sedated. Her hair dark against the pristine white pillowcase, her face pale. Her shoulder was bandaged, an IV protruded from the back of her delicate hand.

He'd reached out tentatively, brushed her hair away from her face, rubbed his knuckles gently across her cheek.

It wasn't enough. That single glimpse, that single touch, wasn't nearly enough. But he forced himself to be satisfied—to walk away. She was going to be all right. He had no right to ask for anything more.

And so he got into his car and came back to Pennsylvania.

Back to a home that was empty without her. Back to a bed that carried a lingering trace of her scent no matter how many times he changed the sheets.

Damn it—even now, even in his office, he could smell her. That slightly musky scent that clouded his senses. He shook his head, scrubbed his hands over his face, rubbed his tired eyes.

Maybe he needed a vacation. Mike had been on his case since he'd come back from West Virginia to take some time off—to get away. But there was nowhere he wanted to go without Riane.

He opened his eyes again, and she was there.

He blinked, certain she would disappear as quickly as she'd appeared, but the image remained.

''Hello, Joel.''

He ignored the sudden rush of his pulse, the tightening around his heart. He'd promised himself that he could get over her, but he needed more time. It had only been a few days. He hadn't even started to heal.

''Riane.'' Her name was little more than a whisper on his lips. Or maybe it was a plea.

She stepped into his office, closed the door behind her.

She was so beautiful, even with her arm in a sling and her face tired and pale, she was the most beautiful woman he'd ever known.

He swallowed, searching for something to say, finally settling upon, "What are you doing here?"

"I needed to see you. I need to know why you left."

"My job was done."

"Is that all I ever was to you?" She sounded casual, as if it was simply idle curiosity that prompted the question, as if his response didn't really matter.

He wished he could be as cool, but his heart was breaking all over again just looking at her. "You know better than that."

"I thought I did." She shrugged. Again, very casual. "But I didn't think you'd take off without saying goodbye, either."

"Is that why you're here—because I didn't say goodbye?"

"I'm here because I never got a chance to thank you."

"Thank me?"

"For saving my life."

"Saving your life?" Joel wondered briefly if he was having some out-of-body experience because nothing she was saying made any sense to him.

"You came after me…you found me. Even though I walked out on you. And I wanted to thank you for that."

"Christ, Riane. He shot you. He could have killed you, and it was all my fault."

"How was it your fault?"

"I led him to you," Joel said, even now horrified by the realization that she'd nearly died because of him. That the life of this precious, beautiful woman could have ended because he'd been unable to put aside his personal quest for vengeance.

Joel shook his head, guilt gnawing at his insides. "He probably hadn't even thought of you in the past twenty years until I started asking questions." He broke off, appalled. "I'm sorry. I keep forgetting—"

"That he was my father," Riane finished for him.

''He was your father,'' Joel repeated. ''And I killed him.'' Even if she could somehow forgive him for everything else, how could she ever get past that fact? How could *he* ever get past it?

''He would have killed you,'' Riane said. ''And me. I wish I could forget it. I wish I could pretend it wasn't true.'' She managed a wry smile. ''It was devastating to learn that the people who raised me weren't really my parents. Although I know now that I was wrong to ever have thought that. They are my parents—in every way that counts.''

''I'm glad you worked things out with them.''

''There are a lot of things in my life that I still need to resolve, but I'm working on them.''

He just nodded.

''That's the real reason I'm here,'' she admitted softly. ''To see if we can resolve what happened between us.''

''I didn't realize it was *un*resolved.''

''When we were in the ambulance—on the way to the hospital—I thought you said you loved me.''

Joel didn't respond. There wasn't any point in admitting his feelings, opening up his heart.

But she wouldn't accept his silence. ''Did you say it?''

He swallowed. ''Yes.''

''Did you mean it?''

''Why are you bringing this up now?''

''Because I need to know if it's really over between us or if maybe we could start again.''

''It's over.''

She looked away quickly, but not before he saw her eyes fill with tears. He hated himself for hurting her, for doing so callously and deliberately. But he knew it was for the best. So he braced himself, prepared to watch her walk out the door. To walk out of his life, taking his heart with her.

Riane stopped in front of the door, hesitated.

Just go, he pleaded silently. *Now. Don't make this any more difficult.*

She turned back abruptly, her eyes glittering. Not with

tears now, but anger. ''Do you really expect me to believe it's over?''

She retraced her steps across the room until she was standing in front of him again. ''My life has been turned completely upside down over the past several weeks, and even though there were times I wanted to pretend none of this really happened, I never wished it away because through all of this chaos I found you.

''You made me believe that everything that's happened doesn't change who I am. And if I'd never found out I was adopted, I would never have known how desperately my parents wanted a child—how much they cherish me because they couldn't have children of their own. They gave me love and security. They taught me to be confident in who I was and what I wanted.

''You taught me to accept who I am, to be proud of who I am. And, damn it, you made me love you.''

He didn't have time to catch his breath, to even think of a response, before she was plunging ahead again.

''So if you can look at me and tell me that you don't care about me—that you don't love me, I'll believe you. And I'll go. But don't you dare tell me you don't want me because you think you know what's best for me.

''Maybe you're not the kind of man I envisioned myself spending my life with. I'd be willing to bet I'm not the type of woman you were looking for, either. But the fact of the matter is that I think we've found something pretty special together, and I'm not willing to throw it away because you have some warped sense of nobility.''

If he'd had any doubts before, he didn't now. She wasn't the type of woman he'd been looking for. He hadn't wanted anyone; he hadn't wanted to admit he needed anyone. It wasn't until that moment—when she'd looked him in the eye and practically shouted that she was in love with him, almost daring him to dispute it—that he realized she was exactly what he needed.

And the tightness that had settled into his chest when he'd driven away from West Virginia finally began to ease.

Joel wasn't sure if she'd finished her speech or if she'd just run out of breath, but she was silent now. He'd never loved her more.

"Are you done?" he asked, pushing his chair away from the desk and rising to his feet.

Riane nodded.

"Then maybe you'll shut up for a minute so that I can say something."

She glared at him and opened her mouth to speak.

He held up a hand. "You had your turn, now it's mine."

Her jaw snapped shut, but the mutinous look was still in her eye. He finally gave in to the urge to touch her, reaching out to take her free hand in his, linking their fingers together. The skin-on-skin contact reassured him that she was real and gave him the courage to say what was in his heart.

"First of all, I *do* love you. I meant it when I said it the first time. I love you even more now."

The clenching in her jaw eased, the set of her mouth relaxed.

"You're not the kind of woman I envisioned spending the rest of my life with," he admitted. "I didn't want to share my life with anyone. I was perfectly happy to be alone and independent, until you came along. You're everything I never knew I wanted, and so much more."

He watched her eyes fill with tears even as her lips curved.

"Don't start crying," Joel warned. "I'm not good with tears, and I'm not finished yet."

"I'll wait," she promised.

"I want to be with you. For now. Forever. But only if you promise not to throw yourself in front of any more bullets. Because if you do anything that stupid again, I'll kill you myself."

She laughed. There were tears spilling onto her cheeks, but she was laughing. Then she was in his arms and they were kissing.

Joel savored the taste of her, relished the softness of her curves pressed against him, marveled at the way she fit so perfectly in his arms. Nothing had ever felt better than holding her, and he knew he couldn't let her go.

He'd tried to do the right thing, he'd tried to walk away, but she'd come back to him. He'd been deceitful and dishonest—he knew he didn't deserve her. But by some miracle he didn't dare question, she'd fallen in love with him. And as he'd vowed that fateful day when he'd found her bound and gagged in the motel, he was going to spend every day of the rest of his life showing her how much he loved her.

He lifted her off her feet and sat her on his chair, kneeling beside her. He could feel a single bead of sweat trickle down his back as he prepared to take the biggest risk of his life. A life that was empty without Riane in it.

"I didn't plan this," he admitted. "I didn't think I'd ever get a chance to do this, but you're here and you claim to love me, so I'm going to take this chance and grab it with both hands."

He took her hands in his and held on tight. "I don't have a lot to offer, and I don't make promises I can't keep. But what I have I want to share with you. And I can promise my love and my loyalty forever."

"That's all I ever wanted," Riane told him.

* * * * *